The

Illuminated

Manuscript

The Illuminated Manuscript

A NOVEL BY RUTH MOFFAT

THE MERCURY PRESS

Cover art and illuminated page art by Dale Jackson
Cover design by Gordon Robertson
Edited by Beverley Daurio
Composition and page design by TASK

Printed and bound in Canada by The Porcupine's Quill
Printed on acid-free paper
First Edition
1 2 3 4 5 00 99 98 97 96

Canadian Cataloguing in Publication Data

Moffat, Ruth, 1942-
The illuminated manuscript
ISBN 1-55128-036-1
I. Title.
PS8576.O345I44 1996 C813'.54 C96-931714-X
PR9199.3.M63I44 1996

CO-PUBLISHED WITH HEARTHSTONE BOOKS

Represented in Canada by the Literary Press Group
Distributed in Canada by General Distribution Services

The Mercury Press
137 Birmingham Street
Stratford, Ontario
Canada N5A 2T1

CONTENTS

IT'S ANGELS. IT ALWAYS has been. We humans just avoid the obvious. We are truly topsy-turvy creatures, and the angels spend our lifetimes trying to right us. This search I am on, for the words to say it, is the quest for the language of the angels. How do they speak? Their language system encompasses the principle that *the word is the thing*... Their word is transparent, clear, visible; but for angels, words are only one component of what I suspect is a simple language. Emotions are what count with angels, much more than the spoken or the written word. The heartfelt word, the clean chord, resonates across the room or across the world and hits one in the solar plexus like a blow. Angels speak by playing on our heart-strings.

PROLOGUE
CANADA — 1832

Caroline Harris yanked the silk thread in an effort to pull it through the coarse cloth lying on her lap. That much accomplished, she clenched her teeth and pushed the needle through the linen, straight into her finger.

"Damn this stupid thing. I hate it. I hate doing it and I'm not going to finish it."

Caroline jumped to her feet, tossing the needlework to the floor. The second figure in the room rose from her comfortable position by the fire. She, too, was doing needlework, but with considerably more success than her daughter. Emily Harris moved reluctantly from the warmth and brightness of the fireside into the shadows at the far end of the room, where Caroline stood still, looking out the window into the blackness of an early winter evening. Emily touched her daughter gently on the shoulder; she could feel the girl's trembling even through the heavy woollen fabric of her dress. This was not the first time Emily had had to deal with Caroline's outbursts.

"Caroline, don't be discouraged." Emily stooped and retrieved the discarded sampler.

She drew the girl back into the circle of firelight and patted the upholstered surface of the bench.

"Come," she coaxed. "Sit here beside me. Your work is not bad at all. You have a wonderful sense of colour. Let me help you with this difficult part of the pattern. Once you are over this hurdle, the rest will fall into place. Stop fighting each stitch, and let the needle guide you. Needlework can be very restful. I can't imagine sitting here without something in my hands. When you are older, you will feel the same way."

Caroline stiffened. She allowed herself to be seated on the bench, but she dissociated herself from Emily's final remark by sitting with her back to her mother and her face to the flames.

"Let me show you how to pull the thread through gently."

Emily, even from this awkward position beside and partly behind Caroline, was able to direct her daughter's needle, and work resumed on the despised sampler.

Caroline had turned thirteen that winter, and the beauty that would grace the adult Caroline was surfacing, although at this exact moment her face was sullen and her skin a mottled scarlet. Caroline was furious. Working samplers was a great waste of time. Her brothers were getting on with their lives. Her older brother, Daniel, had been sent to military school in England years before, and Richard had left in the fall to attend school in Kingston. It wasn't fair. She had finished the village school at the same time as Richard, even though he was three years older than she was. She should have been the one to go away to school. Why wasn't something being done about it? Only Emily prevented Caroline from pitching the useless sampler to the floor a second time. She hated disappointing Emily, but she also hated what her mother's life had to offer. There was so much to do and to learn, and here she was, confined in the house until she could somehow be transformed into a proper young lady. Caroline wanted to scream and scream until someone came to let her out.

The piece of linen slipped from her hands. Caroline loved to watch the fire. The life force in the flames curled and stretched and leapt into the blackness. The flames split and licked the base of the logs. All was colour and motion even as each individual flame sprang into extinction. The tumult in her breast subsided and an icy calm settled over her.

"Thomas. We'll call him Thomas."

The ringing clarity of Caroline's voice broke the silence of the flamelit room and the rhythm of Mrs. Harris' needle.

"What did you say, dear?"

"He's such a beautiful baby."

The vision of the baby danced on the flames and then replaced itself with a new image.

"Oh, no, look behind you... please."

The agony in Caroline's voice brought Emily to her feet.

"Caroline? What is the matter?"

The little red cart with its precious cargo still inside flew wildly down the hill and pitched into the water.

The girl slumped on the bench. Mrs. Harris took hold of Caroline's shoulders and gave them a sharp shake. Caroline opened her eyes at her mother's touch, and Emily's blood chilled. Caroline's dear face had thinned and become as transparent as glass. The eyes fixed blindly on Emily were not the familiar blue of Caroline's, but the bright silver of coins or mirrors, bordered in a band of black. No pupils graced their centers.

The fear Emily felt tumbled into her words. "Caroline. What did you see?"

The pressure from her mother's hands, frantically squeezing her shoulders, penetrated Caroline's trance. She shivered and snapped her head to an upright position.

"Pardon, mother? What did you say? I must have dozed off."

Emily looked closely at the girl's ashen face and with relief recorded the return of Caroline's familiar features. She decided not to press the matter further. Snow was falling about the stone house in thick heavy flakes. Emily felt helpless. This was not the first time Caroline had slipped from consciousness. And each time, when she awoke, she was unable to remember where she had been or what she had seen.

I had an uncomfortable dream last night... Andrea and I were sailing on an ocean, but not together. I seemed to be controlling her boat from another boat (with a guide rope, perhaps)? The waves were horrendous and I signalled her to come about, but I reversed the instructions. I told her to jibe. I had to wake myself before the boat capsized. I will never forget the confusion on her face as she realized what was going to happen. My instructions had been wrong and she had trusted me to tell the truth. The scenery was very beautiful but strange... all shades of blue with enormous waves and strikingly tall ice walls.

I must find Andrea this summer. She is lost and needs our help. But where do I go to find her?

I feel uneasy when I think of you.

It is very hot and airless. The puppy smells a storm and she is right. I have managed to avoid the meeting of the three of us I know must come this summer. Funny how life crises occur at decades! With the best of intentions and quite unconsciously, I have tried to make Andrea in my own image, only better, and I have thrown such a net of affection, intuition and hope over her that she is strangling. How to cut the threads and yet let her know the love is always there for her? How to let her know I will love her whatever she becomes? Or will I? I shall have to go to *The Illuminated Manuscript* to understand myself, my motives and my relationship to my mother. I have become the face in the mirror. I am now the mother, but I never was the daughter. Even all these years later, tears prickle behind my eyes. I shall study my manuscript for the clues that will set me, my daughter and my mother free.

PART I

ELIZABETH

IRELAND — 1800 - 1818

LIKE RILKE, I MUST change my life, not just in theory but in practice. It will be difficult. I have such a nice life. I think I have encountered the "word made flesh," the God language I have been seeking. Tree branches and the tops of fences are inanimate objects, lines on some gigantic page; squirrels and dogs and cats are moving lines on this same page, and humans are thinking objects, free to place themselves on this cosmic page. Wherever this thinking takes me, I am free to go. I saw a pine tree full of cones and it reminded me of birds. If the cones are letters, inanimate (incapable of rearranging themselves) and birds are animate letters (capable of rearranging themselves) and able to change the meaning, where do humans fit? We are both animate and thinking letters, capable of not only changing the meaning but also of creating meaning; each one of us is a letter of God. Where we place our letter is up to us. Free will, you know. I can only go so far, and then I stop.

Thank heaven for my journal. Without it, almost nothing pulls me back into the place where my soul can be at home. We use up words the way we use up our days, without filling them with any real meaning, and so our days, like our words, become meaningless. I ache to use words as if they were jewels, but it is not happening. How do angels communicate with humans? I must think on this, for it is certain that they do.

CHAPTER ONE

He was bent over an opened ledger and did not lift his head when the soft tap came on the office door. Ellen Strathy wondered if he had even heard. The whitened knuckles of her clenched fist had barely grazed the door. The girl waited a long moment, settled the dark green shawl more firmly about her shoulders, and took a deep breath before rapping the center panel smartly.

"Come in, please."

Charles McMaster, the newest and youngest of the assistants to the estate agent at Ballinough House, raised his head.

"Yes..."

His voice trailed off. The girl standing in the doorway seemed disembodied, framed as she was by the morning light.

"Excuse me. I'm looking for Mr. Carleton. He's wanting to see my father."

The cloud of dark hair spilling over her shoulders rose and fell as she spoke. Charles hastened from his chair and beckoned her to enter the office. Everyone on the estate either feared or hated Carleton. Charles had been in his position less than a fortnight and was little acquainted with the workings of Ballinough House, yet he knew instinctively how the tenants felt about the agent. And it wasn't just the tenants. People were not real to Carleton; they were numbers in the ledger. As Ellen Strathy came closer, he looked into her clear, almost colourless eyes and saw himself reflected there. He was confused and raised his eyes until his gaze rested on the frothy mass of her hair, each strand coated with a fine silver mist. Charles was enchanted. What possible business could this beautiful creature with the great gray eyes have with Carleton?

It came as a shock to Charles to have the questions he had raised in his head answered as if he had spoken them aloud.

"I am Ellen Strathy, Stephen Strathy's daughter. Da's indisposed and I've come in his stead."

Charles heard only the surname.

God in heaven, he thought. Stephen's Strathy's daughter. I can't evict this girl and her family.

For those had been Carleton's instructions to his young assistant. "If that lazy sod of an Irishman, Stephen Strathy, puts his head in this office while I'm away, make sure he pays what he owes and pays in full or he gets his notice. No excuses, no delays. Full payment or out he goes. I've been diddled long enough by that one."

The agent's words prodded an unpleasant memory. The image of a dirty overcrowded cottage swung into Charles' consciousness with every horrid detail still intact.

One day, in his final year at the Jesuit-run college in the west of Ireland, Charles had taken an unfamiliar route to the home of a classmate. Deep in thought about the impending examinations, he failed to notice the smashed cottage. He would have walked right past had he not been accosted by a woman who threw herself at his feet.

"Please, sir, have pity on us. We have nothing to eat and the children are starving. Please, sir, give us something, for as sure as God is in His Heaven, one of us will die by morning. It's that desperate."

Charles looked wildly about him. His eyes, but not his mind, took in the battered house and the ditch beside the road. Both swarmed with life. The woman pulled herself to her knees, and before Charles could stop her she had opened her dirty shawl and exposed the empty bag of her left breast.

"I can pay, young sir, in pleasure."

The stumps of blackened teeth in her once pretty mouth were all that he could focus on. He fumbled in his pockets and gave her the few coins he found there.

Father Bernard was the principal of the college and it was to him Charles raced with his tale of the wrecked cottage and the starving woman and her children. Charles had not finished his story when Father Bernard interrupted.

"They've been evicted. No doubt the husband's gone and the rent not paid. They never leave unless the walls are knocked down. It's the only way the landlords can get them out."

"Where will they go? Who will feed them? Shouldn't we help out?"

"Do not interfere, Mr. McMaster. You know nothing of the true faith. Don't presume to know the ways of God. You must not interrupt me, Mr. McMaster."

Charles had been about to ask what God intended for the children.

"You may be very clever at your books, Mr. McMaster, but you are a non-believer. You are at this college only on special dispensation. Do not force us to regret our decision to allow you to study with students of our faith. That wretched woman and her children are suffering for their sins, and to have hope of salvation, they must be cleansed of all earthly evil. Only then can they enter the Kingdom of Heaven. Would you condemn them to eternal hellfire? I must admonish you, Mr. McMaster, not to interfere in things you do not and cannot understand. Good day."

Charles never took that route again. He came to hate both Father Bernard and the Church he represented, but that hatred was nothing to the contempt he felt for himself. He graduated that June with the gold medal and a loathing for all things connected to the Roman Church.

Charles' family had been settled, two centuries before, by order of the English Crown, on vacated tracts of land in the northernmost province of Ireland. The country had been good to the McMasters, who had prospered and acquired more land. After the defeat of the Irish by King Billy, Robert McMaster's branch of the family had moved south and established itself in County Roscommon. The ensuing political climate was favourable to the Protestant farmers, and the black Irish soil yielded rich harvests. Even so, the present head of the McMaster family did not intend to let chance change their fortunes. Robert McMaster, as had his father before him, adopted and strictly adhered to the English system of deeding the land directly and without division to his eldest son; younger sons were free to enter the clergy, the army, or to emigrate to the colonies. The first duty of the head of the family was to the first-born male of the succeeding generation. Charles was the most promising of the McMaster boys, but the farm would go to young Robert. Robert McMaster saw this as harsh but necessary. Following Charles' graduation, his father secured him the post as assistant to the estate agent at Ballinough House, a grand property of better than a thousand acres, owned by an English lord who was rarely in residence.

The girl with the rain-washed eyes stood facing Charles across the table that served as his desk.

"Please sit down, Miss Strathy. I'm Charles McMaster, Mr. Carleton's assistant."

He motioned Ellen to the other chair. It was a mistake. The office took on a more intimate atmosphere and the girl's translucent eyes were only an arm's length from his own. For the second time he saw his own reflection mirrored in the black orbs that centered her eyes. The trembling of her underlip was clearly visible to him and it required all his attention to keep his own voice from trembling as he questioned her.

"I see by Mr. Carleton's accounts your rent has been paid in full only twice in the last five years. Has there been a problem in your family? Your father is ill, perhaps, unable to work?"

The double image of himself drowned as tears filled her eyes.

He lowered his gaze to the ledger and leafed through the pages.

"No, my father isn't ill."

Ellen's thoughts went directly to the scene played out that morning beside her father's bed.

"Now, Ellen, my love, would you be doing your father a grand favour and nip up to Carleton's office to find out what that old weasel would be wanting? He left word with your mother that he had business with me. Well, I've no business with the likes of him that do the dirty business for English thieves. You tell him that Stephen Strathy's family has lived on Irish soil since God created Ireland and the Strathys owe nothing to any man. You tell him that, sweetheart, for if I go myself there is sure to be trouble, and you know how fighting upsets your mother."

Her father's long narrow face with its shadowed jaw was still handsome. Stephen smiled engagingly at the girl and patted a place beside him on the bed. He took her face in both his hands and whispered so those in the other room could not hear him.

"You'll do this wee thing for your father, then? Tell him I'm sick, I'm unable to work the fields. And darling, smile at him when you ask for an extension. For the Saint himself could not resist the sight of your sweet face when you smile. Off you go then, and give him your sunniest look when he asks where I am. For sure that bloodsucking devil will ask where I am."

This last bit of information was spoken almost to himself.

"Yes, da', for sure I'll go. But he won't like you not coming."

"Darling, when he sees your Irish smile, he'll not remember me. Why, a man could forget his own name at the sight of you."

Ellen had backed out of the room, laughing in spite of her concern at the lovely foolish words of her father. He charmed them all.

One translucent tear spilled onto the black silk of an eyelash, where it hung precariously. Charles watched in helpless fascination until the tear dropped and rolled down the curve of her cheek, leaving a streak of silver from eye to chin. He constructed his next question with great care.

"Why can he not manage to pay at least something towards the rent? He must realize this situation cannot go on forever."

To Ellen it was as though Charles McMaster's questions came from some distant world. Didn't this young man understand that there was no money and the Strathys would never be able to pay the rent in full? In her father's mind, he owed nothing. She sighed. How could this well-meaning man, for he was well-meaning, ever understand? He was a Protestant, of that Ellen was certain; Carleton hired only his own kind. How could this young man know that night after night, Stephen Strathy held forth in the public house and stayed until there were no men left to buy him the whiskey that dulled the memories of a glory he had never known? No wonder there was no money to pay the rent; her da' worked the public house, not the fields.

She sighed again. Ellen knew by heart the fateful twist of history that had taken the Strathy lands from their rightful owners and given them to the foreigners from across the Irish Sea. Bad times had befallen the Irish aristocracy before, but none so catastrophic as those wrought by the Battle of Boyne, where the last Catholic King of Ireland was well and truly defeated by William of Orange. With roots in Ireland that went further back in time than those of the Norman invaders, the Strathy family and their feudal home, Kildrum Castle, were, until 1690, the living symbols of an ancient Irish line. All this changed after the defeat on the Boyne. The Strathys were as unwilling to convert to Protestantism as they were to swear allegiance to the English Crown. Their lands were confiscated and broken up and the surviving members of the Strathy family were stripped of their titles and dispersed like cattle throughout the country because they had been loyal to James II and remained Catholic in their own land. In the succeeding century, not one Strathy male accomplished anything of note. The narrow, handsome Strathy face still existed in Ireland, that and the scorn the Strathys heaped on those traitorous Irish families who forsook their Church and knuckled under to the English Crown.

"Sold their souls to the devil," Ellen's father maintained, "to keep their land. And the price they paid and will continue to pay for their lying deeds is a special place in hell."

At this point in his story Stephen would crush his glass in one hand and throw the pieces on the floor, his hand dripping blood from the shards of glass. The barman would open the back door of the pub and call for Ellen to get her drunken father out of his establishment before he smashed it to smithereens.

How could this kind young man with his clean hands and open face know what generations of hate could do to a man?

Her fingers grasped each other so tightly the knuckles on each hand stood out, chalk white against her skin. Another tear slid onto her silk-tipped lashes. Charles could not bring himself to utter the word "eviction." He could neither look away from her nor think of what to say. He did not understand what was happening to him. He managed one further question.

"Have you no brothers able to work the fields? Have you no one to help you?"

His concern was more than Ellen could bear. She had never felt compassion from a stranger. Tears poured down her face.

"There's too many babies to feed and the boys are still too young to work the land without supervision and da's too discouraged to care. He doesn't even try. He drinks to forget he can't look after us. Father Boyle tells him he shouldn't have to pay for his own land that was stolen from the real Irish by the black Protestants. Mother and I do what we can, and manage to feed the little ones, but there is never anything left over for the rent."

Ellen placed her face in her hands and sobbed.

Charles snapped into action.

"I will speak to your father and I will speak to your priest. We cannot have you losing your home now, can we?"

In a single motion, he stretched across the table and cradled her tear-streaked face in his hands. Charles was lost. Ellen, too, forgot who she was. She was content just to be. It was the first time a man other than her father or her priest had touched her. She did not move, and when at last Charles withdrew his hands, her whole being went with him. Ellen was as cloistered from the world as if she were a nun, and just fifteen, she was too young to hold back a portion herself in case this man was not what he seemed.

"We'll get you a position in the house. Mrs. Archer will help me. Would you like that?"

She nodded her assent. Work in the big house. It was the answer to a prayer, and until this moment, could never have been conceived of as a possibility.

"Carleton's not due back for a month. By then you will have received your first month's wages and I can apply them with my own to the debt. Between the two of us, we can pay the rent and no one need ever be the wiser."

She followed him, ghostlike, with her great, pale eyes, and when she spoke it was to whisper, "I couldn't let you do that. It's not right."

"Ellen." He reached over and would have touched her face again but she saw it coming and stood up. "I want to do it."

"I would be very grateful if you could put in with Mrs. Archer for a place for me in the big house. That will be enough."

She reached the door before he could stop her, and turned to drop a pretty curtsy to him. Bright colour had returned to her face.

"How can I thank you? You are the kindest man I have ever met, even though you are a Protestant."

He waited for Ellen outside the back door of Ballinough House each evening that fall and winter, and while he walked her home, they talked of many things, but never of their families or religion or their future. Charles always left before they reached her cottage. It was as though the two of them existed alone, outside of their own time and place.

THE LION HAS NOT only come right up to the door and growled; he has let himself inside. I am hobbled by pain and my world has shrunk from thoughts of Africa to thoughts of "how much will it hurt to swing my legs over the side of the bed?" My body has been brought back to an infant stage… each step must be planned for and thought about. Hanging onto the bed and nosing around in a banana skin for the fruit, I was reminded of a baby rooting around for a nipple, a poignant and painful reminder of how far I have to go. I am a baby in this world.

Andrea is safe and for now I can listen to my inner self made manifest in poetry. Hearing poetry read speaks eloquently to something deep inside me. It articulates emotion that can rise to the surface of my life.

I saw *Romeo and Juliet* danced last night... a feast for the eyes and for the emotions. Karen Kain was Juliet. She floated, she glided, she extended her wings. Watching Shakespeare's poetry danced is almost better than seeing it acted. Romeo, too, was wonderful, but Juliet knew something that he did not. She knew what she had experienced was beyond words. She also knew that if a price had to be paid, then she would pay. Romeo loved on a human level. Juliet loved on a divine level. It is all a matter of scale. What scale one wishes to live on.

I am moving slowly, with no set purpose. I don't feel burnished in use. I know in my heart *The Illuminated Manuscript* is right for me to work with, but how to compose it? How to speak the divine language that it needs? I shall head to the third floor and my old poetry and journals and hope to be touched. One can only hope that divine grace will be given.

It cannot be demanded.

CHAPTER TWO

The village priest fostered Stephen Strathy's hatred of the English Protestants with his own stories of mistreatment and flight from the soldiers of the Crown. Father Boyle had taken his vows during that period of Irish history when the penal laws had been most severely enforced. These harsh laws suppressed the rights of Catholics in education, politics and in voting and property rights. One of the harsher restrictions prohibited a Catholic from leaving all his land to one son; it had to be divided equally among all the sons.

This law proved the undoing of many of the great Irish Catholic families. They simply could not feed their dependants on ever diminishing plots of land. Inevitably, the Irish Catholics ended as tenant farmers on English-owned land. It was a calculated cruelty. The Church itself during this period was forced underground in order to survive; masses were said in fields and in the basements of private homes. Priests were forced into hiding, closeted in attics and in secret rooms to keep them from falling into the hands of the British patrols.

Ellen had heard the story more times than she could remember of how Father Boyle and three other novice priests had taken their holy vows wrapped in sheets and lying face down on the dank floor of a warehouse cellar in Galway. They heard the formal Latin of the sacred ritual whispered by a bishop smuggled in from France. Parts of the ceremony were blotted forever from Father Boyle's memory by the stamp of British boots searching overhead for the renegade priests. Ellen had grown up not knowing which was worse, being English or being Protestant.

Charles and Ellen never knew who told Stephen Strathy that they met secretly. He was there one night as they took the path from the big house to the cottages, and he was drunk.

"You sneaking coward, how dare you come after my daughter? Steal a man's land, rob him blind, and then go after his family. What a sly excuse for a man you are. I should kill you."

Ellen placed her arm about her father's shoulders, as she had countless times before, and spoke gently to him.

"Let's go home, da'. Mother and the little ones will be waiting their supper for us."

He shook off her arm.

"Did you not hear what I said, you slut of a girl? I never thought I'd see the day when my own flesh and blood would take up with a black Protestant. You'll be the death of me. 'Tis enough to drive a man to drink. Get away with you."

He turned to chase her and stumbled, falling heavily across the path. Between Charles and Ellen, they managed to get him home. Ellen's mother stood waiting on the doorstep.

"So he's finally heard, has he? I'd hoped for your sakes it would be a while yet. What will you do?"

"I want to marry Ellen, Mrs. Strathy. Will you give us your blessing?"

"Impossible," breathed Ellen.

"Yes," said her mother. "You have my blessing. Go with him. He is a good man. There is nothing for you here."

"But ma, who will look after you and the boys?"

"Don't you worry about that, love. Maybe this will be the making of your father. Maybe he'll have to provide for us, or I'll go and work in the big house. I'm sure Mrs. Archer would consider me for your position. How he would hate me to do that! I want you to leave here, Ellen. It is your only chance."

There was no time for Charles to think of the consequences of marrying outside his own faith or of his family's reaction to such a marriage. Charles, with his innate hatred of the Roman Church, could not convert, so it was Ellen who left her faith. They were married in the vestry of St. Simon's Anglican Church in Galway on June 3, 1801, with no one from either family to witness their union. They could not return to Ballinough House and so they went to the McMaster farm in County Roscommon. It was only a temporary refuge.

This is not an easy thing to do, this rereading of a story written before it happened. It is as though I wrote the script and then people stepped in to play the parts. It was fiction when I wrote it and now parts of it are coming true. I half wish I did not have to own up to its existence, but it is there, waiting for me, like a face in the mirror. Dear God, I am frightened. I don't know the ending and anything I create could spell disaster for someone I love. What in God's name have I tapped into?

It has been years since I dealt with the written landscape of my mind. I ran from it. I ran to classes and the knowledge of others for answers, not to my own knowledge. There were answers, but not for this. This thing that is happening is too scary to own. I cannot even say it out loud, let alone write it; so I must read what I wrote before and try to work it out. I must not deny what happened and continues to happen. I must come to some understanding of the events, and this manuscript is my best hope. Probably my only hope.

CHAPTER THREE

"Mama says the baby is going to be born and you are to get Dr. O'Flaherty from the village."

Elizabeth McMaster spoke quickly, lest she forget any part of her important message. Her small chest heaved with the exertion of running without stop from her own cottage door, past the stables, down the gravelled carriageway to the gates of Kingsmill Manor, no mean distance for a five-year-old. Elizabeth had been to her father's office on many occasions, but always she had been accompanied by one of her parents. Once she had met a bewhiskered gentleman there, whom her father had called Sir Roger. Papa had held her hand and Elizabeth had made a tiny curtsy to the stout white-haired gentleman; he, in turn, had made a courtly bow and called her a sweetheart. Never had she imagined coming to the gatehouse alone and with such a message. Her dark blue eyes never left her father's face.

"Papa, shouldn't you hurry? The baby wants to be born and Mama needs the doctor to help her."

"Of course I'll hurry, sweetheart. Babies take a little time to make their appearance. Mama will want you home to keep her company while I go for the doctor. Don't you worry, Elizabeth."

Charles swung his small daughter onto his shoulders and closed and locked the door of the slanted stone building that served as his office. The building's twin lay on the other side of the carriageway. The two limestone structures and the massive iron gate hanging between them formed the entrance to Kingsmill Manor. More than a manor house, it was an ancient castle rooted in Irish history and purchased by the present owner some sixteen years before. Sir Roger Kingsmill had converted the rundown castle into a smart country house and had placed his own name on the gates of the estate. The name change had been effected by the stroke of a pen in the registry office in Galway, but improving the productivity of the estate proved more difficult. Kingsmill Manor needed the services of a clever young agent, one who understood both the land and the incomprehensible ways of the Irish tenant farmers. It was all in Charles' favour, to Sir Roger's way of thinking, that McMaster had got himself a Catholic wife. Under Charles' management, the estate was beginning to show some excellent results.

Three years before Ellen's second confinement, the McMasters had arrived from County Roscommon with their small daughter. It was an unseasonably warm day in late fall. The refurbished castle gleamed gold in the autumn sunshine amid lush green lawn picked clean of fallen leaves. At the first sign of the coach turning in at the gates, Sir Roger Kingsmill had started down the drive.

"Welcome to Kingsmill Manor. I hope you will be happy here."

"Thank you, sir. You are very kind. This is my wife, Ellen, and my daughter, Elizabeth. We are looking forward to our life on your estate."

"Let me see the baby."

Ellen Strathy McMaster moved back on the seat to give her husband's employer a better look at Elizabeth. A large finger came out of nowhere to chuck the little girl under the chin. Elizabeth looked curiously at her mother but she did not flinch.

"She's a nice little thing. I like children about the place; makes things lively."

"Do you have any children, sir?" Ellen blushed at her own boldness as both men turned to look at her.

"Just one, a boy, and he's off to school in England. Doesn't even spend holidays here unless I make him. Enough of Rodney. Let's get you settled. You are welcome to any vacant house on the estate."

Charles and Ellen, with Elizabeth half swinging and half walking between them, had found an empty whitewashed cottage set back from its neighbours. It sat by itself on the very edge of the fields that backed the buildings of Kingsmill Manor and extended for some distance up the old mountain range. Something about the house appealed to Ellen even before she had stepped inside.

"You won't be lonely here?"

"No," Ellen smiled at him cheekily. "It will be lovely to be lonely for a change. Besides, I have Elizabeth for company."

Charles laughed out loud at the memory of the crowded farmhouse in Roscommon.

"That's settled, then. I'll tell Sir Roger, and if he agrees, we will move our things in right away."

Charles decided on one of the gatehouses for his office. Ellen had explained to him how the tenants hated having to troop up to the big house with their rents and their complaints. Where it was within his power to do something for the Irish peasants, Charles meant to. The tenant farmers still regarded Sir Roger and his son, as they had the English owners before, as interlopers, and the change in the Manor's name as a blot on the old and convoluted history of the castle. It did not matter that Sir Roger Kingsmill had taken possession of a property that had languished for almost a century under the ownership of absentee landlords whose only interest was the amount of money that could be squeezed from the peasants who worked the land. Not once in the hundred years that followed the awarding of the castle and the lands to the English lord who had fought shoulder to shoulder with William of Orange had a single member of that family bothered to visit the Irish property. They had hired a series of Scottish agents to oversee the estate and collect the rents, and when the crops failed and the rents dried up, the lord's heirs placed the property for sale. Under Sir Roger Kingsmill's stewardship, the estate was feeding its people properly for the first time in generations. That knowledge did not change the fact that the Kingsmills were English, Protestant, and trespassers; the peasants despised them and those that served them. It was into this atmosphere that the McMasters had moved.

With Elizabeth perched on his shoulder, Charles made two stops before coming to his own door. The double row of whitewashed cottages with their freshly thatched roofs shone in the late afternoon sun. It was a rare enough day for this part of Ireland, known for its heavy mists and threatening skies. It was rare, too, for the peasants to be housed in such well-tended surroundings. Poor they might be, but it was clear that each cottage provided more for its occupants than mere shelter. Crisply laundered lace curtains hung at each window, and the swept and tidy paths leading to the cottages boasted neatly laid out vegetable gardens on each side. Charles tapped on the door of the third cottage in the first row. A young woman with a baby in her arms and two little ones at her feet answered his knock.

"I have come to ask for help for my wife, Mrs. O'Neill. Elizabeth here," and Charles swung the little girl down from his shoulders and set her on the doorstep, "has run all the way to my office to tell me it is time for me to go and fetch the doctor. I was wondering if I might trouble you to keep an eye on Ellen and this young one while I'm away to the village."

The young woman fiddled with the shawl covering the baby's head.

"No, no, I can't possibly help you— my man needs his meal and I can't leave the little ones. I'm… I'm sorry for her, but there is nothing I can do."

She stood motionless in the doorway. The hand absently patting the back of the infant's head seemed detached from the rest of her. Charles politely thanked her, lifted Elizabeth to his shoulders and walked down the path.

At his next stop he was greeted by a much older woman. Charles was uncertain whether time or the harshness of her life had given her such a stooped figure and lined face. She did not wait for his knock before opening the door. She looked him boldly in the face and hissed between the stumps of her teeth.

"It's her time, is it? Well, don't be expecting help from us. Go to the castle and ask them."

The door to the cottage was closed with force. Charles did not try again. With Elizabeth still perched on his shoulders, he quickened his pace and hastened to his wife's side.

The location of the McMaster cottage was not the only factor distinguishing it from its neighbours. It was slightly larger than the others and Charles had added a small stillroom at the back for Ellen. She had a knack for working with plants and herbs, turning them into healing tonics and potions. The roughened surface of the stucco supported Ellen's climbing rose bushes and the doorway of their cottage was wreathed in roses. The traditional vegetable garden had been allocated to the rear of the cottage, and was barely visible from the front walk.

"Darling, we're home. I'll have Dr. O'Flaherty here to look after you in no time. Meanwhile, I'll leave you in the hands of the smartest colleen in the west of Ireland."

With that, Charles swung Elizabeth down from his shoulders and deposited her with a flourish on the floor in front of her mother.

"Sir Charles and Lady Elizabeth at your service, m'lady."

The full force of her labour had not yet gripped Ellen, and she giggled at their antics.

"I'll take Elizabeth to help me. She'll be more use to me than a man with a mouthful of nonsense. Make sure you and the doctor don't stop for a few sips to celebrate the impending arrival of your new son on your way through the village."

Ellen laughed to let him know she was only teasing. She was very thankful that Charles was not a drinking man. He kissed her with great tenderness and petted the soft dark curls on his daughter's head.

"You girls be good. I'll be back in time for my tea."

Charles' first stop was the stables, where the head groom was currying one of the well-bred animals that filled the stalls.

"Paddy, I've need of a horse to take me to Ballindooly. Which one can you give me?"

"Why are you bothering me? You know you have the run of the stables. Take any horse except Sir Roger's or Master Rodney's."

Charles was not put out by Paddy's gruffness. No offence was intended and none was ever taken. The man had never learned the comfortable give and take that language affords some people. He found his ease with the highly strung horses entrusted to his care; to hear Paddy talk to the great glossy beasts and to watch them follow his words was a magical experience. Charles had heard him once when Paddy had thought himself alone.

"You're a handsome fellow, Brebeuf... quite a chap with the ladies, but I know how you feel when the weather claps and bangs around your ears. It's terrifying. It's all right, boy... I'll not leave you alone."

The horse had dropped his head so Paddy could stroke his neck. Charles had tiptoed from the stable; from that time on, Charles understood when the groom spoke roughly. Both men knew that Charles would never take a horse without asking Paddy. It was one of the courtesies that set Charles apart from the other agents who had managed the estate.

"I'll take Fair Cloud, please. She runs well and she won't cause me any trouble in the village."

The road to the village was little more than a rough cart track following the curve of the lake. Today, the sky over the lough, usually shrouded in a fine silver mist, was streaked with sunlight like fine watered silk. Charles was too preoccupied to notice. He relaxed somewhat as he recognized the landmarks that told him Ballindooly was just over the rise of the next hill.

Little more than a crossroad on the route to Galway, the village was a collection of stone buildings clustered about the church, a few stores and a public house with rooms above for the unsuspecting traveller. The manse and assorted cottages hugged the fringe of the churchyard, but the church was the only building of any real significance. With the repeal of the penal laws, Roman Catholicism had come out from its hiding places and resumed its rightful status in the lives of the Irish. The tall spire and prominent location of the church spoke of its importance. Charles guided his mount to the doctor's house, which also sat beneath the shadow of the church. As luck would have it, the doctor's buggy was tied to the post in front of his house.

"Hullo, Charles, is it me you have come to see?"

Dr. O'Flaherty appeared from the side of the house.

"Yes, and it's happy I am to have caught you at home. It's Ellen's time. She told me to tell you that the baby's on his way and I am not to come home without you."

The outline of a black-clothed man filled the doorway of the doctor's house.

"I am waiting for the doctor, too, Mr. McMaster, and I am here before you. You'll have to wait your turn. One of my flock is ill and in need of Dr. O'Flaherty."

Charles recognized the dark figure in the open door as that of Father Egan, well-known for his dislike of the Protestants at Kingsmill Manor. There would be little compassion for Ellen or himself from this parish priest. If Ellen died in childbirth, it would be no more than God's justice for Ellen's betrayal of her Church. It was common knowledge in the village that Ellen McMaster had forsaken both her family and her faith to marry Charles, and the townsfolk were waiting for God's wrath to strike.

Concern for Ellen gave Charles reason to ignore the presence of the priest and to halt the abrasive reply that rose unbidden in his throat. Instead,

Charles moved closer to the comforting figure of the doctor and appealed to him directly.

"How long might your services be needed?"

The black-garbed figure intervened.

"We have no answer. It's God's will, not yours, that will determine how long he is needed. Old Mrs. McElhinney is dying, and Dr. O'Flaherty will be with her, as will I."

Charles heart plummeted. Surely the passing of an old, old woman, who no doubt welcomed the release of death, would not take precedence over the lives of a young mother and her child? No one but a fanatic would allow this, but Charles suspected that Father Egan not only would let it take place but make certain that it did take place. Charles made a last desperate plea, hoping he could swing the doctor over to his side.

"Could you come to us when you have done all you can for Mrs. McElhinney? I have no one at the cottage but young Elizabeth. I would be so grateful for whatever assistance you could spare us."

He directed a barely contained look of panic at the doctor. Dr. O'Flaherty glanced at the priest and then touched Charles on the arm.

"'Tis certain I am that you will do just fine, Charles. Babies have a way of surviving even the most inexperienced hands. If I can, I will be there."

The two men climbed into the waiting buggy, and at a smart flick of the doctor's wrist on the reins, the horse pulled away from the post. Charles wasted not a moment in remounting Fair Cloud and riding back to Kingsmill Manor and Ellen.

I have been brought to my knees and slowed to a crawl. I must listen to what the angels are saying. One cannot proceed with speed. I keep trying to stay with language, a language of emotions, not words, not doing, not senses. I must sit and feel what is happening around me. I am such a slow learner. It is a wonder that the angels do not become discouraged with me and give up, but parents don't; and angels are our celestial parents, tied to us by something immeasurably stronger than life. It would take more than human strength to break the bonds.

I was trying to get down to work when the thought came to me so clearly and so rightly that I shook my head in amazement. I am not to rush this project, but to proceed delicately and with great care. This is a fragile substance that I am trying to capture. I must not kill it by overexertion... I am trying to write the invisible as illuminated language, illuminated meaning *fire and light*. How does one write illuminated language? One hits the wall, admits defeat, and then asks for help.

CHAPTER FOUR

Ellen's second child was born as the clock on the mantelpiece chimed twelve o'clock. It seemed a good omen that this baby heralded the beginning of a new day. He was beautiful— crumpled and red, but the shape of his head was perfect and his cries were strong. Ellen sent a silent prayer of thanksgiving to the Almighty God who had so kindly bestowed this second gift of a child, and a son at that. A woman of lesser strength might not be thanking Him for the safe arrival of a healthy baby. Ellen and Charles had been the only adults present during the long hours of labour preceding the midnight appearance of their son. Not one word of complaint had come from Ellen concerning the absence of family, friends, or medical attention. It was not her way to question what could not be.

The lateness of the hour and the dying coals of a spent fire softened the whiteness of the roughcast walls of the cottage's only bedroom. A four-poster bed bereft of hangings dominated the small room. A rocking chair and a carved cradle beside the fireplace were the only furnishings apart from the bed, but even those few pieces crowded the room.

"Charles, are you pleased with our new son?"

The question was rhetorical, asked so she could hear once again the joy in her husband's voice. The man who had toiled almost as hard as she had to bring this child to life cupped his wife's face gently in his hands.

"I am more than pleased, my love. I am the happiest man in Ireland tonight. He is my firstborn son and he is healthy and my own sweetheart bore him bravely. No one in all the world is as happy as I am. Thank you for both my children."

"Thomas. We'll call him Thomas," Ellen said, half aloud, and trailed one finger across the baby's downy head.

"Charles." Ellen raised herself on one elbow; the other arm encircled the baby.

"Charles, can we call him Thomas?"

"My love, call him what you will. Thomas will do just fine."

The man rose from his reverie at his wife's words. He placed more coal on the fire and stirred it into life, then settled back in the chair and stared into the flames. The look on his face belied the softness of his words. Charles acknowledged to himself the grim reality of his son's lonely birth.

Remembrance Day... for perhaps the first time in my life, I stopped to really think what war means. Not the pomp and ceremony that governments use to lure their young men into uniform, but how it feels as a mother to cast her firstborn into the mouth of Baal. Not so very less savage than those ancient gods that demanded human sacrifice. Have we changed? Progressed? I think not. There are still men who want to control all other men, men smart enough to figure out a way to have someone else's son pay the ultimate price. There have always been such men. Whatever happens to them as they near the point of death? Do they fear Hamlet's "undiscovered country"? If they took my son and blew him up to save their vested interests, I would kill.

Another golden morning after yesterday's rain, and yet it is yesterday I want to explore. Sensations of wonder and delight at what other people write, odd combinations of words that are right for what they want to say. It is an electric atmosphere. What strange creatures we women writers are, covered by so many gauzy layers. I am keeping a list of words that ring in my ear, words that sound what they are: majesty, drenched, adroit, sullied, schooled, propitious, propensity, peripatetic, epiphany, oblique, explicit, embellished, fester, festoon, sumptuous.

While swimming lengths, I thought of how much of their lives women spend nurturing. I am filled with a great rage when I realize how much of my creative spirit is consumed in nurturing my husband, my children, and now my father. Who nurtures me? My books, my classes, my thoughts, and other women who understand. It is an uphill battle, struggling to release myself from those close claims of kinship in order to free that part of me that longs to soar and know.

Dale came over with the new painting for the tapestry. It is dazzling. She has captured what Elizabeth wove in a way that is uncanny. I will not change one flower. Imagine, Dale will weave what I wrote. I am overwhelmed by the oneness of it all. There we are, back to pulling unity from a world composed of contraries and disparities.

I AM NOT SURE WHETHER angels like to be written about; and even if they do, perhaps they do not want to be written about by me. The lack of structure in working with the language of angels is scary. Is this what angelic space is… free floating and undefined? Can we humans handle angelic space, what Milan Kundera calls "the unbearable lightness of being"? How does one anchor such lightness to the page? We must find our way back to the beginning, to the place where the word and the meaning were one, where "the word was, in fact, not theory made flesh." It is this clarity of meaning that I must find and write.

CHAPTER FIVE

One of the McMaster children's favourite walks was down the path past the cottages to the rear of the big house. Elizabeth would pull Thomas between the manor and the stable and continue down the neatly raked and gravelled drive to the gates of Kingsmill Manor. She would peep through the window of the gatehouse, and if her father was there and if he was alone, she would tap lightly on the glass to let him know she and Thomas were just outside. This morning, as on other mornings, Elizabeth raised herself on her tiptoes and peered through the window into her father's office. Standing across from her father's desk, and facing her, was a very tall, very thin man. She did not recognize him, and Elizabeth knew almost everyone connected with the working of the estate. Even stranger was the black dress he was wearing. The man looked very angry. She could not see her father's face, but his back was rigid and his neck and head jutted out of his starched collar. Elizabeth knew better than to interrupt; she drew back from the window and turned her attention to Thomas, who had been waiting patiently for his adored da' to appear. Elizabeth put her finger to her lips, then bent to pick up the handle of the wagon. They were leaving without the promised visit to his father, and Thomas set up a great shout of protest.

Charles had made a red cart for Thomas. The little boy loved to try his newly acquired walking skills, but when Elizabeth appeared with the red wagon, he smiled his toothy smile and raised his arms to be lifted into the cart. Off they went, Elizabeth pulling the wagon, while Thomas sat in the back, waving his fat arms at cows or trees or whatever caught his attention. Little was forbidden to the children. Elizabeth had proven herself to be a reliable child, and they were free to explore the barns and stable, the fields and lawns, with their only boundary the road which ran between the estate and the lake. Charles had made a special point of telling Elizabeth she was not to cross the road.

"Da', da', da'," Thomas howled, ignoring his sister, who had knelt beside him in a vain attempt to quieten him. It was there Charles and Father Egan found them.

Thomas stopped yelling when Charles appeared. He watched wide-eyed as Father Egan thundered.

"You see," breathed the priest, "these young ones are living a heathen existence. What kind of a man has no care for the souls of his children? What kind of a man keeps his lambs from their Shepherd? Send the girl to me at the village school. I'll teach her about the true faith and her Father who waits for her in heaven. She's old enough to learn about her heritage and to be saved from the flames of hell. The devil himself will take these children from you if you don't return them to the Church."

Father Egan stretched out a long black sleeve and touched Elizabeth, who was crouching by the wagon, on the shoulder. She recoiled from the bony prodding of the priest's finger as if she had been poked by the devil. All the colour left her face and she ran blindly through the gates and away. When she could no longer catch her breath, she sank in a heap by the road.

"See what you have done, you meddling old woman? I'll thank you to keep your Papish thoughts to yourself. The little ones will grow up without your dark rituals and evil threats of hellfire. If I ever catch you tampering with my children, I'll take a horsewhip to you. Now get out of here."

With that, Charles flung his arm in the direction of the village. He bent down and scooped Thomas from the wagon, and strode up the driveway to warn Ellen of the priest's troublemaking.

When her heart stopped pounding and her breathing returned to normal, Elizabeth sat up and took notice of her surroundings. She had dropped onto the steep border of thick grass that stretched up an incline between the lake and the road. Elizabeth had never been this close to the water before, and she scrambled to her feet so she could leave before her father found her there. The valley was still, and there was not so much as a ripple on the surface of the lake.

"It can't do any harm," she spoke aloud, "seeing as I am already here, to have just one look."

She found herself at the brink of silvery Lough Corrib. There was something floating on the surface. She edged closer and saw her own tear-smudged face. Cautiously, she leaned over to get a better look; her black curls tumbled across her face, erasing her image. She pushed them back impatiently and bent even closer to the water. Something in this face bothered her. Something about the face in the water was not right. She stared. It was the eyes. The longer she looked, the more she understood that the eyes did not belong to her. They were the eyes of a stranger, looking back at her from her own face. Elizabeth drew back, hunched on her heels, and waited. Then she looked into the water again. The stranger was still there; she looked exactly like Elizabeth, except that her eyes were the bright silver of mirrors or coins, and they reflected rather than absorbed the light. The silver of each eye was bound in a band of black velvet. Something else about the eyes disturbed Elizabeth. The black dot where each pupil should have been was silvered out, missing, giving the girl in the lake an odd but not frightening appearance.

Elizabeth was so enchanted with her double that she completely forgot what had brought her to the lake. Elizabeth blinked; the girl blinked. Elizabeth giggled and the girl's blank eyes crinkled with laughter. When Elizabeth could no longer stand the suspense, she leaned over, and with her lips almost touching the water, whispered: .

"Who are you?"

The girl pursed her lips and tried to reply.

"What did you say?"

Elizabeth shifted her head so one ear was very close to the water.

The girl altered the angle of her head at the same time. Elizabeth straightened and once more faced the girl directly.

"What's your name?"

The girl in the water grinned and shook her dark curls mischievously.

Her face rippled and danced on the smooth surface. Elizabeth inclined her head to the girl and barely breathed the words: "You can't talk, can you? That's why you won't tell me your name. Nod at me If I guessed right."

The mirrored pieces of the girl's face swam together, and when her silver eyes locked with Elizabeth's, they slanted downward. Elizabeth had her answer.

"Having a little visit with your fetch, are you?"

The voice came from so close behind her that Elizabeth jumped and would have fallen into the water had the woman not caught her by the arm.

"There now, you'd best be careful 'round the lough. It's that easy to fall in, and no one to see you disappear."

The old woman peered intently into Elizabeth's face. "You be McMaster's young daughter. What brings you here?"

Elizabeth recognized her rescuer as Biddy Connor, one of the estate's grannies, women who had lived their whole lives on the property and who knew everything about the estate. When their husbands died, they moved from their own small cottages into ones tenanted by their sons or daughters. Their knowledge went with them. Elizabeth knew them all by sight; often on her walks with Thomas she had seen them picking berries or gathering herbs, but she had never talked to one before today.

Biddy Connor bent over Elizabeth and spoke to her in a hushed voice. "You saw someone in the water, didn't you?"

Elizabeth nodded.

"Who did you see? Did you know her? Was she young or old?"

"She looked like me, but her eyes were very strange."

The old woman smiled and took Elizabeth by the hand.

"Ah," she said, "I thought as much. You saw your fetch."

"What's a fetch?"

"You mean to say, Elizabeth McMaster, that a great Irish girl like yourself has never heard of a fetch? What might your mother be teaching you, then? Come, I'll walk you home so your folks won't worry, and I'll tell you what my granny told me about fetches.

"I was your age, maybe a wee bit older, when I met my fetch. I was standing on a stool in my cottage, polishing the window glass with my apron, when as clear as could be I spied a reflection in the glass. It wasn't anyone I knew and I was very frightened. I went straight to my granny.

"'Bridey,' she said, 'it's one of those that's crossed over, come to have a peek at you. Poor soul, all she wants is to look; she means no harm. She died when she was just a child, and now she is lonely and wants someone to play with. There's plenty over there to keep her company, but some of them still pine for their life here.' Whenever I meet one, I try to be kind and not run away. It's a sad thing to be always wanting to be coming back."

Biddy Connor slowed her pace. "I never saw my fetch again, although I looked for her. Yours was a young one? That's good. The old ones are the ones you want to watch. If you see an old one, it means they want to 'fetch' someone to their side. The young ones usually just want someone to play with, although it's queer she looked like you."

Elizabeth had listened very carefully to Biddy's story, and had a question of her own.

"You mean you never saw your fetch again?"

"No. That's why I crept up while you were looking in the water. I thought I might see yours. But she was gone."

"Do you miss her?"

"Not so much as when I was a girl. I got married and there was always plenty to keep me busy, what with raising a family and putting food on the table. I had no time to think of her, much less to go looking for her. But now I'm alone, and I wish sometimes I could visit with her, see if she still looks the way I remember her. I will see her again when my time comes. One of them, I hope it's her, will come across for me."

"There is only one history and that is the soul's." — W.B. Yeats

Caroline dear,
I felt I was only the instrument. Someone or something was speaking through my fingers. I feel now as I did then. I am flying blind.

Poems rained down and poured from my fingertips. I could hardly get them down fast enough. What did it mean? I must go back to the beginning of this strange time. Nine years later, can I make some sense of it?

It is a golden day outside, full of yellow leaves and sunlight. I watched a branch heavy with leaves and thought of fruit heavy on a tree and I wondered how these leaves manage to detach themselves from the branch. Weight hasn't caused them to fall. One has splashed onto the window of my room and it is exquisite. And yet, the image of masses of yellow leaves stuffed into green plastic bags intrudes. I do not understand why a single leaf is considered beautiful but myriads of them must be destroyed.

We talked of mother last night at dinner. It was very emotional. She never forgave us for whatever we did to her years and years ago. Dad knows what he did, but I am uncertain. I feel it had to do with the summer I turned thirteen and Dad took my side over hers and that was that. A wall went up between us, never to come down in this life.

We drove through rain and fog yesterday, a very gray landscape. They say your external environment reflects your internal state. Mine must be gloomy indeed. Dad is getting tired. It is time for him to go home. An old dog needs familiar surroundings. I hope I never lose my zest for life and new adventures. Old people hate to line up, or wait, but why are they in such a hurry?

I DESIRE AN INTIMACY with angels. All summer I felt their presence. I had only to walk out under the stars and the possibility of meeting them was there. Lately, life has not had that miraculous overtone that I have come to love... the polish, the patina of angel dust over the everyday. I have everything that life can offer, and yet I yearn for the celestial connection. I have this peculiar feeling of needing to minimize the intellectual part of my being in order to encourage the looking, feeling, recording side of me... more witnessing than interpreting. I must take the self and shrink it... such a difficult task... you spend fifty years learning about the self and then the next fifty dismantling it, so that knowledge can flow right through you into meaning without the controlling aspect of the mind.

CHAPTER SIX

Nineteenth-century Ireland did not appear on any map as a divided land, but anyone who lived there knew differently. Reality daily pitted the pale gentry of the Anglo-Protestant landowners against the dark masses of the Irish-Catholic peasants, but the McMaster family was claimed by neither side. Charles and Ellen never openly acknowledged this fact, but they understood it all the same. It was enough for them that Sir Roger liked them and that the tenants gave Charles a grudging respect. Ellen's nursing skills had made huge inroads in the Irish-Catholic community, and although she had no close friends among the women, she was welcomed into every cottage.

Charles and Ellen had come to terms with the Irish malady. As long as they had each other, their children and their work, they could ignore its presence.

For Elizabeth and Thomas, it was different. They were excluded from the natural world of childhood where children make the rules and play at being adult. Thomas suffered most. Elizabeth had her lessons and the company, whenever she needed it, of the other Elizabeth. Thomas was eight years old, and had never had a friend outside his family.

Thomas had watched from the road as boys older than himself rode their carts down the steep slope leading to the lake. He had been longing to try it himself. There had not been much rain that spring and the ruts in the old cattle track leading down to the lake were hard and fast. The carts roared down the track and the faces of the boys in the carts split with laughter as they landed in a heap on the soft grass at the very edge of the lake. Once, while Thomas watched, an empty cart had landed in the water, and one of the boys had leaned so far out into the lake to catch it before it sank that two other boys had to sit on his legs so he would not slip in after it. Their uproarious shouts had reached the ears of the small boy standing by himself on the road. No one ever asked him if he would like a turn.

From early morning to sunset, Ellen moved about her house and garden with Elizabeth at her side. Elizabeth had been helping her mother since she was old enough to stand. As Ellen stood at the table preparing dinner, she made up games for them to play. Sometimes they were nuns in an abbey, working under a vow of silence, and Ellen would pantomime instructions to Elizabeth on how to knead dough or chop vegetables. Elizabeth often collapsed into fits of giggles at her mother's strange antics. They would be weeding the garden, when Ellen would drop to her knees and hide among the plants. When Elizabeth asked her mother what she was doing, Ellen would whisper they were scouts in enemy territory and some soldiers had just ridden past the cottage on their way to the giant's castle. She and Elizabeth crept silently between the rows of vegetables, thinking of ways to outwit the wicked giant and his soldiers. By the time the last weed had been plucked from the garden, they had devised several methods of escape, each more heroic than the one before.

Thomas' arrival had changed the pattern of their days. Elizabeth was put in charge of the baby for much of the day, while Ellen did her countless household chores alone. They missed each other, but for Elizabeth, minding Thomas more than made up for the loss of her mother's company.

When they visited the stable, Paddy stopped whatever he was doing the minute he heard the rolling of the wagon's wheels between the stalls. He loved to listen to Elizabeth explain some special feature of the horses to Thomas; the little girl had an instinct for the horses. Paddy knew this love as something you were born with, not something you could learn, and as surely as his name was Paddy O'Connor, Elizabeth had it. She communicated with the horses by touch. The first time Paddy saw one of the great beasts nuzzling the dark curls on the top of Elizabeth's head, he had rushed to intervene, but now he knew better. No horse in the stable except Master Rodney's would harm Elizabeth. Paddy watched her teach young Thomas how to hold up his hand for the horses to smell his fingers and let them know they had nothing to fear from him. Thomas roared with laughter as the soft nose hairs of the beasts tickled the palm of his hand, and their thick-skinned lips explored each one of his little fingers ever so gently.

The Manor's cook and housekeeper stopped what they were doing to watch the McMaster children go by, and if Sir Roger glimpsed Elizabeth pulling her small brother in the wagon, he abandoned his work and went to the window, following them with his eyes until they disappeared from view. He had grown very fond of the McMasters over the years. On this day Sir Roger stood in the window congratulating himself on the excellence of his choice of Charles as estate manager. Not only was the man a fine manager, but the wife had also proven to be a boon to the estate. Sir Roger had heard from his head groom and his housekeeper how sick children and sick animals alike responded to Ellen's nursing. She was a Godsend to the place. And then, of course, there were the children.

Sir Roger gazed longingly after them and thought of Rodney. He had brought his only child to Ireland as a motherless infant, and had settled him with his nurse into the pastoral atmosphere of the Irish countryside while Sir Roger had buried himself in the restoration of Kingsmill Manor. Sir Roger sighed. He'd done his best. It had been hard without a wife to tell him how to bring the boy up. If Olivia had lived, it might have been different with Rodney. He'd never know, but it did not stop him from wondering what had turned young Rodney against Ireland. Perhaps it was the influence of his English nurse. She had made no secret of her disdain for the peasant farmers with their strange Gaelic speech and their country ways. He had heard her speak of how she hated her exile in this backward country. No doubt she had spoken of her feelings to the boy. Sir Roger remembered how afraid he had been of losing her; he had never reprimanded her, and now his only child hated Ireland and the Irish. It was a strange world. The nurse had stayed until young Rodney was old enough to be sent to school in England. Sir Roger felt badly about that, too. Rodney had cried and begged not to be sent away. Maybe if he had let him stay, things would have turned out differently. Maybe. Sir Roger shook his head and turned from the window. For whatever reason, Rodney had little respect for his inheritance, and spent his time at the gaming tables of London or in pursuit of the pleasures offered on the continent. He showed no interest in attending university or in settling into an occupation. Rodney came to Ireland only when his debts enforced escape from London, and he remained at Kingsmill Manor only until his father paid off his gambling losses. The old and the new occupants of the estate agreed on one thing: life in the old castle was much better when Rodney Kingsmill was not in residence.

Elizabeth never spoke of her conversation with Biddy Connor or of her meeting with the girl in the water, but whenever she could, she slipped away to the place where she had first met the other Elizabeth. She waited for her to appear on the still surface of the lake and she was never disappointed. Biddy died that summer, and now no one but Elizabeth knew her secret. She wondered who had come to "fetch" Biddy. She hoped it was the one Biddy had seen as a young girl.

Shortly after Elizabeth's encounter with the silver-eyed girl, Charles suggested, if she wanted to and Ellen agreed, that she could study with him at the gatehouse. Elizabeth was wildly excited at the thought of real lessons. Each weekday morning she left the cottage with Charles and returned with him at noon for their midday meal. She was a bright and eager student, and Charles was a more than capable teacher, spurred to extraordinary efforts by the memory of Father Egan's words. By the time Elizabeth reached her thirteenth year, she was much better educated than any of the girls under the priest's supervision. Thomas took his lessons from his mother, but he had been promised that next year, he too could have his lessons from his father at the gatehouse.

Ellen laughed when she heard their plans.

"Will you leave me no one to care for, then?"

Charles replied for all of them. "You care for everyone. There's not a cottage you have not been into, looking after the sick or helping with the new babies. And Sir Roger hopes you will use his library. If any of the Manor's old herbals can help you with healing the tenants, he would be more than pleased for you to use them. Do try and humour him."

Ellen's nursing skills rested on her own natural compassion for anything young or sick, and the rudimentary knowledge of herbal medicine passed on to her from her mother and her grandmother. She had never seen an herbal and had never worked from written instructions.

"I've managed up to now. I'd feel queer going up to the big house and rummaging through Sir Roger's books."

The theory of woman as a two-dimensional being seemed to have the backing of the Church, and resulted in woman cast as either saint or sinner, without middle ground. Her human and divine qualities were never allowed to meld and merge into a fully formed whole being. Why? Was she perceived as a threat to the patriarchal society that was such an integral part of western civilization? Man believed that she must be pure or she was soiled, and we had to choose one model or the other. It is fascinating to see how one gets trapped in the ideals of others.

The end of the year, a summing-up day. Mom died, dad became dependent, and Mary came home. For the first time in my life, I felt I had a sister. Whatever happened in our house that so divided us? Mary was, and is, a treasure.

It is a cold sunny day and the shadows on the thin layer of snow in the back yard resemble a moonscape. I am enchanted with the concept of a whole world in a microcosm, Blake's "world in a grain of sand."

We are so far away from what is really valuable in life that I wonder if it is even possible to retrace our steps and find the right way again. God must be a very patient Being. I think I would have torched the whole bunch of us. And then there are moments of sheer beauty. The lake has a thin skin of ice on it; it is closed and still. Waves under ice are amazing to watch, like regular waves in slow motion, as though the lake were breathing in great heavy gasps. Parts are shiny and mirrored, and I am not sure if it is ice or open water. From a distance they look the same... like so many things. It is difficult to perceive the true nature of something from a distance, and yet, to find out for oneself, one must get close. That presents a danger. I keep feeling that I am waiting for something. Why did mother resent me so?

CHAPTER SEVEN

Ellen McMaster never refused a summons to a sickbed or to a young mother about to deliver a baby. Night or day, no matter what the weather or the hour, Ellen always came. That morning in early May, a frantic mother arrived at the McMaster cottage and entered without knocking. Thomas was at his lessons.

"Missus, please come to look at Rory. He's been gasping for breath all this night and now he's blue and choking for air. We've tried everything, his father and I, but he's getting worse. My man has sent me to get you. Will you come?"

Ellen did not hesitate. She picked up her shawl and her basket in one motion, mentally checking the contents of the basket, pausing only to add a vial from the shelf beside the fire. As she swung her shawl about her shoulders, she issued instructions to her son.

"Now, Tommy, you finish your lessons and I'll be back as soon as young Rory's out of danger. If I am too late for your meal, you can pack their dinners with your own and take them to your da's office. Have your meal with da' and Elizabeth, you'll like that. Now mind, you work at your lessons until the clock strikes twelve."

No sooner had the women rounded the corner leading to the second row of cottages, than Thomas was up from the table and out the door on an errand of his own.

Elizabeth, usually so enthusiastic about her lessons, was sulky that May morning. Twice, she and her father had been interrupted by visitors to the gatehouse, and twice teacher and student had lost their concentration. Finally, Charles gave up any hope of teaching his young pupil that morning and spoke not unkindly to his daughter: "Elizabeth, go back to the house and help your mother, will you? This doesn't seem to be a good time to get your lessons done. We'll try again tomorrow."

Too often, to Elizabeth's way of thinking, had this same conversation occurred. Her lessons were what always seemed to be put aside, as if the matter of her education was of lesser value than most other things. Seething, she left the gatehouse with a quick toss of her dark curls. Elizabeth's studies with Charles were her lifeline to the world outside Kingsmill Manor, a world grown so perfect in her imagination that she needed but go there to belong. For her father to suspend her lessons so casually was a great betrayal of her future. She had no intention of going to the cottage to help her mother. She went directly to the lake, but for the first time since she had met the other Elizabeth, she was unable to catch a glimpse of her. The dark gray surface of the water reflected nothing. She threw herself face down on the bank of the lough to wallow in her misery, oblivious to the world around her. She did not see the red wagon rattling down the rutted track or hear Thomas' squeals of joy as the wagon picked up speed. At the point where the older boys fell from their carts in a tumbled heap of arms and legs, the red wagon carrying Thomas remained in the track, accelerating in its descent. For whatever reason— inexperience on Thomas' part, the lightness of the load— the wagon, instead of veering off the track onto the grass, persisted in its runaway path. As Thomas catapulted through the air into the unresisting waters of the lake, his wild cry roused Elizabeth. She could not swim, and his point of entry was too far for her to have any hope of grasping a part of his flailing body. With horror, she watched her brother sink beneath the dark water of the lough and claw himself to the surface, only to vanish beneath the water a second time and then a third time. In those terrible moments frozen forever in her mind, Elizabeth saw beyond Thomas to another figure, flung into a body of water. From some primordial depths a scream rose in her throat and hurled itself across the lake.

Hours later, Thomas' body was recovered. The bank was lined with people. Every man, woman, and child who lived on the estate was present as the small empty body was lifted from the water and wrapped in a blanket. Elizabeth was mute. She had not spoken since sounding the alarm, nor had she moved from the bank. Her rigid stance was disturbed only by the arrival of the priest, and only those standing nearest to her noticed how she shrank from his presence. Not a word was uttered as the blanketed body of Thomas was handed to his father. Even Father Egan was silent.

"They can be seen only if one knows of their existence."
— *A New Model of the Universe*, P.D. Ouspensky

Britannia and I had a breathtaking cross-country ski... great gentle flakes of snow falling, our road filled with pillows of snow, not a track and barely a sound. I tried very hard to be present to the all-white world. When I managed, it was magical. I do believe the creative process parallels the divine process.

God works in mixed media. He can work in wood or stone or flesh, but not in words. Words are not His medium; they are ours. No wonder I am having trouble ferreting out the divine language, a language— not as we know language— created by the angels to allow them some way of communicating with both Him and us.

"They must speak to us in our language until we learn to speak theirs."
— Robert Burton

The best-laid plans can be sent awry by angels. They constantly remind me who is in charge. I am laughing at my disregard for their input. Journal entry from December 29th: "I think I will get up every morning and walk Britannia, then have coffee at my computer... work 'til noon," etc. It doesn't work. They have other plans. There is a stillness and a peace in the early morning that I remember from my childhood, an expectation of miracles rising in my blood like sap, a lovely feeling lost so quickly in the daytime bustle.

CHAPTER EIGHT

"Elizabeth, I'm at a loss. Nothing seems to help these babies' dreadful coughs. It's been the worst winter for sickness in my memory. Some days I wonder if the syrups I give them do any good at all."

Elizabeth lifted her gaze from the table across to where her mother was stripping greenish gray leaves from a pile of dried plants and grinding them into coarse powder with a small wooden pestle.

Ellen had changed little in the two years since Thomas' death. Her voice held the same lilt, and her eyes, when they met Elizabeth's, were still gentle, although they held a distant look. The great mass of dark hair now coiled in a neat bundle at the back of Ellen's neck was threaded through with silver, and the liveliness that had detailed all her movements was diminished. These changes escaped the attention of most visitors to the stillroom but did not escape Elizabeth's. She had shadowed her mother in the terrible days and weeks following Thomas' accident, and that pattern, once established, extended through months and years. Elizabeth was not fooled by appearances. She had seen her mother, in an unguarded moment, reach to take a hand that was no longer there, and snatch it back as if she had touched a flame. Elizabeth heard the sounds of children laughing and shouting outside their cottage, and watched the pain gather in her mother's eyes and sharpen there. At the first sounds of laughter, Elizabeth would gently place her arm around Ellen and steer her out and around the cottage to the stillroom Charles had added to the rear of the building. Here, working amidst the bittersweet aroma of the drying plants, Ellen was able to reduce the memory of Thomas' death to manageable proportions.

"Of course they do," Elizabeth protested. "Their mothers would be desperate without your help. But the syrup stops their coughing for such a short time. Why don't you give them larger doses?"

Ellen's face whitened and she gripped the edge of the oak table with both hands. Elizabeth bit her tongue. As she cast about for another subject, her gaze fell on the plants she was sorting into different bundles.

"Tell me about the herbs, mother. I've always meant to ask you where you learned so much about them."

"I don't know nearly enough, it seems."

"But you know which ones to use. Where did you learn that?"

Under Elizabeth's gentle probing, the colour washed back into Ellen's face and her fingers relaxed their tight grasp on the table.

"My mother used herbs for remedies when I or my brothers or sisters were sick, or the old people when they complained of aches and pains. I treated you with the same remedies. Sometimes you are lucky and hear of new things, and you store them in your mind along with the old ways for a day when you are frantic and nothing works. It's then that you remember what you heard about the healing properties of a certain plant and you try it because there is no other choice. Every woman does the same. If a particular herb works well, you add it to the ones you already know, and if it doesn't..." Ellen shrugged her shoulders. "You forget it. The good ones last and are passed down from mother to daughter. Each generation adds something new."

She stopped as Elizabeth lifted her eyebrows.

"When you are a mother with a sick child, you will understand how it works. A mother will try anything to save her child."

Once again the conversation had veered towards danger. Elizabeth smoothly changed the tack.

"But you know more about healing than any other woman on the estate. Everyone comes to you when they have an illness in their cottage. How is it that you know more remedies than they do? They all had mothers."

In the long silence, Elizabeth watched her mother's face empty of all animation. When Ellen spoke, her voice was hollow and sounded as if it had travelled a great distance.

"The answer must lie with the teacher. I had a better teacher than they did: my grandmother was the best there was in the west of Ireland. She knew more about what plants cured which diseases than anyone I have ever met. I remember opening the door of our cabin many times when I was just a little girl, and there would be a stranger standing there asking me if my Granny be at home. People came from all over the county and even further for Granny's potions. One day my dad asked her why she didn't sell them and keep us all in splendour. She got very angry. She was old even then, bent over and shrivelled up, but when she spoke she grew taller and seemed stronger and more powerful than even my father. I was awed by her. I can still hear what she said to him."

Ellen's own back straightened as she spoke the old words:

Life feeds on life
Not on gold.
The riches of the Mother
Cannot be sold.

"If I close my eyes, I can see her hunched over the table, crushing herbs into a fine powder and mixing them with liquids that she kept in jars on the highest shelf of the cupboard. She had to stand on the bench to reach them, and all the time she would be talking to herself." Ellen sighed. "I wish I'd listened closer. I would give anything now to be able to talk to her."

She closed her eyes.

"She would send me out to find a special herb she needed. She would describe it to me carefully. I remember what those plants looked like. I was the only child in the village who wasn't frightened of her. The other children ran away from her whenever she left the cottage, and when she died the priest refused to bury her. My mother and I and two or three of the village women had to dig her grave ourselves. None of the men would help us."

"Why wouldn't the priest bury her?"

Ellen's eyes flew open and she turned to face the fire. Since Thomas' death, she had been afraid of this question. The moment the words slipped from her mouth, she wanted to catch them and hide them inside where they belonged. "She was a Catholic."

The words dragged across Ellen's lips. She did not want to remember what the priest had said as he crossed himself over the old woman's deathbed: *She never renounced her heathen practices while she lived. Now she must lie with the Devil.*

Elizabeth persisted. "Then why did he refuse to bury her?"

Ellen did not want Elizabeth ever to know what it was like to "lie with the Devil." She turned back to face her daughter and lied.

"I don't remember."

Less than a week later, Ellen, exhausted after yet another night spent coaxing her honey and herb mixture down small raw throats, admitted defeat.

"Elizabeth, I am going to have to go and ask Sir Roger if I may borrow an herbal from his library. Nothing seems to work. I cannot bear to watch these babies cough their way through another night. Will you come with me? You read so quickly and so easily, we might find something."

The housekeeper escorted them to the library, a room that was dark even in mid-morning. As Mrs. Gooden lit the oil lamps, rows and rows of book-lined shelves became visible against the oak-panelled walls. Elizabeth's whole body tingled with anticipation. Her fingers itched to pull one from its place on the shelf and open it; it didn't matter which book or what the subject. Her lessons at the gatehouse had never resumed after the accident. It had not been discussed, and Elizabeth never mentioned it for fear her part in Thomas' death would be revealed. The gatehouse became a place to be avoided.

Elizabeth had not understood until this very minute how much she had missed her lessons.

Ellen left the manor with two of the library's oldest herbals under her arm, and several new ideas for treating the children's coughs.

Elizabeth remained behind.

"Keep plunging into the unknown, it is the only direction home."
— *Self-Remembering*, Robert Burton

Real life is more painful than writing about life. I am still hurting but not quite as acutely. Imagine not feeling anything! Would you still be alive? For the first time in my life I am beginning to get a hint, a glimmer of what "life" is all about. You don't find answers in books, or, if you do, they are second-hand stories. Life must be experienced from the gut, in the raw, first-hand. On the plane, I had an unusual reaction to my relationship with the ground. The landscape was very white and muffled with snow, yet the pattern of roads and streets and rivers was visible, much like those maps of early settlements. We moved through the cloud cover into bright sunlight and as I looked down on the layered clouds, I wondered which was reality. This, or that place I had left? In either case, I was not afraid.

CHAPTER NINE

Sir Roger's passion for Irish history had begun when he took possession of the old castle. The period when he was adjusting to his widowhood coincided with the discovery that he had purchased, along with the threadbare furnishings of the castle, one of the finest collections of books and manuscripts on Irish history in all of Ireland. His first responsibility was to the estate and he had committed all his energy and resources to restoring Kingsmill Manor to its former grandeur, and the land to a new level of productive self-sufficiency. This mammoth project, under the keen stewardship of Charles, was well underway. Sir Roger, finding himself with time to spare, turned to the library. His reading progressed well until he came up against the Gaelic texts of pre-Norman Ireland. Gaelic, the language of the island's original inhabitants, was still spoken by the Irish peasants. It was essentially a verbal rather than a written language, poetic in its images and rhythm, depending heavily on cadence for meaning. Never tamed by rules of grammar, Irish did not yield easily to those who tried to learn it as a second language. Sir Roger wrestled with the Gaelic manuscripts but made little headway until the day he was called to the library to locate the herbals for McMaster's wife and daughter. Then he heard the lyric sounds of the language that so confounded him, as Elizabeth thumbed through the herbals, reading aloud to herself.

"Can you read Irish, Elizabeth?"

"Of course I can, sir. All Irish people speak Gaelic and those who can read have learned to read Gaelic as well as English. My father taught me that if we allowed ourselves to forget our own language, then we would be well and truly a conquered people." The spots of colour on her cheeks deepened to scarlet as she remembered to whom she was speaking and she looked over her shoulder to see if her mother had overheard.

Sir Roger jumped up and thrust the manuscript he had been trying to decipher into her hands. In his enthusiasm he pushed the girl into the chair he had just vacated, frightening her. "You can read Gaelic. What luck! Sit down right here and tell me if I have got this right."

Before Elizabeth was allowed to leave, she had read aloud and translated two pages in the old leatherbound book Sir Roger was struggling to read. She had also given him her word to return to the library whenever her mother could spare her.

Her work with Sir Roger, if one could call something so pleasurable to both "work," became a feature of Elizabeth's day. She helped her mother in the morning, and they took their meal together, for Charles no longer returned to the cottage at midday. When the meal was finished and the room tidied, Elizabeth wrapped herself in her dark green cloak and accompanied Ellen to the stillroom. She lit the fire and settled her mother among the stacked and hanging herbs for the afternoon. Elizabeth was then free to leave for the castle.

Sir Roger would be waiting for her in the library. At first, she simply transcribed the words from Gaelic to English on the pages he indicated. She did not understand the background of the text, and her translations were awkward. They managed for a few days in this fashion, but seeing her discomfort, Sir Roger encouraged her to ask questions if she wished. Elizabeth queried him so thoroughly after each translation that without quite knowing how it happened, he found himself offering to teach her the history of her island.

"Elizabeth, the best way to learn history is to begin at the end. That may sound strange to you, but it is our own times that are most clearly written for us." He smiled at her and added in an undertone, "There's not a schoolmaster in the country who'd agree with me, but you don't care as long as you learn, do you?"

It was a damned shame that Rodney didn't have the longing for an education that this girl had.

The early winter afternoons sped by in a brilliant succession of English victories, beginning with the Battle of the Boyne and ending with the Anglo-Norman invasion of 1170. Sir Roger's methods reminded Elizabeth of the way her mother used to teach her; he inhabited each historical character that marched across Irish lands. She sat spellbound by the fire while he portrayed the fiercely wicked Cromwell laying waste to Catholic Ireland. She thought it odd that Sir Roger, with all his knowledge of history, seemed unaware that he was part of the evil system that Oliver Cromwell had brought to Ireland. Yet surely, if he knew, he would try to change it. Wouldn't anyone?

In this manner they reached the eleventh century, and it became Elizabeth's turn to read aloud from the old books that recorded the exploits of Brian Boru, the Irish High King who took back his country from the Vikings. Sometimes Elizabeth wondered what the tenants would say, or even Mrs. Gooden, if they could see her standing on a chair before the fire with the master of Kingsmill Manor on his knees before her. History made for some strange alliances. They worked quickly through two hundred years of occupation by the Vikings, not a period beloved by either of them. The Norse invaders pillaged the riches of the Irish monasteries, and the monks, gentle ecclesiastical scholars that they were, were no match for this race of warriors. The monks' only defence was to withdraw into their round stone towers and wait for the raiders to board their ships and sail back down the rivers to the sea. Elizabeth uncovered the information that the Vikings had established the first Irish towns; even Sir Roger had not been aware that Dublin, Cork and Limerick all owed their existence to the Viking occupation. Elizabeth blossomed under the praise he showered on her: "I'm very pleased at your astuteness. You have the makings of a real scholar. I have been called to London on business and I want you to continue your studies while I am away."

Elizabeth jumped to her feet and placed the book she was reading on the library table. Sir Roger waved her back into her chair.

"No, my dear, there is absolutely no need to interrupt your education. The library is here, and the books. Elizabeth, you are perfectly capable of learning on your own."

After Sir Roger left, Elizabeth was hesitant to use the library. It lacked the cheerful intimacy lent it by Sir Roger's presence and she was intimidated by its size and gloom. She would enter the cavernous room, choose a book quickly, and leave. This procedure soon proved to be a nuisance, for as often as not, she would arrive home only to discover that in her haste she had selected the wrong book.

Gradually, her desire to learn overcame her fears and she would curl herself in one of the deep upholstered leather chairs by the fire and read until she could no longer distinguish the faded writing on the pages. In this fashion, Elizabeth first encountered Ireland's Golden Age. Every Irish child, whether Protestant or Catholic, had heard of St. Patrick, the patron saint of Ireland, whose most famous exploit, reportedly, had been to drive the snakes from the island. The Catholic Church made certain that St. Patrick's story was familiar to every Irishman, but it had not been quite so conscientious in the matter of the Golden Age.

Hardly anyone now remembered the great monasteries and the rich Irish culture that had flourished in the sixth and seventh centuries. The Church held history and its secrets by tight reins, relaxing its grip on higher education only for those destined for the priesthood or those outside the faith. Elizabeth was astonished to learn that Irish monasteries were once the centers of the most advanced learning in all of Europe, and that Irish monks had been in demand as scholars at all the noble courts. Elizabeth wanted to share this new knowledge with everyone. Patrick's mission to convert Ireland to Christianity had not been accomplished by force. Always before, she had pictured the saint as a black-robed priest with the features of Father Egan, wielding a cross about the heads of the snakes and the Irish peasants. It hadn't been that way at all! The mystic-loving Irish had embraced Christ and added Him to their own list of miracle-performing deities. And as she read further, Elizabeth shivered, even though she sat very near the fire, for horrible things became clear.

She could not change history any more than she could smother the impending sense of doom rising like smoke from the fine, even-handed script of the monks, nor could she stop herself from reading how easily St. Patrick and his Roman masters had infiltrated the age-old religion of the Celts. She wanted to shout, "Close the gates of your world and look carefully at those you let through. Trust the God, but not the priests." St. Patrick had ushered in the richest period in Irish history, but how could the Celts, who treated all Gods as sacred, all priests as holy, and all sanctuaries as hallowed, know that the grid of Christianity being placed over their land would in time erase their own religion and make them servants to a foreign God? This had not been Patrick's intention, but the result had been monstrous all the same. No wonder the church did not want their people privy to such information! The hours spent with Sir Roger in the library and her own analytical mind enabled Elizabeth to perceive the straightforward design; she wondered why the high priests had failed to see the danger. The Druids were anything but fools, yet they had never sounded the alarm. Were they unwary because they had never felt the weight of Roman rule? Was it because Christianity had walked unarmed into their midst?

Under St. Patrick, the Irish had shared a Celtic Christianity with room for all, and Ireland bloomed. This intermarriage of the two religions, the ancient and the modern, nurtured art and literature and new learning, and peaked in the building of the great monasteries at Clonmacnoise and Kell. Slowly the grand Celtic sagas were restyled to reflect a more Christian theme, and bishops, with all of Ireland spread out before them, built their churches on pagan sanctuaries. Those who followed the old Druid ways were now called pagans, and the term became progressively pejorative. The more Elizabeth understood, the more upset she became. She wished Sir Roger would return; she had so many questions. It was insidious, what had been done to the Irish in the name of Christianity. Even the bones of Bridget, the Celtic goddess of wisdom, and her nine maidens who tended the sacred fire at Kildare, had been picked clean and clothed in a Christian fashion to re-emerge as St. Bridget, midwife to the Virgin Mary; the nine virgins became good Catholic sisters. It would have been laughable if it had not been so cruel. What right had these Christian priests to subvert the Celtic myths and trample on their ancient mysteries?

Elizabeth meant to find the answers to her questions. Lucky it was for her that the Irish holy men had recorded the sagas of their Celtic past before they disappeared into the thick mists of pre-Christian history. Had they an inkling of what was about to happen? Bits of yellowed parchment fell between her fingers as she pulled an old book from its clandestine resting place on the most out-of-the-way shelf in the Kingsmill library. She clambered down the ladder with the book clutched carefully in one hand. Placing it on the table, she pulled the lamp closer, the manuscript untouched except by her eyes for an inordinate length of time. It was a large, calfskin-covered book, mottled with patches of darkened leather. Moisture had all but obliterated the title. She opened the cover gingerly. On the first page was an exquisite drawing of a circle of upright stones, surrounded by gold stars in a night-blue sky. Inscribed in the circle were four lines of poetry. Elizabeth translated them as she read aloud:

> Within the circle of stones
> Two worlds still touch
> And the stones will speak
> To those who listen.

When I write I feel alive and tuned into something larger than my own experience. I used to think a person's journal was like a map of her mind, but now I am moving closer to thinking it is a map of her soul.

I am surprised at how angry I still am at a society that cast me in such a narrowly defined role as wife and mother and then made me feel guilty for trying to be something else. All very convoluted, but the rage I feel is real. I am surprised at how long it has lasted. The other side of this rage is the bliss I feel when I have a new book to read. I actually feel smug, on the brink of some new discovery. All this over a copy of Northrop Frye's *The Educated Imagination*.

A friend's grandmother died this week at ninety-two. She was blind and had had a stroke. Her mind was fine but she had no way of communicating. The week before, this same friend's brother and his wife had a baby girl. It made me think of how connected we women are to the circle of life and of death. How we are all sisters and share the miracle of giving life. How it all flows like water backwards and forwards, life, death, birth... baby, girl, woman, wife, mother, grandmother. We are part of some immense cycle of sisterhood, mythic in its roots, mystical in its existence and magical in its possibilities.

I was there when Mom died. Her eyes flew wide open and stared at what? Her breath grew ragged and somewhat strained; she expelled a great gush of air and she was dead. I saw her life force leave her body in that last great exhalation. She was like a wax doll after, and I felt no grief for her. Where had that actual tangible life force gone? It was physical in dimension— without substance— but it had space, width and length— a whole new dimension to think about, for I do trust my own eyes. I know what I saw. A new year in which to see more than there is.

Who will come?
Who will go?
Who will change?
Who will grow?

LIFE HAS ITS OWN rhythm, but I want to enter that world rhythm, where my breathing resonates with the ocean's breathing... not strained, just conscious that the world is an organism like I am, much larger but accessible to me. I hear and feel how it works. I don't make it happen; I move into it, and when I do a state of bliss ensues. Thank you, thank you, thank you. Somehow, the clean white shell I picked up yesterday is part of this; of course it is; everything is tied together.

CHAPTER TEN

"Two worlds and stones that speak." The words sent shivers up and down Elizabeth's spine. She shook her head, disgusted with herself, and sat up straighter in the chair. She couldn't put what she felt was out there into words, not even for herself. There was something about the Irish, something about herself, that wasn't written into the history she had read. This something kept escaping her. She turned the page. Her nose wrinkled. There was an odd odour in the room and she took a deep breath in an effort to identify it. It smelt old but not musty. She sniffed the air again. It had an earthy fragrance. Her nostrils distended, probing the air for a clue. The smell was not totally foreign. It was as though something familiar was buried in the library. Not possible, she thought, and turned her attention back to the book and her Celtic ancestors. The peculiar scent dissipated. She forgot about it.

The Celts were fiercely independent. Loosely grouped into tribes, they had moved wavelike across Europe and into Britain. Driven from the continent by the advancing Roman legions, they laid claim to Ireland, their last toehold in the western world. The Celts called their priests Druids and worshipped within the confines of sacred oak groves. Elizabeth was disappointed; she had been sure, since reading about the circle of stones, that it was the Druids who had brought these sacred circles to Ireland. She read on, hoping to connect the stone circles to the Druids in some way. The priests received their training in Colleges of the Druids and they could both read and write, but they preferred to commit their mysteries and their history to memory. The Druids feared the written word would atrophy their memories, and there was another reason why they kept the oral tradition: to keep their secrets well-hidden from the common folk. Elizabeth laughed at their wiliness. Who would need a priest if everyone could read about the mysteries for themselves? Priests were priests, Druid or Christian, and they were still hiding things from the people. She closed the book and replaced it on its shelf. She should be helping her mother.

"Elizabeth, would you be a dear and gather some tansy for us? I have used the last of it and we are sure to need more before this day is out."

The stillroom was overwhelmed with requests for tonics to cure the rash of sickness that had come with the last days of winter. Three days of icy sleet had kept all but the most hardy indoors. Elizabeth had not visited the library in over a week. She was still annoyed with the Druid priests for holding their ceremonies in oak groves instead of stone circles. It was far more satisfying to work beside Ellen in the warm, herb-scented room. Here, she was doing something worthwhile.

"Of course, mother. I'll get us some willow leaves as well. If this weather doesn't improve, we'll be in short supply of everything. The McNally children are coughing again, and everyone is complaining of aches and chills. Don't wait supper for me. I'll replenish as many of our plants as I can find. It may be days before I'll be able to go far from the cottage again."

She made this last statement with her head turned towards the window overlooking the back fields and the gray hills where the mountain range began. Elizabeth glanced into the baskets stored under the table and mentally added new items to her list.

"We are almost out of coltsfoot and yarrow. I'll look for them, too."

Ellen stopped what she was doing as Elizabeth wound her dark cloak around her shoulders, kissed her mother gently on the forehead and slipped from the warmth of the stillroom. Ellen was uneasy about the girl, but she could not put a finger on the source of her discomfort. Was Elizabeth too quiet? Ellen cocked her head as if a different angle would provide an answer. It wasn't really that. At Elizabeth's age, Ellen too had been quiet. It was as if Elizabeth's silence held something more. But what? Ellen shook her head. She was becoming too fanciful. Elizabeth was too serious for a young woman, too interested in books and learning. Ellen wondered if she should ever have taken her to the library. She lifted her shoulders and sighed deeply. Who was she fooling? What was the difference between Elizabeth spending her time by herself in the library or in the stillroom with Ellen? The books were not the problem. It was a lack of friends. Elizabeth needed to be with people her own age. Ellen shifted her position so she could follow the thin line of Elizabeth's back moving across the empty fields. Her daughter had grown so tall Ellen hardly knew her. The image of a sunny little girl following a younger Ellen happily about the house and garden was clearer to Ellen than the daughter who had just left her.

Christmas has come to my heart. The girls are safe. Sybil's prayers have brought them to a place of refuge. Thank you. Britannia and I skied into Ragged Falls today... not a soul there. There were great clumps of ice formed over the rocks, forcing the water to channel through much-narrowed passages. Are rocks ideas that have become stagnant, monolithic? This piece belongs with thoughts on "Wooden Archetypes," whereby animate things are transformed into inanimate objects while retaining their basic form. The branches of a willow tree are rain carved in wood, and trees are people trapped in wood, like Daphne in the Greek myth. They lose their freedom of movement and become fixed, like art.

CHAPTER ELEVEN

Kingsmill Manor was situated in a broad valley with the lough running from north to south through its middle. High stone hills extended their great bulk to the east, climaxing in the worn top of an ancient mountain range. More hills, rolling and less formidable, edged the western horizon. The manor house and its cottages, although set back from the water, faced the lake, and the working fields spread their skirts about the buildings. Only two features of the landscape broke the monotony of brown fields. A smooth green lawn rose in gentle waves from the lough to lap the stone walls of the old castle, and to the right of the castle was a large fenced paddock. All other ground was cultivated, including the rocky incline behind the buildings.

Elizabeth gathered herbs where the soil was too thin and the inclination too steep for even the most tenacious Irish farmer to till the land. Those plants clinging to life in the soil at higher elevations were of more interest to her mother than those gathered closer to the cottage. The higher Elizabeth climbed, the more rare the species she found. This day, determined to climb to the very top of the old mountain range, she discovered her way blocked by the sheer face of a limestone wall. She had half expected to be prevented from going to the peak.

Elizabeth glanced at the sky; it was still early. There was time to explore. The cut in the limestone must have been there all along, although how she had come to miss it before, she could not understand. One minute she was facing the flat surface of a stone wall, and the next, her eye had found a narrow slit in the surface, an opening barely wide enough to accommodate her slender figure.

The enclosure she entered was completely surrounded by high stone walls and open to the sky. The mountain meadow, for that is what Elizabeth had chanced upon, was thickly carpeted in wild grasses. She moved slowly, with an ordered delicacy, through the tangled undergrowth. Thousands of tiny flowers poked their heads through the grass, and Elizabeth marvelled that spring had come so early to this place. She knew she should be on her knees, picking as fast as her hands could move, for these plants were different from anything she had seen before. Ellen would be thrilled. But as much as she wished to please her mother, she first needed to see what else the enclosure held. Elizabeth wanted to be everywhere at once.

The stones were there, nestled in the furthest curve of the wall and partially shadowed by its rocky heights. Two were standing upright, or she might have missed them altogether. The rest lay tumbled in the grass and all were coated in the soft gray-green of weathered moss. Tall as Elizabeth was, she was minuscule beside the huge stones. Almost without thinking, her hand moved out to touch the stone nearest her and with that same unconscious movement she scratched at the moss covering the smooth rock face. An energy jumped between her fingers and the stone, and as she pulled her hand away she encountered the same smell she had come across in the library. Elizabeth put her hand to her nose, closed her eyes and inhaled deeply. It was an old smell, very old. At the same time, she noted a freshness in the scent, of life hidden inside, the smell of earth in spring or of a newly dug grave. What was wrong with her? When Elizabeth opened her eyes, two things were true. The smell was real and it had come from the stone.

Elizabeth gathered her courage in both hands and carried it to the gatehouse. Her knock produced an immediate response: "Come in, the door is open."

Charles raised his head, both annoyed at the interruption and curious. The tenants knew better than to disturb him with trivial matters when he was working, and the tap was light. For a moment Charles failed to recognize Elizabeth, framed as she was in the doorway of his office. She could have been Ellen. His face brightened.

"Elizabeth?"

She exhaled the breath she had been holding and unclenched her hands. She spoke quickly, excited.

"Father, I have something I want to ask."

She arranged herself carefully on the straightbacked chair that faced his desk. Somehow, in this setting, the changes in her father, wrought, she was certain, by Thomas' death, were highlighted. She saw ravages in his appearance that had gone unnoticed in the cottage. His handsome face was pale and creased, and folds of flesh moved loosely about his neck when he spoke. He wore spectacles she had never seen before, and the lines of laughter that used to dance about his eyes were now wrinkles. Elizabeth could not remember when he had last smiled at her. His whole life was the running of the estate, and Ellen. In losing a son, her father had forgotten he had a daughter.

Elizabeth made a motion to regain her feet. Charles reached across the desk and patted her arm. She stayed in her chair.

"Tell me what you have come for." His speech was clipped and short, in a hurry to be done with the present. Her one hand gripped the other tightly.

"I've... I've been reading in the library of the big house. I was reading Irish history with Sir Roger, but he's away. Would you mind if I came here to ask you questions?"

"Go on."

For the first time in months he looked directly into his daughter's dark blue eyes and read fear in them. He was astonished. Who was she afraid of? There was no one but him in the office. She said nothing. He softened his tone.

"Tell me what you have been reading and what you wish to know." He ran his fingers across the ledgers on the desk, and clapped his hands.

She cast about for a way to explain.

"I've found stories about an Ireland I never knew existed, of people who lived in Ireland long before St. Patrick came. So I..."

Charles' voice held a biting edge as he interrupted.

"Elizabeth. Not you. Surely you are not studying heathen gods? If it weren't for St. Patrick, we might still be running around half naked, praying to some filthy pagan goddess. Next you'll be asking me about the 'wee people' and the 'faeries' and women who claim to have the 'eye.' Sir Roger never meant you to read those books. Ireland's history began with St. Patrick and Christianity."

The history of St. Patrick and Christianity was not the history Elizabeth sought. The old manuscript and the stones spoke eloquently of another world and another story. There was a world out there other than the one she inhabited. It was not a world of shadows where the gates to heaven were manned by stern men in dark robes. This was a world of sunlight and flowers. The certainty of its existence sent Elizabeth back to the library.

This time she found what she had missed. One line in one old manuscript pointed the way to a world Elizabeth knew was real with every instinct of her being. She read, with a growing sense of anticipation, that "the Druids had been charged with the safekeeping of an old religion." She intuited instantly that the old religion of which they spoke was intimately connected to the giant stones. Elizabeth felt a great weight lift from her, as if in locating the stones she had uncovered a world where her own soul could soar and fly. She stood on the threshold of that world; a world created from a different substance than the one in which her father lived.

This world contained goddesses who raced the wind and whose hair burned in long fiery streamers before approaching storms. It was Macha who placed the curse of misery and misfortune on the men of Ulster for their part in demanding she display her celebrated speed in a race against the King's swiftest steeds at a time when she was six months gone with child. Macha raced and won, and for her prize she claimed the right to curse the selfish men who had forced this contest. The curse would last nine times nine generations. And there was Birgid, who communicated with plants in a secret tongue and who shared with her people the mysteries of their healing powers. But there was one among the many goddesses who spoke especially to Elizabeth. She was called by different names, but it was as Cerridwen that Elizabeth knew Her. She was the mother goddess incarnated in Nature, and Her hands both pushed the wheel of time and held the reins of life and death. She gave the gift of foresight to those who nurtured life. Elizabeth discovered it was Cerridwen who was worshipped in the circle of stones and within that circle every living thing was included; nothing and no one was ever lost or discarded. Elizabeth put her head down on the table and closed her eyes. She was not dreaming. She heard the sound of water falling over rock. Elizabeth stepped across the threshold into a world that became more real to her with each passing day.

Archetype: the original pattern from which copies are made.

I am dying to see Dale's tapestry. What if she has resolved the story and I have not?

I think I am finally coming to understand Sophie and Caroline as well as I know Elizabeth. It is a fluid situation. I must yield to it. Imagine, they are created characters, but they are changing and growing as I write them. When they are between the covers of a book, they will have to stop changing. Until then, all is possible.

Andrea got her driver's license today. I felt a great lightness for her... one more string let go. I imagine our children as gorgeous coloured kites that Mike and I received as presents and our task was to launch them into flight. I see them racing across a blue blue sky, higher and further, and we stand on the ground and watch. I do not feel sad, just exultation that they are so high. No need to bring them down to earth. I couldn't anyway; the strings are cut. They are so beautiful up there, the only bright colours in that blue blue sky. The bad patches smooth out and before you know it, it is kite-flying weather again. Sometimes the wait is years.

The tapestry is breathtaking. I will try and live up to its beauty. I was feeling very earthbound, landlocked, and tied to things when I came across this quotation: "poetry as the practice of magic." Just reading it made my wings start to lift. There is no doubt but I am doubly inspired by those twin balms, sleep and sunshine. I now and then understand a tiny bit more of this complex world we share. Each room leads to another, not better, just endless and sunlit with information. I must not rush through each room; I must go slowly, learn all there is in each room before leaving for the next one. If I am patient I can use this principle to my advantage. Some days I fight it, and all is darkness and dead ends.

There is gorgeous sunshine today. The old dog is warming his bones in the sun outside the kitchen door. It must feel good.

CHAPTER TWELVE

How and where could Elizabeth make contact with the Goddess? She centered her search on the huge standing stones, hoping to find in them "the stones that speak to those who listen" of the manuscript, but they remained silent under her probing fingers. She moved clockwise, from the upright stones to the first tumbled stone and walked around it, inspecting the soft green surface. She went from stone to stone, looking for a sign. She found nothing. Elizabeth had half completed her tour of the fallen stones when she paused and leaned against one of the huge stones. She faced the two standing stones. She looked back to where she had been and ahead to where she had yet to go. There was order in the placement of the toppled stones. Elizabeth ran to where the two enormous stones stood guard and placed herself between them. She could scarcely breathe. Spread out before her was the unmistakable outline of an immense circle. She had found the site where they had worshipped in the old religion.

Whispering the well-remembered words, "this is the place where two worlds still touch," she circled the stones reverently, the old new knowledge sifting through her head, unsure of what to do. She spoke the four lines of the poem over and over again, and with the repetition came a creeping recognition.

As spring came, Elizabeth alternated between the library and the mountaintop. The enclosed meadow became a second schoolroom for her. Inside the limestone walls, she watched in wonder as each petal on a single flower unfolded to the sun and closed upon itself with the setting of the sun. It was here she first felt in the soles of her bare feet the pulse that throbbed and flowed beneath the surface of the earth as if the very ground were breathing.

The enclosure was open to the sky, and as night fell Elizabeth's gaze would shift from the carpeted floor of the meadow to the polished vastness of the heavens, where the stars formed dazzling patterns. Some nights she stayed late to chart their movements across the sky and missed the evening meal at home. On those nights Ellen made some excuse or other to Charles to explain Elizabeth's absence. It was enough for Ellen that when Elizabeth returned, she would run up the path and upend her basket on the stillroom table, a blush of colour in her cheeks as she skipped about the room.

Rodney Kingsmill was in foul humour. He had been forced to travel over pot-holed roads for two nights and two days in an ill-sprung coach. Each jolt had been a painful reminder of his ultimate destination. And this had been after a dismal crossing where the rain had been unrelenting and the cabin had reeked with the body odours of the unwashed Irish. He had arrived at Kingsmill Manor late the night before to find his father gone. Damn his luck! It had deserted him at the gaming tables in London and he had dashed to Ireland just ahead of the authorities. He had counted on his father to sort it out, but no one knew when he was expected back. Although, now that he thought about it, his father had never been there when Rodney needed him. He slouched deeper into the armchair.

Even sulking, Rodney was a handsome man. Excessive living had not yet thickened his waist or spidered his nose with the reddish purple veins associated with the consumption of too much good wine. His full head of red hair crackled with a lively energy that contrasted with the indolence in his blue eyes. He gave those who viewed him for the first time a mixed impression of forcefulness and passion laced with a languid air of boredom. Those who knew him well never felt completely at ease with Rodney Kingsmill. Rodney took what he wanted when he wanted it, and left when he was bored or in disgrace. At the same time, if it suited him, he could be charming and amusing. Rodney Kingsmill was a self-confessed sensualist who, at almost thirty, had done nothing in his life but play.

The girl who strode so purposefully into the library did not see Rodney, but she did not escape his notice. He settled deeper into the down cushions of the armchair and watched her move the ladder into position in the farthest corner of the room. Her freshness was not lost on Rodney. He almost sniffed the air to validate the acuteness of this sense, but stopped himself. He'd trust his eyes, but he'd wager she was a virgin. Elizabeth was standing on the ladder in her stockinged feet, propped against the rungs, reading from a book she had pulled from the topmost shelf. He could see, even from this distance, the luscious curving of her body, and his senses quickened. Here was an unexpected twist. Perhaps his luck had changed after all.

As soon as Elizabeth left the library, Rodney was on his feet, pulling the same book from its place on the shelf. A cursory examination of its illustrations conjured up visions of Druid priests practising their pagan rituals on half-naked virgins. He titillated himself; why was this young Irish beauty intrigued with such heathen trash? It was a question worthy of his attention. By the end of the day, Rodney had made the scant inquiries necessary to find out who she was. He ticked off on his fingers what he had learned about Elizabeth McMaster; she was young and lovely, he had seen that for himself. Mrs. Gooden had been only too willing to advise him on whose daughter Elizabeth was, and the tragic circumstances of her brother's death. Lastly, there was Elizabeth's own curiosity about the carnal magic of the old Druid rites. All the ingredients of a mystery were present, and Rodney meant to unravel it. In any case, he had nothing better to do. He was stuck in Ireland, with no hope of resuming his former life until his father returned to Kingsmill Manor and could be persuaded to pay his debts.

Elizabeth was unaware of the interest she had aroused. Her days were filled to overflowing. She managed her daily tasks in the cottage and the stillroom while immersing herself in the traditions of the old religion. Whenever she was free, Elizabeth went either to the library or to the mountaintop, gleaning bits of information on the old ways from whatever source she could.

Gradually, she came to recognize the earthly face of the Great Mother in nature, but this did not satisfy her. Inside the circle of stones, She was Cerridwen and nature's laws were left behind. Elizabeth longed to see the face of Cerridwen during Beltane, the most sacred of Her festivals. Beltane was traditionally celebrated on the eve of the first day of May, and from the moment Elizabeth discovered this, she directed all her preparations to this one night. She rose early each morning and climbed to the top of the mountain, where she performed her own rituals to please the Goddess.

Elizabeth always went directly to the standing stones, where she shed her heavy farm clothing and pulled a shift of creamy linen over her head. Leaning dreamily against the unhewn rock, she removed her clumsy leather boots and waited for the contact with the stone to propel her back in time. She was no longer Elizabeth McMaster, daughter of the estate manager at Kingsmill Manor; she had shifted imperceptibly into the being of an acolyte of the Goddess. Moving to each plant, and before taking a cutting, she knelt artlessly and uttered age-old words of thanks that came to her lips so easily it seemed she had always known them. She was careful never to destroy the plant, but to take only the necessary part. When all the herbs she needed had been harvested and placed in her basket, Elizabeth allowed herself to enter the circle through the gateway formed by the standing stones. Once inside, she stood diminutive and alone, waiting for the magic of the Goddess to wash over her.

And while Elizabeth carried out her simple rituals, Rodney Kingsmill watched from the cut in the limestone wall. He never tired of seeing her strip the clothes from her body to pull the white robe over her dark curls. This movement loosed a violent pounding in his breast that he mistook for lust. He had dwelt so long in the land of artifice and greed that he no longer recognized his response as innocent, a fragment of some long abandoned memory that called out to a younger, uncorrupted Rodney. But it was too late. Rodney had forgotten what that sensation meant.

Yesterday was our twenty-third anniversary. More of my life has been spent with Michael than with my blood parents. I am a better person for it. Michael is inherently good; not perfect, but a good man. I was lucky to have picked him out. Is it luck or is there some invisible thread that tugs us in certain directions? I have grown and blossomed in this relationship. I don't quite understand the mechanics of it other than to say I have never felt insecure or unloved in our relationship. It is a wonderful thing to be loved wholeheartedly by another human being. It is also an awesome responsibility. He is my life's companion. I will follow him to the ends of the earth.

I was out on the lake last night. It has an enchanted quality... silky smooth and a sky full of star patterns. No wonder the ancients longed to read them. The boat skimmed across the water much like I am skimming across my visible life, very fast and on the surface. My sense of smell is heightened; everything smells sweet and potent. It is a dream world that at times creeps along and at other times spins so fast I can hardly remember yesterday. Am I being lulled by this good life into a soul-deadening complacency? Will it be so great that I will stop looking for that other world I know exists?

On Saturday night, we were out in the boat as night was falling. There was a bank of fluffy cloud over the bay, and inside the cloud an electrical storm was taking place. I felt I was watching celestial fireworks, very dramatic but not frightening. The electricity stayed within the clouds, lighting them from inside. I wonder what the ancients would have made of this? I read somewhere that there used to be fifty senses but now we are down to five. I sometimes have an intimation of one or two of the others, but have not the words to describe them. I hear the flutter of a bird's wings, but it is much better than a flutter: a splash, a beating. No, I can't find the words.

The morning is exquisite, calm, shell pink, and the sun is very tender. I shall swim in a moment. Sometimes there is too much beauty and I become tearful. Is this Shakespeare's "heavenly dew" that bathes our souls? I can't tell if it rained in the night, or if it is a heavy dew. The birds revel in the wet freshness. A chickadee nearly landed on my shoulder, not one bit intimidated by Chester or me. I heard a "barking" in the bay and went down to investigate. There were four loons, and I felt connected to the lead one by an invisible string which pulled him closer and closer. My concentration must have faltered, for he dove and I lost him. Such lovely birds, weighty and substantial. Lots and lots of work today, but not one phrase strung beautifully together. Whatever made me think I could write a book?

CHAPTER THIRTEEN

At dawn on the day before Beltane, Elizabeth was up and on the mountaintop gathering the herbs she needed for the celebration while the dew was still on them. She fasted all that long day. When she went to bed, Elizabeth thought the night would end before she heard her father bank the fire and retire to his own bed and she could slip away.

She had never seen the enclosed meadow night by moonlight. Against the starred blackness of the heavens, the plateau on which she stood appeared to be contained in a small stone cup, but simultaneously, the rounded walls of limestone seemed very far away. She was both floating in endless space and held closely in the gentle embrace of the stone circle. Elizabeth halted her passage at the entrance, where she withdrew a wreath of leaves and winterberries from its hiding place in the thick grass at the base of the giant stone. She lifted a flask to her lips, breaking her fast. Two spots of colour warmed her moon-whitened face. She glided across the circle to where a ceremonial fire was laid. Elizabeth took the live coals from the container she carried and placed them on the heaped straw. She knelt, poised, as still as death, while the reddish glow from the coals spread and caught and held. Only then was she released from the frozen place she had inhabited since Thomas' death. The flames sprang to life. Beltane began.

Here by moonlight and by firelight
I offer herbs of grace
Flowers from your daughter
Who longs to see your Face.

As Elizabeth spoke, she plunged both hands into the basket of herbs and leaves and blossoms and sprinkled them tenderly over the flames. She pressed her face to the earth in front of the fire and buried her fingers in the loose soil.

I feel the pulse of the earth
The rhythm of the dance.
To those in your keeping
Nothing comes by chance.

Elizabeth rose from her position in front of the mounting flames and with her arms outstretched and yearning, called to the Goddess once more.

I know the touch of your Fingers
I know the feel of your Face
O Cerridwen come to me, come to me
In this most holy place.

She circled the fire, chanting,

Come in, come in, O Cerridwen.

Weaving between the stones, her voice barely audible above the crackling of the flames, she danced in the firelight until exhaustion claimed her. Only then did she lie down beside the dying fire, extending her arms wide to either side, head tilted to the night sky with her eyes alive to any movement in the heavens. As she lay on the ground inside the circle, she watched the face of the moon magnify, clocking time effortlessly backward and forward. The round white circle grew larger, until at last Elizabeth could look inside.

The lady of the moon beckons me.
Do you await me there, O Cerridwen?

Her slender figure, lying exposed and luminous in the silvered light of the stone circle, gave a convulsive shudder, and Elizabeth released her hold on time. She drifted downward, unimpeded until she encountered the cold stone of a bench and woke to find herself seated in a garden, her hands still and useless in her lap. It was strange to be idle and alone, and without lowering her eyes, she groped for something her hands had dropped or lost. Rodney took this opportunity to slip inside the limestone wall.

As soon as my hands touched the waxed leaves and I pinched their stiff backs, releasing a bittersweet aroma, I remembered where I was: in the garden of the abbey, where I had just finished collecting herbs from the garden for the sisters. I must have fallen asleep and tipped the basket over, for the plants are scattered across the bench and some have dropped on the ground. I hasten to pick them up. I cannot afford to incur the displeasure of the nuns. Before my mother died, she extracted a promise from her husband, who was not my father, to bring me directly to the religious house run by the sisters of St. Bridget. Even he was afraid to disobey the wishes of a dying woman, and especially one who was rumoured to see more than there was.

I am not unhappy here in the abbey. The ladies are kind, in their own way, to a young orphan, and they make sure I have everything they think I need, but I need more than food and shelter. Mother knew that. She understood my longing to escape the schoolroom and spend the hours of daylight in the countryside. She let me roam the fields and meadows surrounding our house and only cautioned me when she knew I was looking with wistful eyes to the far-off forest. I longed to explore its silky depths, and when I did, I learned the ways of the small animals. I passed patient hours watching birth and also death. I was never afraid there, not as I am now.

Mother protected me from the jibes of my older brothers who considered me a nuisance and some passing strange. She kept me away, when she could, from the malevolent eye of her new husband. I hate him as he does me, and I wish him harm as he does me. I will never understand why she married him! I often came back to the manor with my arms laden with flowers and leaves and berries; prizes I had garnered with my newfound knowledge. The plants had secrets, too, and if I was very still and waited patiently, I might hear a snowdrop whisper of winter's death.

It was a very satisfying life. Mother gave me her herbals and I studied their contents. The old books helped me understand the reasons underlying certain salves and potions, why some plants helped some diseases, and how to recognize which plants cured which diseases. When you know what to look for, it is easy. I became adept at mixing medicines. Some in our household still thought me passing strange, but they needed my herbs when they were sick; they only muttered when they thought I could not hear. They think me strange here, too, but they are kind.

I wake to total silence in my tiny room. Full night and yet things stir. I creep from my cot and tiptoe to the door. There is no one there and yet I hear clearly the accusations being hurled at me. How could he be so stupid as to think that I would ever do harm to Midas? Midas is a beauty and very intelligent. I love that horse more than I love most humans; I'm the one they call when no one can get near him. Harm Midas! He must be mad or desperate! That sneaking brutal joke of a man! Afraid of a thirteen-year-old girl, it's almost worth the fear I feel, rising in my throat and choking me, to hear him snivel to the local magistrate. The eye, indeed, as if it were something evil, and to be feared. The eye is nothing more than the things I have learned from my excursions in the forest and from my mother. The knowledge that so frightens him is only that which I have gained from careful observation of all the things I see. The birds, the animals, the flowers have opened up the nature of their being to me because I cared to look. Anyone can share this thing, this eye, this knowledge that I carry tucked inside me, anyone who cares enough to try.

The sisters let me go. They cannot look me in the eye as I am bundled like old clothes into the back of a farmer's cart to be hauled before the judge and my accusers. No doubt the nuns of St. Bridget are worried what their priest will say to them in the blackness of confession, but how can they let me go, knowing what will happen? They must be very frightened of their God to turn me over, more frightened of Him than of a dead woman. The sisters, for all their cloistered ways, know full well what happens to those accused of witchcraft. Innocent or guilty, the punishment is the same. To be named a witch is to be sentenced to death.

He has convinced them I am responsible for the death of every cow and lamb that has perished in the county this past year, and for the neverending rain that drowned the crops this season. Even my brothers have spoken of my solitary wanderings in the fields and woods and have made my walks seem sinister. I gathered herbs for mother and stopped to watch the little creatures in their homes. If I had such evil power, surely my first act would have been to destroy my mother's husband, but they do not think in simple terms, and I am not allowed to speak. What ordeal will they put me through to test my innocence? I have heard stories of how they flush confessions from their victims. I know now what the small woodland creatures suffered when I cupped them in my hands. No human words of reassurance could still the frantic throbbing in their breasts. My heart beats hammer hard, but no one comes to hold me in their arms, or gently speaks my name. I want my mother.

Trussed up like a chicken and hauled to the bridge over the village pond, I find my fear stretched beyond the limits of my strength. I shake uncontrollably. Lifted by rough hands over the stone cold side of the bridge, I face the water. I look straight down into the depths, and looking up at me is a girl about my age, with silver eyes and a wise face. She smiles when she sees me; her smile moves in ripples across her face, and I am no longer frightened.

The smile that crept across the composed face of the sleeping girl unnerved the intruder. He, by now, using the shadows lining the limestone walls as cover, was standing at the very edge of the tumbled stones. Something made him hesitate to cross the invisible line marking the circle. It might have been the artless smile clinging to the girl's lips, or perhaps something in the stones themselves suggested a power he did not want to test. He stayed outside. Inside, Elizabeth drifted more deeply into the past.

Inside her dream she woke, remembering nothing of where she had been or what she had done. She felt light and airy, as if she had been swimming and had gone beneath the waves and stayed there until she thought her breast would burst into a thousand glassy pieces and then suddenly she had broken through the surface into sunlight and she was free and whole with her life spread out before her.

When I was very young, an old man came to see us. Someone must have pointed out our house, for we did not live in the village, but close to the sea on a cliff overlooking the rocks where the seals came to sun and to sing. The old man asked my mother, for there were only the two of us, if she would give me to the Goddess as a gift. My mother was very sad, and cried, but in the end she agreed and I was delivered to the old man, who was a Druid priest, for safekeeping. I was treated with great respect while preparations for my departure were completed, and the night before we left, there was a feast in my honour. It gave the village strong standing in our tribe to have a daughter chosen by the bard to become one of the virgin priestesses guarding the sacred flame at Kildare. I slipped away from the celebrations and made my way to the shore. I wanted to see the seals who slept on the windswept rocks and say goodbye. I never saw them, the night was that black, but I heard them singing, and their song was so bittersweet it made me cry.

I wasn't afraid when the old man brought me here. There were twelve of us, young girls from all the tribes in the western isles, and we lived together and learned the magic of both worlds. We were taught to recognize the patterns of the Goddess as she wrote in nature and to see her hand in the workings of the heavens. All this was imparted to us by our teachers, who were her priestesses. It was rumoured that one day we would be told the secret of the standing stones. I never saw the old man who brought me here again, or any man for that matter. Men are not permitted to view the sacred flame.

I have been here six winters, and six times I have watched my sisters prepare to partake in the Great Ceremony. This year it will be my turn and I am terrified. What if I see nothing in the Holy Well? Will they send me in disgrace back to my village? But I must not think such thoughts. If the Goddess wills it, I will read the water. If I am found unworthy, so be it. I am hers to do with as she wishes. But I am human and I cannot help but hope to see something in the Well.

I have eaten of the herbs; I am purified and clothed in the sacred vestments; I am well-versed in the ritual I must follow. I am ready. Down, down, down, step by step, I am led deeper into the mountain that holds the hallowed water, where I have never been before. My teachers await me. My eyes are covered and I am led by unseen hands to a place where I must kneel. The blindfold is removed and I am kneeling by a well. A cup is placed in my hands and I drink from it. I look down into the transparent water. Nothing. I see nothing. I panic at the emptiness and think the Goddess has abandoned me. I am judged unworthy. So be it.

But wait, the surface clouds and shifts, and there is a face, an ancient face with haunted holes in place of eyes and twisting curving serpents in her hair. She points one bony claw at me and I can look no more. I run away, but neither fast enough or far enough.

The oak trees are all slaughtered and the mistletoe is ripped from the boughs. I can run no further. I must stop. The soldiers have come with no warning; they burst into the sacred grove and killed everyone and everything they touched. I do not understand their outlandish tongue but I do not need to hear to know their purpose. With their evil metal weapons they slash at whatever they can see and they see everything. I must run to where the stones stand still and get inside their circle. They hold a magic older than that practised by the Druids in their sacred groves. I will be safe there. I feel such fear. Everyone is dead. My legs can hardly carry me. Something has touched me! My face is trapped between dead hands. I twist to see what holds me, and as I turn my robe is ripped from neck to hem and I am naked in the sweet coolness of the night air. I have never known such fear. Where is She? The pain is cruel. The violation of my self is even more inhuman. I have never felt so alone or so abandoned or so far away from Her. Will I ever be whole again?

Elizabeth's very being was shattered like old glass by the violence of the rape. Her bruised body lay crushed and unresisting beneath the rapist's senseless pounding. Her mind had not yet connected with her body, and this lack of response maddened Rodney.

"Damn cold virgins, it's like having a dead woman! What does she take me for, a pervert? Wake up, damn you. Wake up." He slapped the unresponsive girl twice across the face. The brutality of the blows catapulted Elizabeth's disconnected mind back into her battered body. Her eyes flew open and looked directly into his. Rodney was stung by the atrocity of his act. Her eyes were huge and full of painful questions for which he had no answers. He could only mutter incoherently as he pulled himself away from her.

"Sorry, so sorry, you looked so lovely, I couldn't help myself. Don't know what came over me, won't happen again. Look, you aren't hurt, are you? I thought you wanted it, coming up here all alone, driving a man half crazy taking your clothes off. Here, take this, and mind, not a word to anyone."

He threw a leather purse onto the soft ground near where Elizabeth lay, unmoving. Only the taste of salt on her bleeding lips from the tears coursing down her face told her it was real. She closed her eyes. For Rodney, the fun of the hunt was gone. He hated to feel guilty. He turned his back on her and buttoned his breeches.

"Damn country virgin got what she deserved, coming up here in the dead of the night to practise heathen rites. What did she expect?"

He kicked one of the massive stones with a booted foot. Why had he ever thought her worth his while? He would certainly be smarter the next time.

Hot hot weather and I walked to get my hair cut. As so often happens, I was pulled into another time frame, a time before there were cars, when I walked everywhere. It was a gentler, slower kind of life. I was a teenager, scuffing along a dirt road. The feeling was very real. I must have been there.

Both children have had car accidents within the space of three days; no one hurt, but still nervewracking. I keep thinking there is a pattern to all this, if only I could read it. But what then? Could I stop it from happening? It is strange, but I sense strongly that someone or something is trying to get through to me, as though someone were talking to me from a great distance. I can see their lips moving but I cannot hear the words. All very uncanny, and I have retreated to the lake to regain my equilibrium. I love being here where my soul can rise to the surface.

I tap the earth
For that is where
My connection lives.

Lines jotted down on the back of a bank statement. They all matter.

Writing fixes life in my memory; when I don't write, life slides through my mind with almost no recall of events. I have a passion to see as much theatre as I can. It is all tied in with a suspension of belief which is the space I want to enter and explore. Just back from Craftsbury, a rowing camp. It was bliss. There were times when I was part of the lake and sky, moving for one long moment in perfect harmony.

Andrea, you were the best story I ever wrote and then you up and left the page and I was left to carry on alone.

SHADES AND SHADES OF blue in a swelling ocean and thoughts of the relationship between birds and leaves and fish and humans have combined to produce a chance analogy. It seems that each of these components plays the same role within its own cosmos; birds are to the animal kingdom as leaves are to the plant kingdom and both are as fish to the aquatic world. Humans must play this same role in the celestial realm. We are the birds, the fish and the leaves of the divine kingdom. We people the angelic realm, but we cannot see or understand the underlying design any more than birds or fish or leaves can see the larger design of our world. We are in this kingdom, but we are not of it. Everything is predicated on the theory "made in the image of God." It is this image that is translated again and again throughout the different worlds. Each world adds its own piece to the original image, and we humans attach gender to this image, distorting the clarity of the divine design.

CHAPTER FOURTEEN

Elizabeth had not wanted to keep what happened to her a secret. She had wanted to sob out her hurt and shame to her mother and feel herself circled by her mother's arms. It was this instinct to pour out everything about the rape to Ellen that enabled Elizabeth to gain her feet and get away from the meadow whose limestone walls had become the sides of a giant trap. She dragged herself down the mountain and across the greening fields. With each step closer to the cottage came the awareness that she could not tell Ellen what had happened to her. It would be the final blow to her mother's fragile spirit. Ellen willed herself to survive each day. Elizabeth couldn't tell her mother. She could not take that chance. That left her father. He cared about her, but she could imagine his reaction.

"Who did this to you? Tell me. I'll kill him."

"My God! That brute, I'll take a horsewhip to him. How dare he touch you! What kind of an animal is he? That spoiled no-good bastard! He should be shot. Are you sure it was him?"

"How can I tell Sir Roger that his only son has raped my daughter? We'll have to leave. Well, that makes no difference, he's got to be told, and that bastard has got to be punished. Tell me everything, Elizabeth."

"When did this happen?"

"What were you doing out last night? Your mother and I saw you go to bed."

"On the mountaintop, in the middle of the night! My God, Elizabeth, are you mad? Whatever possessed you to go up there at night? However am I supposed to explain this to Sir Roger?"

By the time Elizabeth reached her door, she was so bruised and exhausted that the thought of dealing with her father's rage was more disturbing than any comfort she might derive from telling him. She crept up to the loft and into her bed, crawling under the covers like a hurt animal.

"Elizabeth, it's a heavenly day, far too nice to be bent over a workbench. Go and climb in the hills. There's nothing needs doing here that can't wait for a rainy day. I thought I'd drop by the gatehouse to see if I can persuade your father to give up his ledgers for an hour or two."

Ellen stroked Elizabeth's cheek with gentle fingers. The sun was pouring through the windows, bringing motes of dust to life in the air of the stillroom.

"You need to spend some time in the sunshine, love. You look so pale and tired."

And hearing the words made Ellen look more closely at Elizabeth than she had in months. Panic swept her. The girl looked terrible. She had grown taller without any corresponding gain in weight; where before she was slender, now she was gaunt. There were great blue smudges about her eyes as though she had been badly beaten about the face or had not slept properly in months. Ellen was truly shocked and even more shocked because she had not seen this coming. Where had she been?

"Elizabeth, what's wrong? Are you ill?"

She placed her hand on her daughter's brow.

"You are not feverish, that's something. What on earth can be the matter? Part of the problem, I'm sure, is spending all your time inside the stillroom. You're young, you need to get outside in the fresh air. If you want to help, gather some of those special herbs you used to bring me. You are the only one who knows where to find them."

Ellen moved to the end of the room to check the shelves where the pots of medicines were stored. Elizabeth hadn't been anywhere in weeks.

"That's it. No wonder you look ill. You haven't put your head outside except to go between the house and the stillroom. You'd think it was the middle of winter instead of the middle of June. Now here's a basket, and mind, I don't want to see you back here until it's filled."

What Ellen saw leap into Elizabeth's eyes was more frightening than any illness. She felt a premonition like a chill of icy water.

"Elizabeth, what did I say that makes you look so...?"

Ellen could not finish what she had started to say, for she had no words to describe what she had seen in Elizabeth's eyes. The girl was stone silent, looking into Ellen's face as though it were a mirror. Alarms went off in

Ellen's head. She reran slowly all she had said, editing each word before passing onto the next. She knew, before she reached the words, precisely where the terror had darkened and distended Elizabeth's deep blue eyes into empty pools.

Ellen answered her own question. "It's the herbs, isn't it? When I asked you to get me the special plants? You are afraid to go and gather them. Why?"

Ellen forced herself to remember that first day, months ago, when Elizabeth had struck off across the fields, her dark green cloak the only patch of colour on the gray blankness of the mountain.

"It's the high meadow that frightens you, isn't it? Why?"

The girl flinched as though she had been struck a blow across her face, and her hands shot up to protect herself from further blows.

"Nothing. I just can't go up there. Please, mother, don't ask me. I can't do it. I'm sorry."

And Elizabeth dropped her head on the table and sobbed as if her heart would break.

Ellen ran to her and held her closely as she had held Elizabeth when she was a child and had hurt herself.

"There, there, it's all right. Don't cry. No one will make you go. I've got you. Shh... shh."

And she patted Elizabeth's back and rocked her in her arms until the girl's sobs subsided. Only then did Ellen lift her daughter's chin and look directly into her eyes. She had never encountered such a poignant plea for understanding. Ellen was terrified.

"It's all right, Elizabeth, I won't pry any further. We won't need those herbs until the damp of winter sets in. Maybe by then you'll feel differently about climbing in the hills. In the meantime, you take over my duties in the stillroom and I'll gather what plants we need. But you must promise me to spend at least an hour every day outside in the sunshine. You can work in the garden if you feel you must do something."

Ellen put her arm around the girl's shoulders to reassure herself that she had done the right thing. Elizabeth's body was as brittle to the touch as the pieces of fine china displayed on the top shelf of the Welsh dresser. She was so tightly strung that Ellen felt the slightest increase in the pressure of her arm would cause the girl to crumble into fine translucent powder. She released her carefully, sick at heart.

Home... no time to write, to be. Just rush and do. I do not want to live the rest of my life this way. I am accumulating too much: things, people, projects. It makes me tired and fretful for I know that I am not gaining in my being; my soul needs companionship. I shall try and not race around, beating the clock. Time is to humans as collars are to dogs, a necessary restraint. Just for a moment, sitting in the sunshine overlooking the Potomac, I "saw" the pigeons pecking for food along the promenade as businessmen in their gray suits, pecking away with their heads down, oblivious to the larger picture which I could see from my place on the bench. It was gorgeous— sun, people, music, sky— a greater reality— theirs is only the crumbs on the pavement (probably an apt analogy for the men in the gray suits).

I spent the afternoon at the National Gallery with one Leonardo da Vinci and a roomful of Rembrandts. I was not sure of what I was seeing but it was big... beyond good. Did they paint emotions or did they paint emotionally, from the inside out? What did they see? What am I getting glimpses of... the pigeons, the tree with the ruffled fringe of leaves? A shock of recognition, and Rilke's warning, "you must change your life." I must place the tree in context; I was driving and I saw a tree with a few fragile leaves clinging to its branches; for that moment I was seeing the tree with my heart and it was frail and lovely, frilled like the edges of a chiffon skirt. It was more than a tree, but the words will not hold what I felt. This is where I want to go... this deeper penetration of life... straight to the place of being.

CHAPTER FIFTEEN

Elizabeth would not climb in the hills beyond the fields, not even to gather the special herbs that grew only in the high meadows. She no longer frequented the library, and it had been such a source of joy to her. And what Ellen had seen in Elizabeth's eyes was nameless. It could not be described, nor could it be forgotten.

Ellen saw herself at Elizabeth's age, kneeling on the cold stone floor beside her mother, and then there was a flood of memories: her mother helping her dress for her first communion and the face of the priest as he offered Ellen her first taste of Christ's blood, and the indescribable closeness to something so sacred that she thought she might faint as her lips touched the cold edge of the chalice. Ellen pushed that memory away and replaced it with the wetness of her mother's tears running down her own face as they said goodbye at the convent where her father had sent her to school. It was a better memory. The sisters had been kind to her and she had slipped into the routine of their finely cloistered life as easily as if she had been born to it. There were those times when she missed her mother and the little ones so much that a great lump clogged her throat so she could not speak, but there was always a sister to whisk her away to the kitchen or to the classroom, or best of all to the sewing room where the nuns embroidered ornate designs on the altar cloths and on the vestments of the priests. The nuns worked magic with their needles, and Ellen loved to watch their fingers fly among the gold and silver threads. She remembered to pray fervently that one day she would be asked to embroider the sacred cloths. But that seemed a long way off, for now she was stitching, under the watchful eyes of Sister Catherine, a sampler, a young girl's first piece of needlework: the one thing she had been allowed to take away with her when she left the convent. She had spent two years there, two good years before the money ran out. Her father had been summoned to come and fetch her home. She hadn't thought of the sampler in years.

Ellen sat up straight in her chair.

"I can teach Elizabeth to embroider. I hope I remember how."

Ellen chuckled at the memory of trying to teach her young sister the intricacies of French knots and feather stitches, and then her smile faded. The shadow of her mother loomed over both of them and Ellen heard her say: "What's the good of fancy stitching for the likes of us?"

Ellen had quietly picked up the squares of linen and hidden them in the bottom of the dresser.

A sampler might be just the thing to capture Elizabeth's attention. Ellen got up from the chair and checked her sewing box. There was little in the way of embroidery thread. She would ask Charles to buy the brightly coloured skeins she needed in Ballindooly. They could stitch in the evening if the light was good, and when the weather was fine they could take their needlework outdoors. She was sure Charles would build them a bench. If she could just get Elizabeth's approval.

"Where's that tall good-looking daughter of yours, Mrs. McMaster?"

Ellen started. She had asked Elizabeth this morning if she would go to the library and check the old herbals for some new tonic to give the women who were still rundown and work-worn from the winter. She worried about these young mothers, always pregnant or nursing. They never had time to fully regain their strength before the next baby was swelling their tired bodies. Ellen thought surely, if she looked hard enough, there must be something that would bring the colour to their cheeks. She sighed. It wasn't only the young mothers who worried her. In answer to her request, Elizabeth had given Ellen that pleading look that Ellen had come to correctly interpret as *Please don't make me leave the house.*

Sir Roger continued: "I haven't seen her at the house since my return. As a matter of fact, I haven't seen her at all. Has she got a young man and given us all up? That girl had the makings of a true scholar, always looking in the history books and asking questions. Until I went away, we spent every afternoon reading the old Irish manuscripts. I can't believe she isn't interested any more. Young people, you never know what they are thinking. Take Rodney. He never spent any time on the estate unless I made him, and here, on his last visit, he stayed for months when I wasn't here. And just when I am due to return, he up and leaves without even waiting to see me home. He left a note saying he was bored with Kingsmill Manor and bored with Ireland and he didn't care if he ever came back and I could sell the whole damned place if I wanted to. He knows the estate is entailed and can't be sold. I don't understand any of the young people any more, Mrs. McMaster. Do you? Tell that attractive daughter of yours to come and use the library again. Even if she doesn't want to do that, have her come up to the house and say hello. I miss her."

As an initiate of the Goddess, Elizabeth's spirit had been reaching towards larger worlds than those promised by either sect of Christianity. There was her father's Protestantism, the authorized religion of the estate, but not the tenants' choice. The small chapel tucked in a turret room in the old castle was never filled, and although there was an organ and an organist who came from Galway to play for special services, the music never held the same high clear joyful sound Elizabeth heard when water bubbled over rock. She sometimes felt they deserved the epithet "black Protestants," not for their actions, but for the soulless rendering of their religion. In her view, the religion of the people was even less appealing. The Roman Catholic Church took souls as hostages.

The outrage of the rape had shrunk her world; the only people she saw were her mother and her father, and the only places she trusted were the cottage and the stillroom.

The sampler changed all that. To her delight, she saw in the coloured skeins the same threads nature used in her creations. A magic in Elizabeth's fingers made stitches dance like flames and embroidered stones cast shadows of blue silk against a wall of silver threads; tiny stars glittered knowingly from the purple blackness of the background. She smiled more often now and colour washed the contours of her softly rounded face when she was especially pleased with something she had stitched. Ellen noted happily that Elizabeth was gaining weight.

Ellen's talent for nursing had not remained the sole property of the human population of the estate. She had, when asked, ministered to any sick animal. Generally, Paddy was able to manage on his own. He had a store of remedies he had always used on his precious horses, but now and again he came up against something beyond his skills and he would call on Ellen, who was most in demand when the foals were due. Ellen had often taken young Elizabeth with her, and the two, working side by side with Paddy standing at the animal's head to reassure her, had eased the birthing process for his mares. Ellen used the same methods to soften the birth pangs for the horses as she used for her human mothers, and the three of them had never lost a patient.

The knock on the cottage door was sharp and urgent. Charles answered.

"Sir... it's your missus and the girl we need in the barns with Paddy. One of the mares is in a terrible way. Paddy's needing your missus and Miss 'Lizabeth to help him or for sure the horse won't see morning."

Elizabeth panicked.

"Will you come with me, Elizabeth?"

Quietly Elizabeth gathered her courage and followed Ellen to the stillroom. She trusted her mother and she hated knowing an animal was suffering. She held the basket while Ellen filled it with anything from the shelves she thought might help the animal. The horse was in agony. They heard her screams and the dreadful thrashing of her body the moment they walked into the stable. Her eyes rolled back in her head and her sides were slick with sweat; she was heaving with exertion. The horse was not in foal; she was terribly sick. Paddy, Ellen and Elizabeth worked steadily throughout the night. Paddy held the frenzied animal while the women poured a colic drench laced with restorative herbs down the horse's throat. She retched and groaned but the medicine stayed down, and every half hour they got more of it inside her. By dawn, her thrashing had stopped and her eyes were calm.

She was as exhausted as they were, but she would live. Ellen placed a blanket over the mare and sank down in the straw beside her. Paddy offered to make tea.

"Elizabeth, I'll use your help."

Out of Ellen's sight and hearing, he grasped Elizabeth's arm and spun her towards him.

"Who did this to you, girl?"

It was meant kindly, though the tone was gruff. How did he know what no one else had guessed? Paddy would have been hard-pressed to explain what he had seen in Elizabeth's face. He narrowed his eyes as if he had been asked to verify his thoughts. He knew a breeding female when he saw one, and if this young one was not pregnant then he was a bloody Englishman. He shook Elizabeth's arm, but not roughly.

"Answer me. Who did this?"

Two tears slid down Elizabeth's face. She trembled under his touch, but remained mute. The misery he had seen in the eyes of dumb animals abused by their owners stared back at him.

Paddy watched the women disappear into the thick mist of the October dawn and swore at the empty walls of the stable.

"Damnation, who's got to that innocent child? I'd like to kill him, which is what her father will do when he finds out. God in heaven, it won't be long before everyone knows. She must be," and he counted out the months on his brown fingers, "full five months along." He kicked a bale of hay that lay in his path and went to check on the ailing horse. The mare was doing well.

Later that same day Paddy had his answer. He should have known. He went back into the stall several times to check the condition of the mare, and on the last visit he heard a great commotion and went to investigate. He found one of the young stablehands backed into the corner of a stall by Captain Die. The stallion had his lips drawn back and was about to bite the frightened boy when Paddy intervened.

"It's all right, lad. Back out gently, out you go. I've got him interested in me now. Poor fellow, he's not mean, just restless. He loves to run and race the wind, but we're not to touch him when his master's gone. No wonder he's in such a temper; he's not been properly exercised in almost five full months."

It was as though Paddy dipped his head in a barrel of rainwater, so clear and cold was the image of that early May morning. He had only just arrived at the stable when he was hailed by Rodney.

"I thought you'd never get here. Hurry up now, I need a horse to take me as far as Ballindooly. If you don't step lively and get a saddle on one of these beasts, I'll never make it. No, no, not Captain Die. It's not a pleasure ride I'm after. I have to catch the morning coach to Galway, and if I miss it I'll have your neck."

Rodney's demands brought the stable to life. The horses moved restlessly in their stalls and one of the young stallions started a rhythmic kicking against the door of his stall. Paddy could hear the beat in his brain even now. Paddy had saddled Rodney up in record time and had him out of there. Paddy's face dropped. No wonder Rodney had been in such an all-fired hurry. It all made sense. And if Paddy knew a thing or two about that bastard, he'd forced her. That slimy English scoundrel— he hoped McMaster would take a horsewhip to him when he knew.

Paddy O'Connor had never been one to interfere. He'd learned at a young age that most people didn't want your help and they didn't deserve it, either, but this was different. This young one was in trouble, and she, he'd bet his life on it, was not to blame. But she'd be the one to pay, all the same. It wasn't fair. She clearly hadn't told her mother, and why the mother hadn't guessed was more than Paddy could understand. That mother knew more about the birthing of babies than most doctors, and yet here she was, not knowing her own daughter was five months gone with child. He guessed that when it came to their own, folks saw only what they wished to see, and the closer they were to a problem, the less likely they were to see it.

He wasn't doing any good, dallying about. If he was to do what he knew to be right, he'd better get a move on. There wasn't much time to be had.

That night, Paddy presented himself at the front door of Kingsmill Manor.

"I'd like to speak with the master, Mrs. Gooden."

The housekeeper was shocked. The head groom never came to the house, not even by the back door.

"And what is it you'll be wanting with Sir Roger?"

"That's me own business and none of yours— now tell the master that I'm wanting to see him."

The meeting took place behind the closed doors of the library. When Paddy O'Connor exited the manor, he left behind a very troubled man. The candles in the library burned late into the night.

INSTRUMENTS

If the pen is a metaphorical penis
to write men's stories,
is the needle a metaphorical sword
to castrate them,
or an instrument to keep them
from unravelling?

When women reach middle age dead center, and they have the time to dream or write or paint or read, they have forgotten how. So much time and energy went into creating our increasingly complicated and overdecorated "nests." There is a funny gap where Andrea used to be. I will get used to it in time. I read a quotation this morning: "we reveal our most universal truths when we write about ourselves."

Today I must ask some questions as I write. These women, Elizabeth and Caroline, reject and are rejected by nineteenth-century society, but they do not give up. They search for the something "eternal and divine" they know is hidden out there.

A wonderful weekend at Pethern Point— six of us in such different places— but we can come together and share a common happiness. That is the wonder of old friends— a tolerance for what and who we are and a desire to understand; rare, I think, among peers. The men, by example, have taught me this. I walked the streets of Perth today, hoping for a glimpse of the young Caroline.

I spoke to Andrea yesterday and I am left with a vague uneasiness. Does she know how to judge situations? Does she know what has the potential to become dangerous? I have only myself to blame. At seventeen I knew everything and was mistress of all; at forty-five I know how little I am in control. How to tell her and yet not kill the wonder of a chance encounter? There are no absolutes in life. I am hostage to her taking extra care and she is hostage to her innocence and beauty. If we love, we are always hostages to fate.

HOW DOES ONE WRITE emptiness… space? Is it like painting white in watercolours? Does one simply dip oneself in water and use that to lighten up the darkness? Do I remove myself from paper, the self as ego, personality, and let the lightness slip around without me? I'll try. Andrea is impatient with me, my oldness, my fatigue, my presence; she does not want to understand the hands of time. It is time to go home, but not before I transform this heaviness into nothingness, space. Paint yourself white… lots of salt water (no colour, no self) and let it work itself into the paper/body and see what happens. This transformation really works. I floated through yesterday, refusing to get drawn into Andrea's grumpiness. I swam myself into lightness. Is this baptism? You clean yourself, inside and out, and then dance through the day. Everything seemed to be held in perfect harmony, and as a result I was not one bit fatigued. It is hot and tiring holding onto all that heaviness.

CHAPTER SIXTEEN

A young woman stood steadfastly in the stream of oncoming passengers and porters bearing luggage of all descriptions. They had to part to pass her. This young woman had a small boy in a sailor suit held firmly in each hand. The boys struggled to watch the loading of the ship, which was taking place behind them, while their mother scanned the faces of the oncoming passengers. A stack of boxes piled on top of two large trunks blocked the older boy's view.

"Mother, I can't see what they are doing."

"Be quiet, Daniel. We must stand here and wait until they come. There will be plenty of sailors for you to watch once we board ship."

Emily Jane Harris had decided early in her marriage that she would not spend her life waiting for her soldier husband to return home on leave. That might satisfy some women, but she meant to spend the rest of her life by her husband's side, wherever that might be. That was what God had intended when He joined them together in holy matrimony, and Emily meant to respect God's wishes. Fortunately, God's wishes corresponded with Emily's own, and this coupling of strengths had brought Emily and her sons to this crowded quay in Liverpool. Tom Harris had already been in Canada for five months. He had written her of his assignment. His regiment was in charge of establishing a military settlement in Upper Canada. She read into his letter the understanding that it could be years before he was back in England to stay, and that he missed her and the boys dreadfully, but he could not ask them to give up their comforts for the hardships of a pioneer settlement. Emily knew that life in Upper Canada was rough and full of difficulties for a gently raised lady. She knew because everyone from her father to the village vicar had told her so, but that wasn't going to stop her from joining Tom in Canada. What did they know? None of them had ever been there.

Emily had had no money to purchase tickets to make the trip; the trip to Canada had seemed impossible. And then Margaret had arrived with a strange proposal. In return for escorting a young woman who was with child, and yes, unmarried, to Canada, Emily would receive first-class passage for herself and the boys to Montreal and sufficient funds to allow them to join Tom somewhere in Upper Canada. It was, to her mind, a fair exchange, though she cringed at travelling with a woman of low morals. She had wanted to ask Margaret more about her charge, but Margaret had cut her questions off with one sentence.

"Don't ask me who she is. I know nothing more than I have told you."

Sir Roger had paid a surprise visit to the McMaster cottage one damp evening in mid-October. A chair was drawn close to the fire and as Sir Roger settled himself, a draft blew through the room. All three adults turned to where Elizabeth stood, framed in the open door, well-wrapped in a dark green wool cloak.

"Good evening, sir." The thick folds of her cloak flared out as she dropped a small curtsy.

"I am happy to see you, Elizabeth. It has been a long time since our paths have crossed. I have a matter to address which concerns all of you, but it is Elizabeth who will be most directly affected by what I have to say."

While he spoke, his eyes remained on her face.

Elizabeth shifted uncomfortably inside her cloak. Without unwrapping herself, she took a place on the bench by the hearth.

Sir Roger pulled a letter from his waistcoat pocket. Without opening it or altering the direction of his gaze, he began to speak.

"This letter is from my youngest sister, Margaret, who lives in London. She has written to ask me if I am acquainted with any young ladies of good character who might wish to obtain a position as governess to her sister-in-law's two small sons."

He paused. There was such silence in the room that the rustling of the letter as Sir Roger drew it from its envelope was all that could be heard.

"Emily wishes to join her husband, who holds a commission in the British Imperial Army in..."

There was a general intake of air, held for a long moment and then expelled, as the words "Upper Canada" were dropped. He continued quickly.

"She requires the services of a young lady with impeccable references to make the voyage to Canada with her and the boys, and once there to assume the duties of governess. There will be few of the amenities of English life available in the colony, but it is a fine opportunity for a well-educated young woman of modest background to travel abroad and at the same time obtain a position with a kind family."

Sir Roger folded the letter, replaced it in its envelope and tucked it in his pocket.

"Such a long way," Ellen gasped.

"But a wonderful opportunity," countered Charles.

"I thought Elizabeth would be perfect for the position," added Sir Roger.

All three once more turned to watch Elizabeth. She sat utterly still and her face gave way to her eyes, which had grown huge and very dark.

"Well, Elizabeth, what do you think of this?"

It was Charles who spoke.

Elizabeth hugged herself, as though she were cold in spite of the heavy cloak and her proximity to the fire, and rocked quietly back and forth on the bench.

"Did you hear me, Elizabeth?"

She raised a finger to gently silence him and cocked her head. She heard a faint tattoo being tapped onto the rounded walls of her womb and she stopped to listen. The first time she felt the delicate flutters she had been stitching on her sampler and had wondered what they meant. The next time the touch like feathered fingers had caressed her womb, she knew what was happening. It was the Goddess' way of connecting with her. Elizabeth was supremely happy. She hadn't been abandoned after all. Each time a message was stroked across her flesh, she stopped whatever she was doing to listen, and each time what Cerridwen was saying became clearer to Elizabeth. Now the Goddess had sent Sir Roger with the letter, and in one grand gesture the tangled threads of Elizabeth's life unravelled. She was free.

"I'd like to go to Canada, father." And to Ellen she simply said, "This way is best, mother. Be happy for me."

"Then it's settled."

Sir Roger heaved himself to his feet.

"One more thing. We'll have to leave for Liverpool in three days, or the ladies will miss the last ship sailing for Canada before the ice sets in. Winter comes early there, and blocks passage up the river."

Only Charles was in Ballindooly to wave goodbye to Elizabeth and Sir Roger. Ellen was in no condition to accompany them.

Sir Roger and Elizabeth made an agreeable couple, although oddly matched in age and station, and they travelled easily together, as though this were but one of many trips they had taken in each other's company. Passengers sharing the coach with them speculated as to the propriety of their relationship. Elizabeth's concern lay not in what the other passengers were thinking, but in what Sir Roger thought. She believed he was aware of the real reason for their trip, but she had no way of confirming this. He took great care to establish himself, with her and others, as the kindly benefactor of a favoured employee's daughter, taking a keen interest in her future. She could find no fault with his performance. Elizabeth wondered what she would have said if he had asked if she was carrying Rodney's child, but it never came to that. It quickly became apparent that he didn't want to know and she didn't want to tell, and they fell into their old ways of the previous winter, entertaining each other with passages of Irish history. Each signpost was a signal for one or the other to recall what they had studied together. Had it not been for the changing conformation of the landscape, they might have thought themselves back in the library at Kingsmill Manor. Sir Roger was almost sorry when they reached Dublin.

Elizabeth had never been on board ship before, or even seen the sea, and her companion experienced misgivings as to the wisdom of introducing her to a sea voyage in her condition. But there was no help for it. They had to cross the Irish Sea to reach Liverpool. He soon discovered his fears were groundless. Elizabeth was a natural sailor. She easily adapted to the rise and fall of the boat and the ceaseless motion of the waves. The sting of the salt-laden air stained her cheeks scarlet and sharpened her senses. The prosperous looking man, past middle age, and the fresh young woman bundled in the huge green cloak were a most engaging pair as they walked the deck of the ferry. He answered, as best he could, her multitude of questions. He could not remember feeling such a zest for life since he was a boy. The trip, far from the ordeal he had anticipated, was ending much too soon. He began to wonder whether he was making a mistake in sending Elizabeth and the child to Canada. He'd never met anyone remotely like her. She had such spirit, and she was smart. Life was interesting around Elizabeth, but what could he offer her and a baby? At best, a second-class life in the sidestreets of London, or the ostracism of a small house in one of the more remote Irish counties where he would be an infrequent visitor. No, what he had devised was better. Canada was far enough away for anyone to begin again. She would have a chance of succeeding with the background he had given her. Elizabeth was the young widow of a naval officer accompanying another young officer's wife to the British colony. Once there, she would have to use her wits and his generous allowance to keep her life on course. If his background story was to succeed, the baby had to be born in a new country where records were less stringently kept than in England or even Ireland. After what Paddy had told him, he had come to the conclusion that Elizabeth's ship had to sail and sail quickly. He glanced at her to reassure himself of her well-being. She was leaning over the railing with her chin lifted to sniff the sea air, and the wind snapped her dark curls tightly against her pink cheeks. He could not pull his eyes from her. She might have been a freshly painted figurehead on the bow of some Viking ship. He nodded to himself. Elizabeth would make an excellent passenger on the *Atlantic Star*.

Something brought to mind a poem I started years ago in the back of Seamus Heaney's *North.*

TIMES TWO

I need to visit things
Twice, two times.
Times two for both places and events.
Once to learn the sense of it
And one to sense the feel of it.

Must I live my life twice,
Or only once but on parallel tracks?
I haven't got the hang of it.
Am I a slow learner, a day dreamer,
A sleepwalker in time?

I am reading Margaret Atwood's *Morning in the Burned House.* I recognized myself in her metaphor. That's me, the burned house. It is not morning yet.

CHAPTER SEVENTEEN

The wind rose and the girl's great green cloak whipped about in a gust of rough air and moulded to her swollen body. Emily gasped. Never had she imagined that her assignment lay in escorting so young a person, or one so far advanced with child. It was impossible. She opened her mouth to say as much, when Sir Roger took her hands and placed a packet in them. Looking down to see what he had given her, she lost her advantage.

"I know you will be good to Elizabeth. She is very important to me. After you have seen her arrive safely in Montreal, you are free to continue upriver to your own destination. Everything you need is contained in this package. Take care you don't misplace it."

He turned from the speechless Emily and put his arms about Elizabeth.

"Goodbye, my dear. I shall miss you. Have a safe crossing. Take very good care of yourself."

Emily had to strain to hear this last remark as Sir Roger's voice thickened and dropped in volume. He leaned over to kiss Elizabeth gently on the forehead, and while Emily was considering him in the role of lover to this young girl, he vanished into the crowd.

His charge appeared unperturbed at the rapid disappearance of her benefactor. She tossed the heavy weight of her hair from about her face and, with an air of anticipation, settled her cloak more firmly about her.

"We should have fine weather for sailing. The wind is freshening and as soon as the cargo is loaded, the captain will want to be off. Have you sailed before?"

Emily was still speechless. Elizabeth discovered the round wide eyes of the two small boys fixed on her and she dropped awkwardly to her knees.

"Well, hello, what are your names? Won't you two make the best sailors? You'll want to see everything on board. Come on."

And with that runaway exchange, Elizabeth took each little boy by the hand and started up the gangway. Emily followed helplessly in their wake.

The ship sailed that same afternoon. All four were assigned to one cabin containing two berths and two chairs. Elizabeth cheerfully offered to share her bed with one or other of the boys and Emily gratefully accepted. Before the ship entered the frigid waters of the north Atlantic, Elizabeth McMaster and Emily Jane Harris were friends. Emily stated quite openly to everyone on board that she could not have managed without Elizabeth. Elizabeth seemed to know when Emily's patience had been tried long enough and she would appear from nowhere with a smile on her windwhipped face and wink at the boys.

"I don't suppose you two would care to hear about the giant who wished to cross the sea to Scotland and made steps so he could walk there without getting his feet wet?"

They would be at her side in a flash and be entertained for hours. Elizabeth's good humour was as endless as her supply of stories, which were a rich mix of her imagination and background information from the old manuscripts in the castle library. She loved telling and retelling these Irish folk and faery tales almost as much as the boys loved hearing them. To her original stories, she added magic she had learned from her worship of the Goddess, and some days when she began a story, she was unsure of how it would end. She liked these stories best of all. Day after cloudless day, Elizabeth sat on deck, wrapped in her heavy cloak and flanked closely, as if for warmth, by two small boys bundled in blankets from the cabin. Spinning tales of enchantment from Ireland's Golden Age, Elizabeth attracted more than small boys to her circle. Other passengers and members of the crew, hearing scraps of her stories in passing, found themselves unable to leave until they had heard the whole of some ancient Celtic tale where a world of mystery and magic still existed side by side with the world of men.

At night, after the boys had been put to bed, Elizabeth would bring out her needlework and stitch the same bewitching elements of her stories into her sampler. Emily was fascinated with Elizabeth's skill with her needle, and asked for help with her own embroidery. Emily's work appeared dull and lifeless to her eye when held up beside Elizabeth's. They passed the evenings stitching in quiet conversation, and were two weeks out of port before Emily raised the question that had concerned her since their first meeting.

"When do you expect your baby, Elizabeth?"

"I'm not sure. I think the end of January, or early February."

"Didn't a doctor or your mother give you any indication of when your child was due?"

"I never saw a doctor, and my mother doesn't know I am having a baby."

A great surge of emotion engulfed Emily. She remembered her own first pregnancy and all the love and attention showered on her. And here was this girl, barely past childhood, unwed and friendless except for herself and the boys. There and then Emily, who was no more than ten years older than Elizabeth, assumed the role of Elizabeth's mother.

"Are you frightened?"

"I don't think so. She's there to look after me."

Emily moved closer to Elizabeth, looking expectantly at her, as if by moving nearer she could discover whom Elizabeth meant. The girl's deep blue eyes were focused on something or someone Emily couldn't see, and what she saw reflected in Elizabeth's eyes meant nothing to her. It was puzzling, but it didn't matter. Emily intended to look after Elizabeth and her baby, and it had nothing to do with the payment she had received from Sir Roger Kingsmill.

The weather continued cold and fair and the winds pushed the *Atlantic Star* to new records for a north Atlantic crossing. The captain announced that if they maintained their present speed, they would dock in Montreal well before ice blocked the river. The passengers and crew cheered loudly at the news. The boys and Emily felt the bitter cold more than Elizabeth did, and they made fewer and fewer forays to the deck. But each evening, while Emily sponged the boys and then read to them until they dropped into sleep, Elizabeth walked the deck alone. At first Emily had pleaded with the girl to stay below, saying that as Elizabeth grew more cumbersome, she might slip and injure herself. Elizabeth refused to give in. For it was in the velvet depths of the night sky that she felt closest to Cerridwen. She saw the workings of the Goddess in the intricate design outlined by the bright points of the stars, and each night she travelled further along the Goddess' candlelit path. Elizabeth began to long for night to fall; only then did she feel the delicate tug of the Goddess' needle, sometimes pushing, sometimes pulling her across the stretched canvas of the night sky. The undulating rhythm beneath her feet, the gentle slap of the water against the boat, the pattern of the stars splashed deliberately across the sky, and the trembling life pulsing in her womb all beat in unison. She was a small piece in some splendid work.

When Elizabeth returned to the cabin, she tried to stitch what she had seen on that wider canvas into her own work. Emily could only stare in amazement at Elizabeth's artistry. Each night she created something more exquisite than what had come before, and in front of Emily's astonished eyes, the central figure of the piece changed its shape until Emily could only guess at what the final canvas would look like. One night she saw the image of a great pale horse rising through the foamy crests of breaking waves. He had a long thin horn of twisted silver pointing from his head, and huge drifts of snow-white wings clinging to his back. Another evening, the horse had disappeared and in its place a clipper ship appeared, its full sails billowing as it raced across a storm-tossed sea, its topmost sail thrust skyward, almost touching the outer circle of a crescent moon. And yet, just as Emily had decided the ship was here to stay, another picture surfaced in the stitches and she could see the outlines of an enormous weathered stone, shrouded by folds of brooding clouds, cushioned on a grassy sea, and in its depths, a shadowed face. The magic of the sampler lay in its changing central form; the background remained the same and anchored that night's image to the canvas. The entire border of the work was stitched in glossy threads of purple black, and springing from the silky depths were the cross-stitched points of a hundred tiny stars. Stitched neatly into the lower right-hand corner of the sampler was an inscription:

Elizabeth McMaster
April 24, 1802.
County Galway

One night, when Elizabeth was late in returning to their cabin, Emily became uneasy. The girl had grown distant with Emily in recent days, not in enmity, but in a vague detachment from things and people. Emily struggled to understand what it was about Elizabeth's behaviour that worried her. Even the boys were bored with this new Elizabeth, and demanded more of their mother's attention. And there was more. One of the sailors had brought Elizabeth to Emily during the day and issued a warning.

"Watch her closely, ma'am. I found her wandering in the bow where only the crew should be. It's dangerous for her up there by herself. She could slip and fall overboard, and no one would see or hear her. I wouldn't want any harm to come to her."

"Elizabeth," chided Emily softly, "you mustn't go to the bow by yourself. You could injure the baby. Please, Elizabeth, stay close to me."

"She's calling me. I can hear her faintly, but I can't find her. If I go to the bow, maybe I'll catch a glimpse of her and hear what she is saying."

"Who, Elizabeth? Who is it you are looking for?"

Elizabeth turned to Emily with huge luminous eyes and said simply, "The Lady. I have been searching for Her all my life."

Emily was terrified. The girl had gone beyond the boundaries of Emily's world. She watched with a rising sense of horror as Elizabeth withdrew further from reality, staring for hours at a bare horizon, waiting. When the boys asked for a story, she looked beyond them and spoke in riddles. Emily kept her close by, but she was unable to distract Elizabeth from her patient scanning of the western sky.

While her sons slept, Emily waited for Elizabeth. This was the only time when Elizabeth was not under Emily's direct supervision. Her discomfort grew with each passing minute. Where was Elizabeth? Why hadn't she returned? Emily strained to hear a footfall or a soft tap on the cabin door. When Emily could stand it no longer, she left the boys alone and went to look for Elizabeth. She climbed the narrow stairs leading to the deck, stepped out and gasped. The entire northern sky was shot with great arcs of white light that shimmered and danced in the clear air, bursting into brilliance then sinking into the blackness, only to flare again and again into life. For a moment, Emily forgot why she had come. The white lights crossing and crisscrossing the heavens bathed the whole ship in a radiance that made it easy to identify each object, and she found Elizabeth curled in the circle of her dark green cloak in the foremost part of the bow. The girl was in full labour.

Emily Harris delivered Elizabeth McMaster of a healthy baby girl on the deck of the *Atlantic Star* on December 29, 1818. The child was born beneath the splendour of the northern lights. As Emily placed the baby in her mother's outstretched arms, a beam of light shot from the heavens and exploded in dazzling fragments over the ship, showering mother and child with an unearthly radiance. Emily was stunned by what she saw, and Elizabeth, weak as she was, held the baby up in the brilliant light and whispered.

"The kiss of Cerridwen."

This done, Elizabeth sank back on the cloak-covered coils of rope that had served as the baby's birthing bed and closed her eyes. Emily wrapped the tiny infant in her shawl and went below for help. There was no time to waste if these two were to survive the cold, the harshness of the delivery and the prematureness of the birth. The ship's surgeon was summoned and he checked both patients with great care. He pronounced the baby to be in fine shape, but after his examination of Elizabeth he shook his head and spoke to Emily in a subdued tone.

"She's barely breathing, and she's not fighting. All we can do is keep her warm and pray."

The little boys had been moved to share a bed. Elizabeth occupied the other. They had not wakened during the transfer, nor had Elizabeth. Emily, who had relinquished the baby only to the doctor, picked her up again and went to search the ship for a nursing mother. By noon of the next day, Caroline, for that was what Emily thought she had heard Elizabeth name her daughter, was nursing contentedly at the breast of a young Irish mother.

Much older but no wiser, random thoughts to end the year. Andrea is pushing me away (not me personally, but what I represent). Her youth cannot save her, nor can I. She does not understand the hands of time; nor do I. We are like the ancients gathered around the fires in the winter darkness, hearing the wolves howl. There is something fearful out there, but who wants to name it?

As I see my youth in her, she sees herself age in me and hates what she sees. I did, too. Oh, that unrelenting wheel— no matter how hard we try— do we change anything? I simply must believe we do or I could not go on.

Back to work, but it does not feel like work; it feels like where I want to be. I must not think how far ahead I would be if I had started my journey in university all those years ago. I must not be bitter that a society that recognized only male needs and heard only their voices placed me in the home to rear the children. Where would I be? Never mind. I have the opportunity now. I am not too old and I have learned lots of things, most of which are related to the caring field as opposed to the creating field. I am enraged when I stop to think how passively I accepted the male notion of my life. How dare they think they had the right to carve the pattern of my life? No wonder there were mad women in the attic. They are probably the ones who fought back.

We are having a wonderful snowfall. It is coming down in slow motion in very full flakes like great soft dots in a gray landscape. Maybe we are meant to read everything not only front to back (scientific, rational) but also back to front, like the story "The Yellow Wallpaper," by Charlotte Perkins. Icicles on the edge of the greenhouse window are "like bangs of glass" framing nature's face. These moments of seeing are rare. It is so beautiful out there, and so flat when we recreate it in man's world. Things keep crossing my mind this morning and I know if I do not write them down I will lose them. I always wondered why people, when talking to loved ones, talk about the weather. It struck me as so banal. But now I think of the meteorology of the mind. Are these weather terms a chart for reading what the other is trying to tell us? "It's cold today but sunny. Will the rain never end? The winter has been so long and cruel. It's the hottest summer on record." Is the brain so sophisticated that it can translate emotional life into meteorological phrases to allow the listener the option of hearing only weather? If they wish to stay on the surface, then the weather will satisfy them and that is what they will hear. If they wish to know what is really going on in our lives, then they must learn to read the weather in psychological terms. It is so complex. Will I ever unravel any of the threads?

Early this morning I saw three deer cross the ice— *deja vu*. Russia— during the revolution— crossing the ice with a baby in my arms.

I wore a dark green velvet cloak and a fur-lined hood.

It is hard to see my face.

PART TWO

CAROLINE

CANADA — 1818-1850

CHAPTER ONE

January 3, 1819.

My Dear Sir Roger Kingsmill:

It is with great sadness that I put pen to paper to inform you of the loss of your dear ward and my dear friend. Elizabeth died aboard ship this past week from the effects of giving birth in such unsuitable conditions. She was delivered of a healthy female child, but after her ordeal, Elizabeth never regained consciousness. She was given a proper Christian burial at sea.

The child is tiny but quite hardy, and she appears to be thriving, thanks to the kindness of a young Irish mother who is nursing this baby along with her own child. The compassion shown the unfortunate babe by the crew and passengers has been heartwarming and a support to me in my own grief. During the voyage, Elizabeth became as dear to me as a sister and I mourn her sudden death. I am uncertain as to your wishes in regard to the future of the child, but I have heard from passengers more knowledgeable than I that there is an Order of Catholic sisters in the settlement at Quebec who devote themselves to the care and education of orphaned children. I will leave the baby with them. I trust this arrangement meets with your approval. It may be of some comfort to you to know that Elizabeth, with her last remnants of strength, named her daughter "Caroline."

We are to remain on board for two more days, and hope to proceed upriver to Montreal, but our Captain reports that it is very doubtful that we can continue our journey beyond this city this winter. The weather is perishingly cold and each day brings new snow. The land is buried under layers of white and it is difficult to identify one's surroundings. I will have to learn to adapt to the harsh climate of this new country. I have just received word of a ship sailing for England in the morning, and I will give this letter with its sad contents to its Captain to deliver.

I remain, your servant,
Emily Jane Harris

The north Atlantic wind had swept the deck of the *Atlantic Star* of all but one small group, clustered at the stern of the ship. The black-clad woman and two children, heads bowed, stood apart from the sailors during the reading of the prayer for the dead at sea. They looked up only as the words *We therefore commit her body to the deep* were spoken.

The weighted white form was lifted, poised lightly on the rail as if for flight, and then slipped effortlessly over the edge. Hardly a splash accompanied the entrance of Elizabeth McMaster's body into the fathomless depths of the winter sea.

Ice forced the closure of the St. Lawrence River to all traffic. Passengers of the *Atlantic Star* made what arrangements they could, either to spend the duration of the winter in the town of Quebec, or to go on to Montreal by sleigh. Emily went immediately to the convent run by the sisters of the Ursuline Order and asked in her halting French to speak with the Mother Superior. The nun agreed not only to keep and raise Caroline but also to board Emily and her boys until the ice cleared and they could continue west by river. Emily sent a silent prayer of thanks to her Irish benefactor and the purse he had provided her. The convent needed all its resources just to feed and shelter its own; it was a rare ship that did not leave at least one small being in the custody of the nuns, and a rarer winter when the convent cupboards had anything left in them when spring finally came. Paying guests of any faith were welcome. A few nuns, at odds with the convent's open policy, went about their business with pursed lips, but most of the Ursulines were delighted to have the Harris family for the winter.

Originally the Ursulines had come to New France to assist in the education and religious conversion of the Indian children who circulated freely throughout the newly founded settlement. Many things had changed in the colony in the two hundred years since its creation; there were no longer Indians anywhere near the town, and the Quebec garrison was manned by English soldiers, not French, but the nuns' devotion to the welfare of orphaned children had never changed.

The three-storey building that housed the Order dated back to the early days of French settlement. Its thick walls were as solid and immutable as the rock cliff against which the building stood. Four enormous fireplaces provided heat, but the warmth they radiated never fully penetrated the upper regions, and the top floor, where Emily and the nuns each had a small cell-like room, was always bitterly cold. She was grateful the boys were housed in a dormitory on the floor below, where it was slightly warmer, and even more grateful that Caroline slept cosily in a cradle in the nursery on the ground floor. Daily, Emily gave thanks for the good fortune that had led them to the convent, a refuge from the most severe winter she had ever encountered.

Daniel and Richard provided a lively diversion in the neatly ordered ranks of children already in residence, and Caroline enchanted everyone. One nun attached herself to the little English family and appointed herself as their protector; for even in this selfless atmosphere some jostled for the few material comforts that came their way. Sister Marie Paule saw to it that Emily's chair was placed within comfortable range of the fire, and she gently chastised any child who laughed at the strange language spoken by Daniel and Richard. Her gay good humour in struggling with English prompted the boys to try and speak her language; within days they were chattering in broken schoolboy French to the other children. Their mother overheard them speaking, even to each other, in English dotted with French words. The Harrises would have survived without Marie Paule's kindness, but it would have been a longer, colder winter.

Caroline, beloved by everyone, did not need a benefactress. She smiled and waved her arms and legs in welcome and made chirruping noises to each white-coiffed round-faced nun who came to visit her. Several times each day, they all found excuses to pass Emily's chair, where the baby lay tucked snugly in her pine cradle.

"Quelle belle bébé! Donnez nous une sourire."

And Caroline smiled for them all.

The boys were not the only ones who had an ear for languages. Before a month had passed, Emily found herself listening to and understanding most of the conversations that swirled around her as she sat knitting by the fire.

Still, for all her grasp of the language, she was hesitant in speaking French to anyone but the sympathetic Marie Paule.

Marie Paule explained that the Protestant Harrises were not expected to attend the frequent services conducted in the chapel by Father Hebert. Emily had been concerned that their stay in the convent would involve attempts to convert either her sons or herself to Roman Catholicism. She questioned the boys rigorously on all their activities and was pleased that they were never taken to the chapel. Caroline was often plucked from the warm nest of her cradle, pressed to the tunicked breast of a gray-garbed sister and whisked down a corridor into the shadows at the end of the hall. When Emily saw the baby in a nun's arms, she thought how well-loved Elizabeth's baby was. Weeks passed before Emily thought to question Marie Paule.

"Where do they keep disappearing with Caroline?"

"Emilie. Caroline goes to Mass."

It was as though Marie Paule had hit Emily hard in the stomach. She could hardly manage a reply.

"But Caroline's only a baby?"

"To dedicate one's life to God, c'est important à commencer at a young age."

Emily thought it shameful that the Roman Church demanded attendance at Mass from a baby. Knitting by the fire, Emily could see the life of the convent unfold; each day followed precisely in the footprints of the one before it without deviation. If, by chance, an elderly sister hesitated in the routine, the bells corrected her. The bells dictated the very motion of the nuns' existence. Bells woke them up, summoned them to Mass, called them to meals, and told them when to kneel and pray.

In her narrow cot at night, Emily imagined all sorts of harsh measures being imposed on a little red-haired girl with Elizabeth's face. Emily began to lose sleep. She wanted to snatch Caroline from her cradle and refuse to yield her to the nun who came to collect her tiny charge for the evening service. When the nun came, she clenched her teeth so tightly that her skull ached.

One morning, as Emily sat reading to the boys, Caroline was carried into the room by Sister Evelyne. Daniel noticed the baby first.

"Mama. Caroline looks like a petite réligieuse."

He laughed and held out his arms to the young nun. A white linen napkin had been placed over the baby's finely coppered head, crossed under her tiny rounded chin and fastened snuggly behind her ears. In her white robes, with the nun's crucifix positioned above her head, she resembled a doll-like version of a Bride of Christ. Emily drew back. Daniel's clear young voice bounced off the stone walls of the nearly empty room.

"Does this mean Caroline is a nun, now?"

"Daniel, don't ever say that. Caroline is only a baby."

Emily was stunned by the violence in her response. Was there any other future for a convent-raised orphan?

February drifted into March, and Emily found herself daydreaming more and more by the fire, thinking of how Elizabeth would hate the cold stone walls, the constant discipline of the bells, the bleached existence of the nuns' half lives. Emily would shake her head and jump to her feet. Movement was an antidote to such thoughts. By the end of March, Emily thought she was going mad.

One morning, over the ringing of the bells, Emily heard another sound, louder and even more insistent. Flinging open her window and leaning out over the sill until her toes barely touched floor, she saw a thick-bodied boat, its deck crammed with crates and barrels, moving smoothly from the wharf across the water. The boat's whistle announced the end of winter. The river was open.

I have been to the Barnes Exhibit and received a huge shock when I encountered Cézanne's "Bathers"... all that blue! I am reading Bennett's *Deeper Man* and his model of the inner life, which is composed of four energies: sensation, feeling, thought and consciousness. Each energy has its own body to carry its message. The physical body deals in sensations. Composed of the solid forms (the five senses), these sensations form the physical world. What body does the energy produced by feeling inhabit? It produces a world of emotions. These are not solid forms, but are like hot wires connecting everyone to everything in the universe, messages transferred instantaneously and received through the heart. For example, at the teaching dinner, everything was connected to everything else, from the flowers to the stars in the night sky to the people to the words they spoke. I remember it all in great detail, but it is the feeling that I recall most clearly: like being in love with the whole world.

The October woods on a sunny day are another world, the world of emotions as opposed to the world of words. It is like going from dark into light, but hard to stay there. The old intellect continuously draws one from the emotional present into the world of the mind. I saw this theory at work as I was walking; my mind kept throwing up distractions until I succumbed and left where I was in this beautiful forest for the world of tomorrow. What a shame to miss today. I was simply not here. It is impossible for angels to contact you if you are not home.

CHAPTER TWO

Sister Marie Paule had been Emily's staunchest ally when she made her decision to take Caroline with her to Upper Canada and to bring her up as her own daughter. No one, not even Tom, was to suspect that the little girl was not their own child. They had plotted together, the French Canadian nun with the bright polished-apple face and the young English mother, to have Father Hebert write out a baptismal certificate in the name of Caroline Elizabeth Harris. Marie Paule had persuaded him that the best thing for a baby was to be raised in a family. With the precious document safely in her possession, Emily had booked the first available passage to Upper Canada.

The simple two-day journey to Montreal was the real beginning of their life in Canada. Brisk river air reddened their convent-pale cheeks, and the sharp brightness of the sun dazzled their cloistered eyes. The boys raced about the deck, shouting with the sheer joy of hearing their own voices, defying their mother's best efforts to control them. Even Caroline refused to close her eyes and go to sleep. She lay in Emily's arms, wrinkling her nose at the puffs of wind that played about the deck, trying to catch them in her tiny hands.

The docks of Montreal were clogged with people and goods. Everyone wanted to get to Upper Canada. For those with sufficient means there was transportation. Emily's initial euphoria at her release from the deadness of the convent soon wore off as she encountered the difficulties of a woman travelling alone with two young children and an infant. The inns where they lodged were often dirty, and they slept four to a bed. Emily worried about the children catching some terrible disease and she would sit up half the night. They spent days waiting in smelly crowded common rooms for coaches that never came, and Emily had to endure the bold stares of strange men, who sometimes questioned her on why she was travelling to Upper Canada without a man. It became bearable when they travelled by boat. There, at least, the boys could sleep on deck where the air was fresh, and she and Caroline had a small cabin to themselves. Food was plentiful, although ill-prepared and badly served.

Daniel and Richard were full of questions about the changing landscape, and when Emily didn't have the answers, there was always someone near at hand who did. Soon Emily began to share in the boys' excitement. When they spotted a great swath of mud-brown water flowing into the distinctly green waters of the St. Lawrence, the Captain told them they had crossed from Lower Canada to Upper Canada. The muddy water was from the

Ottawa River that formed the eastern boundary of Upper Canada. The passengers, including Emily, cheered, and the boys, encouraged by the general rowdiness of the adults, dashed about the boat, bumping into the crew and the passengers and throwing their hats in the air. As they proceeded upstream, the river became shallower and dotted with thickly wooded islands. The boat moved slowly, and those on board caught glimpses of slim brown figures running swiftly between the trees. Once they passed a flotilla of birch-bark canoes that skimmed the water, leaving no wake to mark their passage. At night, the fires of Indian encampments lit up the sky, and the boys were deliciously frightened at the thought of coming so close to the wild savages about whom they heard so many fearful things. Once, after Caroline cried all night, Emily left her in Daniel's care in the morning while she tried to sleep. She woke to hear Daniel talking to the cranky baby.

"Caroline," he said, looking directly in her basket. "If you don't stop crying and be good, we will give you to the Indians the way we almost gave you to the sisters in Quebec. How would you like that?"

Emily flew off her bunk and gripped his arm so tightly that he winced in pain.

"Stop it. Don't you ever say anything like that again. Caroline is your sister. Do you hear me? She is your sister."

She pinched his flesh until tears sprouted in the corners of his eyes.

"I mean it, Daniel. Caroline is ours. I can't believe you would say such a wicked thing."

Emily sat on the bed, sobbing into her hands.

Long after Richard had fallen asleep on the deck, Daniel was awake, watching hordes of fireflies blink their lights on and off in the blackness and thinking of his mother. He had never seen her cry before, not even when Elizabeth died, and today marked the first time he had ever been afraid of her.

Emily had had no real word as to the whereabouts of Tom's regiment since leaving England. She made enquiries at every stopover, but no one knew for certain where the Royal Engineers were located. Emily soon discovered that Upper Canada ran on rumour. Some thought the Engineers were building fortifications in Kingston, some people said York, and an innkeeper told her they had been recalled to England. Emily blanched, leaning up against the counter for support, and whispered, "It can't be true."

He admitted, amid great shouts of laughter from the men drinking in the tavern, that he had made up the story. Emily had no choice but to push further into Upper Canada. She made the necessary arrangements for them to travel on to Prescott, an overland trip of some fifty miles. The rapids in the river made further passage by boat impossible; only baggage was forwarded by the flat-bottomed bateaux. Passengers were transferred to coaches that travelled over roads that were two lines of deep ruts cut through the fields by the wheels of heavily burdened wagons and marked haphazardly by great holes into which their coach sank and swayed precariously.

The spectacular beauty of the countryside kept Emily from feeling the full discomfort of the journey. Wherever she looked there were fields of wildflowers and birds of species she did not know. In the distance, the river sparkled in the spring sunshine. They passed log houses of a kind she had never seen before, and at each house the farm folk paused in their work to wave and yell words of greeting to the passengers in the coach. The boys loved the trip and every time they stopped for water or to change the horses, Richard shouted out at the top of his lungs: "Is this it, Mama? Is this where we are going to live?"

While skiing yesterday, I felt light pass right through me. I was moving down the trail, but there was no *body* getting in my way. I was all light and sunshine moving over the snow. I shall remember this for years. Sitting at the Jackson cottage with the fire blazing and harp music in the background, two lovely cats and many nice thoughts and conversations, I am desperate to record all my thoughts, all the beauty I hear and see and touch. I long to capture it and hold it, and in the holding, understand what escapes me: the colour, the sounds and most of the words. The birds are wonderful— chickadees, nuthatches and woodpeckers. The woodpeckers are the best of all, downies and hairies; the hairies are the large ones. I love almost everything I see. If only the writing would move, I'd be happy— I think.

Our abortion law was overturned on Thursday, a landmark decision. But for whom? We are left to wrestle with our souls. What is life? At what point is it life? Do we die to save it? What deity gave us such complicated ethics to deal with? How would it (he, she, the being) deal with this question? I think this being would come down on the side of life. Remember, this being sees every little sparrow fall. I worry that language can obfuscate anything, like using "viability" instead of "life," "fetus" instead of "unborn baby." What power lies in the word, or rather, what power lies in who defines the word?

I would have loved to know my mother as an adult, not just as a mother, but somehow we never got the chance or took it. Why? I want Andrea to know me as a real person and I hope we like one another. Today reminds me of those ski days long ago at Mont Tremblant... a sky so blue and clear that it sings, and snow full of moisture. Just to remember conquering those runs is enough... I don't mind giving up the reality as long as I have the memory. Time ticks in my head and I feel I must rush to finish something, everything.

CHAPTER THREE

Word had reached Tom Harris by a kind of backwoods network that his wife and children were enroute to Perth, and he was at the wharf as the scow carrying his family came into view. It had been over a year since he had seen them. As Emily stepped from the boat and into her husband's arms, the river reverberated with the cheers of weary settlers. Even the battle-hardened soldiers under Tom's command stopped unloading boats to watch while

Emily gently detached herself from Tom's arms and placed the baby in them. Their eyes misted with unfamiliar tears and their rough banter was stilled as a strange tightness gripped their throats.

"Emily, this is no place for a gentlewoman. And the children! Whatever possessed you to bring them to this wilderness?"

She knew he did not expect an answer. He was thrilled to see them. She stood on tiptoe so she could rub her wet face against his and murmur in his ear, "Oh, Tom, I missed you so."

Without removing his arm from Emily or giving up the baby in his other arm, he turned to the two boys standing awestruck on the dock.

"Are these my sons? Why, Daniel, you are almost grown up. You brought Mama and the little ones all this way by yourself?"

Six-year-old Daniel swelled visibly and nodded his dark head seriously. Daniel would grow taller than his father and be of slighter build, but there was no mistaking the relationship between the two. Tom bent over to get a better look at Richard, and that little boy, usually so boisterous and outgoing, watched in terror as the strange adult face came closer and grew larger. He burst into tears and hid his head in Emily's skirt. Of the three children, only Caroline produced a smile when Tom lifted her up to his face.

"And who are you, my pretty?"

The baby opened her blue eyes as widely as possible and laughed at him. He touched her tiny nose and she laughed again, crossing her bright eyes in an effort to follow his finger. Captain Harris was captivated by this little creature nestled cosily against his chest.

"She's Caroline Elizabeth Harris, my darling, and we have brought her all this way to meet her papa."

Perth had been conceived by the British military as part of an alternative transport system to the St. Lawrence River. The War of 1812 had provoked paranoia in British North America, and the Imperial Army was under strict orders to secure the interior of Upper Canada for England. The Crown did not intend to lose a second colony to the Americans. An inland waterway was proposed, to bypass the section of the river vulnerable to American raids, and the policy was to encourage the rapid settlement of immigrants loyal to Britain. As Perth grew, her population was comprised of two distinct groups: civilian immigrants given encouragement by the Home Government to locate there, and soldiers freshly discharged from the Army. There were few jobs in England for the soldiers returning from the Napoleonic Wars, and Upper Canada was the ideal place to reward those who had fought for the Empire with land and a small pension. This policy served England's interest well. The officers among the soldiery chose to settle in the town itself, whereas the enlisted men, for the most part, took up their land grants outside the town. The bush surrounding Perth was thickly forested, with trees so tall and closed packed together that the men who worked to clear their land rarely saw daylight.

By 1822, the initial trickle of immigrants to Upper Canada had increased to a steady stream of impoverished British families looking for the free land offered to those who settled in the new province. With the threat of an American invasion all but over, the need for Perth to remain a military settlement diminished, and the District of Bathurst was transferred from military to civilian authority. The little town on the Tay was named the capital of the District, and assumed the responsibilities accompanying such a designation. Streets were laid out in a regular fashion and wooden sidewalks were installed on the main street. A jail and courthouse were built. There were now seven stores in town and four churches, as well as taverns. The number of private residences within the town's boundaries had escalated from the few cabins present on Emily's arrival to more than fifty in 1823. In that same year, a young Scottish doctor settled in Perth and a schoolmaster was hired to teach those boys whose parents were willing to pay for their sons to read and write. Perth had come of age.

Still, Perth was a pioneer settlement, located far from the commercial centers of Canada, with few of the amenities of the middle-class English household available. The little community scarcely held its own over the always encroaching bush. Things were manufactured by the residents themselves, or they did without. For the Harris family, the basic elements of survival had been met; their log cabin was adequate, and once Emily had mastered the techniques of cooking over an open fire, they ate well. There was an abundance of fish and game, and Tom had been able to negotiate the purchase of a cow. Once a week, Daniel delivered milk to their closest neighbours and returned with their surplus eggs. Emily could not bear to have chickens about the place. When Tom had brought the subject up, she coloured a deep scarlet.

"There are some depths, Tom, to which I am not prepared to sink. Raising chickens is one of them."

The topic was not mentioned again, and Tom forbade the boys to make clucking noises with their tongues when Emily was working in the garden.

Emily, Emily, whatever possessed you to come to this wilderness? Tom's words echoed through Emily's head fifty times a day. Emily had never worked so hard in her life. Each time the question insinuated itself into her mind, she had a different answer, but all of her responses were associated with a taint of madness in her character, as in, "Only a mad woman would choose to live under these conditions" or "I must have been insane to think being together as a family was more important than living decently." And she would push back the tendrils of hair that had fallen over her forehead during one of her vain attempts to coax the red coals of the fire into flames, and open the door to let some fresh air into the smoke-filled cabin.

They were very fortunate, Tom told her, to have secured this three-room cabin. The frontiersman who built it had abandoned it in favour of the west, where there was more land and less regulation. Emily laughed aloud when Tom told her this. Imagine, someone finding Perth too civilized for their taste! Most families spent their first winter in a lean-to of some nature. She supposed she was lucky, and gave a great reluctant sigh that sent Caroline into fits of giggles.

"What are you laughing at, miss? Just because you like to poke about in the dirt doesn't mean I do. You and your brothers love all this backwoods nonsense and, if the truth were known, I suspect your father doesn't mind it, either."

Emily would swoop down and lift Caroline from where she played on the earthen floor and whirl her around the tiny room, humming a tune from some long-forgotten concert.

"Never mind, my beauty. By the time you are old enough to go to dances we shall be safely back in England. Whatever possessed me to come to this wilderness?" And Emily would mimic herself as she put the baby down.

"I didn't get married to be left at home to raise my children without their father. I don't care where he is posted. I want to be with my husband."

And Emily would roll her eyes until Caroline fell over on the floor from laughter.

"And here I am."

I am reading *The Mad Woman in the Attic* and feeling very angry. These thoughts came to me in a dream; I want them remembered but I do not know why. Do they throw confetti at a bride because it is the shredding of her story? Do all women wear red shoes, and what do they mean? As a child I saw a beautiful film called *The Red Shoes*; I never understood it, but now I wonder: are the red shoes a symbol of the pull between our creative lives and our maternal lives?

I am in a routine... boring but productive. I read and write and walk and swim and think. The contemplative life suits me and I can see more clearly now. That is one half of the coin. I have little yen to leap into the fray and change what I see. All must run its course and work through to its end or its beginning. Caroline is my medium of change. She works for me, poor thing, and takes all the journeys I never will.

I HAD A LOVELY DREAM where an owl came to visit me. He was all soft feathers, big round head, and eyes. I was walking through the woods when I came across him; he was not frightened of me. I stopped and watched him and thought how lucky I was to be here. Are dreams a form of memory? Watch what happens to yourself in a dream: you are both the observer and the observed. I felt this dream and saw it and my mind did not take over and intellectualize. I woke up feeling very light and happy.
I cannot seem to hold onto
what is real. It slips through
my hands like water,
and I am left with
rags and bones.

CHAPTER FOUR

"Ma, there's someone here to see you."

Since Tom had left with a survey party three days before, Emily and Daniel had been working steadily to turn a patch of earth behind the cabin into a vegetable garden, but its dimensions were miniature, more appropriate for herbs than for vegetables. Nothing in this country came easily. She wiped her forehead with the back of her hand. How brown her arm was. She looked over at Daniel, who had stopped work to watch her.

"You caught me woolgathering, Daniel."

They both bent over their hoes again.

"Ma!" Richard came careening around the corner of the cabin. He had been left to mind Caroline, who was walking and required someone's full attention every waking moment.

"Richard, how many times have I told you not to call me ma? It sounds so common. Did you leave Caroline alone?"

"Yes, ma, I mean no, mama. There's a lady here to see you and she's watching Caroline. You'd better hurry or she'll go away."

Emily wiped her hands on her apron and rolled down the sleeves of her dress before rounding the corner of the house. She recognized the young woman as one of the two women, besides herself, in the group of settlers with whom she had travelled to Perth. She hurried to greet her. Emily rarely saw another woman. As yet, there were no other wives of military men in Perth. Those women, Emily concluded, were much wiser than herself. The girl was much younger than Emily, and very shy.

"Mary, how good of you to stop by. Tom's been away all week and if you want to know the truth, in spite of the company of these rascals," she waved her hand to include all three children, "I've been lonely. How are you and Stephen making out?"

The Caseys had been the youngest couple in their party, and Emily had taken them for brother and sister, not man and wife. She was surprised when Tom had called out Mr. and Mrs. Stephen Casey and assigned them a lot number. Their land was located far from town. Emily thought how lonely it must be for a girl of Mary's age to live way out there; it was bad enough for her, and she lived in town and had children. She took Mary's hand and gave it a squeeze to let the girl know how happy she was to see her, but the girl's hand was lifeless. Emily looked more closely at her.

"You must be tired. Come in and sit down. Daniel, fetch Mrs. Casey some water. It's much too hot for tea."

She turned to draw the young woman inside the cabin and caught her staring at Caroline. The toddler was sitting on the grass with the late afternoon sun behind her. Her features were blanked out by shadows, and the sun had highlighted her curls into a copper halo.

"Mary? Why are you staring at Caroline?"

"Is your baby Irish?"

Emily swung around to face the girl. "No. Why would you say something like that? Because of her red hair? Lots of people who aren't Irish have red hair."

Emily ran to Caroline and lifted her from the ground, pressing the little girl against her breast.

"I'm sorry, Mrs. Harris. I didn't mean anything by it. She reminds me of my sisters' babies. Ma always said, if it's in the family, red hair will out." Mary reached out to touch one of Caroline's bronze curls. "I hope my baby has red hair."

"Why, Mary, you are having a baby! How wonderful. I'm not surprised you are thinking of home. A woman always wants her mother at a time like this. Sit down. Walking all this way in the heat can't be good for you. You must take better care of yourself."

"That's really why I stopped by, Mrs. Harris. You're the only one I know who's had three babies and I wondered... if it wouldn't be too much of a bother to you, could you help me when my time comes? It would mean a lot to me and Stephen."

Emily placed Caroline on the dirt floor and hugged the girl.

"Of course, I'll do whatever I can. There's one thing you must do for me, though."

She took a step back, so the girl was at arm's length from her. Mary looked frightened.

"What's that, Mrs. Harris?"

"If I'm to help deliver your baby, then we must become friends. Isn't that right?"

The girl nodded shyly.

"And if we are to be friends, then you must call me Emily, as all my friends do. I should say used to do, for I haven't any friends here. You will be the first."

She laughed at the look in Mary's eyes and for a second time gathered the startled girl in her arms.

"Everything will be just fine."

And that fall, Emily delivered Mary Casey of a healthy boy, the first settlement child to be born in Perth.

Food was plentiful after the harvest, but other things needed replenishing. When Emily's supply of English soap and candles ran out, she had to learn to make them. Emily went straight to Mary Casey with her problem, and Mary, who had never used store-bought soap or candles in her life, taught Emily all she knew.

Emily learned quickly, and her new skills were put to good use during that first winter in Perth. It was not as dreadful as she had anticipated. It did not seem as perishingly cold as the one spent in Quebec, and there was so much to do, the days flew by, with never enough time for her to finish the tasks she set for herself each day. Yet it was somehow very satisfying to climb into bed at the end of a long day bone-tired but unbowed. Most nights, by the time Tom had been to the shed to see the cow safely bedded down and then back to the house to bank the fire and cover the sleeping boys, Emily herself was sound asleep. He would creep into bed quietly and try to keep his feet from slipping across the cold sheets to toast against the warmth of his wife's body. But sometimes when he blew out the candle and crawled in beside her, Emily was wide awake and waiting for him. Those nights made all the other nights and days, where they seemed to do nothing but work from dawn to dusk, melt into nothingness. Emily would lie awake in the darkness long after he had fallen asleep and think of her old life in England. She hardly recognized herself in that Emily. A half smile would curve her lower lip. What a pampered child she had been!

Tom's superior officer arrived in Perth one day from Fort Henry with a small party of engineers to reconnoitre the lakes and rivers linking Kingston to Perth; they were specifically looking for sites where locks could be built to connect these bodies of water into one smoothly flowing waterway. The possibility of hostilities breaking out between Britain and the American colonies was now remote, but the Army was still pushing for an inland supply route. They had not relinquished their dream of a Rideau Waterway. The British parliament was balking at the cost, and the proposed construction was at a legislative impasse. Major Willoughby spoke to Tom in private.

"I didn't like to say much in front of the men, Harris. Parliament is hedging on the funding for the Canal."

Tom nodded.

"If it doesn't come through we won't be here long."

"They'd pull the whole regiment out?"

"No, I'm sure they'd pension off the men and bring just the officers home." He put a hand on Tom's shoulder. "How long is it since you've been in England? Four years, five? If that Bill doesn't pass we'll all be home for Christmas. I'd like to see your wife's face when you tell her. She's a plucky one! I can still see her standing in front of me with a baby in her arms and two small boys at her side, and hear her saying, 'I've come this far to be with him. What's fifty miles more?'" Major Willoughby smiled. "You wouldn't catch my wife out here. They all hate to leave England, and the ones who come can hardly wait to get home. I'll bet she'll be overjoyed when you tell her."

The men shook hands and Major Willoughby swung himself into the saddle. "Good luck then, Harris."

Tom was not sure how he felt about the Major's news. Recall to England would merely be a temporary posting. His unit would be sent off to some part of the Empire where conflict was inevitable. Tom's regiment had reached Upper Canada too late to participate in the War of 1812, and he felt this reflected on him badly. The men didn't seem to mind— they obeyed his orders cheerfully— but Tom himself felt somewhat of a fraud in uniform. The senior officer in this command, he was the only man in his unit who had never been in battle. It wasn't right. He wanted to see active duty. On the other hand, he was a good administrator, and had derived great satisfaction in seeing Perth evolve from a backwoods settlement to the thriving centerpiece of the district.

In this frame of mind, he set out for home. Jim Betts, a local farmer with a wagonload of logs, hailed him from the road.

"Hey, there, Capt'n Harris, you're just the man I want to see. When's the Army going to build that sawmill we've been promised? It's a disgrace, with all these new people coming into town, to have to go elsewhere to get our logs done up into boards. Here's twice in as many weeks I've had to stop what I'm doing and hitch up a team and drive miles to get my logs cut." He spat in the dust.

Tom agreed. It was a disgrace, and if what he had heard from Major Willoughby was right, nothing was going to change. The Army would spend no more money in Perth unless the Rideau Canal became a reality. If the town wanted a sawmill, they were going to have to build it themselves.

Tom shook his head. "You can't count on the Army; they'll do what suits them. Beats me why no one else has done it. There's no reason why a smart man can't build a sawmill in this town and run a very successful business."

Jim Betts leaned over the side of the wagon as if he had some confidential information to impart. "You're right, Capt'n Harris, you can't count on the Army. I know just the person for that sawmill job. You do, too. Hardworking, well-liked, knows the country like the back of his hand, and if you ask me, I'd tell you straight out that he's in the wrong line of work right now."

Tom's boot played with the loose dirt on the road. When Jim came to the part about the "wrong line of work," Tom's foot worked faster and faster until he had churned the dirt into a cloud of dust. He held up his hand, signalling no more.

Jim Betts tossed one more word over his shoulder before he touched the reins to the horses.

"Interested?"

The loaded wagon was almost out of sight before Tom replied.

"Maybe," he said. "Maybe I am."

Tom waited until all three children had gone to bed before he spoke to Emily. She was feeding wool into the spinning wheel and watching him.

"I've something to tell you."

"I'm not surprised. You've been nervous as a cat all evening." She stopped the wheel. "Tom, good news or bad news? I've been bursting to ask you ever since you came through the door with that look written across your face. I'm not a child who has to be protected. I can take whatever it is you have to tell me."

"It's not bad news, Emily. It's that I don't know myself what to make of it."

"Just tell me. I can't stand the suspense another moment."

He told her everything the Major had said and watched the colour come and go in her face. When he reached over and took her work-roughened hands between his own, she was trembling. And then he told her of his meeting with Jim Betts. By the time he had finished his story, her hands were steady and she was staring at him.

"So what will you do?"

"I don't know. I want to be fair to you and the children. It's a hard life for a woman here. Don't think I don't know that."

"But could you be happy here, Tom? Could you give up the Army? You were raised to be a soldier."

"If I really think about it, there hasn't been much soldiering to do. I've had far more association with the farmers and the townsfolk than with the military. There have been times when someone's shouted 'Captain' and I've wondered whom they meant."

He smiled, and Emily watched as a soft distant look filled his eyes and spread across his face. He seemed as vulnerable as Daniel.

"I believe I'm happier here than anywhere I can remember. A man can grow in this country and so can his sons. But you, my dear, aren't you pining for home and gentle English ways?"

"Sometimes, I wish I were in England, especially in the winter. But most times I never think of England, I'm so busy. And would you like to hear something strange? Just now, when you said 'home,' a picture of Perth flashed through my mind, not England. Can you imagine that?"

"I can. Emily, I am going to build a sawmill."

She threw her arms around him and pulled him to her. "But if we are going to stay here, I'll want a proper house."

The sawmill was in operation by the fall of 1824. Emily's stone house was started soon after, and took over a year to complete. It was not the largest house in Perth, but it was the most elegant. Built of multicoloured sandstone by Scottish stonemasons who had recently immigrated to the district, it had an abundance of large windows, a gracious front door, and a wide verandah running the width of the house. Inside, fine mouldings outlined the ceilings in the main rooms and there were five fireplaces, each with an exquisitely carved mantelpiece. Emily never intended to be cold again. They moved in a month before Caroline's sixth birthday and on the first night in their new home, the boys laid a fire in each of the five fireplaces. Emily and Tom, with Caroline swinging between them, strolled through the house, stopping to admire each and every detail in the well-lit rooms. When the tour was finished and they were descending the curving staircase to the entrance hall where Richard and Daniel waited for them, Emily could contain herself no longer.

"It is perfect, isn't it?"

Her smile widened to include more than the marvellous stone house.

Andrea will be nineteen tomorrow. I feel nineteen, and I am her mother. I keep getting glimpses of my mother in the mirror. It is very unsettling. We burn or bury what we do not wish to reveal, but the secrets must come out somewhere. Is this manuscript a woman's twentieth-century journey through a nineteenth-century landscape?

Why are we so surprised when someone dies? Is it the manner of their passing or the time? Surely we cannot be surprised by death itself? It comes to all of us. I saw an airplane move across a perfectly clear blue sky and for a moment I thought I was seeing a shark. Is our sky the sea of another world?

Sometimes I don't want to think deeply and look for the profound. I just want to look at an old lady in a pale blue hat sitting on a bench in the first spring sunshine. I don't want to worry about what her life was like; I just want to enjoy her pale blue oldness. Old age is pale blue.

A VERY SHAKEN woman records these past twenty-four hours. Who is she? Where has she been? I woke up yesterday feeling better than I have in months, the body alive, not chained to pain. I could actually move almost normally. Britannia and I walked down the stairs to the beltline; I was entering a world I had never seen before. It was snowing and there was a newness, an anticipation… I was seeing, not with my eyes, but through them. My eyes were windows, not judges. The intellect was not interfering with the process… just self seeing this particular world for the first time. Is this the pre-lapsarian state, our condition before we ate from the tree of knowledge? Is this the place God cast us into, a space where the mind is the interpreting or translating factor, not the heart? Is this what losing Eden means? Are angels here to help us find the way back?

CHAPTER FIVE

Caroline lay crumpled on the tumbled bedclothes, still and lifeless as the doll she had been playing with when the fever struck. Emily knew that at any moment the terrifying convulsions could begin again and the little girl's body would be wracked by spasms. The fever had come like lightning on a fine summer's day. One minute Caroline had been playing happily in front of the fire, and the next her limbs had flown every which way and she was shouting deliriously.

"Mother, mother, save me, save me." Her arms shot straight up in the air and her legs stiffened like iron pokers. Emily was beside her in a flash.

"Caroline? What is the matter?"

Fear trickled into Emily, gathering speed, invading her body and leaving chunks of ice in its wake. By contrast, Caroline's body was burning to the touch.

"Mother, don't leave me. Wait for me." She screamed and struggled like a wild thing in Emily's arms. "Don't you see her, she's going, she's almost gone. Oh, let me go, please let me go to her."

Emily tightened her grip, terrified that Caroline would harm herself in her frenzy.

As suddenly as it had begun, the thrashing stopped. There was absolute stillness in the room. Even the fire seemed motionless. It was Caroline who spoke to Emily but she spoke with Elizabeth's voice.

"My mother's gone. And Sophie's gone without me."

The fire leapt back to life as Caroline slumped unconscious in her mother's arms.

Tom carried Caroline up the curved staircase and placed her carefully on the bed while Daniel raced for the doctor. Emily followed them blindly, unaware of her feet making contact with the steps. It seemed an eternity before Daniel returned with Dr. Cameron. She forced her mind to focus on his words. To ensure she missed nothing, she repeated his instructions back to him verbatim.

"Keep her quiet. Bathe her frequently in cool water. Watch her closely throughout the night and pray the fever breaks. Yes, Doctor, thank you."

Her manners masked an empty Emily. Her real self was sorting frantically through layers of veiled lifetimes for something to barter, to trade, to exchange, anything that would let Caroline live. She sat beside the bed, placing cool cloths on the blistering skin and changing them when they no longer served their purpose. Tom and the boys took turns bringing buckets of cold water to the room, and tea for Emily.

Only once did Emily leave Caroline alone. During the second night of her illness, when the fever showed no signs of weakening, Emily capitulated. She walked silently through the sleeping house to her own room where the pine chest lay at the foot of the bed. It still held the precious linens she had brought from England. On top of the carefully folded sheets and table linen was a package wrapped in creased tissue paper. Tom was snoring gently. Emily lifted it from its resting place and carried it from the room.

There was no abatement in Caroline's fever. If anything, the flushed face on the pillow was rosier and the skin hotter and dryer to the touch than when Emily had left. She bent over Caroline, placing her left ear on the little girl's chest. Had the rhythm of her breathing changed? Was it quicker? Shallower? Instinct told Emily the crisis was nearing. She wasted not a moment in stripping the nightgown from the child and bathing her whole body with cool water, replacing each cloth as it warmed with a fresh wet one. She worked like a mad woman, and still the fever raged.

In that long hour preceding dawn, all hope drained from Emily. She opened the package she had brought from the chest and spoke out loud.

"She doesn't have to belong to me. Just let her live."

The sampler spilled across her lap, scattering colour. Emily lifted the candle and held it over the canvas. The candlelight picked out ruby red and emerald green silken stitches, and reflected their brilliance into Emily's eyes, dazzling and confusing her. She replaced the candle on the dresser, determined to follow the lines of the design and not be waylaid by the shifting splendour of midnight blue, indigo and turquoise. Elizabeth's sampler was more extraordinary than Emily remembered. Once she had seen the outlines of a clipper ship, a flying horse, a mammoth monument, and now she could distinguish only colour and the cold glitter of tiny stars around the edge. The center of the piece was a garden gone to seed, lush with overblown flowers bursting through the borders. Emily could almost smell the ripe perfume of the blossoms. She felt uncomfortable with the sampler in her hands; it was heady to the senses but disconcerting to the mind. Still, it did belong to Caroline. Emily placed it on her pillow.

Caroline's fever broke the next day. She sat up in bed, weak but clear-eyed and rational. She drank the nourishing liquids that Emily brought her. Those in the stone house breathed a great sigh of relief and Emily whisked away Elizabeth's sampler from the pillow and replaced it in the pine box beneath layers of wedding linen.

Caroline was scarcely better when Daniel brought home a note from the schoolmaster addressed to Captain Harris. The town still thought of Tom as the Captain, and after his resignation from the Army had been accepted, it seemed a friendly term and not a title denoting rank. Emily wished it had been Richard who had brought the note home. A tongue-lashing could deal with Richard. Emily frowned and turned the letter in her fingers as if the contents could be divined by touch. Richard was not the problem. Before the schoolmaster had been hired, Emily had been in charge of teaching both boys their letters. Richard had chafed at her attempts and she had tired of chasing after him to study. He was not a dull student, and Richard was adept at figures. His problem and hers lay in keeping his attention. He abandoned his books on the slightest pretext; games, friends, or even chores all had prior claims on Richard's time. The village school and its Scottish schoolmaster had worked wonders with her younger son. She was happy to pay someone to keep Richard at his desk. With difficulty she pulled her thoughts from Richard and back to Daniel and the note.

The school which was working out so well for Richard was not advanced enough for Daniel. He had often already mastered on his own, concepts the schoolmaster was just introducing to the other students. When he told her these things, Daniel was not complaining. It confounded him that everyone did not understand the workings of these principles as promptly as he did. Even as a little boy, Daniel had had a curiosity that strained Emily's own knowledge and baffled Tom's. He had never been discouraged from asking questions by a lack of answers; Daniel had the scholar's faith that someone somewhere had an explanation, and if he persisted, he, too, would find it. Emily had known from the first day that the log schoolhouse and its young schoolmaster were only improvisations in Daniel's education, and yet she clung to them as if by her very tenacity she could change the direction of what had to be.

Tom and Emily sat on the verandah in the warm May air, waiting for the schoolmaster and watching the light fade from the evening sky. Tom had changed his dusty work clothes for a coat and clean trousers. He loved the mill, and no matter what Emily said, he was not content to remain behind the counter.

"If Daniel's playing truant, I'll have to take the whip to him."

They both laughed. Tom had never been able to administer corporal punishment to the boys. When they needed disciplining, it was Emily's hand on the ruler.

"Tom, be serious."

"Daniel is the best student MacEwen has or will ever have."

"That's the problem. Daniel has outgrown the school. There's nothing more for him to learn there."

"My God, Emily, the boy's just turning thirteen. I think that's too young for him to go into the business."

"I do, too."

It was decided before the schoolmaster ever reached the porch that in September Daniel would return to England to enroll at Tom's old school.

"What's the matter, Caro? What are you doing?"

Sean Casey crouched beside Caroline, trying to see if her eyes were open. She lay still as death, hoping he would run inside and tell her mother. A fly landed on her face, walked delicately across her cheek and climbed the bridge of her nose. She clenched her fists, hoping Sean would not notice, yet willing him to brush the fly away. Nothing. The fly began to move again, crawling with exquisite slowness down the slope of her nose. Her lips quivered as she imagined its filthy feet landing on her mouth. Flies were always swarming over the horse droppings on the road. She sneezed and sat up.

"Hi, Caro. My mother said I was to come and cheer you up, 'cause you can't go to school."

"I can too go to school."

She took the measure of the boy with her eyes. Although much younger than she, he was about the same size.

"I could go to school if you helped me."

"What do you want to go to school for?"

"I just do. Now go into the privy and pass me out your clothes."

He jumped to his feet.

"What do you want with my clothes?" he yelped. "What will I wear?"

"Just do what I say."

Caroline pushed him towards the privy.

She had him in the outbuilding and out of his homespun shirt and britches before he realized what was happening. She pulled her dress over her head.

"You can wear this."

The little boy watched speechlessly as Caroline stepped out of her pantaloons and into his shirt and pants.

"Now give me your hat, and don't cry. Boys don't cry. What's the matter? It's only for a little while, so I can see what school is like."

Sean began to cry with real intensity.

"Stop that, Sean, or I'll never play with you again."

He was hiccuping sporadically as she closed the door of the privy.

"You don't have to stay in there. You can come out."

She hitched Sean's britches around her waist and tied them up with a piece of cord she found in the barn. She was lucky it was warm enough to go barefoot.

Caroline got as far as the middle of the schoolyard before she was challenged. Mr. MacEwen himself saw the small figure crossing the yard and sent Daniel out to investigate because the lad was always finished his assignments far ahead of the next best pupil, and the schoolmaster was tired of finding Daniel's eyes fastened on him, like a pup that never tires of retrieving sticks.

"Daniel, see what's up. That lad looks too young to be enrolling in school."

As Daniel neared, the boy dropped his head and dragged his feet.

"Where are you going?"

"To school," came the muffled reply from under the wide brim of the straw hat. "I'm late."

There was something familiar to Daniel in both the slight shape of the boy and the tone of his voice.

"What's your name?"

Caroline was taken aback, and she raised her head.

"Caroline, what are you doing here? What are you wearing? Wait right here. Don't move an inch or you'll be sorry."

Daniel went back inside the classroom to report to Mr. MacEwen.

"He's lost, sir. I'll take him home. I know where he lives."

"Caroline, it's a good thing it was me who was sent out to investigate. Whatever possessed you?"

She thinned her lips into a narrow line and refused to answer any of his questions. It was only as he marched her up the walk to the house that she spoke.

"We'd better see if Sean is still in the privy."

Daniel rolled about on the grass, choking back his laughter at the sight of young Sean sitting in the privy dressed in Caroline's clothes. Caroline was mortified. While the two children exchanged clothes, Caroline extracted a promise from both Sean and Daniel never to tell anyone what she had done, "on pain of a cruel and violent death."

Girls are their mothers' daughters and their fathers' dreams.

I am trying to find a voice for women who were never heard, who never had their own voice or who never heard their own voice except late at night or in a poem. I am one of their spokepersons, like it or not. This rage I have must be channelled. Such power I would have at my disposal if I could harness it and unleash it at my discretion.

My heart is soaring on music, poetry and philosophy; not pulled earthward towards people, but flying inside. What a way to go! "Old Women and Love," a poem I heard on the radio this morning, with phrases like: "the rustle of blood" and "firecrackers in the far woods stir the memory of the misty-eyed girls we were." I share this happiness with all who wish to feast, not devour, the riches of the mind. We can eat sensuously, deliciously with the eyes and tongue and ears; taste and touch and lean back on the classical cushion of the past until the hunger grows and we must return, yearning, to the table. If I have to, I will go alone, or share; I do not care, but go I must. There is magic in the land and in my hand today.

In Eliot's *Murder in the Cathedral*, the language is beautiful and the women speak as a chorus. I saw them as a sisterhood, faceless, suffering, solid, rooted in the earth, and very knowing outside the patriarchal strictures of the Church. Archbishop Becket was the spiritual father who literally threw himself between his flock and the forces of evil. Martyrdom is the boundary for evil, as is the circle of the women's world; both represent the line which no devil dare cross. One line, "action is suffering and suffering action," rings through the piece; this is what makes the wheel turn and yet follow an eternal design. One sees this design in the heads of puppies and the faces of babies.

CHAPTER SIX

Emily had never seen a summer go by so abruptly. She found herself unprepared on the wharf waiting for the boat that would take her son on the first stage of a trip back to England. Her family, and much of the town as well, judging by the number of people on the bank, were there to see Daniel off. Emily spotted Mary Casey in the crowd, her latest baby in her arms. Emily waved and managed a smile of sorts. It was abnormal for Emily to feel uncertain of herself, as if she were sending Daniel off to a war. She pulled herself up short. It would be years before she saw him again, and yet she was proud that he was leaving to enter a different world than that which Perth could offer. Emily wondered if Tom was experiencing these same contradictory feelings. She had an urge to run to where he had taken Daniel aside and say, "He doesn't need to go away. He can learn everything he needs to know right here with us." She smiled and nodded her head as people greeted her and she noted Tom surreptitiously wipe his eyes with the back of his hand before he clapped Daniel on the back and slipped something into his hand. Emily moved close enough to overhear what he was saying.

"Daniel, not to worry; everything is paid for as far as Liverpool, and there you will be met by your aunt and uncle, but you might need this. You work hard, Daniel. I know you will do us proud. Don't forget to write your mother. She is going to take your leaving pretty badly. Be good, son."

Watching the two of them together, Emily had a quick intimation of the Daniel that would return to her, no longer a tall thin boy with a slash of dark hair falling across his brow. He would be a man whom she would scarcely know and she, in turn, would be a stranger to him. She closed her eyes so no one could see the tears welling up and threatening to spill over onto her cheeks.

Richard and Caroline, who had been hanging over the bridge above the wharf, were now pushing and shoving their way through the crowd, anxious to tell Daniel they had seen a boat in the distance.

"I saw the boat, it's almost..."

Caroline yanked Richard's arm. "Let me tell. I saw it first."

"Tell me what you saw."

Daniel listened carefully to Caroline's description of the large flat-bottomed boat being poled upriver. When she had finished, he leaned over and whispered in the little girl's ear.

"Goodbye, pumpkin. Remember, no more bullying Sean Casey."

She pulled back from him, drawing herself up to her full height by sucking in her stomach. Caroline narrowed her eyes to blue slits and hissed, "Daniel, you promised not to tell."

"Calm down. I haven't told anybody."

And he ruffled the crest of her red hair.

Caroline shook off his hand, furious.

"Caroline, what's to become of you?"

Daniel had been honest with Caroline about the village school. No girls. "Do you want to be the only girl?"

"I don't care about that. I want to go to school."

The rumour that the Misses McIvor were to open a school for young ladies was a Godsend. Emily could not have contained Caroline's insatiable desire to learn for another year. She had already read every book in the house, including most of the Bible, and she was constantly at Richard and Tom to make up sums for her to do. Emily had prayed that the girls' school was more than a rumour, for her own resources had long since been exhausted.

Caroline was up before the sun her first morning of school, dressed in her Sunday best and with a big black taffeta bow hanging lopsided in her red curls. When Tom and Emily came down to breakfast Caroline was standing by the back door with her lunch pail in her hand.

"I hardly closed my eyes all night 'cause I thought I might be late for school. Hurry, pa, eat your breakfast." Caroline pushed a bowl towards him and watched as he ate his porridge. "The teachers will be very cross if I am late."

Richard stepped in from doing his chores in time to hear her last remark. "Holy cow, Caroline, it's only seven o'clock."

She ignored him, concentrating all her efforts into hurrying her father. "Drink your coffee up, pa, and let's go. I can't wait."

Caroline arrived home at noon. To the kitchen in general, and to Emily in particular, she announced: "I'm not going back. They don't know anything and it isn't a real school. We sit at the Misses McIvors' dining-room table. There aren't any slates or brushes. There are hardly any books, and they wouldn't let me touch the books they have. They said I was too young. But I already know how to read. It's stupid."

Her lunch pail landed on the floor with a thump and Caroline dropped beside it. Emily traded glances with Tom across the table. He shrugged his shoulders and stood up.

"I'm sorry, Caroline. That's a shame. I'll see you both tonight."

Emily fixed her daughter with eyes that brooked no nonsense. "Caroline, have you been fair to give up so soon? This afternoon it might get better. If they learn something you want to know, you will be sorry that you didn't go back. I think you should try again, unless you want to be a quitter."

The little girl's eyes flashed defiantly and her lower lip protruded. Without any warning, her face softened.

"All right, I'll go back. But this time I'm taking Sophie with me. She doesn't know how to read or write. Maybe they can teach her."

Sophie had first come to live with the Harrises when they moved into the new house. Caroline had never slept alone before; she had always had the boys for company. It was frightening until Sophie came to share her room and her life. Sophie was Caroline's exclusive companion; Caroline was the only one who could actually see Sophie, although the boys claimed Sophie was responsible for any trouble they got into. Sophie became as much a part of the family as a beloved pet. Emily hadn't the heart to discourage Sophie's presence; she counted on the passage of time to take care of that.

In the meantime, Sophie went everywhere with Caroline except to church on Sunday. Sophie didn't like their church. According to Caroline, Sophie had said, "God doesn't live in a house, no matter what you call it. He lives in the forest with the trees and flowers and animals. He hates being locked up in a church and He won't go there."

Once, Richard jokingly asked Caroline what Sophie did on Sunday. Caroline had fixed him with a steely glance and replied, "She never told me, but I think she walks in the woods. Sophie likes to be alone among the trees."

Since leaving England, Emily had subconsciously marked the passage of time in winters. Caroline had been born in the winter; they had come to Perth at winter's end; they had moved into their stone house as winter set in; and this was her fifth winter without Daniel. Emerging from a Canadian winter unscathed was counted as a year well-lived. Life was difficult for the women in these pioneer communities, but winter added a cruel dimension to their already heavy burdens. The piercing cold, the snow, the frozen lakes and rivers, and the overriding fear that it would never end, chilled the women's spirits. Their calendar year ended when spring began.

This winter differed from those that had come before only in the length and degree of the duration of the cold weather. There had been no January thaw. The freezing temperatures had been constant since the advent of the new year, and here was February with no sign of a respite from the arctic cold.

Each day, Emily wrote a small note in her fine handwriting in her journal. Often, it was just a mention of the weather or what she had served the family for their main meal of the day; this was a more precise way of tracking time than waiting for the winter to end. She was writing in her notebook when the ringing of a bell penetrated the thick stone walls. She stopped in mid-sentence and counted the number of rings.

One... two... three... and then a long pause, and once again one... two... three rings and silence. There was a fire.

The snowclad streets filled with life as every soul in the village responded to the summons of the bells. By the time Emily negotiated the snowy streets, the fire had gained a solid foothold in the house that served as the girls' school. A line of figures stretched from the hole chopped in the ice of the river to the porch of the frame house, each man intent on grasping and then passing the contents of each bucket intact to the next link in the human chain. Emily spotted Tom out on the ice, and Richard closer to the house. She ran to where Richard stood in the line and barely breathed the words.

"Where's Caroline?"

"She's safe, ma. I saw her myself. Pa spoke to her before he started with the buckets."

He was short of breath and his face was red with exertion as he transferred the heavy buckets without interrupting the demanding pace imposed by those on either side of him.

Emily's eyes moved precisely and swiftly over the crowd until she found the burnished head of Caroline, tucked safely among the hatless heads of the students huddled at the rear of the school. Emily's heart stopped racing and she asked the person closest to her, "Is everyone accounted for? Did they all get out?'

"I heard someone say the little Quinn girl is missing, but one of the other girls said she thought she saw her leave. Probably, she was so frightened, she ran home."

As Emily watched the cluster of schoolgirls that included Caroline, she heard a great roar of air escaping as the roof of the house collapsed. Everyone jumped back as the flames leapt to new heights, and sparks scattered in a wider circle. The inside of the house was exposed, revealing the flaming spectres of tables, chairs and the fiery outline of a staircase. Emily stiffened as all but one of the girls scurried away from the shooting flames. The one girl stood alone for a long moment, and then walked deliberately towards the burning building. Emily did not know whether she heard Caroline's cry above the crackle of the flames or whether she had read her lips.

"Sophie— Sophie's in there."

Emily saw Richard yank Caroline from the steps of the blazing back porch and drag her to safety. Emily reached Richard in time to help him hold the girl upright. Caroline had fainted.

The service for Moira Quinn was well-attended. The tragedy of the girl's death was compounded by the hostile weather. The ground was too frozen to admit the coffin. Moira's body had to be stored in an empty root cellar for interment in the spring.

There was no service for Sophie. Only Caroline mourned the death of her childhood friend, and no one had any hint of the magnitude of Caroline's loss.

Lines from Liz Zetlin's *Scented Red*:

A woman, a child, a ghost
they will all be
in the river together
all at the same time,
each in her own time.

What a terrible price we pay for safety. We pay this price as women, and look what has happened to us. Andrea will not pay that price. Rilke's eighth elegy instructs us to place death behind us and look outward; each moment is huge. I close my eyes and sunshine dances on my eyelids, a warm liquid gold. I am rocked by the sound of the water lapping in the boathouse; the wind is talking to the trees and I am here.

Fairy tales are a way into one's own life; they break things down into their essence and allow meaning to shine through. Fairy tales sweep away the clutter from our lives and give us back the essentials. Is an astral body necessary as a home for the soul? We need to create a place where the soul can live. Sometimes when I am swimming across the bay I picture a second ephemeral body floating just above mine. William Blake drew ephemeral bodies. I wonder if he saw them, or only intuited that they were there? Two lines are present in my life: terrestrial, with its linear and sequential structure; and celestial, with its non-linear and triadic structure and its cosmic dimension. Sometimes they overlap, and if one is very alert, one can see a pattern between the two. These glimpses are very rare.

CHAPTER SEVEN

Some of the girls had been glad when the Misses McIvors' school burned down. They said so in front of Caroline.

"Only old maids need an education! Boys don't like girls who are too smart." They looked pointedly at Caroline and giggled. She thought they were disgusting, always trying to attract attention to themselves when they were around boys. She caught a glimpse of her reflection in the hall mirror.

"You really thought some miracle was going to happen that would magically admit you to some institute of higher learning? You are daft, girl. You are as stupid as the other stupid girls. What made you think you were different? No wonder no one wants us in their schools. We are stupid. Stupid, stupid, stupid..." She stuck her tongue out at the red-haired girl in the mirror and crossed her eyes. "And as for you, Caroline Harris, you are ugly as well as stupid." It wasn't surprising that everybody, including her own brother, hated her.

At Mr. MacEwen's log schoolhouse, Caroline had given no thought to her future; she had been totally caught up. She was taught real subjects by a trained teacher, and in this atmosphere she reached, in a short span of time, the same levels of achievement as Richard and his friends. The schoolmaster used her youth and gender as spurs to goad his senior class on to greater excellence. Caroline, a willing if unwitting instrument in his strategy, had become universally despised by the class of 1831. It was a matter of importance only to a few that this class wrote the best examinations of any graduating class in the brief history of the school. For the majority of the students, their classroom education was at an end. Their strong young bodies were put out to work the family farms, while their freshly turned and fertilized young minds were laid to rest. In recognition of the outstanding results obtained by Mr. MacEwen, the town fathers voted to increase his yearly stipend.

From inside the stone house, Emily watched Caroline, in a fury, abuse the old chestnut tree. She guessed at how much Caroline was hurting, but she was powerless to help; Caroline would despise what Emily could offer her: an apprenticeship in household science, a poor substitute for Greek and Latin.

Secretly, she agreed with Caroline, but that was the way it was. Emily let her gaze slide down the figure of the girl now leaning against the tree and made mental notes of how the waist of Caroline's dress was bunched halfway up her back, and above it the flowered material was strained almost to the tearing point. And yet the girl was bone thin. Emily followed the flow of the hem to where skin curved whitely around the black tops of her boots. There was a harsh honesty about Caroline, Emily decided, that, when softened by the onset of young womanhood, would mould into elegance. Emily herself was the product of a long rebellious girlhood that had nourished her resistance to tradition and allowed her to travel all the way to Perth, where she had slipped with ease into her prescribed role. Emily did not want to break Caroline's spirit, but neither had she any wish to see her become a pariah. It was a thin straight line a girl had to walk; she could make only so many deviations before being banished by her elders. A web of fine wrinkles creased the corners of Emily's eyes. These next few years were going to be difficult.

She found herself wishing Sophie might return for just a year or two to befriend Caroline and give her someone to talk to. Emily turned abruptly from the window. This was madness.

Emily was lonely, too. The British Government had decided to go ahead with the building of the Rideau Canal system, as much for economic reasons as for defence, and in the last two years the eastern portion of the province had been inundated with soldiers, workmen and thousands of new immigrants. Construction was at an all-time high in Upper Canada, and Perth, as part of the system, benefited from the increased activity. The Harris sawmill and lumber yard were hard pressed to supply the demands of the canal contractors and maintain good service for their regular customers. Tom was scarcely home except to sleep. Each time he hired more men, business increased at the same pace, and he no longer took the time to walk to the stone house for his midday meal.

Caroline was delegated to carry Tom's hot-dinner bucket to the mill, a task she liked as much as anything Emily suggested. She escaped the house and her mother's watchful eyes, and scuffed along the road, deliberately raising dust with the toes of her boots. She hoped Emily would become discouraged with the coating of dirt on the black leather and let her go barefoot, as she had every summer before this one.

There were a great many wagons on the main street, for the most part filled with unfamiliar faces. Their otherness played havoc with Caroline's adolescent mind, and she invented scenarios in which she took the starring role and cast the strangers in supporting parts. If they were young and pleasant and smiled as Caroline assessed their potential, she assigned them decent roles. But when she detected a hint of malice, or the shadow of some unspeakable perversion in their faces, they were doomed to die as villains, sometimes by her hand and sometimes by their own. Her stories kept her from arriving at the mill punctually, but her father never noticed she was late or asked why his dinner was lukewarm; he was rarely at his desk when she arrived. She would find him in the yard, helping a workman stack newly cut boards into neat piles, or loading them onto a wagon for delivery to a site along the river. Caroline waited while her father ate, ostensibly to return the bucket to her mother, but really because horses and wagons and men were always coming and going and someone was usually at her father's elbow, needing his advice. It was deliciously noisy. The men didn't talk, they yelled, and their rowdiness excited the animals, who lifted their great heads and snorted in sympathy. Over and through these other sounds was the constant buzz of the saws. The lumber yard was breathing, and Caroline along with it. The rasp of the saw buzzed in the soles of her feet, and from there it vibrated the length of her body, separating into tingling fragments and ending in each of her fingertips. She could not remain still when the saws were humming.

Sometimes, when her father was unusually busy, he would send her to his desk to check an order or pick up a bill, and she would stay at the sawmill as long as there were errands to be run. By summer's end, Caroline was spending more time at her father's desk than he was, and when the time came to wave Richard off to school, his going didn't seem nearly as unfair to her as it had in June. Caroline was quick, accurate and agreeable, and her presence in the office left Tom free to supervise the yard. The men, both employees and customers, became accustomed to seeing Caroline behind Tom's desk, and no one hesitated to ask her to calculate costs and board footages. There were a few raised eyebrows from those coming for the first time to the sawmill, but no audible comments and no complaints. Emily shut her eyes as to her daughter's whereabouts, and during the long summer evenings, when Tom was at the mill, she basked in Caroline's good humour.

Colours are taking on a new dimension... red is lipstick clear and pink has bubbles in it. Waking up is wonderful. The sun on your skin, the water to move through. Life is nature. A dragonfly landed on my hand this morning;

he was chrome yellow and patent leather black. Time is not quite suspended, but it has definitely changed direction. I listen to what my body and mind tell me and do it then, instead of waiting for some self-imposed schedule of getting my work done first. The habits of a lifetime are hard to break, but it is coming. Write those thoughts while you think them, swim when you need to, and eat what your body asks for. Above all, listen, listen, listen. Last summer I discovered it all begins with a question; this summer I discover the answer lies in the silence.

"What goes around, comes around" really does hold true. I wonder how many others of those old sayings have the grain of truth in them?

I had a nasty car accident and only now have stopped shaking. My God, the collision took forever and then it happened so fast— time stopped, time speeded up. I remember it all in precise detail. I am having a summer of warnings. The brakes on my car went on July 18th, and my car accident was on August 18th. Do I take precautions? I don't think so. Life is for those who dare to live it. So full out, my dear, and the devil take the hindmost.

Morning and a walk down the road with a long-eared, long-legged pup to put everything into perspective. The quiet, the warmth and the solitude are healers. I let nature surround me, soak into me, and I can feel my center righting itself. A few days of this and I will be healed— a strange summer— hot and full of trauma, little, big, assorted. Just when you feel you know the answers to some of the questions, you get slapped back into size.

THE PEN feels too thick and wet for my hand… like a puppy's tongue, adorable but slobbering. I have been reading Rilke on Cézanne. You must literally fight to stay present, here, where you are. The mind always wants to race ahead. I saw a great maple tree hanging over a tennis court and the colour of it took my breath away: Rilke's shock of recognition? The same thing happened on a walk. A branch of brilliantly coloured leaves floated in front of me… unattached to anything earthly. Words attach themselves to emotions and drain them of their feeling. Is this what criticism does to art and literature and people? The power of the word is used to disenfranchise the work from its emotions. Words become the control, and transfer value from the emotional to the intellectual. We humans have a great need for control. How then do we communicate, if not in words? By touch, by deeds, by our lives!

CHAPTER EIGHT

A peculiar offshoot of the building boom was the entrance of society into the towns and villages of Upper Canada. It came on the arms of British officers, assigned to engineer the massive Rideau Canal project, in the persons of their wives. Upper Canada was not the backwoods it had been ten years before. There were schools and churches and farm girls for hire as domestics, but perhaps most compelling was instant social standing of a kind unobtainable in England. The women came out in numbers, and with them their lace-edged linens and their crystal and bone china. Entertaining in Perth no longer involved the whole community, but became the private preserve of those hostesses who wished to advance by clambering over the backs of those deemed less desirable. Genteel functions for the ladies of the town proliferated and soon became the order of the day. The lack of an invitation to even a single event could occasion great despair. Emily, of course, was on every guest list; her position in Perth was unassailable.

"Emily, my dear, where's Caroline? You must bring her to our little soirees. Isn't it time she was introduced in the proper circles?"

"I'm afraid you will not find Caroline at tea parties."

"Why not? Is she too busy cutting wood at the mill?"

A burst of giggles from several ladies in the circle camouflaged the exact position of the speaker. Not everyone in town wished Emily well; her good fortune lodged snugly in more narrow throats. She lived in the best house, it was generally conceded, in Perth, and had both sons away to school, one of them at a smart English university. If this were not enough, her husband operated by far and away the most successful business in town. Emily gasped and then smoothed over the little faux pas with a cough. She had been away from England so long she had almost forgotten how the game was played.

"Of course not. Caroline, cutting wood? How droll! She's in the office, helping Tom with the accounts. He's been so busy, and it's impossible to find someone who can add and spell as well as Caroline can." Emily looked around the silent circle, daring anyone to challenge her. The woman seated on Emily's right, a recent arrival in town, picked up the lagging conversation.

"Caroline is thirteen? Just my Rebecca's age. I've seen your daughter in church. This brings to mind a great concern. The Major and myself were shocked there have been no arrangements made for our young people to join the Church of England. In England, Rebecca would be receiving instruction by now. I have taken the liberty of speaking to Reverend Gordon about starting a class, and I assured him there was a demand. We can't let our standards drop just because we are so far from home; our young people will grow up as heathens. Can I count on you to send Caroline to the confirmation classes, Mrs. Harris?"

Not only did Caroline not contest Emily's request, she was actually eager to go. Emily would have been less delighted had she understood the reason underlying her daughter's zeal. Caroline had no conventional desire to join the Church and be part of a wider Christian community; rather, she viewed the classes as a singular opportunity to feed her fierce appetite for knowledge. The subject of religion suited her as well as any other.

The church was empty when Caroline arrived for the first class. Reverend Gordon had already preached two thunderous sermons that day, and he was tired and in ill humour. He could have smacked the snooty woman who had cornered him and demanded he organize these classes. The prospect of leaving his own fire to face a room full of half-grown boys and girls was irritating. Some fancy busybody from England was stirring up trouble where there had never been any. Her kind tested his Christian charity. What was she trying to do? Out here, if you wanted to join the Church, you went every Sunday and regularly put a little something in the collection plate. After a time, no one questioned whether you belonged or not. That was your church, and you were a member. Why did she want to import elaborate rituals from England? It was a pack of nonsense having young people receive instruction. Any decent person could learn all they needed to know from listening attentively to his sermons. If the Church of England didn't watch what they were doing, they would end up just like the Roman Catholics with their Papist rites and ceremonies. He'd come out here to get away from the pomp and arrogance that was creeping into English ministries. Damned women were always complicating things. He hauled himself out of his chair and hooked his clerical collar together at the back of his neck. With any luck, he promised himself, he'd be back in his chair in an hour.

A single glance told Reverend Gordon that Tom Harris' red-headed daughter was trouble. She sat right up front in the pew directly under the pulpit. Every time he lifted his eyes from the Book of Common Prayer he encountered her look of wild-eyed ardour. His collar tightened and threatened to strangle him. By the end of the first class, he had developed an antipathy to Caroline that bordered on the fanatic. He raced through the Catechism, had them repeat the Creed after him, and ordered them to memorize both for the next meeting. He dismissed the class and exited the pulpit in the same breath.

Since the town fathers had voted to have a spur canal built to connect Perth to the Rideau Canal, there were even more strangers in town than usual, and all of them, at one time or another, passed through the lumber yard. Caroline handled their curious glances and muted remarks by ignoring them. She did not want to jeopardize her position at the sawmill by complaining to her father. The trick, she discovered, was to think of the strange men not as people but as trees. She calculated how much each would fetch in terms of clean board footage after they had been planed and trimmed. Caroline became so adept at converting them to stacks of lumber that she was startled if addressed directly.

"Hey, girlie, don't that red hair make you hot?"

Caroline's head was bent over a ledger.

"Hey, you, girlie. Let's get a look at what goes with all that hot red hair."

He was a short man dressed in the rough homespun of a labourer. His powerful upper torso made the rest of him, including his head, appear undersized. Ordinarily, he could not have gained such easy access to the office, but everyone in the yard was busily engaged and the stranger was free to wander about the lumber yard. His close-set eyes, constantly on the alert for anything left unattended, had panned the yard. A splash of colour in the office window had drawn his attention, and he had strolled over to investigate. It was Caroline, shaking her head over some figures that did not tally. The stranger had looked behind him; everyone was still occupied. He slipped inside the office and closed the door. The first she knew of him was when his calloused horny hand touched her throat. Danger circulated in the small room as surely as if he had stropped the blade of a knife on her throat. Caroline had seen a wild dog once. She had been a little girl, picnicking with Daniel in the woods behind the town. They had been packing up their basket when an ugly guttural sound had filled the clearing.

"Don't move a muscle, Caroline. Stay exactly as you are and do exactly what I tell you. Whatever happens, don't move. Watch his eyes."

She had withstood the vicious glare of the animal's crazed yellow eyes for what seemed like hours, until the dog had finally lowered his head and slunk back into the woods.

She stood up and faced the man across her father's desk. That dog was still alive. Would he crush the life from her, or remember where he was and worry for his own safety? It was not decided until she curled her finger into claws and bared her teeth.

"Get out of here."

He backed off then, snarling.

Through the window, she saw him slinking from one stack of lumber to another, until he finally reached the gate.

Caroline never knew which one of the workmen told her father or what exactly he had seen. That same night, she asked to be excused from the table, saying she was tired. Later, lying in her bed with her door open, she heard her father talking to her mother.

"Emily, you had better speak to Caroline about coming to the mill. There are some very rough characters about the town, and every one of them ends up at my lumber yard. It's no place for a girl, let alone my daughter. Keep her home where she belongs."

Caroline was waiting inside the door for Reverend Gordon to arrive for the confirmation class. He nodded curtly and made a motion to pass by her.

"Excuse me, sir. I have some questions about the class last week."

"Now is not the proper time for questions. Take your seat, please."

She sat in the same place as she had at the first class. The rest of the young people sat bunched together in the back pews, the girls on the right side of the church and the boys on the left. Caroline and Reverend Gordon formed their own congregation in the front.

Caroline listened conscientiously to everything he had to say, and when Reverend Gordon was summing up, she raised her hand. He ignored her. She waggled her hand back and forth.

"What is it?"

"Is this the proper time for you to entertain my questions?"

God damn the little snippet, challenging him with his own words. "Yes, girlie. Get it out and get it over with."

Caroline was stunned by the malevolence in his voice. She forgot why she was there.

He tuned his voice to the furthest pews and thundered, "It seems the cat has got the red-haired girlie's tongue. Thank God for that."

Great peals of laughter rose from the back of the church and rolled towards the pulpit where they crested and broke across Caroline's back. She hunched lower in her seat, hoping their shouts of derision would not find her, but the laughter searched her out and grew more uproarious, echoing back and forth between the stone walls of the church and bouncing off the backs of the wooden pews, until everyone in the church, with the exception of Caroline, was shaking with laughter.

Caroline shredded the damned list of questions with her nails until not one word remained intact. She remained huddled in the pew while the church emptied, and made her way home reluctantly, praying she would not meet anyone along the way. Caroline was unwilling to concede final victory to Reverend Gordon or to her peers, but marching into the parlour, she announced with a funereal air that she had withdrawn from confirmation classes. Emily jerked upright in her chair.

"I thought you liked them?"

Caroline dismissed her mother with a wave of one gloved hand. "I am going to speak to Father Benoit and ask him to give me instruction in Roman Catholicism."

As she spoke, a picture of a white-robed, beatific Caroline focused in her mind. The image expanded and she saw in the background, their eyes round with disbelief and tinged with envy, the familiar shapes of Reverend Gordon and a good portion of the town's adolescents. It was a beguiling tableau.

"I want to give my life to Christ. I shall become a nun."

Emily swooned.

How quickly the summer goes... read young womanhood. The air is nippy early in the morning. I am sitting on the dock at sunset in a gentle rain, puddles on the water and a golden sky. No wonder humans treasure gold; it mirrors the sun. It has become unbearably bright and each letter I write has a yellow aura. This must be what the monks saw before they illuminated their manuscripts: letters edged in gold.

I have learned to slow my pace and savour the moment this summer, though the temptation is to race through each day instead of looking at the greens of the forest, the surface of the lake. Yesterday the waves were exactly the same shape as the seagulls' spread wings. I move through time as though it were a substance, like air or water. Is time a substance with chemical properties? What a thought— I could change my medium.

The world wakes up slowly these late August mornings. It is dark and cobwebby with heavy dew. The lake is white with mist, and the girls (Britannia and Bailey) and I are lost in the forest. We like it. They see a jack rabbit and chase it. The cobwebs fascinate me, millions of them strung between every means of support. Who spins all night and why? There are two sorts of webs. One is the wheel, flat and spoked from the center; the other is pyramidal in shape, three-dimensional and fuzzier in texture. Such a world of miracles, all fitting one into another like a Chinese puzzle.

Endings take a long long time. Tomorrow I leave and I will only be a visitor until next summer. What will this year bring? I am not crazy about this vault into the Middle Ages but it has its advantages. I don't have to rush home to put little ones into school. A writer must be an observer of life and a socializer must be in the thick of life. I don't think the two are compatible.

If I don't get this down, it will never go away and let me sleep. I am forty-six years old and my younger child has left for university. I too can go. There is a course being offered on all the things I think about and wonder at and I am afraid to take it. Why? A strange Chagallian mishmash of Marlene's course, Liz's poetry and my own writing is churning around in my head, begging for the fragments to come together. Perhaps the pattern is not a quilt, but a woven coverlet placed over the lives of sleeping women?

Is there a journal within my journal waiting to be written, and is the starting point today? Do I write her journal? Why hers and not my own? Am I some product of an earlier age that begs to be unlocked? Is my life a key? It's confusing, and all I really want to do is sleep, but she won't let me unless I agree to write her story. I have not capitulated yet, but I know in my bones that I will.

CHAPTER NINE

The letter from Daniel, announcing his homecoming in time for Christmas, was almost more than Emily could bear. She threw herself into a frenzy of preparations; Caroline was allowed a temporary respite. Emily's abundant energy was redirected into producing a Christmas all of them would remember forever.

Richard came home first. Kingston was the best place in the world, but now that he was home for the holidays, Perth satisfied him immensely. He was a lad who relished life wherever he lived it. It was good to be home, he thought, as he strolled across the bridge joining the residential section of the town to the business district. A chap needed roots. When Richard spoke of himself in the third person, as he had done since going away to school, Emily and Tom exchanged amused glances. Richard didn't mind. The pater and the mater were a trifle old-fashioned, but he liked them that way. A chap might change, but a chap's parents ought to stay the same. Otherwise, one would never know what to expect. When Richard smiled and threw back his shoulders, he was unmistakably his father's son. The shy glances he attracted from the young ladies he passed on the way to the mill were not at all unwelcome. He whistled a cheery tune and adjusted the thick woollen muffler he wore so the broad coloured stripes showed to their greatest advantage. The chaps at school all had scarves like this, but he hadn't seen another one in Perth. It felt great to be home. Even his sister wasn't as bad as he remembered.

The young man had waited half the evening to claim a dance with Caroline Harris, and as the band rested their instruments and rustled the sheets of music on their stands, he saw his chance. His measured arrival at the row of chairs edging the polished surface of the dance floor coincided with the delivery of Caroline, by her most recent partner, to her mother's side. Emily was seated with the other matrons, engaged in seemingly carefree conversations, but all the while her eyes and theirs followed the pairings of the couples on the floor.

Had she danced with that young gentleman more than once this evening? No, that was last week's dance at the Officers' Mess in Merrickville. Sarah Rowan is giving a certain officer a rather large portion of her dances.

"Emily, don't forget to give me your recipe for ladyfingers. They were the best I have ever tasted."

Wasn't that the third time young Duncan had sought out Susan McGee?

"Of course, Charlotte. I'll send Caroline over with it in the morning, if she ever gets out of bed after all this dancing. She hasn't sat out a single set."

Sometimes Emily could not resist underlining the obvious; these same women never hesitated to apply their sharpened tongues to her when Caroline had broken their rules. Caroline was by far and away the most sought-after young woman in the District, and Emily meant to enjoy her daughter's popularity. Charlotte's face, beneath its mask of powder, coloured. Emily had hit her mark. The ladies gave their full attention to the activity on the dance floor.

Surely Lucinda Morris could do better than that coarse sergeant?

"Excuse me, Miss Harris. Roderick Kemp at your service."

Caroline lifted her perfectly arched eyebrows and ravished the young officer with the astonishing blue wetness of her eyes. Caroline's eyes appeared to swim in a sea of tears. Roderick Kemp was not much older than twenty; had he not rehearsed his lines in advance, he would have stumbled badly over his request. Caroline Harris' beauty took some men by the throat and shook them until they were speechless and barely breathing, and Roderick was one of them. Disgusted by his behaviour on first meeting Caroline, he had promised himself it would not happen a second time.

"We were introduced by Major John Haslett, my commanding officer, several weeks ago. I was hoping you might remember me."

Caroline's full bottom lip curved slightly upward and she inclined her head in recognition of his honesty.

There had been so many parties since Thanksgiving, she had quite lost track of whom she had met and where she had danced; those details were in her mother's keeping. Caroline's role at these functions was to simply be there. Rather like being displayed in the window of a dry goods shop, she mused, and giggled at an image of herself laid out·stiffly among the bits and pieces of dressmakers' ornamental trim on a background of black velvet. Her inner eye passed quickly over braided strands of metallic threads, loops of jet-black silk and satin-smooth strips of pastel ribbon. When she heard music, she felt herself lifted gently from the velvet background and placed between the unfamiliar fingers of a prospective buyer. She realized that the young man was waiting for her to extend her hand. She did so hurriedly. He enclosed her long fingers in his own warm hand, swallowing hard at the contact with her flesh.

They stepped out to the music. She, a mere half head shorter than the fresh-faced officer, with her long skirt billowing, swept across the floor with no visible means of support other than his hand. He, in turn, held on to her as proudly as if he carried his country's flag into battle. He was as dashing in his narrow, impeccably tailored dress uniform as she was elegant in her silks.

She's too flamboyant to be ladylike. I'm glad Emmeline is modest. Imagine having all that coarse red hair hanging down your back. It's disgusting. You would think Emily would do something about it.

Emily saw the same fiery mane rippling across Caroline's shoulders and was conscious for the first time of Caroline's good sense in eschewing both fashion and Emily's own entreaties to pin up her mass of hair. The light from a hundred candles picked up the bronze highlights in her loose curls and tossed them indiscriminately into the night. Her progress on the dance floor was charted easily, as if she were a runner in a night-blackened forest holding a flamelit torch above her head.

She hasn't replied to our invitation for the Christmas social. You'd think she would have better manners. Honestly, Emily lets her get away with murder. I hope she comes. Dear God, if she refuses, half the young officers will stay away.

This particular matron pulled her eyes from the spectacular sight of Caroline on the dance floor and looked for Emily so she could wave and reassure herself of their friendship. She sighed and thought of her own daughter, still seated by her side. *If only Dorothea looked like that, how simple life would be.*

Emily did not fail to notice what a comely couple Roderick and Caroline made. Maybe Kemp would be the man to pierce the aloof exterior that Caroline presented to the world. A young woman, no matter how lovely, lost some of her desirability if she became a fixture on the social scene. Freshness was a prized commodity in this market.

She held her breath as Caroline and Roderick glided by the row of chairs. Emily modestly lowered her eyes, but not before she had stolen a quick sideways glance down the line of matrons. Every eye accompanied each movement of the pair.

The girl was a beauty, there was no denying it. Dorothea's mother shifted weight from one ample haunch to the other. *How hard the chairs were, as cold and unobliging as the Harris girl.*

A real handful, she sniffed. *Why, everyone remembered how Caroline made a fool of herself in the confirmation class and then went to the R.C. priest for religious instruction. Imagine being that spoiled and willful! If she'd been mine I'd have locked her in her room 'til she came to her senses. The girl does practically anything she wants and always has; for certain, Emily has lost control of her daughter.* Dorothea's mother shook her head in disgust.

Once again, Roderick and Caroline swept by. Emily weighed the pitfalls involved in rushing a girl with Caroline's temperament into an early decision. How fragile was the footing beneath Emily's feet. One misstep, and disaster could ensue, but she would have to manage this as she had managed everything. She wished Caroline to marry well, but she wanted Caroline to know the delirious intoxication that came with the simplest collision of flesh, the delicious weakening in the legs that made one want to sink to the ground and writhe in ecstasy at the sight of the beloved. Emily was a hopeless romantic.

Her Dorothea was no beauty, but she could be counted on to do what was expected of her.

Dorothea's mother leaned over and patted her daughter on the hand.

The girl started at the caress. She had been watching Caroline Harris and wondering what it felt like to be that beautiful.

It must be heaven to be sought after by half the young men in the District! More than half if the truth were told. Strange; she didn't look very happy. If she'd been Caroline Harris she would have never stopped smiling.

Dorothea straightened in the chair, remembering her mother's admonishment: "You can tell a lady's character by the uprightness of her carriage." She saw Caroline bestow a smile on her dancing partner. Dorothea struggled to an even more upright position.

Maybe Roderick Kemp was the man Caroline would choose? He was a fine catch, if the gossip at the tea parties was to be believed. It was rumoured he had an uncle with a distinguished title and great tracts of land in Scotland and there were whispers among the mamas, which the girls heard second-hand, that Roderick was to be his uncle's heir. Wouldn't that be something if Caroline Harris married him!

Dorothea hoped it was true, not for any genuine feelings of goodwill towards Caroline; she didn't give a fig about her, nor did any of the girls, but the sooner Caroline retired from the field, the better for the rest of them.

The men clustered around Caroline like fruit flies on a bowl of ripe peaches. It was a good thing the young men were practising Christians, not heathens, or there'd be no husbands left for any of them.

The music ended. Caroline, as if on cue, stopped in the middle of a turn and carefully withdrew her long cool fingers from the moist palm of her companion. Roderick ushered her back across the floor, returning her reluctantly to Emily. She made an exquisite partner, but he was honest enough to know his presence had not caused the faintest stirrings in her senses. Her azure eyes had looked right through him. He knew by heart the look he would receive when next they met. He would be greeted by those same thickly drawn bronze eyebrows raised quizzically.

"Thank you, Miss Harris. You were a delightful partner. Shall I trust you to remember me?"

Caroline tossed her head, showering copper sparks onto the floor. Instead of speaking, she ran her tongue gently along the edge of her upper teeth and pushed against them with its wet pink fullness. Roderick retreated, weakened by his own desire. He barely made his way across the room to where his fellow officers were gathered. God, but she was beautiful!

Caroline wondered what she had said or done to send him on his way so quickly. No matter. He would either be back, or he would not, and in any case she had forgotten his name.

Dorothea snickered as a vision of Caroline Harris, half naked with a feathered headdress stuck in her red hair, snuck into her head. Caroline was holding court before a campfire while a collection of salacious suitors, their oiled brown bodies gleaming in the flames, vied for her attention.

Dorothea laughed aloud. Heads turned in her direction and she whipped the smile from her reddened face. Another of her mother's maxims came to mind. *Young ladies should be seen and not heard.*

Andrea leaves today. The air is full of tears. I want to intellectualize another world from the comfort of the dock; Andrea wants to live it. For me it is a theory; for Andrea, it will become a fact. She has gone. My body feels like a lump of clay, numb and shapeless. I simply cannot help myself or anyone. There is such a heaviness inside me that I cannot even celebrate our thirty years together. What a good man I married, caring, decent and trustworthy... not visionary, but feet for my wings.

Britannia has brought an old deer haunch onto the dock. She thinks she is very clever. The angels must feel like this when we bring them gifts. Are we like animals to them, or children? They love us, but they cannot comprehend the level from which we operate. Will how I treat Britannia give me some clues as to how higher beings feel about me?

A really sensational weekend of friends. The men are having a tough time; they see their dominant position in society being undermined. It must for them be akin to a woman's loss of physical beauty. One minute you are there, glowing with no effort, and the next you are fading away into lumps and wrinkles. The "me" is still inside, fresh and lovely, but it isn't there on the outside. Does all the gorgeous stuff move inside? For the men, power, money, success is their currency in life... how can this move inside? The point is, it can't; and they are bereft. In spite of this, they are angels, baby angels maybe, or dropout angels, or even angels-in-training, but angels all the same. They will hate me for finding them out.

CHAPTER TEN

The year concluded snowlessly, unusual for Upper Canada; not a flake had settled on the frozen ground. The streets of Perth were tracks of hardened ruts, where crackly troughs of ice formed between the lines and shattered at the slightest touch. The river stopped its flow and froze in sheets of smooth black ice. The town itself was suspended in a crystalline countryside, hard, cold, clear. The intense blue of the sky deepened each day as no snow fell to warm the air and blur the sharpened edge of the horizon.

Caroline heard the knock, but before she could reach the door, it had opened. A tall, bright-faced man in an army greatcoat was standing in the hall, stamping his feet and rubbing his gloved hands together.

"Brr... is the weather always this perishingly cold?"

Caroline stood by the door, nonplussed. Who was this soldier with the snooty English accent who had pushed his way into her house as if he owned it? What nerve he had to engage Caroline in small talk.

"Close the door, will you, love? No sense in inviting winter in to stay."

Caroline drew herself up to her full height and thrust out her chin. In her most chilling manner, she fixed him with ice-blue eyes and enquired pointedly, "May I be of service to you?"

"You may, if this is the Harris house. Where is everyone, and who might you be? No, don't tell me. Caroline, the little carrot-topped girl, all grown up."

He stepped back to have a better look at her. "And beautiful to boot. Come here, brat, and give your big brother a hug."

Before she had a chance to gain her equilibrium, she was engulfed in the folds of his coat and soundly kissed on both cheeks by a brother she was struggling to remember. His face was hard and cold and rough against hers, but the embrace was very pleasurable. She closed her eyes and inhaled the warm fragrance of his skin. She might have stayed longer with her face buried in Daniel's neck if Richard, hearing voices, had not appeared. He shouted and pounded Daniel's back with even more than his customary gusto.

"Ma, where are you? Get out here. Hurry up, it's Daniel."

The vigour of the welcome caused Daniel to back away from the young giant who was pummelling him.

"Take it easy, Richard. You'll beat me to death before mother has a chance to see me. And say, you are not as ugly as I remember."

Daniel reached over and ruffled Richard's curly hair. The brothers grinned wickedly and threw their arms about one another. This was accomplished with much laughing and slapping of backs. Caroline, meanwhile, had slipped away and found Emily.

"Mother, take your apron off. I'll look after supper. You have a visitor."

Emily hung up her apron and patted her hair before going into the hall. Her two sons were standing side by side, as she had dreamed they would.

"Daniel," she cried out, and before he could open his arms, she sank onto the bench, dropped her head and covered her face with her hands.

"Now, ma, cut that out. Daniel's fine. What's there to cry about?"

Richard frowned. Tears made him uncomfortable. Daniel knelt in front of the weeping woman and held her gently by the shoulders, talking softly, his face close to hers.

"Listen to me, mother, I am to be given a commission to serve in Upper Canada— probably in the west, but that's not so far away as England. I'm home for good." He raised Emily to her feet and motioned to Richard.

"Be a good lad, will you, Richard, and fetch father from the mill? I've waited years for us to be together. I can't wait any longer."

Caroline left the kitchen and stood in the shadowed recess under the stairs to watch the reunion between her mother and a brother she did not recognize. This handsome uniformed man with the hint of command in every word he spoke bore little resemblance to her memory of Daniel. The brother who had left ten years ago had been her first teacher. Daniel had taken her into the woods and taught her the names of the trees and plants. If she closed her eyes and conjured up those long-ago days, she could see him reaching up and picking a leaf from each tree she identified correctly, and feel the warm imprint on her palm where he had traced the shape of the leaf with his lean brown fingers and spoke its name. The memory of his touch triggered other memories that pushed to the surface of her mind as surely as the first spring snowdrops he had showed her had pushed through the receding blanket of snow. And the delicate turquoise eggs! Wonder filled her now as it had when he had lifted her up to peep inside the nest. Daniel had waited patiently beside her all one morning for the first tiny head to make its damp appearance in the world. How could she have forgotten him? Tears prickled behind Caroline's eyelids as her memories of Daniel erased the face of the stranger who embraced her mother.

A week before Christmas Eve, Emily gathered the whole family together for evening carol service. It had been many years since the pew occupied by the Harrises had had its full complement of worshippers. Emily's hand searched out Tom's as she sang the familiar words of the carols, whose age-old joy was written across her face as she reviewed her own Christmas blessings in the persons of her family. There, at the far end of the pew, was Richard, first in as always, his naturally high colour made ruddier by the stinging cold of the midnight air. She would never have to worry about Richard. He was content; he could not conceive of a situation where he would not be welcomed. With a barely perceptible shift, she brought her daughter into view. Emily was usually immune to Caroline's beauty, but tonight Caroline was luminous in the darkened church, as though she had absorbed candlelight into her skin and eyes and hair. Emily's gaze fell on Daniel, kneeling beside her, his head angled away, his fine dark hair curling softly into his collar, his face turned helplessly towards Caroline. Emily withdrew her hand from Tom's comforting clasp and touched it to her heart.

Daniel's mornings found everyone, including a tousle-headed Richard still warm and rumpled from his bed, gathered around the kitchen table. Even Tom delayed his departure for the mill. The talk was of England and Daniel's school years. Caroline circulated around the kitchen, tidying as she moved, and refilling the teapot as it emptied. "Mother, if you don't need me, I think I'll walk along the river and cut some boughs for the mantelpieces."

Emily nodded without taking her gaze from Daniel's face. "Wear something warm, dear. I can't remember such a spell of cold weather. You must find it frigid here compared to England."

Caroline smiled and slipped out the back door. It was pleasant for a change not to be the center of her mother's world. The cold air snapped at her face, flicking colour into her cheeks and adding a kick to her step.

Caroline took the path following the river upstream. She loved the iced-over river. It appeared to be hard and smooth, but beneath this frozen skin the water flowed loose and fast; she spotted a throb of movement pulsating under its coat of ice. It was enough to satisfy her and she moved on, too cold to remain in one place for long. A thick stand of fir trees bordered the bank, and Caroline remembered the original intention of her outing. Fingering the pockets of her heavy skirt and finding nothing, she spoke out loud. "Damn, damn, damn... I'll be damned if I'm going back empty-handed. How could I forget to bring a knife?"

She knelt and stripped the lower branches of a white pine with her bare hands. Its needles brushed her face with silky fringes, hampering her attempts to break off the boughs. She crawled in closer to the trunk, muttering to herself. “Imagine coming out without something to cut boughs with. What was I thinking?”

“Do you always talk to yourself when you chop trees, or is there someone here I can’t see? Don’t tell me. It’s the mysterious Sophie you’ve got in there.”

Caroline pulled back, losing her woollen cap to one of the branches, and crawled out from underneath the tree to face Daniel.

“What are you doing here? I thought mother would still be questioning you on every moment of the last ten years.” Caroline softened her bantering tone. “She did miss you dreadfully.

“I missed all of you. It was lonely growing up without a family. Here, let me help.”

Daniel pulled a knife from the pocket of the heavy jacket he had borrowed from Richard and expertly stripped several boughs from the tree. He stacked evergreen branches in Caroline’s waiting arms until she nearly disappeared under the pile of pine boughs. When only the top of her head could still be seen, Daniel plucked her knitted cap from the bottom branch and pulled it over her curls, tugging it until her eyes were covered and she was laughing.

“There, that should be enough for one day. Let’s go home.” He started to walk away.

“Wait, don’t go,” she giggled. “I can’t see anything.”

“Need help? Why didn’t you say so? Give me the branches. I’ll carry them. It’s strange. Someone told me you pioneer women could handle anything.” He transferred the bundle of evergreens from her arms into his own. Caroline giggled and straightened her hat.

“You have been listening to mama too much. She means *she* can do anything.” Caroline leaned against him as she walked, and smiled up at him. He looked down at her, smiled back and dumped the armload of pine boughs over her head. Caroline yelped.

“There, see what you have made me do.” Daniel stood back to survey the damage. Caroline was heaped in greenery. He swore softly. “My God! Was she a mirage?”

To his eyes, Caroline appeared part of the winter landscape. Her slender figure wreathed in dark green boughs seemed rooted in the ground, and her eyes mirrored the intense blue of the heavens. She was all earth and sky.

Together they picked up the spilled greenery and walked slowly home. At first they were hesitant of speech, but as they moved the gentle swell of camaraderie picked up momentum and flowed between them as naturally as water. After that day, Daniel joined her each morning as she left the house. They walked for hours beside the frozen river and on the narrow paths between the pines, and they did not lack for things to say. She never tired of hearing of his travels or his school or the books he had read, and he, in turn, encouraged her to tell him about life in Perth. No snow fell and each day was colder and sharper than the one before. The blazing fireplaces and pine-scented rooms of the stone house radiated warmth and cheer. A profusion of young ladies paraded up the walk to call on Caroline and Emily. When Richard was in, he had the door open and the visitors inside before the bar on the brass knocker had been released from the gloved hand that raised it. Caroline and Daniel exchanged amused glances. After the guests had departed, Caroline would throw her arms in the air and announce dramatically: "I don't understand. Why the sudden interest in my company? Do you suppose those silly girls have at last come to their senses and realized what a charming person I am? Can there be another reason? If there is, I wish someone would let me in on the secret. I'm tired of being so popular."

At this, Richard would turn scarlet and leave the parlour as his sister and brother screamed with laughter and clutched their shaking sides. Alone again, they picked up the thread of conversation they had dropped and continued their discussion as though there had never been an interruption. Emily often paused in her chores to listen to the rhythmic ebb and flow of their speech, and a great happiness would well up in her and threaten to spill over into tears. They were good friends, that was all, in spite of the years they had been apart.

I did a crummy thing this morning. I read Andrea's journal from beginning to end, almost compulsively. I felt rotten, deceitful, intrusive, but I could not stop myself. I am not very proud of me. It made me laugh and cry, but most of all it made me terrified for her. She is such a risk taker and I love her so. Remember that the artist Jack Shadbolt does twelve pictures before he gets one that pleases him; she pleases me. I am but one of the pictures that have gone into creating her. I want to shield her from pain, but that would cripple her more than if I cut off a limb. I must let her fly— no strings attached. Just one thing, Andrea; if you read this, remember never to pity me. I would hate that more than anything. I am sorry. I hope you never know.

I spent yesterday with my daughter and for the first time I looked at her outside myself. I saw her as Andrea, a fine young woman sorting out what she wants to do with her life and sorting out who she is. I like her and I like her friends.

I must hurry and learn it all— so little time. I think it will be blindness that slows my quest. Funny, you always assume one thing and it (what lies in the forest) has another name. Oh, it is hard to second-guess fate. The lake is closing down, gray and blurred, ready for a winter's sleep. I have run back through the woods to write this down:

The image of her mother's face
was stitched in stars
across the forehead of the sky.

Only the entrance to the forest is hidden; once inside, the paths are all laid out.

I had a dream in which I lay in bed with a stranger; I don't even know if it was male or female. I woke up in a panic, terrified to find out who was beside me.

I am dazzled by the colours of the leaves outside my window. They make me want to paint, for I cannot reproduce the reds in words: dark red, almost rust in the shadows, orange red with the sunshine, reddish pink, with light shining right through the leaves and real red, clear scarlet, against the gray fence, framed by the black bark of the trees.

THE SKATING PARTY

Richard arranged the party, he said, in honour of Caroline's sixteenth birthday. In reality, her birthday presented him with the opportunity to indulge his own high spirits. Richard thrived on action. It had not taken him long to size up the state of social functions in the town, and he had wisely surmised that the youth of Perth yearned inarticulately for some other form of entertainment.

The night he chose for Caroline's party, an infinite black sky powdered with stars roofed a sharply frozen world, and the bitter cold kept the adult members of the community from lingering along the lake; they soon retired to the warmth of their own fires, leaving the young people to celebrate. Groups of youthful skaters, red-cheeked with cold and the prospect of adventure, roamed the polished surface of the lake, unsupervised except for Richard, who seemed to be everywhere at once, organizing a cluster of laggard skaters into a game, whistling for them all to change partners. All the while, he piled log after log onto an already overloaded fire. The towering flames threatened the safety of those closest to the blaze, but no one noticed. The pace of the games accelerated faster than the skaters' skills, and there were many spills accompanied by much raucous laughter.

Caroline glided among her guests, more at home on the frozen lake than on the varnished floors of that fall's dances. For a time she was the center of the merriment, responding as gaily as any of them to Richard's directions. She stayed until the level of the horseplay rose to unmanageable proportions, and then she directed the long curved arcs of her blades towards the farthest shore. As she veered away from the flamelit games, she felt the pulse of the water trapped beneath her bladed feet and heard the giant pines whisper as they swayed seductively in the icy air. Caroline answered their message with her body, relinquishing all thought. She danced and spun and swirled and stopped on the very edge of the lake, waiting for the music to catch up with her.

A dark figure broke from the shelter of the pines, drawn from cover by the enchanting movements of the skater. He walked to the ice and bent to attach the wooden skates he carried to his own black boots.

"Caroline, give me a hand while I try these damned things. I don't want everyone laughing at me as I make my skating debut."

The girl stopped her spin not three feet from the kneeling man. Her face was rosy from her flight and her eyes were dilated and unfocused in the blackness. For one exquisite moment, he drank in her beauty. Was she Diana, the moon maiden come down to pay a visit, or was she Ondine, the mermaid who swam beneath the surface of the water? In either case, he was certain she was unreal. He leaned forward and put out his hand to dispel the image. Blood rushed through his body, for it was flesh he fingered, not quicksilver. He jumped back, but not in time. She had already stooped to lift him to his feet.

"Daniel, I'm so happy you decided to come. It's the most perfect night for skating. I'll teach you. No one will laugh; we are all alone." Her face grew rosier as she spoke. She thrust out both her hands in her confusion. "Here, take my hands and follow me."

Caroline tucked her mittens in the pocket of her skirt and pulled him. The black depths of her eyes never left his face; she glided slowly backward across the ice, holding him with her opened palms. He slid forward, following her body, while his mind screamed, *Stop, let her go.* A scarlet stain crept up Caroline's throat and spread like dye across her face. What was happening to him was happening to them both, and still she did not drop his hands. She knew, and she accepted. They moved closer together, advancing until the tension was unbearable. They had to break away or touch and so they kissed, delicately, as children do. Then their wanting overwhelmed the softness of their lips and he clasped her with a strength he did not know he possessed and she unlocked the dark red velvet of her mouth to let him in. The moment held them unblemished in their beauty until they remembered who they were.

Hand in hand, they stumbled to the edge of the lake, sickened by desire. Their fingers loosened, and he disappeared into the darkened line of trees from where he had first appeared. She was left standing forlornly on the shore of the polished lake, waiting to be wakened from this nightmare.

Caroline was up at dawn, but she was not the first to rise. She found the note anchored by his skates on the hall bench.

Forgive me for leaving so abruptly. I hope that you will understand. I cannot bear goodbyes. I must join my regiment immediately and I will write and let you know where I am posted. I will think of you often and the happy times we had this Christmas.

All my love
Daniel

She ran to the door and opened it, but even as she looked, the faint outlines of his departing footsteps were being erased by the steadily falling snow.

And then there was graduation. Tears streamed down my face as I watched him graduate and simultaneously remembered him being placed on my stomach. Thank you for loaning him to me and me to him. This part is nearly done. We spent the day at the Cloisters in New York. It has a special feel, like Picnic Point. Sacred space. This thing— no words to say it— is everywhere. I saw a sculpture entitled "Fragments of an Angel," and then I met him as we travelled from the museum to the hotel. He was driving a

New York City bus and he was a huge black man. He cared for each of his passengers and taught us, for the ninety minutes of the ride, just what could be accomplished if we cared for one another without regard for age, or colour, or gender, or economic position. For that ninety minutes, we all became better people.

I planted magical flowerpots today. I filled the carved gray urns with columbine, French geraniums, daisies and dusty miller. I am reminded of Ophelia's flowers in *Hamlet*, and Perdita's garden in *The Winter's Tale*. Somehow that same lovely mix of kind and colour took place in the pots. I cannot stop looking at them.

FOUR TIMES IN MY LIFE I have tapped into something. Twice it happened while I was walking on the beach in Australia, once in Apollo at a teaching dinner, and once on the deck at Lake of Bays. It is that extraordinary feeling of being in love, not with a person, but with a bigger entity, a world being who encompasses everything. When one is in love with a person, there is an actual change in one's physical chemistry. Knees shaking, breathless, excited. It is a wonderful sensation. Nothing compares with it, except if one has that same feeling for the whole world. Tapping into the world soul and encountering that boundless love with its accompanying physical symptoms is the same experience, expanded into infinity. You burn brighter, as though you were breathing different air.

CHAPTER ELEVEN

Emily stared into the shadows. What did Tom know about Caroline? She knew more than anyone and that wasn't all that much. Emily rolled over on her back and replayed what she had seen or thought she had seen that past Christmas. It was not possible. Her imagination had overheated in the drama of having everyone at home. Daniel and Caroline were a brother and sister enjoying each other's company after years of separation. But why had Daniel left so quickly, and without saying goodbye? She closed her eyes and turned over, burying her face in the pillow. Her mind flickered from memory to memory: two young people walking up the path, their arms filled with evergreen boughs with eyes only for each other; the two of them before the fire, Caroline seated at Daniel's feet, laughing aloud with a note of happiness Emily had never heard in her voice before, their joy so palpable she had been afraid to enter the room. Worst of all was her memory of Daniel's face at the evening carol service. She had watched him as Caroline knelt and lifted her face to God. Emily had seen her son breathe in her daughter's beauty.

"God," she prayed, "make it not be true."

It snowed steadily through January. The stone house lost its clean hard shape beneath layers of muffled whiteness, and the village could be seen only from the windows of the second storey. Richard left for school and Tom went back to work. When the holidays ended, Caroline and Emily were left together inside the house to strangle in a conspiracy of silence. No word concerning Daniel or his untimely departure had ever been uttered by Emily in front of Caroline, or, for that matter, by Tom or Richard. Caroline sometimes wondered if she had only dreamed that he had come! And then the longing for him spread wave-like through her body, and she was sure he had been there. And she, Caroline Harris (the blood in her skull thickened and pulsed ominously at what she had done) had fallen horribly, terribly, in love with him. It was too hideous to imagine, but it was real. Daniel had come. She emptied her mind of him, for she missed him dreadfully, and it was only by an act of will that she could think of other things. Her gaze drifted aimlessly about the room, stopping of its own accord at the whited-out window. Was there something out there? Something she had forgotten, some reason why the blank face of the snow-filled window held her attention? And Emily's face would skate across the empty window, daring Caroline to question her. Did Emily suspect that Caroline had wanted to make love to her own brother? Still wanted to? The girl cringed and hunched her back in anticipation of the blows she was sure would come. When none did, she flung the ugly question far away from her and ordered it to stay there.

It hurts to think of Caroline that winter. She was so young and terribly in love, and perhaps, worst of all, she had to live with the person she had wounded most. Nothing was offered by way of a diversion, not even the simple pleasure of walking by the river. The mounds of snow sapped everyone's reserves of energy and precluded all but essential trips. No one in living memory could recall a winter like this one. Caroline was eating little and sleeping even less, and night was the time when she concocted dreadful dialogues between herself and Emily. They all began with the same question.

"Where have you been, Caroline? Why are those twigs caught in your hair?"

"Nothing, mother, nowhere... I fell... on the path. I cut my hand."

And Caroline would hold up an unscarred palm for Emily's cruel inspection.

"A likely story... you slut, you unnatural child. I wish you were dead."

"Where have you been? I've told you a thousand times not to go out on the ice. It's dangerous for a girl. You've been out on the ice, haven't you?"

And before Caroline could explain, her mother's hand would appear from nowhere and strike her across the face.

"Don't lie to me, you ungrateful girl. I know where you have been. Who were you with?"

"Some of the girls." The words stumbled between her teeth as if they were the blades of a novice skater on a clean patch of ice. "I didn't get hurt. I didn't fall through."

"You stupid bitch, of course you are all right. You would be. It's Daniel who has disappeared. You killed him. Why couldn't it be you?"

Caroline writhed in self-disgust throughout these imaginary performances and wished her mother's final words were true.

Each winter day brought new forms of the same horror. She lost weight; the alabaster skin that had carried its own luminescence across countless dance floors dimmed and her eyes looked bruised and haunted. There was no one she could talk to, and nowhere she could hide from the loathing she fancied lurked behind Emily's every glance. Caroline could not bear to meet her mother's eyes and took to burying herself in housework, dragging out each small chore to worn perfection. She watched helplessly as more snow fell and even familiar outlines were changed into new and puzzling white shapes. The path filled in as quickly as her father cleared it. She missed her father's neutralizing presence, for he had noticed nothing. He never made the trip home for the midday meal. One round trip through the treacherous banks of snow was all that he could manage in a day.

Each morning, Caroline watched from the window in her room as her father shovelled his way down the walk and calculated how much time had to be lived through before there was the chance of hearing the scrape of metal on stone and seeing his snow-coated figure fill the doorway. For that hour, after his return, the demons left her. She was able to relax and listen to the stories he brought home. Sometimes she raised her eyes and tried to read her mother's mind. When Emily dropped her eyes or looked away, revulsion for her actions would rise in Caroline's throat, threatening to choke her.

Tom's stories were the two women's only link with the outside world. He told them of farming families isolated for weeks at a time, barely able to move from house to barn to feed their livestock, of trappers who knew the country around Perth like the backs of their hands losing their bearings within a half mile of town and having to abandon their lines and hole up in their cabins with whatever supplies they had. Tom said the only good thing to come out of the prolonged storm was that everyone, old-timers and newcomers alike, agreed it was the worst winter ever, and it wasn't over yet. It wasn't often they could find something to agree about.

Emily and Caroline, confined to the house, pursued a narrowly prescribed routine which allowed them to work side by side (many of their tasks required two pairs of hands) but precluded any but the most banal of conversations. It was as though they had signed a pact, agreeing it was better to say nothing than to speak the truth and destroy one another. When the last chore had been stretched beyond its capacity to provide further employment, the two women retired to the parlour to await Tom's return. It never failed to amaze Caroline that both of them, in a large house with many empty rooms, were drawn day after day to the same location. They sat as strangers do, on the edges of their chairs, alert to any sound the other might make. Even as Caroline acknowledged the bizarre nature of her behaviour, she seemed incapable of changing her routine. Some days she arrived to see Emily seated carefully in her chair by the fire, her sewing basket by her side. Conversely, there were days when Caroline was the first to arrive, and it would not be long before she heard the rustle of her mother's skirts on the bare floor. She would look up, book in hand, in time to see Emily cross the threshold.

From the doorway, the room issued a warm invitation. A fire blazed in the hearth, throwing long shards of light against the black marble facing of the fireplace. Tall candles burned steadily in their polished brass holders. Freshly filled oil lamps shed pools of light. Silence lay like dust about the room. Emily stitched on a piece of needlework; Caroline read and reread the same page of her book. More often than not, she gave up all pretext of reading and the book dropped unnoticed from her hands into her lap while she stared into the flames, listening for the scraping sounds her father's boots made on the doorstop.

The first time it happened, Caroline shrieked. Emily jumped from her chair in alarm. The embroidery fell from her lap and her needle rolled across the floor and disappeared between the cracks of the pine boards.

"What in heaven's name is the matter, Caroline? You scared me half to death."

Caroline, who by now had regained her wits, was on her knees scrambling after the needle. She kept searching as she replied, "I'm sorry, mother. I didn't mean to frighten you. I was daydreaming. Here's your embroidery. Let me get you another needle."

Emily nodded her acceptance of the explanation, but the tension in her body did not diminish as the girl left the room. It had been years since one of those queer spells had come over Caroline, but Emily remembered vividly how she had felt on those occasions: cold, helpless, terrified.

The next time, Caroline held her tongue. There was little point in screaming. There was no one who could help her. The face in the flames was for her alone; her punishment, her guilt. She would see him in the flames as long as she yearned for him to touch her. It was Daniel, trapped beneath black ice, eyes dilated wide with fear, nose and lips flattened to grotesque proportions by the thickness of the ice, his mouth opened, gasping for air. He came into the flames quite regularly now. It was almost impossible for her to sit in front of the fire without this ghastly image rearing up. His face was so distorted by the ice and flames, she might not have known him, but his voice was unmistakable. "Caroline, Caroline," he called, "help me, give me your hand. Save me."

God help me, she thought. The flames thickened before her horrified eyes like blood on an open wound, and smoothed into a sheet of black ice. The face began to take shape beneath the opaque surface. Her ears pricked for his cry and tears collected behind her eyes. She stretched out one hand to the flames. The pain in the tips of her fingers stung her back to consciousness. She straightened her slumped body and spun away from the fire. This had to stop, or she would be mad by spring.

LOVE POEMS

Is love the constant placing
of a hand into the flame?
And if so, must I,
like the moth,
die before I know?

Is love so gossamer thin
that it will tear
if I should dare
to touch your hair?

My fingertips already risk
the rising heat.

Does desire extinguish fire
or fan the flame?

In passing through the flame
I stand aside and watch
the hard edges of myself
dissolve like sunshine
in the air.

Here at my beloved lake I feel at peace. I love this place and I love my solitude. To fully enjoy it, I must come to terms with the darkness. I must make friends with the night and come to know blackness as I know the light. Then I won't ever be afraid. I reread my journals sometimes; it gives me pleasure to recollect things I wrote. I have not explored any of these thoughts, just recorded them. Are they lying there, gathering dust, or are they simmering and stewing to nourish me later?

There is such carnage on the dock, and I seem to be powerless to stop it. As each baby bird leaves the nest to try its wings, Britannia pounces on it (she is just a baby herself). It is disgusting. I shake her until she drops it but the baby bird is so unnerved that it frantically hops away, falls off the dock and drowns. I rescued one yesterday and put it back in the nest. The adult birds threw it out. Needless to say, the adults hate Britannia and swoop her at every opportunity. I feel helpless; three deaths in two days. My old people, and there are so many of them, are wearing away and I feel badly for them. The end of life should be a sunset, all soft fire and glowing colours, sinking into darkness. Why do we want to prolong the day? I must make friends with the night.

CHAPTER TWELVE

"Mother," she cried. "I need something to keep me busy until this blasted snow stops." Caroline was wild with need.

Her gaze fell on the brightly coloured silk threads spilling across her mother's lap.

"I know this sounds peculiar coming from me, but do you think I could do needlework? Would you teach me? I know I used to hate it. I remember throwing a piece across the room."

She chuckled nervously, watching to see Emily's reaction from beneath half-lowered lashes. Her mother's shoulders relaxed, as though a great weight had been lifted from them, and then, as if recalling something else which lay between them and had been forgotten for the moment, Emily stiffened and made a motion as if to speak. Caroline cut her off.

"I told you it was a crazy request. I don't blame you if you don't want to, but I'm older now and I really want to learn. It's time I became acquainted with the finer points of domesticity."

Emily fairly leapt from her chair in an effort not to waste a moment of Caroline's transformation, and as she was crossing the room, she chattered happily. "Will this weather never end? You are as pale as a ghost, my dear. We all need some fresh air, but you especially. You're not used to being inside. Of course I'll teach you. Nothing would please me more. You know, Caroline, I just may have that piece you started long ago, the one you flung across the room, stored away somewhere. Could you bear to finish it? I don't know when we will be able to get out and find something new."

Emily paused on the threshold, waiting for Caroline's decision.

"It doesn't matter, mother, as long as I can get started right away. I don't remember what the old piece looked like. I was such a spoiled child, it will seem brand new to me."

Emily retrieved Caroline's sampler from the top layer of the pine chest and placed it on Caroline's knee.

"There," she said, smoothing the linen square, "I thought someday you might have a use for it. I'm glad I saved it."

Caroline threaded the needle her mother handed her and pushed it through the tiny openings as if her very life depended on the execution of a perfect stitch.

One day, only a hint of palest green hazed the winter bare branches, and the next, the trees were lush with leaves. The heat of summer took the place of a spring that had never come. Caroline did not resume her walks along the river; instead, she spent what leisure time she had in church. Caroline had rarely missed attending church on Sundays, and she now increased her attendance to include the morning and the evening services and any weekday service required by the episcopal calendar. She listened intently to each word uttered by the Reverend Gordon, hoping against hope that something in his message would lighten her painful load of guilt, but nothing expiated her sin. She knelt on the hard floor between the high straightbacked pews, turning over each word the way a child turns over stones. She was not surprised when there was nothing there. Caroline searched through the words of each sermon because there was nothing else to do and nowhere else to go.

"Excuse me, miss. I'm sorry for interrupting your devotions, but I have been waiting over an hour for Reverend Gordon. Do you know where I might find him?"

Caroline blushed at being found on her knees by a stranger. As she struggled to regain her feet, she wondered what he was doing here. At this time of day, she usually had the church to herself. She stood up, restoring the blood to her cramped legs, and was eye to eye with a man not much older than her brother Richard. This young man needed feeding; his skin was rough, and in places so dry it was scaling off in patches.

"I am sorry you didn't speak to me sooner. I could have saved you an hour. Reverend Gordon has been called away, and I've no idea when he might return. He was saddling up his horse as I arrived, and called out that he was off up Lanark way to an emergency. He didn't mention he was expecting anyone, or I'd have watched for you."

Caroline looked down at the young man's hands, flexing in and out. How thin and white they were. His hands, more than anything, made her want to help him.

"Perhaps they can tell you something more at the manse. It's just behind the stand of trees you passed on your way in. Mrs. Gordon should be at home."

Caroline slid from the pew, brushing the front of his black jacket with her bare arm. It was then she noted the starched white collar pressing stiffly against his throat. He looked distinctly hot and uncomfortable. He was young to be a minister.

"I am sorry you have had such a long wait."

He remained motionless for several minutes before leaving the church and taking the route she had suggested; it took him that long to regain his composure from the unexpected contact of the girl's bare arm against his chest. A recent graduate of Wycliffe College in England, John Paterson had newly arrived in Upper Canada to take up his first position as an ordained minister. The rare afternoon tea to which he, as one of several divinity students, had been invited, where the cups of tea and the plates of cake had been passed by the daughters of the local vicar, had in no way prepared him for the sight of Caroline. His mind replayed the image of her kneeling; the masses of copper hair falling about her neck and the easy curve of her spine had set his heart pounding. That was negligible compared to the impact of her eyes, like huge luminous lamps turning on him. He had caught every detail in that glance, including the tears trembling on her lashes. He had actually contemplated reaching over to brush away the tell-tale tears and begging her to tell him why. Fortunately, before the impulse was relayed to his hands, his mind had intercepted the message. He was still admonishing himself, long after she had left the church. What foolishness. The girl was probably crying over some party invitation, or her indulgent papa had refused to buy her yet another gown, or, a welcome thought teased him, some young man had disappointed her in love. He frowned. He must be mad to be thinking such crazy things. He didn't even know her name, and already he had her jilted by an anonymous lover. John Paterson put Caroline's face firmly behind him and marched down the steps in the direction of the manse.

It was common practice at this time to send newly ordained ministers to the colonies to serve, as needed, under the supervision of more experienced clergymen. This practice benefited both master and apprentice. It eased the young ministers into the rigours of ecclesiastical life, while providing the overworked elders with a steady supply of educated assistants. Only graduates with the most impeccable connections had the option of remaining in England for their theological apprenticeship. John Paterson was not one of those. Reverend Gordon needed help and was more than grateful when the Bishop of Upper Canada wrote him to say John Paterson was on his way. John, in turn, accepted his placement stoically. He had hoped to be sent to work among the Indian tribes in the north and the west of the colony. Upper Canada was being settled so swiftly, the Bishop was scarcely able to fill the demands of his own people for clergy. John was assigned to Perth until such time as he was ready to assume the responsibilities of his own living.

Reverend Gordon was jubilant at John's arrival. The early morning weekday service was the bane of his religious life. He was not an early riser, and every morning since he had his own church Reverend Gordon had secretly wished that no one would attend and he could strike the service from the church calendar, but it had never happened, not in twenty years of preaching. There was always someone sitting expectantly in a pew; rarely more than five, and in inclement weather his congregation could sink as low as two. On John Paterson's second morning as assistant minister of St. Luke's Anglican Church, he was held accountable for the early weekday service. From that day on, John scrupulously prepared and delivered what he hoped was perceived as an inspired sermon to the same four or five people. The three McEwen sisters, accompanied on occasion by their elderly brother, rarely failed in their attendance. They were joined with equal regularity by Caroline Harris. The days when Angus McEwen appeared, there was a great fussing and rustling of skirts as the maiden ladies changed positions and resettled themselves in the pew so as to give Angus the most advantageous and comfortable place. There was not always consensus on where that particular place was. John enjoyed these mornings the most, for the shifting and settling of the McEwens allowed him more time to admire Caroline.

Caroline's face swam across the surface of whatever sermon John Paterson was working on. Worse was during prayers, when his thoughts strayed from the words he knew so well, and before he could control it, he had looked up to try and catch a glimpse of the bright curls he had dreamt about the night before. It was more than just her beauty, he told himself, that kept steering her to the forefront of his mind. He was impressed by her devotion to the church and by her self-effacing deportment. She made no effort to charm him. Each summer morning his skin tingled deliciously at the sight of her, and each warm evening she wound through his thoughts and spilled her phantom curls across his page.

One evening in late August, Tom Harris was smoking his evening pipeful of tobacco when a young man walked up the path and called out to him, "Good evening, sir."

The man's face was familiar. What the devil was his name?

"It's John Paterson, sir, from the church. The light's bad this time of night. Pardon my dropping by unannounced. It's not my way to thrust myself on people, but when I decide on a thing, I speak my mind directly."

The curate standing beside the porch steps was a whey-faced, sober individual despite his youth. While Tom watched in amazement, the young man vaulted up the stairs, landing in front of Tom's chair.

"Sir, I wish to wed your daughter, Caroline."

There was a long pause.

"Sir, this comes as a shock to me as well. I had no intention of marrying, but since meeting Caroline I've been unable to concentrate on my work. I'm determined to resolve this state. If it's God's will, she'll have me. I have been offered my own charge in the small community of Fergus, and I am of the opinion, as are my superiors, that a minister of the Church of England should have a wife by his side when he takes on a new charge. Would you not agree, sir?"

Tom followed the young man's line of thought as best he could, but the question had been sprung on him. He nodded dimly, and John rushed on.

"Caroline is truly a spiritual woman, so different from many of her age. You, sir, are to be commended on her upbringing."

John grasped Tom's hand, pumping it up and down. Tom Harris clamped his teeth about the stem of his pipe.

Until tonight, Tom had scarcely been aware of the young man's existence.

"Mr. Paterson, your request comes as a complete surprise to me. I must consult with both my daughter and my wife before rendering a decision. Thank you for your courtesy in speaking to me. Rest assured that if Caroline and her mother accept your suit, I will not stand in your way. Good evening to you, John." The name sounded foreign to his ear.

After John left, Tom relit his pipe and sat smoking in his chair. Surely Caroline wasn't old enough to marry. He'd ask Emily.

They had not yet lit the lamps when Tom came in, and in the semi-blackness he could not distinguish mother from daughter.

"A strange thing's happened. The curate's asked for Caroline's hand."

The words rolled across the room and split open on the hearth between the two women.

"Emily, she hardly knows him. You can't be interested in being a minister's wife, can you, Caroline?" He turned from one to the other, waiting for an answer. "I'll see Paterson in the morning on my way to the mill and tell him it's ridiculous."

Caroline stood, her height distinguishing her from Emily.

"Father, if you and mother have no serious objections, I would like you to consider John Paterson for my husband. He is a good man and a good minister. I could help him."

Emily said nothing until they reached their bedroom. "Whatever do you suppose gave that young man the gall to ask for Caroline's hand?"

"Don't be too hard on him, Emily. Caroline's quite a beauty, and she goes to all his services. In my day, any young lady who went to church every morning either had an interest in the preacher or something mighty terrible to confess. He must have decided it was the former. He knows a good thing when he sees it and he wants to get it before some other fellow does. But I hate to think of her as a minister's wife. Can't you think of a more suitable young man?"

Emily nearly dropped the candle she was holding.

"No, I can't, Tom Harris, and I'm surprised to hear you running down the clergy. Caroline could do worse."

Emily blew out the offending candle and climbed into her side of the bed.

Everybody has a horrible secret. Such a thin veneer covers most of the faces around me... we are paying lip service to the non-existence of racism, sexism. I wonder how little it would take to crack the whole thing wide open? We

all use masks. I am reading May Sarton's *Journal of a Solitude*. What I need, when I need to know it, always seems to be there. At what point does one throw over the outer life to lead the real (inner) one? I guess I'll have to trust that that will come when I am ready. She even uses some of my favourite words: centered, dull, errands and housekeeping. How lovely to meet someone in the writing life who is so much further along the road, a guide.

The sun is shining and we are in the most beautiful of cities, Capetown. It is a town of dark brown people with soft faces, or blue-eyed blondes with fleshy faces. I am in a state of disbelief. I need time to move between worlds; even the language is strange. It must be so uncomfortable going through life as a stranger without a guide. Is that why we have these spiritual guides, like Jesus? "Put your hand in the hand of the man from Galilee." We long for too much control when what we need is to let go. Even in writing we give way to the form at the expense of the theme. We live on the lines of the text, but we don't write the lines or even understand them, and our children will not even want to read them. A fitting end to a world that craved form above substance.

South Africa has some of the most beautiful scenery I have ever seen. How to describe mountains with an ocean on either side? The trip to the Cape of Good Hope is like driving down the spine of the world. There are the most beautiful white wild beaches with no one on them. I want to share this beauty, this wildness, this hidden truth. It is a different story with the people. They are a nation under siege, defensive, closed and somewhat paranoid. I feel their anger, barely contained, longing to thrash out at my North American background, but worse, the men look upon me as a threat. To what? The women are submissive, but subversive, I think. Oh, what a corner these white South African males have painted themselves into.

THE HAIR RISES on the back of my neck: it came clearly to me that we are here on earth as God's spies.

Shakespeare knew this and wrote it in *King Lear*. Our task is to report back to Him, to tell Him what is happening so far from the light. We are pilgrims, crossing time and space to somewhere else. This is not home for us, despite our best efforts to domesticate this place. We cannot build our "nests" here. It is foreign to us, wrong for us, but where should we build? Must we take to the road like real pilgrims? Pilgrims may be what God calls his spies.

CHAPTER THIRTEEN

The granite base of Fergus society was comprised of solid, diligent Scots strangled by the poverty in their homeland and forced to emigrate to Canada. They had come to this site on the banks of the Grand River in the Queen's Bush, and created with their bare hands, men and women together, the town of Fergus. When the call went out for a minister, the infant town contained twenty cabins, a store, a grist mill and a cemetery. The logs for the church had been cut and laid in piles between the gravestones. The Patersons moved from farm family to farm family until the townsfolk could them build them a proper manse.

After sixteen years, Fergus had begun to seriously challenge nearby Elora in all manner of ways. Two-storeyed businesses lined the main street, and a boardwalk running the length of the north side kept the ladies' skirts from trailing in the mud in spring, and from the pools of dust in summer. The town side of the Grand River boasted a straight line of small stone cottages for the millworkers' families, and on the other side, cows grazed on the lush river grass. There was a proper school and three churches, and halfway up the hill between Fergus and Elora was the brooding exterior of the county poorhouse.

The manse was the logical place for the women to meet, in spite of its tiny parlour. The church was too cold on weekdays and too intimidating. It was God's house on Sundays, and the rest of the week, the church belonged to Reverend Paterson. An aura of austereness about the man made them uneasy, though they had no trouble listing his accomplishments. He served his congregation tirelessly; he was a learned man— they prized his education above all else, and never failed to mention it to anyone outside their own congregation— he was the most competent of pastors, conscientious in the performance of his duties, and mindful of his role as a moral leader. But there was an unspoken perception of something lacking in the man. In their hearts, the women felt he disapproved of them, although he never said so, and they maintained a respectful distance.

Aloofness was not possible with Caroline. Her arrival heated up a room as if the earth had moved a fraction closer to the sun. The men were stirred by her flamboyant beauty, unseemly in a minister's wife. They were confused, and angry at her for the disturbing thoughts they hoped marriage had stowed safely behind them. They muttered among themselves and watched how she conducted herself. The women were dumbfounded by the contradictions she presented: Caroline was the red-haired picture of an outrageously beautiful young woman, and on the other hand, she was concerned for the harshness of their lives, and she toiled selflessly on their behalf. It was the first time these women had had an advocate outside their own families, and for some, it was the first time they had ever had an advocate. Caroline did not go about her work in public, but Fergus was a small community, and someone always happened to be at their window, or a husband driving on a snowy road, saw Caroline walking the mile or more to an outlying cabin. It was common knowledge in the town how she paced the dirt floors of such cabins with a colicky or feverish infant in her arms so the worn young mother could have a few hours of sleep. Every tramp for miles around knew there was a pot of soup and a bundle of clothes waiting at the manse, no questions asked. That the stories of her good deeds were exaggerated in the telling was in keeping with the nature of a small community, as was the endless speculation by the female folk on the origins of Caroline's barrenness.

The front room of the manse struggled to contain both the women and the large rectangular frame over which they worked. The ones seated closest to the hearth were most at risk, as the heat thrown by the flames roasted their backs and stained their faces scarlet. Every so often they redistributed themselves, rippling in a clockwise direction with no discernible break in the rhythm of their stitches. The women knew instinctively and simultaneously when the discomfort of one of their number was approaching the unbearable level. Using the latest shift in position as cover, Caroline eyed the newest member of the group. Sarah MacVittie was a colourless slip of a girl wed to the village blacksmith. She had arrived in Fergus the previous month in response to Angus' request to his old mother back in Scotland for a bride. Mrs. Matthews, the postmistress, helped Angus write the letter and then told everyone in town what he had written.

"I'm in need of a wife to give me some bairns and there is a great shortage of unclaimed females in this part of the world. You'd be doin' me, as well as yourself, a service in sending me out a bride." The town had waited breathlessly to see who Mrs. MacVittie would send. "Sarah was an orphan," Mrs. Matthews reported to all and sundry, "raised in the same town as Angus, but very young. Why, she was barely able to walk," the postmistress calculated the age difference on her fingers, "when Angus boarded ship for Canada."

Angus was so anxious to become a family man he would have married Sarah the very day of her arrival in Fergus if John, at Caroline's request, had not opposed it. The Patersons suggested a period of settling in would be beneficial for the girl, and offered her the use of the loft bedroom in the manse. But the smith was adamant; the wedding took place the next day.

Caroline's only contact with Sarah MacVittie was at church on Sunday mornings. Sarah's appearance at those weekly meetings unsettled Caroline. It was true, Caroline told herself, the girl had most unfortunate colouring. Her hair and eyes and skin were all in varying shades of brown, running the gamut from dull to faded. Sarah's appearance, even in optimal circumstances, would never be vibrant, but still, to look at this empty husk of a girl was frightening. It was as if the life were being pressed out of her.

Caroline had made a point of speaking to Angus the day before. The burly smith was bent over the forge, bare to the waist, when Caroline entered his shop. She waited until he had straightened his thickly muscled back and replaced the bellows by the fire before she spoke.

"Angus, how are you and Sarah getting on?"

He made a motion towards the hook, where a workman's smock was hanging, glaring at her in the intense heat. She smiled, relieving him of any responsibility for being seen half dressed.

"Well enough, I suppose. She's sickly, though, cries all the time."

Caroline swallowed hard, remembering her own tears in the first year of her marriage. She had cried every night, although she made very sure John never heard her. Marriage had been a nightmare, and unlike Sarah, Caroline had not been ill. She shuddered. Illness, she admitted to herself, had once looked like the only solution to the dreadful mess she found herself in. For Caroline was certain, halfway through the first year of her marriage, that she did not love her husband, and was never likely to.

"Sarah needs to get out, to meet people and make some friends. I'm sure you are doing all you can to make her happy, but she needs the company of other women."

Caroline looked encouragingly at the blacksmith, hoping to see his harsh expression soften under her warm words. She went on, "Your wife is very young. She's probably homesick, missing her mother."

As soon as the words left her mouth she wished them back. Sarah had not a relation in the world. Her mother died in the workhouse, and no one knew who her father was. Angus took no notice of Caroline's slip, and she continued quickly to the crux of her visit, as if the idea had just occurred to her.

"Have her come to the manse tomorrow afternoon. Some of us meet on Wednesdays to quilt and chat and have a cup of tea. It will be a nice outing for her and give her a chance to make some friends among the women. I can count on you to send Sarah to us, can't I, Angus?"

The smith had kept his promise and his girl bride sat huddled in a padded chair, all but swallowed by its plush interior. Under a ragged fringe of mouse-brown hair, her face was forlorn; much, Caroline thought, like a dog who has displeased its master but has no idea of what it has done to cause such anger and, consequently, has no hope of righting the unfathomable wrong. Caroline leaned across one corner of the wooden frame and touched the girl gently on the hand holding the stationary needle.

"Sarah, is this confusing to you? Did you not do quilting back home?"

The girl shook her fine hair and answered in a thin voice, "They taught us how to weave and knit but I've never seen fancywork like this before. It looks very difficult."

Caroline reached down and pulled a bit of material from the basket at her feet. "Fancywork, that's a good one! Quilts use up all the bits of cloth and worn-out clothing no one wants. Everyone keeps a ragbag. We make our quilts from scraps; but it is nice of you to call it fancywork. Would you like me to show you how to cut a square? Then you can lay it on the frame and stitch it to the backing."

Sarah shrank further into the folds of the chair.

"It really is the easiest thing. Once you have the pattern cut, it's a simple matter to copy it over and over again. We attach the square to the backing and then to the other squares, with neat tiny stitches, and by spring we have a finished quilt."

Caroline watched the needle quiver in the girl's hand. She'd not be able to handle scissors at this stage.

"Would you rather help me stitch my square?"

The fringe of hair bobbled up and down.

Caroline took the girl's hand and guided the needle through the first sequence of stitches, gradually releasing the pressure until she could withdraw her hand, leaving Sarah to work on her own.

"There, Sarah. I can hardly tell which are your stitches and which are mine. You have the knack of doing it already."

The girl sat straighter in the chair. There was a lull in the regular hum of conversation and Sarah's words, intended only for Caroline, became communal property.

"Where do the patterns come from?"

Feet shuffled under the frame as the women stirred in their chairs. Where do the patterns come from? No one had ever raised the question. Where did they come from, indeed! They came from patterns they had always stitched and had known by heart since childhood: the Irish wedding ring, the log cabin, the star, the double chain and countless variations. Sarah's disconcerting question brought old memories to mind, of distant mothers quilting before peat fires. Collectively they ruffled through old pictures, remembering how they had longed to be old enough to place their own stitches alongside their mothers'. And now they were the mothers, and they decided who could work beside them on their quilts.

"Mothers. We got the patterns from our mothers."

The girl looked expectantly from one woman to another, but they had nothing more to say. Each had reached back as far in memory as she comfortably could. Caroline came to their rescue.

"Oh, among the group of us, we know more patterns than we could ever quilt; it's the colours that give us trouble."

At this there was an outburst of laughter.

"I got John to agree to let me have the group meet here, and asked him to build us a quilting frame. And then I cut up two of his best shirts because I thought blue fabric would look better in the quilt than what we had. Is it any wonder he was cross with me?"

"Angus would kill me if I ever cut up one of his shirts."

The woman on the other side of Sarah reached over and patted her hand.

"Don't you worry, dear, no one is going to ask you for anything of Angus'!"

A gray-haired woman at the far end of the room spoke directly to the girl.

"You just bring yourself, Sarah. Tell Angus, Jean Campbell says he's to see that you don't miss any meetings. It's good for us and good for the poor folk who receive the fruits of our labour."

For the first time since Caroline had known her, a wave of colour swept across the girl's cheeks.

Caroline had come to terms with the permanent absence of ecstasy in her marriage; this done, she managed very well. Time and maturity schooled her in the benefits of hard work and devotion as solid blocks on which to base a life and raise a family. But there was no family, outside John. He exulted in the wife he had chosen. Caroline was more worthy in his eyes because of her charity than her beauty. In danger of sinning on the side of pride, in contemplative moments, he thought beyond her beauty and her goodness to the one area where she had failed him. There were no children. Why? John had examined and re-examined every detail of their marital relations. He could not find an earthly reason for their childlessness. John was a normal healthy man who loved his wife and enjoyed the act of procreation mightily, although he had trouble admitting it. She aroused him with her simplest motions at the most inconvenient times; in the beginning of their life together he had had to caution her not to brush against him as they walked from the church to the manse, the only time he had ever turned away from her. No, he concluded, if there was a human fault, it did not lie with him. He insisted Caroline visit a doctor in a distant town, and there, in the waiting room of a retired army doctor, Caroline was sentenced. She overheard John and the doctor discussing the results of the examination while she was dressing.

"No physical reason why Mrs. Paterson cannot bear a child?"

"Nothing in your wife's anatomy or history."

"We must be patient, then. He works in His own time and in mysterious ways."

Caroline stopped buttoning her bodice, a wry smile contorting her face. His ways were no mystery to her. She had forgotten, but God had not. Her incestuous love for Daniel had caught up with Caroline.

Their return to Fergus marked a change in their relationship. Before, whenever he had leaned over and parted the silk strands of her hair, exposing the soft white of her neck to her lips, a shudder had run through her body. She would mouth the words, *Dear God, please not tonight*, into the pot of stew she was stirring. Some nights He heard her, and on the nights He ignored her plea, she lay still, steeling herself to silence as John knelt over her, hoisting her nightgown above her head. Caroline lay smothered in layers of flannelled rage and railed at a distant Emily. It was horrible! How did other women endure it? Why hadn't Emily warned her? The hope that she might conceive had kept her compliant, but after her visit to the doctor, she reassigned her rage.

As the years built one upon the other, John and Caroline, each in their own ways, carved their places in the community. Interest in Caroline's childlessness paled and then faded into nothingness. Eventually, John forgot to ask if she had any cause to give him hope.

This process of becoming is unrelenting. I keep pushing things down and they keep pushing up. I ache brilliantly. Whatever is happening to me? I am pieced into squares like an unstitched quilt. I am full of rage, contained but barely. The more I read and talk and think, the more I realize how manipulated I have been by a patriarchal society. It told me what I wanted and fed me goodies to keep me from taking real power. What brass! What nerve! What arrogance! This understanding has made me want to make a quantum leap into something quite unknown to me. I want to make a commitment to something bigger than me and my family. I want to make this world (not just my world) a better place, greener, richer (but not in the material sense; in the sense of human potential). Our systems have failed us miserably; it is up to each and every one of us to step outside ourselves and see what is really going on. Wake up, Ruth, and read between the lines. This morning's paper held an advertisement for a doggy boutique in Holt Renfrew, a doggy boutique with luxury doghouses, for God's sake, and there are real people sleeping in the streets. We are a society gone mad. And yet, I was at the airport waiting for Dave when a plane from Rome arrived, and all the old people came off to meet the new babies. I kept getting tears in my eyes as families matched up. What was half, now was whole. We really do pour the best of ourselves into our children. We just do. I would not have it any other way.

Frances Yates' *Giordano Bruno and the Hermetic Tradition* is leading me to the conclusion that all living things are designed to a greater or lesser degree to draw down the higher or celestial influences. We are images designed to attract these higher influences. Ficino and Bruno tried to explain this theory, as did Plato and Hermes Tristemegistrus. Shakespeare tries to show us how this works with his characters. Think of Hermione in *The Winter's Tale:* Macbeth in *Macbeth;* Cordelia in *King Lear.* We are all little tuning forks being played upon by planetary forces. Our task is to transmit this knowledge in our being. We cannot do anything directly, but we can convey, indirectly, the message of the Gods in our lives.

CHAPTER FOURTEEN

How Caroline survived these barren years had as much to do with her proximity to the Elora gorge as to her own character. The gorge, located on the outskirts of the town, was claimed by the citizens of Elora as their own. Caroline was enthralled by it. The height of land overlooking the steepest portion of the gorge was her preferred viewing point, and she returned there as often as she could find an excuse to slip away. From this perspective she could not ignore the violence in the river as it forced its way into the narrow entrance and carved the high straight sides to suit its passage. Where the water boiled and clawed at the sandstone cliffs, raw energy was released and wafted up the chanelled walls into the waiting nostrils of Caroline Paterson. It acted as an intoxicant on Caroline's spirit. After visits to the gorge, she returned to Fergus with a visible spring in her step. What was there about the place that stimulated her? she wondered.

Local folklore provided only the faintest outline of a legend. The gorge was a sacred place to those Indians who still hunted along the banks of the

Grand River and fished in its clear waters. Nothing in the legend explained the spell it had cast over Caroline. Calling on the sick and the elderly shut-ins of the area, she was able to piece together more of the story. The old people loved her visits, for she never cut them off in the middle of a story and she never told them she had heard that same story many times before, even if she had. Elderly Scots were a canny bunch, and soon discovered that any mention of the gorge guaranteed their visitor's full attention. They told her stories about the Indian tribe living downstream from the gorge when they had first settled here, and her eyes would light up from the inside and she would stay by their sides for hours. They doled out their memories in fragments to keep her coming back, dropping pale hints of love and treachery. As if by chance, old Mrs. Black spoke one day of a great chief with magical powers who roamed the valley looking for the remnants of his people, although no one she knew had actually seen him.

Sometimes, as Caroline walked the path through the forest leading to the edge of the gorge, her mind drifted and floated above the ancient trees. She imagined she could see bright-skinned figures sheltering in the shadows that played about the woods. With each twist in the trail, she held her breath in hopes of coming face to face with a single line of straightbacked Indians moving silently along the track, or even, she allowed herself to dream, with the great chief.

Never had Caroline needed the gorge more than that spring. The winter had taken forever to wear itself out, and the process had exhausted her and sickened many of the weaker members of the community. There had been three deaths since Christmas and one had been a child. This day she stepped outside and sniffed the freshening puffs of air, the tell-tale scent of warm decay which told of spring. She looked at the muddy track linking the two towns and decided to risk an early trek to the gorge.

"Good morning, Mrs. Paterson. Is it not too soon to be thinking of walking to Elora? The frost is barely out of the ground, and for sure there's one more snowfall in the sky."

"Oh, Mrs. Matthews. How did you know I was thinking of going for the first real walk of the spring? I hardly knew myself."

The postmistress moved her lips in a semblance of a smile, not knowing whether to be flattered or insulted. She had never been able to get a handle on the minister's wife. It annoyed her, and yet there was nothing in Caroline's reply she could report as rude. She watched Caroline out of sight.

The day warmed and dried all but the deepest ruts in the track. It was not at all impassable by foot. Caroline breathed deeply of the sweet air and walked as jauntily as any girl half her age. The entrance to the gorge path came before she had begun to look for it. But what did it matter? The years of winters melted away and Caroline and each tree in the forest lifted their heads and celebrated. Birds dashed recklessly from tree to tree, whistling furiously. Tall dark trees with tightly clenched tufts of greening buds arranged themselves in patterns she had never noticed until today. The path led her to a different place on the gorge from where she customarily went, and someone had arrived before her. A brown-skinned woman stood poised on the very brink, her arm upraised as if in salutation. Caroline froze, afraid her slightest movement would dislodge the woman and send her crashing to the waters below. She crouched noiselessly on the path and heard the winter-heavy water surging against the limestone corridors; droplets, launched by the river, sprayed against her skin. She felt rather than saw the woman turn and walk towards her. It was not until she spoke that Caroline knew for certain the woman was real.

"Have you come to this place in search of the Great Spirit?"

Caroline nodded, afraid to speak.

"Come." And Caroline followed her to the very edge of the cliff.

"Do you see Him?"

To Caroline's amazement, a craft of glistening white birch bark entered the narrowest part of the river, and while she watched, a man stood up in the frail swaying craft and spread arms that were not arms but great wings. They gleamed like sunshine or a blessing in the clear air, for they were crusted with tiny bead-like shells of a lustrous white. He rode the length of the gorge, dropping his arms only when the canoe reached the calmer waters of the lower gorge. She heard the tinkle of a thousand shells before he disappeared from view, and then she remembered the brown-skinned woman. She, too, had vanished. Caroline went in search of her. The path she took no longer traced the precipice, but descended gently to a valley where she had never been. There was no urgency to her movements. The slender track wound beside the strong-willed river, and here and there Caroline stooped to cradle a perfect snowdrop between her fingers. She marvelled that something so fragile and exquisite could muster the strength to break through the heavy covering of the earth. On and on she walked, until the hum of the river lessened; the path had veered from the water's edge. There was no sign of the woman.

The walk was sheer enchantment for Caroline. Each turn and twist of the footpath revealed some new wonder. She revelled in the sensation of discovery and when the path halted abruptly at a clear-running stream, she moved upstream, hoping to find a rock to serve as a stepping stone. Here, sparkling in the hollow of an icy stream, she spotted a pearly glint in the water. Caroline rolled up one sleeve of her dress, plunged her arm into the stream, and was stunned by the bitter coldness of the water against her skin. Before she had a chance to withdraw her arm, she was face to face with a reflection in the water, a reflection of no one she had seen before, a girl with glossy black hair swept back like wings from sun-warmed skin. The girl was looking back at her. To raise her own eyes and look into the girl's required all of Caroline's courage. They were as transparent as glass, holding the gray mist of a late August morning in their depths. And in the center of each black pupil was a tiny reflection of Caroline herself.

CAN I SOLVE THIS ENORMOUS
puzzle I have been handed?
I— who love language, the flexibility
and the fullness of words, the richness
they can loose upon the world—
have come to the conclusion that the higher
level of beings does not communicate in words.
Help! How can I share this if I cannot say it?
Listening to opera, I reverberate like a tuning
fork to the emotions conveyed in song…
I cannot describe this with words. Rilke
does… somehow, in poetry. Painters, on
canvas, and opera singers, in arias, make
known the underlying reality of our world
emotionally. I must speak with an excess
of love, and write my life in feelings.

We took the overnight train from Nice to Geneva, passing through unknown landscapes into unknown towns, hurtling towards what? I thought of the French Jews being shipped across France and I wondered how they stood it. I wondered what they thought. I wondered how I would have managed. I wonder if we have learned anything at all.

Once you pollute your soul, nothing is as clear and beautiful again. One must be on guard against this. My skin is a barometer, my outer set of signals. I must listen, as though I were a lightning rod, a conductor of charged emotions, my own and others'.

One must be honest with one's self to write, but there are things in my life that must be kept hidden, that I don't want read by anyone. I could live a secret life, but that knowledge destroys my vision of myself. How quickly we are humbled. Just when we think we know ourselves intimately, we are forced to reconsider.

I am confronted with hepatitis, a souvenir of our African sojourn. I know now why people lose hope. Life feels very gray and overwhelming and there is no strength to beat it into shape or knead it like dough. I sleep, eat and read. My energy is sapped by the least effort. I want to slide into the inner life but I am missing the key.

CHAPTER FIFTEEN

So engrossed was Caroline with the reflection of the girl in the stream that she lost all sense of time. Cloud covered the pale afternoon sun before she felt the numbing cold circulating through her body. She shivered violently and pulled her hand from the icy water. The girl's face rippled into a multitude of wrinkled copies and vanished from the surface of the stream. No matter.

Her face had imprinted itself on Caroline's mind and now the likeness floated before Caroline. Absentmindedly, Caroline fingered the shell she had plucked from the stream bed while her eyes had remained fixed on the shimmering image of the girl. She followed her blindly, conscious only of keeping her in view. Caroline need not have worried. The vision hovered just beyond her reach, stopping when Caroline stopped and moving forward when Caroline stepped forward. By the time they arrived where the trail met the road, Caroline knew the girl was playing a game. A wisp of a smile touched Caroline's lips, and her smile mirrored the one worn by the girl. Caroline's thoughts were far away from Fergus as she approached the town.

"So you have finally decided to come home, Mrs. Paterson."

The strident voice cut through Caroline's trance, banishing the image of the girl and stopping their game in mid-flight.

"Wherever have you been? Those walks of yours must take you halfway 'round the county. I have been waiting for you since noon, and the Reverend didn't even know you had gone until I told him. You have a letter. It came right after you left. It's not from your mother; leastways it is not like the other letters you get."

Mrs. Matthews reluctantly handed the letter to Caroline, and Caroline suddenly realized how chilled she was.

"I am sorry to have caused you so much trouble. I went further than I intended."

"Be it bad news that you have got?"

The postmistress' eyes raked the seal on the envelope and willed Caroline to break it open then and now.

"Oh, I think not. I must be off home and give John a good meal. Poor man had to make do for his dinner. Thank you so kindly for delivering my letter. Good day."

Caroline moved away slowly, with deliberate grace, stopping here and there on the main street to exchange greetings with the townspeople who crossed her path. Her calm manner belied the rage Mrs. Matthews' words had loosed inside her. I will not, she vowed silently, give that woman the pleasure of seeing me lose my temper.

The letter rested in the pocket of her dress, rubbing against the shell she had scooped from the stream bed. Caroline gained the privacy of the manse before she broke the seal and read the letter.

March 19th 1851.
Oakwood House
Kingston

My dear Caroline,

I do regret having to write to inform you of our mother's poor health. Until this week she would not hear of either father or myself making known to you the serious nature of her illness, or even, for that matter, the knowledge that she was ill. Dr. Wilson told us this Christmas past that mother had only a matter of months before succumbing to the dreadful wasting disease she has contracted. I am now convinced the end is near, and you, as her only daughter, would wish to be by her side. Mother, herself, has requested that you come. Just two nights past she summoned me to her bedside and whispered that you must come. The urgency with which she spoke quite frightened me and she repeated once again, "Get Caroline, I must speak with her." I left immediately for my home in Kingston and have sent this letter posthaste. I pray you will not be too late.

With great affection, I remain your brother,
Richard

I am desperately confused, and yet not unhappy. Can one come to terms with contradictions? I love the lake and I want always to share it with those I love, a wide range of folk, old and young, male and female, human and non-human. If there is magic in this old world, then it is here, at Picnic Point, the rock, the outer dock, the shoreline from the canoe and in the early morning or at twilight. Such a short road from magic to despair. I feel like a great gray swimmer trying frantically to climb onto a dock, but I keep getting pushed down by huge waves. Hepatitis has struck a second time. I thought I had it under control. When will I learn? I control nothing. God, what is down the road? Writing my confusion helps. Desire lives on the skin and responds to sunshine and soft air, but does it have to be directed at someone, or can it just be?

I am not at home down here... and I don't want to get too comfortable. I am a visitor who has put on a physical body to explore this world. I am a diver who suits up in order to visit an environment not my own. All this equipment— wet suit, flippers, air tanks, mask— is heavy— it weighs me down, and yet I need a weight belt to keep me down. My own world must be very light. What did I come to see in this underwater world? Was I simply curious, or was it something more? It is risky to trade one's natural environment for a strange one; there is always the potential for getting lost or having one's gear break down. To get into this world is easy; one simply suits up and jumps from the boat, but to get back to the boat we must swim to the surface and climb the ladder, one rung at a time, carrying all this extra equipment. It is a potent image for humans.

CHAPTER SIXTEEN

When Caroline walked through the front door of her old home, she knew instinctively that her mother was still alive. Stripping off her gloves, she untied her bonnet and removed her cloak. She placed them, as she always had, neatly on the hall bench. Memories of the last time she had stood here rushed like blood to her head. The house looked exactly as she had left it as a bride of one day. She closed her eyes, putting her hand on the post of the wooden bannister. Emily had waited at the bottom of the curved staircase as Caroline made her way down, arm in arm with her new husband. Emily had looked beseechingly into her daughter's face as Caroline drew closer. What had seemed strange to Caroline at that time did not seem so now. Marriage, even at its best, was a long journey for a mother to send her daughter on alone.

Caroline hurried up the stairs to her mother's room. Emily was alive, but barely. The ample-bodied, well-groomed matron who had managed all their lives so effectively and with such efficiency had vanished. In her place was a supine spectre. Caroline tiptoed to the bed, touching her lips in passing to her father's cheek. She gently stroked Emily's thin, blue-veined hand lying forgotten by its owner on the counterpane, and was rewarded by a tremor from the transparent eyelids. Emily's eyes flickered open and lit on the face of her daughter. Hers were haunted eyes in a sunken face of angled bone and paper-thin skin. Had she not known it was her mother lying there, Caroline would have drawn back in horror. As it was, she paused to catch her breath before leaning over the wasted form, searching the bared blueprint of the face for traces of her mother. She strained to capture something of their common past in the pillowed face, but there was nothing. Caroline looked over helplessly at her father, who put a hand to his eyes and stumbled across the floor, closing the door as he left the room. Caroline lifted the hand abandoned on the quilt in her own, hoping to transfer warmth to her mother's cold and lifeless fingers lying curled against her palm.

"Caroline," croaked the death's head, "is it really you?"

"Yes, mother. I am here."

"Come closer."

Caroline touched her ear to her mother's lips.

"Go to the blanket box. Get the package from the bottom, the one wrapped in tissue paper."

Caroline was astonished that her mother's wasted body still contained the power to speak. She had hardly heard what Emily said. "Mother? What did you say?"

"Hurry, Caroline. Get the sampler from the blanket box. It belongs to you."

The pine chest had been in her parents' bedroom as long as Caroline could remember. In the log house of her early childhood, the blanket box had stood at the foot of their big bed, and it was still in the same place. She raised the lid and a scent of crushed herbs and dried flowers rushed out, mingling with other less recognizable smells, reminding Caroline of things she had long forgotten, and hinting at others. She unpacked layer upon layer of starched and folded linens, treasured baby clothes, bits of yellowed lace, and Emily's wedding dress. Caroline lifted each item from its place and laid it on the floor at the end of the bed. One package lay unclaimed on the bottom of the box. Emily struggled to raise her head.

"Bring it here, Caroline. Sit beside me as you open it." Her head fell backward onto the pillow.

The only light in the room was from the fire, and at first Caroline had difficulty in knowing what the package held. It was needlework of some kind; her fingers felt the raised outline of the stitches. She shook it out and held it up. It was a sampler, the sort of piece Emily had encouraged Caroline to work on years before. Narrowing her eyes and holding the linen closer to the flames, she picked out words, cross-stitched on the bottom:

Elizabeth McMaster
April 24, 1802.
County Galway

"Who was she?"

The bony hand grasped Caroline's tightly. "She was your mother. She died in my arms on board ship, while we were sailing to Canada."

For a long moment the eyes of the two women held. Questions hung awkwardly between them, like frozen garments on a winter clothesline.

"How did she die? Where was I?"

Emily struggled to lift her head once more from the pillow, and she reached up to touch her daughter's face with cold fingers. "Caroline, she died giving birth to you. I took you and never told a soul except the nuns. You were all alone in the world and I couldn't let you stay with them. I brought you with me to Perth and passed you off as mine. I never told your father. Forgive me." Tears slipped into lines already deeply etched on the old woman's face.

"Forgive you? You saved me from becoming an orphan. You loved me. You raised me as your own. You are my mother. What does Elizabeth McMaster mean to me?"

Caroline let the sampler slide to the floor and gathered Emily in her arms. She was so frail that Caroline feared the slightest pressure would cause her fragile frame to crack and shatter into a thousand pieces. She placed her lips on the tissue-thin skin where once her mother's cheek had bloomed. She whispered, "Mother, should I forgive you for giving me a home with a mother and a father and brothers?"

And then it forked through Caroline like lightning, igniting her with the knowledge of what might have been. For a moment the pain was so intense she thought she would die. Part of her hoped she would. It was too much to bear. Gradually, the storm subsided and Caroline understood she would not die. Life did not give up its place without a fight. She would live, and regret, instead of guilt, would fill the empty spaces in her soul. She threw back her head and howled her loss to the heavens. Her hands clenched and unclenched and her fingers curved and stiffened into claws. The woman on the bed could not look upon such agony. She closed her eyes and would have stopped up her ears had she been able. Caroline choked back her anguish and once more reached down to cradle the wasted body of her mother against her breast. She rocked Emily, crooning over and over again, "I know, I know, I understand. What could you do? You did the best you could. It's all right, I understand. It's not your fault."

When Emily at last appeared to be comforted, Caroline placed her on the bed and covered her with a quilt as tenderly as if she were handling a fallen bird. The delicate eyelids fluttered faintly and then closed. Caroline gently kissed each gossamer lid, whispering, "I love you, mother."

Emily slipped peacefully into sleep.

Night gathered the shadows of the darkened room about the two women. One slept, and one kept watch and wondered about herself.

"Elizabeth McMaster." Caroline tried the name on her tongue and found it strange but not distasteful. "Irish, she must have been," and smiled to herself, "then so am I. My father, was he Irish, too?"

The questions marched around the room and halted always at the end of the bed, where Emily lay drifting into something far deeper and more lasting than sleep.

"Did she know she had a daughter before she died? Why did she leave my father? Am I like her or him? Why didn't he come looking for us? Maybe he died, too?" Caroline checked the parade of questions. They would have to wait their turn. Right now, the frail, still warm body of this mother demanded all her loyalty and her love.

Caroline shivered. The room had suddenly become cold. This won't do, she thought, and rose to put more wood on the fire. Doing so, her booted foot caught the edge of the discarded sampler. She picked it up and carried it to the hearth. She tossed a birch log on the coals. It caught and flared brightly and showed Caroline the magic of her mother's legacy. In the firelight, a winged white horse flew into the midst of dancing stars whose patterns changed and reformed into other designs while she looked on. It was a trick of the flames, but then she felt the pulsing in her fingers. A circle of stones ringed the borders of the needlework; the stones seemed to vibrate between her fingers, alive in Caroline's hands, magic knotted in the cloth, waiting for the touch that would unlock it. The woman who had created this work was no ordinary artist. She had stitched enchantment with her needle. The sampler tugged at doors in Caroline she had closed, she thought, forever. She longed to throw them wide open, but not yet.

The only mother she had ever known lay poised on the edge of death, waiting to cross over. Caroline wanted to watch with her. Emily lingered throughout that night and all the following day without regaining consciousness. Tom and Richard, helpless in their grief, railed at the inconsideration of a son and brother who could not be found. Caroline said nothing and kept her vigil by her mother's bed. Death came lightly on slippered feet in the hush that preceded the dawn on the second night of Caroline's watch. It came so carefully that Caroline was scarcely aware that her mother's hand, which lay within the circle of her own, had lost its imprint of warmth.

The service for Emily Jane Harris was held in the same church in which her only daughter had been wed. With few exceptions, the faces that had witnessed Caroline's marriage were the same faces that came to bury Emily. Daniel was not among them.

I have time now to listen. I keep Adrienne Rich's *The Fact of a Doorframe* beside my bed. I am trying to move gracefully through each day, not to hurry and not to hurt anyone. The conflict between the creative life and the maternal life is always there. At times, the tension overwhelms me. I crave beauty, thoughts and words, always the words. My skin is like a page, holding desire in its smooth brownness, opening to the sun, to someone's love. My lungs gasp like my pen spilling thoughts across a page— no form, no structure, just breathlessness.

I cannot make a deal with the forms in which I live. Form holds us back. Society must undergo a sea change if we are to evolve. Somehow I must find the courage for anarchy, but change of this dimension is not possible from within. A great load has been lifted from my heart. I have taken off my mask; it was too tight. I thought I could live two lives (my inner one and my outer one) but the gap is widening; the contradictions are too great. I have been daughter, wife and mother, but never me, and now, for the second half of my life, I must be Ruth, whoever she may be. What does she like? What are her real feelings? Is she a good person, and on whose terms?

My hand is so light it must hold a pen to keep from flying away. The fire is all flames and shadows and the music makes me ache inside. Will I ever have the courage to freefall, as Adrienne Rich says we must? "No one who has survived to speak the new language has avoided this."

CHAPTER SEVENTEEN

After a decent interval, Richard returned to Kingston and his law practice, with his family. Caroline was left to settle her father as comfortably as possible in the circumstances. Emily had managed Tom Harris' children and his home so efficiently that he had never had to give much consideration to the domestic side of life. He had been free to pursue his business and to involve himself in local politics. Emily had played her part so well, her husband was unaware of how much effort she had put into running his home and raising his children. He was lost without her, and clung to Caroline.

She hired a girl from an outlying farm to keep the house as spotless as her mother had, and trained the young woman to prepare the food her father liked. He seemed satisfied as long as Caroline supervised the running of the house and gave her full attention to him in the evenings. Under Caroline's careful management the stone house resumed some semblance of normality, and the hole that Emily's death had opened shrank to a manageable size. Caroline wrote each week to John, covering her lengthy absence with her father's need. John wrote back, assuring her that he was managing and that he understood her father's need for her far outweighed his own. She was not to hurry her return to Fergus on his account.

The days were not hard to fill. Caroline dropped back into the routine she had followed as a girl. She tended to the house in the mornings, and after the midday meal she worked in the garden or walked alone along the riverbank. In the evenings she sat and talked with Tom about the sawmill, and whom he had seen and chatted with that day. Their conversations always came round to Emily and their life together. He spoke as though he knew her from the inside out, and yet he had no idea that his only daughter was, in fact, not his. The contradiction in their conversations bothered Caroline immensely. How had Emily lived with this secret? What had she been afraid of? Would Tom have treated an adopted daughter differently? Not possible. After Tom had gone off to bed and Caroline was alone by the fire, she would retrieve her mother's work from its daytime hiding place and hold it up to the firelight.

She emptied her mind into the flames and watched as the white horse, with his pearly horn, took flight. Tiny stars danced wickedly in the corners of the fireplace. At her touch, or so it seemed, the circle of stones expanded until she was overpowered by their closeness and their promise of a secret knowledge. Night after night, the sampler cast its spell: the white horse flew higher, the stars grew brighter and moved provocatively in the flames, and the smooth gray stones loomed larger, custodians of an old wisdom.

Gradually, the day existed only as a bridge, and she was impatient for night to fall. Caroline busied herself with hard physical labour, scrubbing floors and walls and cleaning every cupboard in the house. During one of these forays she came across a small packet of letters, neatly tied with a narrow velvet ribbon, in the bottom drawer of Emily's dresser. They were well thumbed and obviously precious enough for Emily to have saved them. Caroline took them to the front porch to read. The letters were from Daniel, and documented the portion of his life he wished to share with his family in Perth. It was a pitifully thin record of a young man's life. He had returned to his regiment that fateful Christmas and been assigned to duty in the western reaches of the province, a frontier post where young men proved themselves or disappeared into the white wilderness that lay outside the barracks. She read of hardships and of a promotion; she read of how he loved the untamed land and the people who lived there. There was a silence of several years, and then one last letter. He had left the Army and left the town. He told of trapping to survive and exploring where no white man had ever been before.

It was a strange tale, with no explanation of why he had left or where he could be reached. Caroline hid Daniel's letters inside the folds of her mother's sampler, and tucked both away in her old room.

The town's widows found excuses to visit the stone house. One baked a pie from the wild strawberries her grandchildren had picked; she hoped it would tempt the Captain's appetite. She would be by the next evening before supper time to collect the plate.

"It's no trouble," she assured Caroline. "The walk will do me good."

Another widow had brought a book belonging to her late husband that she hoped "dear Tom" would enjoy. She would stop by some evening and see how he was getting on. Tom grew sleek as an old cat with all the attention, and plump from having pie twice a day. Emily had never made pastry more than once a week.

One evening, both ladies arrived within minutes of one another, and there were great protestations: "Oh my, I couldn't stay," and, "Well, perhaps for just a minute." Tom brought another chair from the kitchen and settled her alongside Caroline and his first caller. Caroline and Kate, the hired girl, exchanged amused glances as each widow tried to outstay the other. This happened often.

Soon enough, the sun would go down and the mosquitoes would drive the least hardy of the widows indoors or home. The smoke from Tom's pipe protected him from all but the most ferocious insect attacks, and on these warm evenings he came inside only to go to bed.

Caroline stayed long enough to be polite and then excused herself. She went to her room and lifted the packet of letters and the sampler from their hiding place and lay down on her bed, while voices murmured from the porch and Kate closed down the kitchen. Shadows gathered in the corners of Caroline's room, and it was not long before she heard one visitor make her departure, and then the second followed the first, unescorted, down the path. Silence, then the sound of chairs scraping along the porch and her father's heavy tread on the stairs. She heard the door to his room close.

When she could no longer bear the memories filling her room, she got up and went barefoot, in her nightgown, into the garden. With her feet deep in the sun-warmed earth and the bittersweet smell of freshly crushed herbs filling her nostrils, she read and reread Daniel's letters. It was too dark to see the words; Caroline knew each page by heart. When she finished with the letters she sank down among the plants and spread her mother's needlework across her lap. The winged horse, under the stars, was more bewitching than she could have imagined. She was confused; was she seeing the horse in real starlight, or by the brilliant points of light stitched to the canvas? The one merged and melted into the other, and it no longer mattered which was real as long as she could see what her mother had stitched for her. For the first time, it was all right to want Daniel to make love to her. She lowered herself onto the warm dark earth and dug her fingers deep into the soil. Magic came in waves of memories and washed her out to sea.

Midsummer's eve has come and gone, and the first day of summer finds me looking out onto a fog-filled bay. One is free to imagine what lies in the fog, since the eye no longer perceives physical outlines. There could be anything out there in all that whiteness. And my phone is acting up... all my ties to reality are disconnected.

Britannia found a nest of baby birds on the ground. She barked and barked, but did not hurt them. When I went to investigate, at first I did not recognize what I was seeing: little yellow beaks opening and closing like flowers. They are very fluffy and seem quite healthy. What kind of bird builds its nest in the grass? Guy Green came with the answer. Meadowlarks.

There was a deer on the road this morning; she reminded me of Britannia, that same lift to her head, that same quizzical look. Two female animals, one domesticated, one wild. What is the relationship between them?

I counted on my mother to teach me about the traditions of womanhood; after all, we were twinned by blood and something else, our knowledge of the feminine, the creative and nature. I trusted her to teach me about those things, and instead I got the patriarchal rundown about manners and ladylike behaviour— above all, be pretty and marry well. She failed me as I am failing Andrea. This book is for her.

Sitting on the dock and thinking about why Sylvia Plath and Virginia Woolf committed suicide. If you are going to be an artist (painter,. writer, musician, dancer) then everything must go into the creative energy. Everything gets consumed by the fire— family, husband, children, all precious relationships— nothing can be held back, and even then there is no guarantee of greatness. I have withdrawn my spirit from the relationship; I see it dying in front of me. This time, there will be no rescue; they must make their own way, as I must. I will miss being loved.

The lake is flat, not a cloud in the sky, and my two girls are asleep at my feet. For one silver moment, I saw joy. It flew across that perfect sky on the wings of three precisely spaced ducks. I saw it. And I knew I saw it.

PART THREE

SOPHIE

CANADA-IRELAND — 1851-1854

THE THOUGHTS ARE coming thick and fast. My first reaction is to panic and run for my pen; I am so afraid of losing them. Then I settle in, and let them settle in, too. I take a deep breath, say thank you, and start… No longer knowledge on paper, what I write is rinsed in my emotions and placed in a deeper part of me. We go back and read old things with new eyes, and always the old yields more. Is this because we have gained more being? Does this principle hold true in life? When we have gained a new level of being, do we come at life all over again? The way to gain being must be through our emotions.

CHAPTER ONE

The weather was warm and fair, without the plague of blackflies that made travel in the back country so unpleasant in the late spring. Day after day, Caroline remained upright in the big canoe. She watched with eager eyes the panorama unfolding on either shore. The further north they paddled, the wilder the landscape became, and with the wildness came a beauty she had never experienced. Giant fir trees challenged the very sky for supremacy; no clearing broke the dark green thickness of the shore. Occasionally, a black bear waded into the water. The boatmen laughed at her astonishment, and told her he was fishing. She laughed with them.

The boatmen were boisterous, but kind and anxious not to offend their female passenger with rough language or unkemptness. Caroline had to hide a smile as one after another of "les gars" arrived bloody from the application of a blunt-edged blade to a week's growth of beard or, having subdued a bushy black beard to neatness, they allowed a fellow paddler armed with a pair of shears to trim a shaggy head of hair. Some of the men were French Canadian by birth, descendants of the voyageurs who had travelled this route a century before, and some Metis, the golden offspring of fur traders and Indian wives. Whatever their background, the men paddling the big canoes up and down and across the lakes and rivers of Canada West were united in their love of the wilderness and their hatred of the regulations superimposed on the country by an advancing population. At the same time, their free-spirited lifestyle was endangered by the Hudson Bay Company, which sought to impose its own economic dictates on the frontier lands to the north and west. But paddling their big canoes, these full-throated, big-hearted men were truly at home. They sang the songs of their people as they battled the swift current of the Ottawa River with sturdy paddles that functioned as extensions of their own hard brown arms.

Portages became more numerous as the river wound still further north, until one day they branched west into a smaller river. Now they portaged more than they paddled. The men organized and carried out each trip with speed, oblivious to the weight of the packs they transported. The passengers had only to move themselves along the paths that ran alongside the white water foaming madly over the rocks. Initially, Caroline's movements on land were slow and clumsy, but she was soon as swift as the crew in navigating the trails.

One glorious day in midsummer found her alone on a large rock suitable for their next launching point. She had learned to recognize places on shore that provided the safest and easiest access for the loading of goods and passengers. The men now trusted her to go ahead and scout the shoreline for a place to launch the boat. Stretched out on the hard surface of the lichen-mottled rock in the full warmth of the summer sun, Caroline closed her eyes and let her thoughts turn inward. Not since her days in the gorge above Elora had she been so completely content to let each day dictate its own rhythm to her. The urgency of her search for Daniel was not forgotten, but it had softened with her growing awareness of the landscape.

There was a slight tremor on the warm rock beneath her right hand. She shifted leisurely to a sitting position. Not two feet from the spot where she was basking was the coiled body of a large reptile as mottled as the rock. The fathomless slits of his eyes fixed Caroline with a stare, and only the rapid stabs made by his darting tongue betrayed life. She was transfixed. Moments passed and stretched taut between them. Neither blinked or dropped their eyes. In time, Caroline found herself less frightened and more curious. Her previous experience with snakes had been confined to the small striped variety that had slithered quickly through her garden before shyly disappearing into the shrubbery.

This fellow was unlike those in her garden, coloured in the exact shadings of the granite rock. The diamond configurations along his back matched worn patches of moss. As she watched, he unwrapped the thick rope of his body with great dexterity, and detached himself in one continuous motion from the rock, as though a portion of the stone on which she sat had moved. The only hint of his reality was in the slowly widening ripple of water lapping the rock on which they had met.

Caroline's adventure had begun when she met with Major Edward Wilson, the commanding officer of Her Majesty's Army in Canada West, who had reluctantly granted her an interview. Her letter was lying on his desk when Caroline entered his office.

"Captain Tom's daughter, are you? Why didn't you say so? I took you for some meddling woman wanting to blame the Army for some imagined wrong done to her son or husband. I remember Tom Harris well from our days together in the Royal Engineers. Whatever possessed him to give up his commission? Land hunger, I'll wager. It can get to the best of them. It states here that you are looking for Lieutenant Daniel Harris. Your brother, I presume?"

Major Wilson waved aside the beribboned packet Caroline extended to him. "I don't have time to read your personal correspondence. Tell me when you last heard from him and from where."

Major Wilson listened attentively to the short tale of ex-Lieutenant Daniel Harris. He pursed his thin lips and exhaled extensively through his nostrils before replying, "Goddamn country! Excuse me, Mrs. Paterson, but that wild rotten country out there corrupts them. Yours is not the first story I have heard from that district. Desolation and loneliness, then the Indians get to them, and perfectly decent young men from good families go native. One morning they slip out of their barracks with their guns and their army boots and they never come back. We hear stories of them living with squaws in dirty Indian villages, but when we send a detachment to bring them back, they are never found. That damn country can twist a good soldier into a shape his own mother wouldn't recognize." The Major stared at Caroline with what could pass for compassion. "Don't go looking for him now, knowing what you are likely to find. Forget him. In all likelihood he's beyond saving."

"Major, I mean to find Daniel, no matter where he is or how he is living."

The Major's face hardened into its original arrogant lines. "I can give you every detail of his life in the Army right up to the day he deserted. If you find him, and I doubt that you will, we will shoot him. Do you still want that information?"

His iron gaze pinned her against the chair, but Caroline did not drop her eyes.

"Yes."

She did not move.

"Was there something more, madam?"

"If you were travelling to Sault Ste. Marie, how would you get there?"

The Major deliberated, allowing his eyes to travel the full length of her body. "I, Mrs. Paterson, would go by canoe with the Hudson Bay people up the Ottawa River and across to Georgian Bay. You will have to catch a steamer making the trip across the Great Lakes to Lake Superior. The wait between connections is tedious, but you will find that out for yourself. Good day, Mrs. Paterson."

Their route across the upper reaches of the province was the same one taken by Samuel de Champlain and his Indian guides. In this part of the country, little had been disturbed in hundreds of years. They moved from the Mattawa River to the lake called Nipissing by the people whose canoes had skimmed its surface since before time was recorded. Day succeeded golden day, and Caroline's skill at portaging was equalled by the speed with which she made camp. When the boatman in the bow spotted a piece of promising shoreline and the big canoe headed for land, Caroline was up and out of the craft before it came to a full stop. She coaxed the coals to life with pine needles and bits of wood. As the fire flamed, she added one by one the logs the men brought to her. Two tents were pitched in the time it took her to bring the fire to the desired flame on which to cook the evening meal. No orders were issued, but everyone shared in whatever needed to be done, and then in the meal; coffee in tin mugs was handed round, and for those who wished, a bottle of rum was passed from hand to hand. Caroline loved to draw her knees up to her chest and wrap her arms about them, and listen to the men tell tales as wild and lovely as the land through which they travelled.

Two lovely days, warm and spring-like. I feel myself opening to the sun, just as the ground is. When I walked outside into brilliant sunshine, I thought: it must be like this inside God's mind... absolutely bright, clear and dazzling.

I heard an aria in *Philadelphia* sung by Maria Callas and it pierced me; I heard it in my being, not with my mind, but with my heart— a different kind of knowing. The Henry Moore exhibit at the Art Gallery triggered another kind of knowing. There are cabinets full of treasures he collected to work from, natural shapes... bones, shells, fossils, rocks and corals. I looked from this collection into the room where his sculptures are displayed, and the big room contained the shapes of the cabinet *writ large*. Do we humans contain the larger self (God) inside ourselves in the same fashion as the Moore display? Somehow the boundaries set by mind and reason must dissolve in order to let us see small perfect human shapes evolve into huge cosmic shapes. Do the angels give us access to knowledge (the tree of knowledge) but it is up to us to interiorize this knowledge, to translate knowledge into being? Did we eat of the tree of knowledge too soon... before we had been properly prepared? There is much meaning in the old myths, but how to read them?

CHAPTER TWO

They lived by the sun. As the great orange circle slipped beneath the earth's rim, the bedrolls were unbundled and paddlers and passengers alike threw the blankets that served as trade goods over heaps of fragrant boughs. Rarely was Caroline ready to sleep when the men retired for the night. She got into the habit of sleeping outside the tent. Some nights, as she lay on her bed of freshly cut pine boughs, Daniel would come unbidden and lie beside her; always a young Daniel, resplendent in his officer's dress uniform. She could not banish him this second time, and so she let him stay. With a shy, half-teasing smile, he would clasp her to his tunicked breast as she softened and melted in overlapping waves of desire. She opened her lips to let him kiss her but he ignored her mouth and kissed her hair and eyes and neck instead. His hands moved beneath her nightdress to the hardened tips of her breasts, and she arched to meet him. But as she pushed upward into emptiness, she remembered John and her marriage vows, and Daniel faded and receded to some distant place. Caroline faced the night alone, her aching body hunched inside its hot, flushed skin, staring up at the night sky, waiting to be relieved of thought by a dreamless sleep. In the beginning, she saw only vaulted blackness pierced by thousands of stars, some sharp and sparkling, some faint and misty, and some spread in a thin web across the sky. Her own longing paled beneath the immenseness of the heavens, and she lost herself among the countless stars above her head.

The nights when Daniel did not come or when he fled without touching her were not so unbearable now that she had the stars. A faint light would surface in the twilight and flame to a blue-white brightness in the purpled heavens, quickly followed by another and another until the whole sky displayed a cosmic splendour. Her eye traced flawlessly hundreds of star patterns, yet she was unable to name them or grasp their meaning, as though she looked at markings on an old map, at places she had been before but had forgotten. Awareness trembled on the fringes of her mind, of a memory she used to have and had somehow lost, and then, without warning, the memory would slip, evaporating into the curved black space of night and time. A sense of loss overcame her and she would fall into a troubled sleep, dreaming of things she could not summon in the light of day. The sun was high in the sky before she could shake off a terrible sense of bereavement.

The paddlers steered the canoe along the southern shore of the lake from one fir-tipped rocky point to another, ever mindful of the spirit of the lake which could quickly churn a placid shining surface into a wave-tossed trap. The cloudless weather persisted, the lake was far behind them, and they were but a day's paddle from the great bay which was the gateway to the north, a land that still belonged to those who could accommodate themselves to its harshness. Massive rocks thrust their pink crystal contents up along the shore, fracturing the sunlight into glassy fragments and throwing pieces into the green waters of Georgian Bay. Stone outcroppings crested the water, suggesting many more beneath the surface, and dark green fir trees stood duty on the granite islands. It was colder. Although the summer sun still shone brightly through the day, the nights were sharp and the rock and water declined to hold the heat. The landscape through which they paddled was stronger and less kind to travellers than the route they had followed to the bay. Caroline's old sense of urgency was rekindled by the increased tempo of the boatmen's strokes once they entered the bay. The boat flew through the unresisting water at a killing pace that continued until they heard the roar of the falls.

They landed with a flurry at the government dock in Sault Ste. Marie, and before the passengers and boatmen scattered to their various lodgings, one of them pointed out the customs office to Caroline.

"The customs officer might be able to suggest someone who would know what happened to the men from the fort on St. Joseph's Island. That's the way things get done up north. Somebody knows somebody who knows something. Not like the Army, where it's all written down."

Sault Ste. Marie had declined since its early days as a strategic military post and the center of the richly profitable fur trade. As Caroline made her way up the hill to the small frame building, everything looked shrunken and shabby. In the customs building, a pleasant older man, not unlike her father in appearance, listened to her story and read the three letters from Daniel she handed him.

"Your best bet, missus, is to try and get old Jimmy Big Fish to talk." He pointed out the starched figure of an Indian standing on the wharf. He was so still Caroline had not noticed him when they landed. For a moment, she wondered if he had just arrived, but she would have passed him on the path.

The official continued, "He's come here every year since forever.

According to him, his people guard the falls— sacred waters that the white man doesn't understand. He's probably crazy from the firewater those old Indians all drink, but he's your only hope of getting information about a soldier posted here all that time ago. No one else ever stays in town long enough to remember anything. Get yourself a bottle of whiskey from Lindsay's store, and make him talk before you hand it over. Good luck to you, ma'am."

Sometimes, mankind makes me sick. Imagine a coyote shoot in Quebec with prizes for the biggest, the best and the most beautiful dead coyotes. Their corpses are to be laid out in the local skating rink. I am having trouble with things being hurt. I saw a gorgeous nine-pound lake trout pulled up on the ice by a fisherman— alive and wonderful, tossed into a snowbank to gasp its life away. I hated it.

I went to a classmate's art show entitled "The Myth of the Seven Sisters (Madonnas)." It told of the lives of Italian peasant women. The show was, like their lives, both poignant and heartbreaking. One installation was a christening dress worked in lead; the bridal chamber was also worked in lead. There is a hint of endurance in the use of lead, and the will not to be broken, but also the reality of the heaviness and the dullness of their lives. Kartz has transformed the myth of her mother's life into her art... she has kept the symbols but changed the material. I am in awe of what Kartz has achieved in reworking the fabric of her mother's life.

I feel very nourished and warm, but life is running through my fingers at such a rapid pace. The look of the winter sun... the fierce blue of the winter sky; a big sky, they say. Sometimes things frighten me... how do some things happen? Do I will them? If so, I must be very careful. I feel very attractive inside... in love with life, with people, with language. I must be mindful not to appear too foolish. Imagine having to bottle up an excess of love for the world. Denis de Rougemont's *Love in the Western World* provides some insights into love in the courtly tradition. Love, as in sexual love, is the human route to spiritual love, the all-inclusive love that wants only the welfare of the beloved. This thesis was very dangerous to the Church. The Cathars in the thirteenth century practised this kind of spiritual love (woman-centered) and they spoke of it in the language of earthly love (the troubadours). It was a coded, secret language.

Time is curved space
If we walk a straight line
We will drop off the end of the world.

CHAPTER THREE

"Sir, excuse me. Are you Mr. Big Fish?"

Caroline was very unsure as to how to address him. She had never asked a favour of an Indian before. His narrow figure seemed rooted to the dock. He did not indicate by so much as a flicker of his black eyes that he had heard her speak. He remained as still and stiff as carved stone as she extended the bottle of whiskey towards him.

"If you could tell me. Have you ever heard of a Lieutenant Daniel Harris who was stationed here fifteen years ago? I'd give you this."

The bottle shook; she had to support its weight with both her hands. The Indian turned; his disgust for the bribe she offered scorched Caroline's face. "Who asks for Dan Harris?"

Polished specks, like mica, glittered in the black stones of his eyes. Caroline could not pull her eyes away. The ready reply— "His sister"— formed and was about to slide expertly from her lips, when she sensed his wariness. She caught the lie and relaxed her grip on the proffered bottle. It fell to the ground and rolled into the river. She faced him and answered his question without withdrawing her own direct gaze.

"His family wants to find him. His mother died not long ago and he should know."

"And you, why do you want Dan Harris?"

She pinkened under Jim Big Fish's scrutiny and answered herself as much as him. "I love Daniel Harris and have travelled many hundreds of miles to tell him this."

He was unmoved by her confession. He probed each angle of her face as he had before. She did not flinch.

"You wait here. I'll come back for you in three, maybe four days. We'll talk then."

He gazed once more at the white water jumping from the falls, and the interview was finished.

Days passed with exquisite slowness. Caroline walked and read and searched the river for any sign of the Indian's return. She would wait out the winter in Sault Ste. Marie, if need be, for the man to return and bring her news of Daniel. She never considered that he might not come back as he had promised.

Early one morning, she was startled from her sleep by a sound, and lay still, trying to identify the noise, a splash, like heavy rain on glass. She got to her feet and went to the window of her room. In the first light of day a tall straight figure was standing across from the hotel. As Caroline appeared in the window he stepped from the shadows and raised an arm, in greeting or command; it was not light enough to read the difference in his face. He disappeared in the direction of the town wharf. Caroline dressed, taking time only to wrap Daniel's letters and her mother's needlework into a tidy bundle and place them in her packed and ready valise. He was waiting at the river, and he was not alone. In the bow of the frailest canoe Caroline had ever seen sat an Indian woman of indeterminate age, who looked gravely at Caroline and uttered not a word. Jim Big Fish indicated by a wave of his hand that Caroline was to sit in the center of the light craft. She did so confidently, thankful for the skill she had gained in the weeks spent in the big canoe.

They were off before the sun had fully climbed over the eastern edge of the sky. By noon, the birch-bark canoe and its three occupants were skimming the waters of Lake Superior. Not one word had been exchanged. Caroline sat passively in the middle of the boat and watched dreamily as the canoe moved effortlessly over the transparent water, as if it had no weight or substance. The water was clearer than glass. The bottom of the lake was rocky and heaps of stone, piled not quite haphazardly one upon the other, appeared close to the surface. It seemed that if she had trailed one long finger in the water, she would have scraped the stones, and yet the blades of the two paddlers probed the water deeply and touched nothing.

For two days, they moved continuously west along the northern shore of the great lake, stopping when the sun began to fade and departing again at first light. Caroline was too tired at night to do more than eat the food the silent woman placed before her and then to fall asleep immediately. During the day, she hesitated to disturb their partnership and the rhythm of their paddles, and soon it didn't matter. Her questions and their imagined answers were forgotten.

Towards evening of the fourth or fifth day, the canoe veered to the right, towards the flat rock wall looming hugely above the surface of the lake. Markings on the wall took shape and form, and soon Caroline was close enough to see the paintings on the rock grow larger and become the outlines of birds and fish and animals. The thin craft found a slit in the granite wall and slipped in behind the monolithic rock, rippling to a halt. Caroline disembarked and followed the man's moccasined feet up the footholds he seemed to know by touch. The climb up the sheer rock face was too precarious to risk a backwards glance; Caroline felt the woman follow in her footsteps, and the threesome ascended the stone front of the wall in single file, gaining the summit, where the rock levelled out into a dark green line of trees. There was no stopping. The Indian continued through the trees along a path imperceptible to Caroline. She moved as quickly as she could, half running in her determination to keep his lean back in view. In spite of this effort, she lost him. Stopping to measure where she was, Caroline was conscious once again of the Indian woman beside her. She found herself in a small clearing circled by the black-barked spines of thickly planted fir trees. They walked on a needled carpet that cushioned the rock-hard surface of the granite. A mound of mossy green with a small cross surmounting it came unsummoned to her sight. The Indian woman spoke to Caroline for the first time: "You loved Daniel Harris."

The question was rhetorical. Beside the cross on the grassy mound, Caroline sank to her knees, buried her face in the soft green sides of the grave and wept for her lost love. Nokomo knelt beside Caroline and gently stroked her hair. Each stroke was accompanied by a word or phrase uttered so softly that Caroline was uncertain whether she heard the story from the woman's lips or only imagined it through her fingertips.

Long ago, when the world was fresh and new, there were just two stars shining in the heavens. One star was larger and brighter than the other, and the people called this star the sun; the other star, though not as bright and not as large as the first, warmed the earth with its light all the same. This smaller star the people called the moon. The earth was green and rich with growing things because there was never any darkness or winter. The people did not know what it meant to be cold or hungry, for when the sun went to bed, the moon came out, and with her smaller flame, she warmed the land. The people were very content and happy.

One day when the sun star was at its brightest, the moon maiden who lived with her mother, moon, asked permission to visit the earth and learn the ways of the people. At first, the moon refused to allow her daughter to leave; she feared for her daughter's safety. But the poor girl was so unhappy with her lonely life and pleaded so pitifully that finally her mother relented and gave her consent for the girl to visit just one village.

"You may stay with them as long as my light remains warm and bright, but when you hear the people of the village complain of the cold, you will know it is

time for you to return to me. With the last sparks of my dying fire I will shoot a moonbeam across the heavens to carry you home, and your light will nourish my flames. Together, our light will grow strong and we will once more warm the earth. Promise me, when the moonbeam comes for you, you will leave the earth and return to your place in the heavens."

"Yes, mother, I promise."

The moon maiden was so happy that she hugged her mother tightly, and the people paused in their work, looking up into the sky, wondering why it had grown as bright as day. While they watched, a small luminous star shot across the heavens and a great shout went up, for surely this portended something momentous. The star disappeared from view, and the moon's light shone clearly and steadily, as it had always done. All the people forgot what they had seen, except those in the village where the moon maiden went to live. This was the village of my tenth father. The moon maiden was so beautiful and gracious that she enchanted everyone. She taught my people the secrets of the heavens and we, in turn, taught her the ways of the tribes. Our village prospered more than those of the other tribes and soon the word of Moon Star's (for that was what my people called her) visit spread and the other tribes grew jealous and wanted her to live with them. Most of all, they wanted the secrets she had told our tribe. For the first time, there were rumblings of discontent among the villages, and Moon Star was sorry at the trouble she was causing my people. There was no sign of her mother's light dimming, and the earth was as warm and green as when she had first come, but Moon Star was frightened.

She went alone to the shore of the great lake near my tenth father's village, trying to think how she could avert the tragedy of tribe fighting against tribe that she knew would come if she stayed on earth. It was while she sat by the edge of the water, lost in thoughts of the unhappiness she was creating among her friends, that a beaver, logging on the shore, felt the swirling currents of her misery. He left his partly felled tree and swam to Moon Star's side. She told him the story of the almost warring tribes and he offered her his help. He told her of a wondrous tall tree with beautiful blue-green needles, the tallest tree he had ever seen in the forest, rising almost to the roof of the world, and he offered to take her there so she could climb to its highest branches and wave to attract the moon's attention. Meanwhile, a fish swimming nearby overheard Moon Star's story, and put forth the suggestion that the moon maiden clothe herself in the silver scales that covered the fish's body and swim in the moon's reflection on the surface of the big lake, and in that way draw her mother's eye to her plight. Moon Star placed her long white arms about them both and drew them close.

"Thank you for your kindness, but mother's light is still so bright, Fish, that there is almost no reflection on the water. As for Beaver's tree, I would have to wait for many lifetimes before the tallest tree in the forest could lift me high enough in the heavens for mother to notice me. I was selfish. I never should have come to visit the people."

Her lovely luminous eyes filled with pearly tears and she wept for the wars she knew would come.

Meanwhile, a spider, who had been busily weaving on a nearby branch, dropped a silken line beside the shell-like ear of Moon Star, and whispered her solution to the stricken girl.

"I could spin a web from the topmost branch of Beaver's wondrous blue spruce tree and you could wrap yourself in a shining cloak of Fish's silver scales. Then you could climb ever so carefully into my web and swing to and fro in the sky. Surely your mother would notice such a bright sparkling object flying back and forth in the empty heavens, and come to investigate."

This was the best idea of all, and Moon Star felt a glimmer of hope that the coming tragedy could be avoided. But first, she said, she would wait one more week, and trust her mother to send the moonbeam for her.

Moon Star had barely set out on the trail that led to the village of my tenth father when she was confronted by a breathless deer who blurted out a tale of treachery and evil. Moon Star was to be kidnapped by a neighbouring tribe, and held captive until she revealed the mysteries of the heavens. The trap was waiting for Moon Star at the next turn in the trail.

She could linger on the earth no longer. Moon Star fled to the shore of the great lake where her friends waited, and between them they put the spider's plan into action. Clothed in her sparkling silver dress, Moon Star climbed to the top of the giant spruce tree and met the spider, who had just finished spinning her finest web, as strong as the string of the hunter's bow and as light as the down in the milkweed's pod. The web hung from the top branch of the tree like an enormous teardrop. Moon Star, enshrouded in the silver coat, stepped gingerly onto the web; the motion caused the fragile lines to move, and as she lowered herself into the center of the silken mass, the web, with Moon Star clinging to its threads, began to revolve. Slowly, and then with gathering speed, it exploded with light. Her friends, waiting on the ground, held their breath. As they watched, the moon caught sight of this strange magnificent object shooting lights across her heavens and she advanced majestically across the sky to investigate. The beaver, the spider and the fish breathed easier as they saw their plan begin to work.

However, Moon Star's dramatic appearance in the heavens had drawn other watchers, one of whom had waited in the woods to capture her. This one, cheated of his prize, pulled out an arrow, feathered in white, and fit it to the tensed string of his hunter's bow. Her friends by the shore looked on in horror as the arrow sped across the sky and lodged in the scales of Moon Star's silver breast. By this time, the moon was close enough to the whirling shining disc to recognize her daughter's face, but she was too far away to save Moon Star from plummeting in a tail of silver sparks into the very center of the big lake. She raced to the place where Moon Star had plunged into the water and searched the smooth surface frantically for the face of her beloved daughter, but Moon Star was gone. Her mother saw only her own pale reflection streaking the water. There was a terrible tearing sound, and then the world went black. The moon meant to punish the people for the death of her daughter. She extinguished all her lamps. The terrible tearing sound, so my tenth father said, was the sound of her heart breaking.

"Let them feel cold and hunger and watch their children die, as I am cold and hunger for the sight of my only child."

From the heavens came a shower of pure white shells that fell over the lake, and the people said the moon was shedding tears on the watery grave of Moon Star.

The soft dark eyes of the storyteller studied the spent form of the woman crumpled on the ground and continued with her story.

My people believe that even though the moon saw the mortally wounded body of her daughter plunge into the icy water of the great lake, she still hopes one day to find Moon Star, and each month she lights one small lamp and searches the waters. When she does not find Moon Star, she lets her light dim and fade until her hope springs alive once more, and then she begins her journey across the night sky to the lake. We believe, as she believes, that one day she will find Moon Star, and mother and daughter will be reunited. When that day comes, she will light all her lamps and banish cold and darkness from the earth.

I AM ENJOYING being a watcher and a listener. This morning, I heard the sound of brakes being applied sharply. It evoked a clear memory of New York in June. I walked by the school where both Michael and David had been students, and the boys playing soccer on an October morning were repeating a timeless pattern. Only the natural world requires a time dimension. I understood for the first time something about "out of time." That scene just was and is and will be. Humans see through a time filter; angels don't. In their realm, light and flight are the defining features; time is non-existent.

Andrea and I are having a lovely time... much like having a soft breeze touch your face... no one is in charge; we are just here, the two of us in this beautiful place. Perhaps for the first time since I met her I am beginning to know the real her. How it must have hurt and confused her for me, her mother, not to know her. I was the child; she, the mother. Tears well up inside my eyes for the little girl I never let be herself. From pink dresses and hairbows to dollhouses, I tried to make her into a paper cutout of what I thought a little girl should be. She must have been very strong inside to survive... she knew her own essence and fought like hell to hold on to it. Why can't we learn these lessons young? Thank God I am learning them now. We are just two women linked by blood who love each other, learning about who the other is. I guess the Christmas hurt had to happen or I could not learn. That angel was carrying a cudgel.

CHAPTER FOUR

Nokomo looked at her companion, who had fallen into a deep sleep. When Caroline awakened, the woman rose from her position alongside the grassy mound and beckoned to Caroline.

"Come with me."

Those were her words, but Caroline heard promises from the ground that lay between them. She followed the slender figure deeper into the woods, pausing only when the woman did. They entered a second clearing, smaller than the one before. This enclosure, too, held a mossy grave. The woman knelt beside this mound, and Caroline asked, "Who?"

"My daughter," was the reply.

And Caroline felt the tie of kinship that only blood and grief can really share. She crouched beside the woman and placed her pale hand over the golden one, kneading the ground of her daughter's grave.

"I am so sorry."

And without thinking she placed her hand on the woman's head and stroked her hair.

In place of a wooden cross, this grave was marked by a heap of small white shells. The woman took one polished shell from its thick pad of moss and placed it in the palm of Caroline's hand.

"Hope," was all she said, and closed Caroline's fingers around the shell. The women smiled shyly at one another and stood up, brushing bits of moss and pine needles from their clothing. They walked together from the clearing, through the trees and down the less steep side of the granite bluff. The woman set a punishing pace, but Caroline, with her lightened, empty heart, had no trouble keeping up.

They arrived at the village tucked into the curve of the lake before the sun had completely sunk beneath the western rim of the lake. Dogs barked and raced between the tents, knocking dark-eyed children and cooking utensils to the ground. The black-haired women who tended the cooking fires only smiled and replaced the fallen child or pot to its original position, but their eyes watched the two women who walked side by side through the middle of the camp. Caroline stopped when her friend stopped and waited while she lifted a blanket which served as a door to a sleeping tent. A young girl appeared, hunched in the doorway, straightening as she recognized the woman who called her. She was a girl Caroline had seen before, a girl with shiny sleek hair that sprang back from her head like wings, and a complexion tinted the colour of an evening sunset. Her eyes were clear as water as she smiled at Caroline and extended a slim golden hand, which Caroline took as if in a dream. From outside the charmed circle created by the two of them, she heard the voice of her friend.

"This is my daughter's daughter, and your Daniel's."

Caroline heard her own voice speak as if from a great distance. "What is your name, child?"

"The people of my mother's tribe call me Waussnodae, but my father called me Sophie."

I am just here in this lovely spot... enjoying it and myself, and in doing so I please the gods. This is what they wish for us, not mindless joy, but conscious joy... to be fully here, in this beauty.

Lines for the beginning of something: "She was here for the second half of her journey, although 'here' may be too generous a word: 'more here,' perhaps. The first half just slipped away in a splendour of things and children. She had nothing to show for the time she had spent but a few poems, a cabin in the woods, and a knowledge that all this is about something bigger."

I am watching this woman learn... as Rilke says, "more than this single life."

CHAPTER FIVE

Caroline settled into the rhythm of life in the camp as if she had been born to it, the same rhythm had run through her life in Fergus, and if she thought further back, it had been there in Perth. For the most part, the camp was a community of women, the men being absent for long periods on hunting trips. Caroline was comfortable with the routines of women. Cooking, cleaning, and caring for their children were as timeless as the women themselves. Then, too, the camp lived on sun time, as Caroline had on the journey west. Each morning, when the pink light washed the birch-bark lining of her tent, she rose from her pallet of pine boughs and walked to the lake, where she quietly took her place beside the other women, adjusting her movements to theirs as they gave order to the camp. But it was Sophie who made her feel at home, and it was to Sophie that Caroline looked for instruction. A glance, a lifted hand, a smile was all the encouragement Caroline needed.

Each day Caroline grew more confident and ventured farther from the camp in search of wood for the endless feeding of the cooking fires. Some days she, not Sophie, would grind the corn and fill the iron kettle with what would become that day's meal, and Sophie would leave the circle of the camp to forage for wood and cut fresh boughs for their sleeping pallets. Both she and Sophie took turns carrying water from the lake, and tending to the curing fish in the communal smokehouse. There was one task they always shared. When the sun reached the place in the sky where it could climb no higher, Sophie appeared wherever Caroline was working, a reed basket dangling from each slim arm. She beckoned to Caroline, and the two of them would leave camp and slip into the thick dark forest that came to very edge of the village.

It seemed a random choice of which of the many narrow paths that laced the woods around the camp, but it was always the girl who chose and led. They filled their baskets with the plants and berries that grew in profusion in the late summer. Each carried a small knife and Sophie showed Caroline how to strip the paper-thin bark in sheets from the birches without injuring the trees. The rolls of birch bark, Sophie explained, were essential: they were shaped into canoes for transportation, and circled around poles for shelter; containers were made to store food, and they recorded their history on birch-bark scrolls.

They talked but little as they worked, speaking only to exchange information on the usefulness of certain of the plants they gathered. Of the future, they spoke not at all. Once, Caroline did probe the past, and asked the girl about her parents. They were collecting driftwood on the shore, following the curved line of the lake, when a sudden motion of Sophie's reminded Caroline so much of Daniel that she gasped. As the girl turned with her arms filled with wood she might have been a younger Daniel come back to offer Caroline his gift of Christmas greenery. The question Caroline had hoped never to ask of Sophie escaped.

"What was your mother like?" Caroline stopped abruptly, hand to her mouth and wide-eyed with distress at what she'd asked, but the girl seemed unperturbed. She repeated the question.

"What was mother like?"

Sophie paused, as if everyone should know what her mother looked like, or as if she could not remember. "Mother," she said again, as if the word could conjure up the face.

"Mother was tall and slender, not unlike you, Caroline. She had a very gentle face and the kindest voice. She loved my father, as you did. I think when he died, she did, too, only we didn't bury her right away. I missed her very much until you came."

The sleek wings of Sophie's hair curved forward as she spoke, covering her face. At the place where she uttered the words, "until you came," she lifted her head and swung the glossy strands away from her face, proferring a shy smile. It was a lovely gift. Caroline reached out to touch the girl's cheek.

The days filled and overflowed into nights circled around fires where the charmed tongues of the grandmothers unfolded the memories of the past. All the women knew the legends of their people, but Nokomo gave life to the stories told in Sophie's village. When Nokomo told of the beginnings of the first people, she became Mother Earth; her voice sank to rich moist depths and listeners heard the voice of the land itself. When Nokomo shrieked the cry of the eagle denied its prey, and howled the hunger of the wolf pack in winter, the dogs slunk inside the circle of firelight, and the soft skin on the inner arms of those who listened retracted and froze. Late at night, when the bright-eyed children had fallen asleep in their tents, Nokomo spoke to those who stayed to stare into the red-eyed coals of the banked fire, telling of the Wendigo, the spirit man who stalked winter camps in search of human flesh. Her dropped voice echoed the hollow sound of his footsteps as he hunted in the haunted white landscape. When the cooking fires had cooled and died and hunger had reduced the people, the Wendigo appeared in the land and tracked the weak, the timid and the lonely to their winter lodges. Nokomo's listeners shrank inside themselves and drew nearer to the dying fire. And each looked around the circle and wondered if she might be the spirit man's victim in the coming winter.

The village treasured Nokomo's wisdom and her knowledge of what had gone before, and they treasured her as she unwound the mysteries of life and death in the legends of the Ojibwa people. The puzzle of existence was examined and illuminated nightly in the glow of the fire. Nokomo had the knack of telling a story so that, to each who heard, a different meaning was revealed. Caroline was as spellbound as any of the women; she laughed when they laughed and shivered when they did, but none could match the concentration Sophie gave to Nokomo and her stories. Sophie, straightbacked and cross-legged in the firelight, was mesmerized by the magic in her grandmother's voice. Sophie listened with her whole body to each shadow and shading of meaning; to Sophie the legends of her people were as essential as the food she ate.

Caroline eyed the stars in the night sky as Nokomo told the stories and wondered if Nokomo knew the meaning in their patterns. One night when everyone but Nokomo and Caroline had gone to bed, Caroline drew Nokomo's attention to the uncountered clusters of stars, some mere slivers of light and some as clear and brilliant as mirrored glass. There was no moon to distract their eyes from the spangled field of stars that roofed the sky, and Caroline soon lost herself in the beauty and vastness of the scene. Nokomo's musical voice commented on the panorama that played above their heads. She pointed out the constellations.

"Look, Caroline! Do you see the Great Bear of my ancestors fleeing across the sky?"

And Caroline, following Nokomo's fluent fingers, saw the outline of a bear grow before her eyes. She laughed softly at the discovery and mused aloud. "Why was he never there before, Nokomo?"

"He was always there." She directed Caroline's eyes lower in the southern sky. "There, do you see the Seven Hunters waiting for the Great Bear?"

At Caroline's nod, she continued.

"They have stalked the Great Bear through the spring sky since the Great Spirit gave them life and still he flees before them. It is not to be."

Caroline smiled at Nokomo's interpretation and Nokomo spoke once more.

"You are wise to look to the sky, Caroline, for the legends of my people say, while it is the roof of our world, in the world beyond, it is reality. If we wish to know their secrets we must learn to read their signs, and their signs, Caroline, are in the sky. All knowledge of the other world is written in the stars. Do not neglect the stars, Caroline, for they hold the undistorted patterns of the past which are our future. And as their world reveals its truths to us in star maps, our world etches its truths in nature's patterns." Nokomo's voice became more urgent and demanded Caroline's full attention. She reluctantly withdrew her gaze from the magic of the night sky to face Nokomo.

"Caroline, the patterns were created and chalked in the sky long before there were people on the earth. Just as the hunters must stalk the Great Bear and he must flee, we, too, must follow the celestial pattern, or it will fade and die and live only in our legends."

The black velvet sky with its embroidered pattern of stars stirred a faint memory in Caroline, and as she moved to touch one starlit thread, it disappeared, leaving her breathless with the closeness of her recall. She no longer heard Nokomo's words, so thrilling was the longing that engaged her soul.

How uncommonly important the correct use of language is. Each word must say what it means and keep its integrity, or the lines blur and mist and the meaning shifts and some unscrupulous purveyor of language can abuse this trust. It is a constant watch.

My body is saying nice things to me... it is very fit and lean. Too much Bermuda could do one in... it is so beautiful. Where is its dark side? I can see myself in the Bermuda of the tourist brochure, the lovely daughter, the perfect wife, the good mother. Look deeper, touch the raging, the erotic, the earthy, the envious, the huge cave-like Ruth. That is where the power lies, not in that passive mealy-mouthed female who apes the patriarchal system. The dark Ruth screams when wounded, roars when hurt, and loves passionately. She does not think of consequences or tomorrow. Death is better than being conquered. The dark side of women's lives is told in their diaries and journals, not in the stories men write about us. Men wrote what they wished to read: "the good little woman, tamed and domesticated." I want to write the wild side, about women who go down to the depths of the sea to retrieve their souls.

CHAPTER SIX

One morning Caroline woke before the camp, leaving a sleeping Sophie in their tent, to find the landscape transformed. A glittering net had dropped in the night from the heavens, dressing the earth in a fine coat of silver threads. She moved towards the lake, leaving dark footprints on the frosted ground and clouds of breath in the clear sharp air.

The pleasant rhythm of the summer camp was broken by the onset of frost, and for the first time Caroline felt uneasy there. The women worked harder and faster, collecting, harvesting and storing in birch-bark containers all that could be used for food. The men became more visible around the camp, dragging the frail canoes high on the beach and examining each seam for weakness or tears. Caroline was swept along in the current of activity, and her initial discomfort paled in the excitement generated by the coming change.

One group after another loaded their canoes with their share of the communal food and dispersed with little fanfare to undisclosed wintering grounds. Each group left according to some ancient timetable chosen by the senior hunter in that extended family. Some families stayed close to the mouths of the many rivers that emptied into the big lake and hoped the storms that blew from the huge expanse of water would not be too severe; others ventured inland to take their chances on surviving the cold and darkness that was to come, by portaging to a place where the hunting had proved successful in other winters. The people scattered during the time of cold and ice, thereby increasing the odds of their survival; when the warmth of the spring sun released the earth from the snow, the people and the land would once more be reunited.

At last it was the turn of Jim Big Fish, Nokomo, Sophie and Caroline to leave the camp. They made up a third of the families in four canoes. Jim was the senior hunter in their group and he still hunted with a bow and arrows, the traditional weapon of his people, preferring their results to those brought by the guns so many of his brothers now used. The game that had been so plentiful in his youth had been slaughtered indiscriminately; settlers often killed more with their guns than could be eaten. Jim had to go farther and farther from the village in search of the deer that provided the staples of life. Jim had discovered the place where they would winter on one of his extended hunting trips last summer. Sophie showed Caroline where the deer had made hoof-packed runs between the trees, a good sign.

Caroline was too burdened by her pack and the need to follow the twisting trail to give more than a passing glance to her surroundings. Her plodding feet were in heavy contrast to Sophie's, who danced along the path, taking in every point of interest and never missing a step with her moccasined feet although they walked along a granite ridge that rimmed the short side of the rectangular lake fifty feet below the ridge. Ice formed a thin skin on the water's surface, and pine and spruce covered the area around the lake. Sophie stopped and waited for Caroline to catch up before she pointed at a stand of trees to the right of the path. Caroline followed Sophie's outstretched arm and saw nothing. She narrowed her eyes, hoping this would help her focus, but nothing more than trees surfaced, until Sophie whispered, "Look over there, by the tall birch tree. He's heard us."

As Caroline's untutored eye scanned the stand of birch, she was at last able to distinguish the broad rack of the stag's antlers from the overhanging branches. She drew her breath in sharply at the sight of the magnificent animal and stared. When Sophie touched her softly on the arm, she withdrew her gaze and heard the girl say, "Let's leave him be, shall we?"

Jim Big Fish had chosen well. The deer were plentiful and the cooking pot was always full. When Caroline remembered time, she thought perhaps they had wintered half the season, but she had no idea how long winter lasted in this distant place. On days when the sun made a veiled appearance, Sophie would draw Caroline from the warm oblivion of the lodge and lead her through waist-deep drifts until they reached the shelter of the woods, where the hooves and pads of animals packed down the snow and made their passage easier. Deer and fox and rabbit used the paths that Sophie and Caroline walked, and the girl showed the woman the faint bird-like track of a fieldmouse, to where it ended in two drops of blood. Sophie raised her head and scanned the snowy forest until she saw the pillowed outline of a great white owl perched stationary on the top of a jagged tree, and she pointed him out to Caroline. The world had lost its colour and its shape. Without Sophie to guide her, Caroline would never have found her way back to the lodge.

Caroline spotted a bundle on the ice; she watched it heave convulsively and stop. She called to Sophie, and together they descended the ridge to the edge of the frozen lake. The deer was young; this year's fawn, a female, whose left hind leg had fallen through a weakness in the ice, lay trapped and helpless. Every so often she thrashed and kicked and tried to free the fallen limb. The smooth thickness of the ice gave no purchase to her efforts. As Caroline and Sophie neared, they read the fear in her large dark eyes. She made one last effort to free herself and failed, and seemed to recede into the gray-brown shelter of her coat. Sophie ventured gingerly onto the ice. When it held, she went farther until she stood above the fallen deer. Caroline followed more cautiously, and as she reached the far side of the deer, Sophie lay down on the ice and motioned Caroline to do the same. Between the two, they managed to free the animal's leg from the iron circle of the ice and slide her carefully to shore. She made no move to gain her feet; her rescuers took turns carrying the young animal to the safety of the lodge, where Sophie sank beside the deer and tried to warm her with her body.

Nokomo came to see what they had found, and knelt and probed the injured leg with a sure touch. The young deer's trembling lessened. Nokomo disappeared and returned with a bowl containing a mixture of grain and herbs and a warm liquid which she placed beside the animal.

"Try and get some of this into her. She needs her strength to fight the cold and the shock of being handled by humans. I don't think she has frozen that back leg. She should survive. Wrap her in this and keep her warm."

Nokomo handed Sophie an old worn deerskin. Sophie, who had not released her hold on the fawn since entering the lodge, took the skin from her grandmother and said passionately, "I'll feed her and look after her. I'll make her live." She tightened her grip on the soft gray fur. Nokomo's eyes sought Caroline's and held them for a long moment.

Caroline found the communal living conditions imposed by the confines of the lodge disturbing. Smoke filtered to the farthest corners of the room, stung her eyes and made her cough. No less irritating was the constant presence of eleven other humans and one dark-eyed baby hanging in a cradle board above their heads. Caroline swore he watched each move she made. Sophie and Nokomo did not mind the crowded stuffy atmosphere; they both threw back their heads and roared with laughter when Caroline complained of the baby spying on her.

On days when the wind and snow made outside trips all but impossible, Nokomo would entertain them with stories of the First People. At first, it seemed she was singing to herself or chanting to the solemn baby; but she was drawing everyone from the corners of the lodge with the magic in her voice. When the words, "Long, long, ago, in the days before the people walked on the earth," floated like smoke across the hazy interior of the lodge, even the serious baby smiled at his own good fortune.

The young animal grew stronger day by day, and soon humans could touch her without triggering the violent spasms of fear she had shown when Sophie and Caroline first found her. Although she tolerated the others, it was Sophie's company she sought, and the girl often listened to Nokomo's stories with the deer curled at her feet. Each day Sophie would leave the smoky warmth of the lodge to collect the sprigs of cedar and bits of bark that the animal loved. Since the rescue of the deer, the weather had been ferocious, with the winds hurtling snow and pellets of ice across the lake at great speed, slowing only slightly when darkness fell. Caroline stayed inside, no longer irritated by the smoke-filled room, and waited for the storm to end. In fourteen days, only Sophie and the three men had ventured outside; the men to check their traplines, and the girl to forage for her pet. The herd of deer that had promised so much to the Indians on their arrival at their winter camp had vanished, and the hunters' traps yielded nothing, as if the violence of the storm had driven away all life but that huddled in the lodge.

Caroline, who had never experienced hunger, began to feel the desperation, and thought of food constantly. The baby still hung stiffly in his cradle board, but no longer did the bright button eyes follow Caroline around. Instead, a listless cry seeped along with the smoke into the dim interior of the lodge. On the fifth night, the hunters again returned with nothing, and the storm still howled wildly outside the lodge. Caroline overheard Nokomo talking with Jim while the others slept.

"You and the men will have to go to the hunting grounds by the big river. There is nothing for us here."

"Nokomo, this morning we could hardly find our way back down the ridge, so wild was the wind and blowing snow... but you are right, there is no other way. I'll leave Feathered Arrow to guard the lodge, and we'll go at first light."

Caroline saw the woman shake her head. "Jim, take both hunters with you. You must find food and you will need the strength of three men to carry it back."

"And how will you feed the women and children while we are gone?"

She fixed him with the full force of her bottomless black eyes and replied, "Don't you think of that, Jim Big Fish. I'll keep our people alive until you return."

Caroline fell into a troubled sleep in which she and Nokomo stumbled without rest through thick drifts of snow, searching for a bright-eyed baby swinging from the branches of a tree always just ahead of them. As they came closer and reached to lift the baby from its perch, the branches became the antlers of a giant stag that vanished into the swirling snow with the baby dangling perilously from his horns. She woke unsatisfied by her sleep and disturbed by her dream. She sought Sophie, and was dismayed to find her sleeping place already vacant. Caroline stepped across the women to gain access to the covered entrance of the lodge. She would have ventured out into the blizzard if Nokomo had not prevented her.

"Waussnodae has gone to find food for the animal, Caroline. I, too, am waiting for her return. She will be fine."

The skin covering the entrance to the lodge lifted and wind and snow whipped through and raked the waiting women.

"This is the cruellest day of the storm. The wind lashes the snow against your face like pebbles. I could only get a handful of boughs for Shadow."

"That is more than your own people will eat today, Waussnodae."

Caroline stroked the snow-coated strands of Sophie's hair with chilled fingers.

Nokomo drew a hunting knife from the folds of her soft leather skirt and lifted Sophie's head from where she had hidden it in Caroline's lap.

"It must be done, and quickly. That baby won't live through the day without nourishment."

Nokomo looked directly into the girl's tear-filled eyes, and spoke softly. "Waussnodae, you are the only one who can save us from the Wendigo. Do not let the spirit of your mother's people die because you cannot do what must be done." She placed the long slim blade in Sophie's rigid fingers. "My daughter's daughter, help us."

Nokomo rose from her kneeling position by the entrance and made her way to the fire.

Caroline could hardly grasp what she had heard. Not only was the child to lose her pet, but she was to be the instrument of its death. It was inhuman. Caroline moved to where Nokomo sat impassively in front of the fire and begged.

"Let me do it, Nokomo. She loves that animal, and she is too young to have to do this thing. Let me."

Nokomo's worn face looked compassionately at Caroline, but her haunting voice inked lines on Caroline's face.

"If that was all there was to this, I would kill the deer myself. This must be Sophie's gift to her people, given of her own free will."

ANGELS ARE genderless, weightless and colourless, but they clothe themselves in gender, weight, and colour in order to enter our world... angelic camouflage. Their world is light and clear. Imagine functioning without the weight of sex and substance. They come, I think, to teach us how to convert knowledge (words) into being (flesh)... the word made flesh. You work and work and think nothing is happening and suddenly you really understand, in your body, something you have heard all your life, but not felt. The word made flesh, that is what Christ brought to us. He showed us that knowledge can be transformed into being, right here, right now. Just as our bodies lose moisture as we age and become dry and brittle, so do our souls. We must constantly apply what Shakespeare calls "heavenly dew" to keep our souls from drying out and cracking. We must literally bathe ourselves in "heavenly dew." What is this "heavenly dew?"

It is so difficult to write one's inner life, but to write it in code is almost impossible. Adrienne Rich writes it best. I use her *The Fact of a Doorframe* like a map, a guide to a foreign country. Maybe my own poetry will bring some answers. A close relationship is something I cannot live without... the hollow lady is not for me. What one pays for a close relationship is the self—the sublimation of myself in my children. They become the creative works. I am becoming more sensual in my middle years, more aware of my skin, my mouth, my breasts, as if I am finding something new inside all that middle-class clothing and morality.

"Becoming conscious is an unnatural act," said Adrienne Rich.

I wonder what happens to Mike and I. We have such a long history, but so much is separating us, a gulf too great to throw my arms across. Tears trickle down my cheeks. I don't want this to happen, but I can't stop it. I am standing on the edge and I am afraid to look, but the net must go.

CHAPTER SEVEN

The weather changed, not so much as a coming of spring but more as a shrivelling of winter. The icy air hovering over the lodge by the lake was pushed aside by lively puffs of wind carrying the scent of fresh uncovered earth and opened water. Ragged patches of soaked snow in the shaded northern edges of the clearing yielded daily to the heat in the noon-high sun. There was food in the camp. The half-remembered fear of hunger, centered in the pits of people's stomachs, shrank with the snow.

Sophie showed the most effects of the winter's ordeal. She had grown very tall and lean, and with this spurt of growth, she had pulled inside herself. Sophie emerged into the spring sunshine, honed and hardened to a cutting brilliance. Caroline no longer accompanied her on daily excursions away from camp, and as the days lengthened, so did Sophie's absences. Caroline sensed the girl's need for solitude, and had to resist her own need to intrude in Sophie's life. Caroline was acutely aware whenever Sophie slipped away from the lodge, but she never raised her head or indicated how distressed she was by Sophie's departure.

Sophie had come to hate the confines of the lodge. Someone or something always cried for her attention. Part of her longed to run away and never return, and part of her knew that it was impossible. Now, she could wander in the woods by herself, and pretend she lived alone. Each day she travelled further and returned later, until one day, with night about to fall, Sophie discovered she was miles from the ridge bordering the northern boundary of their lake. She could not find her way back in the dark. Sophie had been daring this to happen, and the prospect was pleasurable. Hunger was not a problem. Sophie had trained her body, since the horrible time when the people in the lodge were eating Shadow, to accept smaller portions of food taken at longer intervals. She had not tasted one morsel of the deer; she had existed without food for five days and nights, and Caroline had been certain she would die.

Sophie's immediate concern was for shelter. She was wearing only the light clothing of the day traveller; the days were warm, but the nights of early spring stung. While there was still enough light, Sophie stripped several small spruce trees of their lower branches and heaped them inside a circle of piled rocks. Inside her stone shelter, Sophie was protected from the wind and insulated from the flat cold of the granite by the springy thickness of the spruce boughs. The darkness was not as unnerving as she had expected; the silence was. With the coming of night, it was as though a blanket had been thrown over the land, muffling any sound. Her ears probed vast stretches of stillness. Each nerve stood ready to receive the faintest signal, but nothing disturbed the silence, and in the total darkness, not the palest glimmer of light from a distant star slid through the deep blackness. Sophie drifted in and out of sleep, straining to keep alert. Even so, she missed the arrival of the great bird. His powerful wings spread across the night sky like passing clouds, and his passage was hushed by the thickness of a thousand feathers. He glided to a halt on the edge of the rocky nest where Sophie slept, and tucked his head beneath one folded wing.

Sophie woke, or thought she woke, to an enchanted landscape. The snow hung thick and soft, but did not fall, and the ground was dead and stripped of vegetation, white, but not with snow, and windless. Light came from beneath the ground and made her feet and legs seem luminous. She wandered over fields of desolation and a stab of loneliness pierced her breast; she found herself stumbling and crying. She lay down and closed her eyes and she was warm and enfolded in great white wings and she was almost happy. It was a struggle to wake a second time, and the landscape was the same, but not. A sense of danger permeated the land, breathing peril while Sophie waited. Menaced, hunted and stalked by an unknown predator, all she had to fight with was her will to live and a single white feather that had floated to the barren earth. Sophie's lean brown body tensed and flattened on the smooth face of the ground; her ears curved forward and heard the rush of air expelled by the hunter. Her clear gray eyes darkened to the mirrored black of polished granite and narrowed for the fight. She lay still, hardly breathing, unwilling to reveal her position until she saw her adversary. He strode into view and loomed over her. His strong taut body nearly defeated her resolve. She wanted him, but his face saved her. The hunter wore a mask of moonlight, cruel and cold and illuminated by a phosphorescence from somewhere in his skull. His sockets, in a fleshless face of stone and bone, saw everything and nothing; he was relentless, an eater of souls. She froze, and chose to live: hands clawed, teeth bared, and eyes alive with knowledge. He paused, confused by the obstacle standing in his path, and was maddened when he understood it was his crouching prey that faced him, one on one. The rigid curve of bone delineating the empty sockets arched, and he reached for the bow and arrows slung across his back. It was too late. Sophie pounced and ripped the carved stone mask from his skull. He screamed with rage and loss, covered the gaping hole with empty hands, and slunk away. Her talons lost their sharpness and returned to fingered flesh, and her fury folded like great wings back inside her slender female frame. Tears trembled but did not fall from her transparent eyes, now flecked with black. When at last sleep came to Sophie, she dreamt no more.

The skins of the winter's fur harvest were washed and stretched and tacked to wooden frames for drying in the sun, and on the lake, the hunters tested the water worthiness of their canoes. Mist was still clinging in cobweb thin shreds to the trees when Sophie appeared in the clearing. The women stopped and the men put down their paddles, letting their canoes drift, as Sophie strode through the lifting mist with the great bird perched on her wrist, his smooth head curved forward like the bow of a boat. Those on shore fell back at her approach. Caroline, who longed to throw her arms about the missing girl, was hesitant to break the spell cast by Sophie and the bird. Nokomo, gaunt with the winter's hunger and still hollow-faced in spite of plenty, went to meet the girl.

Nokomo looked keenly into the face of her granddaughter and held her with her eyes. "You have seen in the forest with the eyes of a shaman, my daughter's daughter, and you have triumphed. Well done, Waussnodae."

When she grasped her granddaughter by both arms, a tremor rippled through the body of the bird, but he remained on Sophie's wrist, encircled by the arms of the two women.

"Come," Nokomo said. And she drew Sophie towards the entrance of the lodge. Sophie touched the great bird gently on the head before she straightened her arm and flung him skyward. He faltered, then launched himself with an immense surge of power from his outstretched wings. He circled the lodge and then spiralled higher until the human eye could follow him no longer. One by one, those on the beach resumed their chores until only Caroline stood motionless, face tilted to the sky, looking to where the bird had been and wondering what it was that she had witnessed.

In the bluish haze of the lodge, Nokomo indicated with a nod that Sophie was to place herself where Nokomo usually sat. She uncovered an otterskin bag from its concealed position near her sleeping pallet and pulled a deerskin bundle from its mouth. She took the bundle and placed it in front of Sophie. Nokomo opened it and handed items, one at a time, to Sophie. When all four had passed through Sophie's hands and lay accounted for in her lap, Nokomo spoke.

"This, Waussnodae, is the medicine bundle of your mother's people—it has been mine to keep until such time as you were ready. That time is now. You must treasure it, safeguard its contents, and only share its secrets with your people."

Nokomo rewrapped each item and placed it in the deerskin pouch. She tucked the bundle deep in the otterskin bag and caressed it one last time before pressing the sleek fur into Sophie's hands. The girl did not speak immediately, and when words came, they were uttered in a voice that neither she nor her grandmother recognized as hers.

"It will be done, Nokomo."

And Sophie withdrew a single white feather from the pocket of her skirt and placed it with the other items in the deerskin pouch.

"This is my promise to my people."

The otterskin bag was then concealed by Sophie near her sleeping place.

I have my most memorable dreams just before waking... if I have others, I don't remember them. This morning I dreamt Mary published an article in *The Globe and Mail* called "Literal Silk"; somehow writing was the way back into art. She wrote under our maiden name. I read it and I was jealous. Everything placed in memory must be infused with emotion.

Yesterday, on the cross-country trail, it was exquisite: clear, cold, diamond snow... sun and that deep intense blue sky. I skied to Hawk Lake and stood on the ice in the middle of the lake. There was fresh snow and sunshine. I was in the center of a perfect O... now I understand the O's in Shakespeare's plays. O as in awe... O as in the connection to perfection. One must simply marvel.

CHAPTER EIGHT

Their packs were heavy with furs but their feet skipped swiftly over the rocky track, and the women and children sang. They smelled the river first, a clean fresh scent that comes from the rush of air above fast-moving water. They heard the clamour of a stream swollen by melting snow and boiling in its efforts to leap and jump its banks, and their feet skipped faster. When they reached the river, it was alive and eager to run to where its mouth joined the waters of the big lake.

Year after year, they went back to the same maple-sugaring grounds; the utensils they used in the making of the sugar had been left in a small storehouse. The four canoes reached the site— at a narrow neck of the river, just before it fanned into a shallow marshland and entered the big lake— almost simultaneously. A loud shout went up as the people recognized the landmark line of sugar maples.

An aura of festivity hung over the camp as tents were pitched, fires built, and the cooking pots filled with the remnants of the hunters' last kill. The men tapped the trees with their knives and plugged the holes with hollow sticks, while the women and children hooked birch-bark buckets to the trees and waited for the sap to run. Clear cold nights and warm sunny days caused the sap to flow, and early each evening, the women collected the thin liquid from the containers on the trees and poured it into a huge black kettle. The fire that boiled the sap and reduced it to a thick syrup burned lengths of maple logs to a white-hot heat. The children laughed and pushed around the fire, trying to steal some of the sap before it went into the big black pot. Elders smiled knowingly as the thin liquid trickled down the children's throats, tasting like water. The fire thickened the sap into sweetness. Hot streams of syrup were poured onto bits of snow the children found hidden in sheltered spots in the woods and then carried gingerly on sheets of birch bark to the fire. On the patches of snow, the syrup cooled and hardened into the sticky sweetness that they tasted with their memories before it touched their tongues. Surplus syrup was poured into birch-bark cones and stored in hide containers under the watchful eyes of Sophie and Nokomo. When the flowing sap was exhausted, the little party moved on, eager to join the wider tribal family that waited for them at the summer grounds.

They made their way along the shore of the lake, watched by silent loons cruising the cold, transparent waters. The loons spoke only to give warning of coming storms, allowing the people time to beach their canoes and reach the shelter of the woods before the thunder crashed and the lake writhed in anger. Some days, they paddled over rock-coloured water along fog-shrouded shores, and out of nowhere would appear an island or a massive rock. Time was measured in the days still remaining until they reached the bay, where the pitched tents of their people would greet them. Each day's journey brought them closer to the longed-for reunion.

Caroline was seated in the bow of Jim Big Fish's canoe with Nokomo resting in the middle. Sophie was paddling in a neigbouring canoe. Caroline's position in the boat afforded her first sighting of all landmarks, but nothing was familiar to her until the smooth surface of a rocky wall rose above the water and she recognized the painted figures on its face. She, Nokomo and Jim had returned to the place of the sacred paintings on the rock. As the four canoes approached the cliff, Jim allowed his boat to lag behind the others. When the forward boats had rounded the wall and disappeared from view, he directed his canoe to the concealed slit cut in the surface of the rock. Caroline was the first to disembark and she helped Nokomo from the boat. Jim looked long and hard at the two women standing on the ledge, but instead of climbing out of the canoe, he pushed it firmly from the edge and raised his paddle in a salute. Without a backward glance, he stroked round the wall and out of sight. Nokomo watched quietly until the craft had vanished and then she turned to her companion.

"This time, Caroline, you must help me climb the face."

The women made the treacherous ascent slowly, with Nokomo in the lead and Caroline below in case the older women lost her footing. It was a long and arduous climb to the summit, one fraught with anxiety for Caroline. She had been unaware of how deeply the trials of the winter had ravaged Nokomo. Less than a year earlier, the slender woman had made the ascent easily. Now she was skin and bone and each toehold was gained only at the expense of enormous effort. Caroline feared the woman could not continue, but Nokomo seemed to gather strength for one last rally and pushed herself over the top. She collapsed in Caroline's arms, depleted and rendered voiceless by her efforts. The sun had sunk almost to the horizon before Nokomo lifted her head and spoke.

"We must go on, for I will not find the path in darkness. Help me to my feet, Caroline, and we will find the way together."

Nokomo did not hide her need for assistance from the younger woman, and as Caroline half lifted Nokomo to her feet and placed a supporting arm about her shoulders, she finally understood what Nokomo could not say. The older woman's frailty was not the result of the winter's hardships; rather, the season's hunger had masked Nokomo's illness. From the lightness of the body she half carried, Caroline knew that the woman could not see another winter. Tears welled and swam in Caroline's eyes, but she forced them back, and she and Nokomo made their way into the green black depths of the forest. Caroline knew, but did not know she knew, where Nokomo was taking them. The mossy mound of earth that marked the place where Nokomo's daughter was buried did not startle her when they came upon it. The women sank into the softness of the needle-strewn ground, and Nokomo buried her face in the velvet greenness of the grave. The shadows deepened, and darkness drew a blanket around the shoulders of the waiting women. They shared its warmth.

"She must go with you, Caroline."

Silence slipped around them as Caroline considered the meaning of Nokomo's words.

"You, my chosen daughter, must take her. She will need guidance, someone who knows their ways, and you are the only one. You love her, and still it will be hard for her."

"Why must she go? She is happy. There is lots of time for her to learn our ways."

Caroline was pleading for her own reprieve as well, but it was not to be. Nokomo took Caroline's warm fingers in her own and traced a pattern on her palm.

"Do you remember the first time we sat in this place, and your despair at finding Daniel dead?"

Caroline nodded, and then shook her head disparagingly at her own lack of hope that day. Daniel's death had brought her Sophie, Nokomo, and a life that had made her previous existence pale and unimportant by comparison.

"I cannot know what Sophie saw the night she spent in the woods, but this I do know: what she saw has set her apart. She can no longer follow her wishes or mine. She is not of this time. For her, time is but a curve in space and she must find her own place along the curve and do what she must do. I must send her, you must accompany her, and she must go."

The melodious voice came from somewhere deep in Nokomo's breast and pleaded for Caroline's support.

"She cannot stay, however much we wish to keep her. It would destroy her and us. Take Sophie to her father's people. It is a beginning. You can ease the way for her into their world. What she saw is of that world, of this I am certain. Go with her, Caroline, for I cannot."

Caroline nodded.

"Will Sophie come back, Nokomo?"

"You ask what should not be answered, Caroline."

Caroline lowered her head, letting the hot tears fall into her hands. Nokomo relented.

"Knowledge of this kind cannot be given from one to another. Each woman must come to understand its meaning in her own way and in her own time. It cannot be taught. It must be searched for and sought after, but there is no guarantee that it will be found."

The women spent the remainder of the night together, pressed against the moss of the grave, watching the movements of the stars. In the morning, Nokomo woke Caroline and touched her thin cheek to the bright strands of Caroline's hair.

"Follow the path to the village, Caroline. Find Sophie, and send her to me."

I revisited two dreams of a year ago that had puzzled me. Today I can read them. Must one distance oneself from a dream to read it? I was up north and backing out of a driveway in a heavy snowfall; I was terrified of going off the road and getting stuck in a snowdrift. It happened. I backed into the ditch. But instead of panicking, I got out, lifted the car right out of the ditch, left it on the driveway and hopped onto a dogsled. I raced down the road behind a team of dogs. I still feel light and young and free, standing on the sled running down the road. I was stuck, but my soul got out of that heavy old car and hopped onto its own mode of transportation. The second dream was even easier to read. A friend of mine from long ago was walking across the floor of a bank in a cheerleader outfit. She looked very young and lovely. I was on a balcony overlooking the scene, quite out of the action. I did not know what to do. This dream is a metaphor of this person's life; she spent it on the floor of a bank. I no longer envy her.

Two generations and two differing approaches to the physical life. They do not aspire to things the way we did; this makes them somewhat careless of what we care about, but they are very careful of nature and the environment. The men and women interact beautifully; no sexist jokes, no patronizing positions and no defined roles. The women are lovely to look at without it being a huge production, and the men cook or clean up as easily as the women. And as for sex (I still have difficulty with that word; for me it is and has always been "making love"), they seem to accept it matter-of-factly, as a private matter between two people.

CHAPTER NINE

On the porch of the company store at Sault Ste. Marie, the factor fingered the bales of furs brought by canoe to the post. Caroline, conspicuous and uncomfortable in her European clothing, stood to one side while their pelts were assessed. Sophie darted from the porch to the waterfront; she had never been to the Sault before. In the past, Nokomo had always been the one to accompany Jim to the trading post, but this year she was too ill to make the journey. Jim waited impassively for the factor and his assistant to handle each skin and determine a price. When the business was completed, Jim handed Caroline the cash he received.

"For you, to take her with you."

She nodded and placed the money in a side pocket of her reticule. Sophie stood trembling with excitement. At first, the cluster of buildings about the waterfront claimed Sophie's attention; she circled each one, peering in windows and jumping back if someone appeared; but when a wagon pulled by two huge horses ambled down the main street, Sophie was spellbound. She could hardly concentrate on what her grandfather was saying.

"Don't forget your mother's people, Waussnodae."

Caroline averted her eyes. Jim was also saying: *Don't forget your mother's mother.* He knew, as did Caroline, that when and if Sophie returned to her people, Nokomo would not be there to greet her. Jim left them on the porch and walked down the path to the wharf. He knelt in the canoe, pushed off, and in the same motion lifted his paddle to salute the two women. They watched him until he disappeared from view.

Caroline took Sophie by the arm and directed her along the track that led to the Stone House Inn, where Caroline had lodged on her first visit. It was clean and comfortable and safe for women travelling on their own. Caroline had mulled over Nokomo's instructions in the days before they left the camp. Nokomo had said, "Take Sophie to her father's people." To Caroline, that meant Captain Tom Harris; she would take Sophie straight to Perth. After, there would be plenty of time to return to Fergus and John Paterson.

"Do people live inside these places, Caroline?"

The Stone House Inn was the largest building Sophie had ever seen; to the townsfolk, it was the oldest building in Sault Ste. Marie. Built early in the century as the grandest private residence west of the St. Clair River, the house had fallen into disrepair when its owner, a Mr. Charles Ermatinger, a fur trader and entrepreneur, had returned to Montreal to live. In the past two years, the large stone house had been partially restored to its former grandeur through the unceasing efforts of David Pim, an Irish immigrant, and his Canadian wife. Sophie found herself in a lobby the size of their winter lodge. Sofas and chairs were arranged companionably about the room and small tables held books and papers. Heavy velvet curtains of a dark green colour were pulled back from the windows and sun flooded the room.

Despite the warmth of the day, a fire was blazing in the hearth, and the cosy nature of the room was further enhanced by the arrival of a small bustling woman of indeterminate age who radiated cheerfulness.

"Good day to you, ladies. Will you be needing a room? Mr. Pim, Mr. Pim, come and see these ladies to our finest room. You must be tired to pieces after your trip. I don't recall seeing you in these parts before, or have I?"

Mrs. Pim stood on tiptoe, the better to peer into Caroline's face as closely as her own conception of good manners would allow. Then she chuckled at her mistake. "It's wrong I am, for certain you are the lady who stayed with us last summer. We wondered what had become of you."

A little gentleman with a mop of curly white hair poked his head through the door. He was even tinier than his wife.

"What's all the fuss, my dear? You've got nothing better to do than to shriek and distract a poor man from his chores? It's you that will be complaining when there is no wood chopped for the fire."

Sophie stared at the two strange little people conducting this rapid-fire exchange of words. She giggled as she remembered sharing a two-week hunting trip with her grandparents and them not speaking this much during the whole trip; while here, in less than a minute, these two had used up an entire season's supply of words. Did all her father's people talk this much? Caroline covered her mouth with a gloved hand to hide the laughter that wanted to bubble out, but Sophie saw the amusement in her eyes and understood she was to smile only on the inside.

The next morning Caroline and Sophie set out to meet the dressmaker recommended by Mrs. Pim. Mrs. McLellan was a widow who took in boarders and did fancy sewing for the ladies of the Sault. A young woman with a pleasant open face answered their knock.

"Hello, ladies, please come in."

"Good morning. I am Caroline Paterson and this is my niece, Sophie Harris. Mrs. Pim at the inn gave us this note to deliver."

The woman motioned them into a tiny room dominated by the unclothed figure of a dressmaker's dummy. She read the short note, folded it neatly into squares and placed it in the pocket of her dress. Caroline handed the widow the package containing the fabric that Mrs. Pim had picked out for Sophie. Mrs. McLellan shook out the material and held it up to Sophie's face. "Lovely. The pink brings out all the warm tones in her skin without highlighting the brown."

The woman made two bunches of Sophie's straight dark hair and lifted them from the nape of Sophie's neck.

"What do you think, Mrs. Paterson? With a new wardrobe and hairdo, Sophie will only look wonderfully exotic."

Sophie rolled her eyes at Caroline and was about to speak when Mrs. McLellan draped the flower-sprigged fabric over the dummy's naked frame and busily pinned the material to the padded form. The sight of the headless dummy, swathed in pink, attended to by the kneeling woman, caused Sophie to whoop with laughter. The seamstress looked up, her mouth filled with pins, and Sophie laughed even harder. Caroline too was overcome with giggles. Puzzled, Mrs. McLellan stood up and backed away from the fat fabric-draped figure. The dummy did look ridiculous. Its flower-printed bosom was thrust aggressively towards the three women, and as if conscious of the boldness of this behaviour, it had dropped the fabric sharply to its waist. The material pulled in tightly to emphasize the wasp waist of the dummy. No sooner had this been accomplished than the fabric, in defiance of all laws of gravity, rose and billowed in bunches across its well-padded hips. The dummy was the epitome of the Victorian model of fashion, a headless mannequin with an hourglass figure. Sophie, choking on her laughter, queried, "Is this how you want me to look?"

Caroline and Sophie were conspicuous among the passengers boarding the *Regina*, the steamer on which Mr. Pim had booked their passage east. That they were women travelling alone was sufficient to draw attention to them, but Caroline's sojourn among the Ojibwa had given her porcelain complexion a warm tone enhanced by hundreds of pale golden freckles, and her fiery hair, softened over the years to a gleaming bronze, was plaited in a single braid. She looked lovely, but not in a European manner, the current mode of excellence for every colonial lady. This disturbed the other passengers. But they could place Sophie. That she was breathtakingly beautiful, in the full bloom of young womanhood, was of no account. What mattered was her mixed blood. The dark straight hair swinging crisply about her narrow shoulders framed a face exquisitely tinted with the golden pink of the sunset sky. Sophie's aloofness belied the intelligence that shone from her clear gray eyes, an intelligence that saw beneath the polite smiles and genteel conversations.

She and Caroline kept their distance. They took their meals alone and were the topic of much speculation by the other passengers. One afternoon, the captain announced that the vessel had developed a problem with the boiler, necessitating immediate repair. They pulled into a bay with a wide sand beach and the crew ferried the passengers to the shore where a picnic lunch was served. The day was clear and warm for early June, and Sophie and Caroline decided to take their lunch into a small clearing in the woods within earshot of the beach. They spread their shawls on a patch of grass and leaned against a fallen tree, their food lying uneaten on the log. Sophie unbuttoned the top two buttons of her serge travelling costume and Caroline did the same. They closed their eyes and let the hot rays of the midday sun beat on their uplifted faces and bare throats.

Perhaps it was the smell of the food carried on the breeze or just the natural curiosity of bear cubs that brought the animals within touching distance of Sophie and Caroline. Sophie was instantly aware of their presence, and with no more movement than the raising of an eyelid, she opened one eye. The cubs moved cautiously across the clearing, stopping now and then to sniff the mild air. They were comic little creatures with shaggy black coats and an aura of bravado. She wanted Caroline to share the clumsy antics of the cubs, but Sophie knew her slightest movement would send them crashing back in terror to their mother. She watched, motionless, as the bolder of the two climbed onto the fallen log where their lunch lay, and batted the food to the ground. As it fell, a tremendous noise reverberated throughout the clearing, and then a second. Caroline opened her eyes in time to see the backs of the two panicked bear cubs running for the shelter of the woods. A further shot rang out as the two women dashed back to the beach.

There was great excitement among the milling crowd. One of the boat's passengers had shot a large black bear that had been spotted berry-picking on a rise of rocky land. The man had needed three shots to fell her, and he was arguing with a sailor as to whether the carcass could be skinned and brought on board before the steamer was ready to depart. The captain was consulted; they could lose no more time. They were ready to pull anchors. He remarked that the daytime heat would make the transportation of the freshly killed corpse distasteful to both passengers and crew. It was a shame not to keep and mount such a specimen, but the captain assured the gunman that black bears were very common and, no doubt, there would be another opportunity to obtain such a prize. The mother bear was left where she was felled.

Sophie's horror changed to pure hatred. Her narrowed eyes and thinned lips veiled to all but Caroline the depth of her loathing. She watched the people board the steamer unconscious of the evil they left so carelessly behind them. To Caroline, she hissed, "Tell me. They are your people. Why did he do it?"

Caroline looked helplessly into Sophie's flat mirrored eyes for as long as she could stand it and then she had to look away, ashamed.

The other passengers basked in the transparent sunshine of each cloudless day and slept serenely under starry skies, rocked by the lapping of the water against the boat. Ahead of schedule, the captain eased his vessel into the berth at Detroit, the western terminus of the newly completed Great Western Railway which stretched from Hamilton in the east across the fields and forests of Canada West to the American city on the banks of the Detroit River. Detroit was the link for a hundred towns and villages to the commercial centers of the world. With the advent of the railways, new immigrants could make their way with comparative ease into the unclaimed lands to the west. Peace had come to Europe and her population was bursting out of her glutted cities and over-tenanted farms. When they arrived at the ports of Boston, New York, Quebec and Montreal they found they had been deceived by unscrupulous agents; no land was available. Once again they packed their belongings and boarded trains and boats and headed inland to find the land they had been promised.

At the docks in Detroit, Sophie stepped from the steamer's gangplank into a crowd of people swarming over every inch of space and filling every empty crevice with the boxes and bundles that accompanied their exodus. Each man was intent on securing passage for himself and his family on the next transport west. Women and children were crushed against the wooden sheds, and people shouted and swore in many languages. Arms waved, money changed hands, and the noise rose to ear-splitting proportions. Sophie shrank from the crowd and yet she could not ignore the faces that swam around her. She read greed and hunger in their eyes.

"Where are they all going, Caroline?"

"West, where we came from."

"What do they want?"

"Land, Sophie."

"What do they want with the land?"

"Sophie, every one of these people," and Caroline waved her arm to include the mob of bodies on the packed dock, "wants to own property. There is none left in the countries they have come from. The government surveys each section and then sells lots. As each section is bought and then filled up, the government opens new sections further to the west."

"People pay money to the government for the land?"

"Yes. They can then farm the land or build a mill on it or even sell it again if they want. It's theirs."

As far as Caroline could see, men were pushing and shoving in their eagerness to be the first to book passage.

"They have all come here to buy land?"

Sophie's face flushed and then went ashen, and her eyes contracted to slits of steel. She had difficulty controlling her breathing. The words boiled from her and scalded Caroline. "You cannot sell land. It belongs to everyone. You share the land with the other tribes, with the animals and the trees. How can your people sell what they don't own? It doesn't belong to your people. It doesn't belong to my people. It belongs to the earth mother. Surely your chiefs understand this? What would happen to my people if the land we hunt and fish and build our lodges on were sold? What would happen to the Ojibwa if the forests were cut down and the animals killed by the onslaught of land-hungry settlers?" Sophie's eyes glittered like bits of polished stone on a wave-washed beach. She waited, but Caroline had no answer.

Their journey together to Perth elapsed as cautiously and delicately as if they were near strangers who had met accidentally and travelled together. The atmosphere was bizarre and disconcerting, as if an abyss had opened at their feet and each stood frozen on the edge, unable to lift her eyes and look across at the other.

Perth had not changed; the stone-lined main street bisected by the ribbon of water was exactly as Caroline had left it the year before. Her father's house was as solid in its lush green setting as the town itself, and yet, as Caroline climbed the few steps to the familiar door, she felt dread. A woman, not quite a stranger, opened the door at Caroline's knock. The widow with whom Caroline's father had been keeping company prior to her departure recognized Caroline immediately and called into the cool shadowy recesses of the house.

"Tom. Come quickly. It's your daughter and some Indian girl."

THIS CRAVING FOR illumination reminds me of Irish monks and their illuminated books. I have started to paint in watercolour, not my medium. The paper feels sloppy, and I have no direction other than a strong desire to paint an angel's wing; a vested interest, as Anne would say. I want to be the brush, and have my body work the paint… in the water, I leap, but in my fingers the brush is stiff and strange. Do I want to paint my own watercolour on the world? I like painting with the white; it is a different white than the paper, and in order to paint white I must first put black down, then see where the lightness is and use that entry to let the image come into being. This, of course, is the same process we follow in life; one must remember to keep light, very light, not directionless, but not in charge, and then there is the possibility of illumination.

"You can really only steal from people who live magically, and for me everything has meaning." — *Cassandra*, Christa Wolf

I am Australia-bound, flying through the night discarding time and countries. My first morning at Dundryad— a paradise for dogs and horses— I got up early and went out to rub the boys' noses, two weanlings that I have fallen in love with. Next to the barn are the babies, three little fillies that need to be loved and talked to— and all the while, the birds are singing and the sun is trying to break through a heavy sky. I think this may be the "real" life I have been searching for... not man-made, and not wrestled into submission. Now to the dark side. The boys will have to be broken and sent to the track, and the fillies will become brood mares in the reproduction business. Is this why we become so hardened, because we hate what we must do? Why can't we stay in the garden and love one another? Why must we send "our boys" to the racetrack and "our girls" to the maternity ward? Are we trying to package something for profit that is better left untouched?

Mary and I are unpeeling layers of whatever shaped us. I always felt mother was not able to look after me properly, and Mary told me that mother was playing out some scenario that included one twin/daughter/sister having to die. A very scary situation, and one in which the old pattern must be broken. Speaking of scary situations, there is something sinister at the subconscious level brewing here at the farm. I feel it. There is a lack of quality care for both people and animals. Mary feels it, too (that is why she came back). It is as though there is a tragedy waiting to happen.

We drove the Great Ocean Road. I am in awe of the topography. It is as though great chunks of the continent were torn away and the waves continue to eat at the rest, timelessly and inevitably. The sandstone cliffs are the form, rigid and structured, and the ocean is the theme. The one transforms the other into fantastical new shapes. In my analogy, the form changes, not the theme. Does this analogy hold for society? The structure is male and patriarchal and is constantly being worn away by the female theme. Too simplistic, perhaps, but truth is often simple and elegant. This ties in with Christa Wolf's theory of woman as magic and man as wanting to possess and dissect this magic.

Is spiritual growth a thinning of the body, so we become light and transparent— like glass— so the spirit can shine through? Do we still carry "clouds of immortality" about us? As soon as I come into the city, things speed up. When I am at the lake, time flows around me with me inside it. In the city, I try and master time; it is a contest. In the city, I live on top of time, and sometimes under it.

I can forgive almost anything but meanness and hypocrisy. I wish I was by the ocean; the cry of a seagull almost did me in. Shall I tuck this away to be taken out and savoured, or shall I bury this so deeply in my psyche that it will not be exhumed in my lifetime and my face shall become pinched and mean? I feel like a snake wanting to shrug off the skin of my old life. I want to live with birdsong and water and blue skies. I want to share and become translucent. I don't want to be the keeper— doling out my life in tidy portions. I want to spend it in great luscious chunks. Make yourself transparent and let everything flow through you, leaving a small residue of pure joy like sunshine on your skin. I noticed yesterday that when I am most in a state of flux, my face is at its most attractive. What a price to pay not to look mean and pinched.

CHAPTER TEN

A man couldn't mistake his own daughter, could he? It was Caroline in the doorway. Well, thank God. Tom Harris had never understood her running off to look for Daniel. He felt a twinge of anger, and was about to say so when Margaret shook her head. Margaret was a sensible woman. You'd never catch her playing such a damned fool trick. It was Margaret who had reminded him that Caroline was a grown woman with a husband, and it was up to John Paterson to worry about his wife's behaviour. Tom barely knew the man, and had never understood why Caroline married him. After Caroline had been gone for some months and a third letter addressed to Caroline had arrived in Perth, Tom had sat down at Emily's old desk and written to the man, saying that Caroline needed time to recover from her mother's death and had gone to visit Richard. He hoped half-truths would suffice, for he could not bring himself to write that Caroline had left her father's house to search the wilderness for a son Tom had given up for dead, and she should have, too. It was easier to let John Paterson think that Caroline had gone to Kingston. Tom sometimes believed it himself.

In spite of all this, Tom was overjoyed to see her. During the nights when he had been unable to sleep, picturing Caroline lost and hungry, prey to any wild animal, Margaret's warm flesh had been his sole comfort.

"Pa, you can't imagine how good it is to see you!" Caroline threw herself into her father's arms.

"There, there." Tom held her awkwardly. "Whatever possessed you to go away like that? Never mind. You're safe and sound."

They stood, arms about one another, faces touching.

"Now, you two, do you want the whole town to watch your reunion? People here already thought it was mighty queer, Caroline going off like that and leaving you to fend for yourself. Do your carrying on inside, if you must."

Suddenly Caroline remembered why she had come. She removed herself from her father's embrace and guided a reluctant Sophie across the threshold.

"Pa, I want you to meet Daniel's daughter. May I present Miss Sophie Harris, your granddaughter? Sophie, this is your grandfather."

She took their two hands in hers, as proud as any mother, and placed Sophie's slim golden fingers in her father's large square hands. Tom turned in confusion to Caroline.

"Caroline, where is my son? Who is this girl?"

"Tom Harris, it's as plain as the nose on your face. This is your son's by-blow from the wrong side of the blanket. No wonder you never heard from him, too busy with his Indian trash, living like animals in the woods. This half-breed must be his. No doubt he's afraid to come home to decent people. It's disgusting."

Sophie wheeled around and raced down the path to the street. By the time Caroline reached the gate, Sophie was gone. Tom followed from the house, and before Caroline could decide in which direction Sophie might have headed, he caught up with her.

"Is what Margaret says true, Caroline? Is she really Daniel's daughter by some Indian woman?"

Caroline looked keenly at the man who was her father. For the first time, she noticed he was old, a shell of a man, well-dressed and well-fleshed, wearing the hollowed life of his advancing years fearfully. She replied carefully and with great pity.

"Yes, father. Sophie is Daniel's daughter. Her mother was an Ojibwa and Daniel loved her very much. Now they are both dead. I brought Sophie back so she could have a chance to know her father's people, and for you to know her. It was a mistake."

The ground beneath her feet felt soft and springy and the river moved lazily against the bank; this was not the frozen landscape of Caroline's dreams. She found Sophie, tearstained and untidy, huddled against a crumbling sandstone ledge that overlooked the river.

"I want to go back, Caroline. I want Jim and Nokomo. I hate my father's world. I know why he left. Please, let me go home."

Caroline gathered the weeping girl in her arms and pressed her glossy head to her shoulder. "There, there," she murmured, echoing her father's words, "I know, love. They are frightened. Their fear makes them cruel."

She patted the girl maternally as she soothed her. "Let's not give up yet. We'll spend the night in the Red House Inn, and in the morning we'll take the first coach away from here. I don't belong here, either. I wonder if I ever did?"

Hours later, when the women were settled for the night in an upstairs room of the inn, there was a tap on the door. Caroline lay in the room's only bed; Sophie, disdaining the softness of the mattress, was sleeping soundly on the floor, close to the opened window. Caroline placed a wrapper around her shoulders and went to the door. Her father stood there, hat in one hand, and a package in the other.

"Caroline, your mother would be ashamed of me. My own daughter comes home and has to stay with strangers. It's not just Margaret's fault, Caroline. I can't see you and that girl living here; it won't work. Folks don't like Indians. It would be hell for both of you. Take her home. John being a minister and all, I am sure folks up your way will be kinder to her. I want you to take this money. Don't shake your head 'til I tell you where it came from. When your mother died, she left money to each of you children, although where she got it beats me. This is your share, and Daniel's. At least you and the girl won't be dependent on the charity of others. Goodbye, Caroline. Don't think too badly of me."

Caroline took the purse he offered and squeezed his age-spotted hand.

"Goodbye, pa. Don't worry about us. Sophie and I will make out just fine."

Caroline put the money in the side pocket of the reticule where she kept what was left of Jim Big Fish's money. As she rummaged through the bag in the dark, trying not to disturb Sophie, her hand encountered the coarse linen of the rolled-up sampler. She hadn't looked at it in a long time. Caroline pulled it from the bag. It was dark in the room and impossible to see the design. She climbed into bed and placed the sampler on her outstretched legs. She passed her fingers over the surface; the raised stitches seemed to convey a message of their own. Caroline strained to read them with her fingers. Who was her real father? Would he have reacted differently to Sophie than Tom Harris had?

I am reading Anne Carson's *Eros*, a wonderful analysis of desire, with some very tempting metaphors. But the thesis is disturbing— desire is only maintained by space. As soon as wholeness is achieved, desire dissipates: not a great recipe for a long-term relationship. The alternative seems to be the anxiety of not knowing, the state of being unbalanced.

I am unreasonably happy today... lit from the inside, like a candle. I am content to exist in someone else's sunshine. How lucky I am to find this out before it is too late. This pushes back the edges and makes me understand I cannot rush through today in order to set up tomorrow. I feel as though I have emerged from an enchanted spell; it is wonderful to be free, but also a little sad.

CHAPTER ELEVEN

The streets of Fergus were deserted at noon hour, and Caroline debated whether to walk straight to the manse or to check the church to see if John was there. She spoke aloud, "We'll go into the church."

Sophie lifted one straight dark eyebrow as Caroline pointed to the church.

"Your husband works there, Caroline?"

Sophie's brow arched in disbelief. Caroline viewed the church and cemetery from Sophie's fresh perspective. The two shared one lawn, for the church elders were a thrifty lot, and it had seemed pointless to clear more land than was strictly necessary. The gravestone-studded grass gave the church a chilling air, as if the congregation needed a constant reminder of its own mortality. To enter the church from the street, one had to walk between the rows of markers; there had been graves before there was a church, and the sanctuary of the church was gained by walking gingerly among the dead.

Sunday services must have presented a macabre spectacle to anyone watching from the street. Caroline chuckled at the thought. No wonder Sophie had raised her eyebrows. Caroline laughed out loud, and her good humour was infectious. In moments, both women were overcome by gales of laughter.

"In answer to your question, Sophie, yes and no. John works in the church, not in the cemetery. He looks after the living, and conducts the services for the dead. However, once they are buried he leaves them alone. Oh, I don't mean that. I mean, once they are in the ground he doesn't disturb them."

Sophie laughed harder.

Caroline continued, "I hardly know how to explain it to myself. How can I possibly explain it to someone who has never been inside a church? I'll let John try. Let's go inside and see if he's there."

She caught Sophie's hand, and the two of them cautiously picked their way around the gravestones in the churchyard and wound up inside the front door of the church. It was noon, but the light that filtered through the windows was subdued. Hushed silence greeted them.

"No one's here. We'll go to the house. John must be home for dinner."

The manse remained exactly as she had left it more than a year ago, a sturdy stone cottage standing squarely in the center of a neatly trimmed lawn. The frilled edges of a blossoming vegetable garden were visible at the cut stone corners of the house. No flowers brightened the green and gray of house and lawn, although it was midsummer and the gardens in town were a mass of blooms.

"I am glad he planted the vegetables. I am sure he has had so much to do there wasn't time to tend to the flowers."

Disappointment coloured Caroline's words. The cottage had looked so lovely garlanded with climbing roses and surrounded with beds of flowers. She had wanted Sophie to see it at its best.

"Hello, hello? Are you here, John?"

No reply was forthcoming. Caroline pushed the door wide open and led

Sophie inside. The stone walls kept the house cool even in the heat of summer, and the women shivered in their light dresses.

"Who lives here, Caroline?"

"Why, Sophie, I do, and John does, and I hope you will, too."

The back door opened and Caroline hurried to the kitchen.

"John, it's Caroline. I am sorry I couldn't write and let you know when we were coming. We didn't know ourselves. Come and meet Sophie, my niece. She's going to stay with us. We've just this minute arrived by coach."

There was a pause as the startled man looked from one woman to the other. As he was about to speak, Caroline brushed his cheek with a soft kiss and said, "How are you, John? You look tired."

"Caroline, this is a surprise. Your father wrote that you had gone to stay with your brother. I wrote you regularly, but I didn't hear from you for such a long time. However, you are back and that is all that matters. Your niece is welcome to share our home. I hope you will be happy with us, Sophie." The solemn man shook the girl's hand with as much warmth as he could muster.

"Now, Caroline, the women of the parish have been taking turns bringing me my noonday meal. As soon as you have Sophie settled, I would like you to fix my dinner. I have not enjoyed depending on others."

"Yes, John."

Caroline and Sophie exchanged amused glances. Caroline had been away a year and had returned with a girl he had never seen before, and yet there were no questions, only the request that his dinner be placed on the table as soon as possible. It was a strange reunion.

Fergus was happy to have Caroline home. She was one of them. She had worked beside them, nursed them when they were sick, and grieved with them when death had struck. They had resented her leaving and her absence, but they were prepared to take her back.

They were not quite so willing to take in Sophie. She was too exotic and too beautiful for the townsfolk's taste, but she was Caroline's niece, and they wanted Caroline to stay. They were prepared to accept Sophie on their terms. Sophie, too, wanted to please Caroline, and so she tried to make herself agreeable, but compromise was not always possible. Her peers were in awe of her unusual appearance and her obscure ancestry, while the older female population vacillated between annoyance at her distant poise and gratitude for her grasp of herbal remedies. Sophie had, with Caroline's permission, taken over Caroline's old role of village apothecary, and had expanded the range of cures available. Sophie had found the remains of Caroline's herb garden tucked forlornly in a back corner of the yard and wildly overgrown. She had worked tirelessly to restore it, scouring the countryside for new plants and succeeding in making many of them grow. The colour of a flower or the shape of a leaf would give Sophie the clue she needed as to its use. She was never wrong, and the villagers valued Sophie's natural cures. Even Dr. McGee would send a patient with a lingering ailment to try Sophie's herbs. Caroline looked on contentedly as Sophie, with her knowledge of nature and nature's remedies, created a niche for herself in the working life of Fergus. Caroline herself was very busy, making amends to John and the community for her long absence.

It was John who voiced the first complaint to Caroline.

"You must know this cannot continue, Caroline. She never goes to church. Only this morning, Mrs. Robertson asked me why Sophie was walking through the fields on Sunday morning as they were hitching up the buggy to come to service. This makes a mockery of my ministry. I don't mind people laughing at me, Caroline, but I would be remiss in my duty to Sophie and your brother if I did not bring her into the fold. You will have to speak to her, Caroline. This cannot continue."

The second mention of Sophie's disdain for Sunday service came from a less kindly source. Mrs. Matthews, the sharp-eyed postmistress, whose pious feathers had been ruffled by Caroline's abrupt departure from the town, and then had been disturbed again by her unheralded return, cornered Caroline after the Sunday service.

"Mrs. Paterson, your niece is not in church again. Is she a Christian, or is she a heathen? Should you be letting her give her homemade cures to sick people? What does she put in them? Who taught her? I think she should be supervised, Mrs. Paterson. You never know what those savages are up to and what evil schemes they are concocting. She is a heathen, isn't she, Mrs. Paterson? Has she ever darkened a church door?"

Caroline's warm colouring had flushed and then bleached ash-white during the postmistress' tirade. Now her face and neck flamed red. As she gathered her strength for a defence, the offensive Mrs. Matthews turned and started down the steps, pausing only to unsling one final arrow at Caroline and the waiting congregation. "Of course she's been in the church. I forgot. The day she arrived in town, the two of you were doubled over with laughter in the graveyard, and then you both went laughing loudly inside the church. I think you owe us an explanation of where Sophie really comes from."

Caroline tensed at the insidious interpretation put on their behaviour in the churchyard. John drew himself to an even straighter and more rigid stance than normal and the congregation held its collective breath. They dispersed without exhaling it.

Not a word was spoken during the walk to the manse. Once the privacy of their house was gained, John leaned towards Caroline, his dark eyes boring into her white face.

"She will change or she will go. I don't care if she is your brother's daughter. I cannot have my position jeopardized." He pointed to the loft. "Go and tell her."

Caroline climbed the ladder, dragging out the scaling of each rung. How could she possibly explain to Sophie that she had to go to church? There was no other way.

It is like existing in a vacuum; there is no fresh air, and sometimes there is no air. He wants me, but only on his terms; he does not feel capable of change. He wants me to feel tenderness; if I do, I am undone. For twenty-six years I became what he wanted, the perfect wife and mother. And now I am choking in that role... choking. Is this the beginning of freefall? Shall I just inch up on it? Somehow, when one thinks of a freefall, one thinks of a great leap into space, but I seem to crawl to the edge and hesitate.

I am moving like an express train down the tracks, to where? Wherever it is, I feel explosive; there is so much loose rage roaring around. I am beginning to see the origins of this outrage— not mine, but the world's. The Greeks, through mythology, demonized the "irrational" as seen in the Dionysian principle. They had to have control, predictability... and the cost was huge. The female form was fixed to the hearth, and my God she was kept there for over two millennia. I want to scream my fury and make up somehow for all those wasted lives.

CHAPTER TWELVE

Caroline was lying beside John, wide awake. She felt rather than heard the almost imperceptible imprint of a bare foot on the ladder leading to the loft. She slipped from the room without disturbing John. Caroline was waiting at the foot of the ladder as Sophie, shoes in one hand and travelling bag in the other, negotiated the narrow rungs. She started when she saw Caroline, and nearly lost her balance. Caroline placed a finger to her lips and motioned the girl to the kitchen. She mouthed the words: "I'll get my clothes and be right back. Wait for me."

She dressed quickly in the faint pinkish light. They left the manse by the back door and crossed the dew-soaked grass to the fields bordering the Paterson property, then followed the fencing to the road that linked Fergus to Elora and beyond. It was not until they reached the safety of the road that Caroline turned to Sophie and spoke out loud. "Before we leave, let me show you something. I would have taken you sooner, but I was so busy placating John and the rest of the town that I wasn't paying close enough attention to you." She hugged the girl and her eyes pleaded for understanding. "I should have known how unhappy you were. I am sorry."

They walked in cordial silence along the road, not yet made dusty by the heat and traffic, arriving in Elora just as the town was stirring. Early morning activities were confined to houses and barns, and the women reached the cover of the trees that masked the trail unnoticed. Caroline wanted Sophie to walk the path she had discovered the spring before she left Fergus. She wanted Sophie to see the stream. It was strange that only now did she remember where she had first seen Sophie's face. She had meant to show the path to Sophie, but somehow life in the village hadn't allowed both women to slip away at the same time without being noticed. Caroline had tried her best to avoid causing talk. The right time had never come.

The women shared the sunrise that was spreading golden pink fingers through the woods and touching the water in the gorge with mirrored streamers. The river was less boisterous than Caroline remembered, and the noise of the rushing water less deafening, but the woods were more enchanting and mysterious in the half light than they had been in full sun. She watched as Sophie took shape and colour from the sky and the water. Caroline could scarcely keep pace with Sophie's dancing feet, for Sophie had discarded her shoes and her bundle some way back, and Caroline had ceased to lead the way. She looked on affectionately as Sophie melted into the trees and then rebounded along the path, dappled with light and shadow. She laughed aloud at Sophie's antics, and the sound reverberated across the limestone walls and drowned in the rush of water pouring through the gorge. Sophie appeared on the path, then disappeared and reappeared at will; Caroline was charmed by the magic of the game and followed as swiftly as she could. The trees opened to let Sophie pass, and Caroline, in Sophie's wake, managed to slip through before the way was blocked. She was breathless attempting to keep Sophie's fading figure in sight. She ran wildly down the path, here ducking under a low-hanging limb and there leaping over a fallen log; in spite of this, Caroline lost her.

"Caroline, Caroline, who is she?" Sophie's question echoed through the light-streaked trees. Caroline redoubled her efforts to catch up with the girl and ran to where the sound of Sophie's voice had come from. She found her standing in the middle of the stream, staring down at something in the water. There was no one with her. Caroline waded into the shallow water and touched her gently on the shoulder.

"What is it, Sophie? Who did you see?"

The girl turned slowly at Caroline's touch, and Caroline's blood chilled as Sophie's face thinned and became as transparent as glass before her eyes. Too startled to scream or back away, she watched as the face of a stranger filled Sophie's face. A woman with black curls and deep blue eyes regarded Caroline quite solemnly from the depths of this glass. She was not quite a stranger, and Caroline closed her eyes in an effort to remember where she had seen this dark-haired girl before. When she opened them, moments later, Sophie stood once more before her in the stream. Caroline looked around, but it was hopeless, as she had known it would be. The girl had gone, and with her something precious had vanished. A sense of loss swept over Caroline and she wept softly. Sophie leaned down, picked up a tiny white shell from its bed on the bottom of the stream, and handed it to Caroline.

"Don't be sad, Caroline. I saw her, too. I am going to find her. Shall we go together?"

The tears dripped unchecked down Caroline's face as she nodded her assent, and with the help of Sophie's outstretched hand, pulled herself from the stream.

I did not want to go to an old friend's surprise fiftieth birthday. We had lost touch over the years and I didn't feel capable of new beginnings. I don't know why, except this friend had always been very special, an alter ego, my masculine counterpart. He has an innocence and a curiosity to match my own. In any case, something made me go, and I could not stop hugging him. It was like reclaiming some part of yourself (not a sexual, but a psychic one). It felt good and right to be there. We went in to dinner and my friend and his lady, who is warm and lovely, came in, changed from cocktail clothes into wedding clothes. They had been married at six o'clock and had kept it a secret from all but their most immediate family. The emotion in that room was so high, it was palpable; almost everyone shed a tear or two. This family has been through a war and now it is starting to heal, openly and with all their friends there to lend support. I do not think I have ever felt so much love radiate from one room. Imagine, I nearly missed this!

I have opened my eyes for the first time since the spell was cast. Such a powerful spell, and the lesson to be learned is never to name the well from which you will not drink. Two years almost to the day! I love the sense of liberation from my senses— the spell was lovely, but scary. I am able to move ahead intellectually, but I don't feel nearly as alive. How does desire relate to intellectual closeness? I feel as though I am radiating love outward, and in turn I am attracting strong feelings from outside myself. Quite lovely sensations, but disconcerting. I feel very tender, very loving, very fragile, and in some respects, very open. I am so happy that I know now that love is not exclusive but inclusive... it takes one in. Love does not shut anyone in or out. It is like Bachelard's definition of poetic space... a passing back and forth, from intimacy to immensity.

CHAPTER THIRTEEN

There had been no kind way to leave John. The Church was a hard substitute for human love. Caroline knew John loved her, and she knew her defection would destroy his capacity to love. Her soul would be accountable for the rest of her life. It was as though she was about to tip a kettle of scalding water into their lives, knowing that both she and John would be scarred, but unable to imagine the degree. What was the alternative? To lose Sophie?

A sealed letter bearing John's name lay on the bureau in the bedroom. Caroline and Sophie were halfway to Guelph in the coach before he read it.

Montreal was a rude jolt to Caroline's peace of mind. Daily, as the women made their enquiries of the shipping companies as to the dates of sailings, Caroline came face to face with her Irish ancestry. The waterfront of the city swarmed. Faces without hope, thin and spotted, hardly looked up as the women passed. Too weak to beg for help, they fell and were stepped over and ignored by the citizens of a city bent on fortifying itself against the afflictions of the Irish. If there were other immigrants, Caroline did not meet them. Those imprinted on her mind were always Irish and always wretched. Montrealers went about their business and tried to keep the contagious diseases, bred in the unsanitary holds of the ships and brought ashore on emaciated bodies of the Irish, confined to the waterfront. Caroline and Sophie were warned constantly by well-meaning travellers about the dangers of contracting infection, but it did not stop them; they went daily to the docks. Caroline could not help herself, and Sophie would not let her go alone. Each day when they returned to their lodgings, Caroline sat on the bed and held her head in her hands, rocking back and forth, asking the same questions of herself over and over again. "What have they done to deserve this? How can I leave them to suffer? What if I have walked by and abandoned someone who is related to my mother, to my father, someone with whom I share blood ties?" When she came to this question she would raise her head from her hands and stare at Sophie as though Sophie's face held the answer.

She thought of them even as she slept, tossing and moaning. And then the questions would begin, as though Caroline was moving from person to person, from group to group.

"Do you know me? Does anyone recognize me? Have you seen me before? Do I look at all familiar? Do you know me?"

Caroline lost weight, and when Sophie urged her to eat, Sophie would see in her the haunted eyes and hollowed cheeks of the waterfront Irish, and she was frightened. It was a relief when the word came of a sailing.

Steamships now plied the ocean routes linking the old world with North America. They were faster and more efficient and, for those passengers who could afford the fare, more reliable than the clipper ships. Caroline and Sophie had been fortunate in securing an outside cabin on the *Prince Albert*, sailing for Liverpool. They boarded the ship one evening and the next morning woke to find themselves underway. When they dressed and went on deck, already the scenes of human wretchedness that had distinguished the waterfront had receded into the stone fronts of the storehouses. The buildings blurred into the background, and in a short time only the cross on Mount Royal marked the place where the city stood. Sophie hoped that each mile that separated them from the Montreal waterfront and the sight of the pitiful Irish refugees would lessen Caroline's pain, but it was not to be, for even here, moving downstream in the middle of the river, were reminders of misery. Each ship they met sailing upriver passed near enough for them to see the crowds of Irish packing the decks.

Sophie and Caroline knew the full horror of the Irish story, how they had been forced from their homes by famine and the greed of their absent English landlords. They had seen hundreds of families packed like animals onto dirty ships. Caroline knew about the fever sheds that lined the waterfront behind the docks.

It was said in the city that those who lived through the nightmare of the voyage survived only to succumb to the nightmare of cholera that arrived with the rats. She could no longer stand to look into the Irish faces on the decks of the passing boats; she lowered her eyes and stared into the river, but she did not go below. The last sight she and Sophie had of Quebec was Grosse Ile, the quarantine island lying above Quebec City midway in the river. Rows and rows of white wooden crosses lined the hill leading from the rocky shore to the hospital. Caroline thought of her own mother and her death. What marked her grave? Caroline retrieved Elizabeth's needlework from where she had packed it.

The end of a spell. What has it meant? I met angels, not literally, but figuratively and symbolically. I learned to ask for help and I received it. Endings are quite difficult, because beginnings must then be made.

Yesterday, I saw an "angel" in the woods. She deconstructed into a perfect little hemlock tree with a fallen log propping her up, and she held a dead leaf out on a branch as if it were a star.

Andrea will never be what I dreamed for her... she must be her own dream, and I must learn to love it as I love her.

I had a dream in which there was an image of a person encased in clay (much like a clay pot); the pot cracked and let the divine human out. The concept seemed to be: as one is born and lives one's life, dirt and clay accumulate on one's being until one finally becomes the clay figure and the divine human is walled up inside.

CHAPTER FOURTEEN

Day after day, Caroline sat in her deck chair, the sampler lying on her lap. The embroidered linen square, and the few words about her birth whispered to her by a dying woman, were her only connections to her Irish past. As the skyline retreated, she listened to Emily's voice again and again in her head: "Elizabeth McMaster was your mother. She died giving birth to you, on board ship. You were all alone and I couldn't let you go to strangers. Forgive me." "All alone" gave Caroline to understand her father was not with his wife, was not a passenger on the ship. Where was he? Waiting in Montreal? And what was his name? The sampler carried only the name that Elizabeth had been born with. Why had her father let his pregnant wife sail all alone to Canada? Why would any man allow his wife to embark on such a strenuous voyage in her condition? It didn't make sense. Were they running away from disapproving parents, debtors? And if they were, why weren't they together? Elizabeth McMaster had been only one year older than Sophie when she died giving birth to Caroline. Tears welled up in her eyes and spilled over the edges until they dripped onto the bright silk threads of the sampler.

The north Atlantic crossing proved easy for the steamship. The weather was flawless, clear and cloudless, day after day, and night after starry night Sophie and Caroline and other like-minded passengers wrapped themselves in warm cloaks and came on deck to avail themselves of the fresh evening air. Some expressed an interest in the stars and their formations, and those with some knowledge of astronomy shared their information with the others. Soon, a cluster of starwatchers gathered at the stern of the ship each evening to chart the different constellations. Sophie was the darling of the group. She knew all the constellations, but not by the names the others knew. And Sophie knew how each had come into being, for Nokomo's stories had answers to all their questions. Sophie's rich colouring intensified in the salt night air, until she glowed like a flame nourished by pure oxygen. Her face competed with the stars for the starwatchers' attention. They sat, circled around her, held spellbound by the stories she had first heard from Nokomo's lips and committed to memory by repeated tellings. Sophie wove the legends of her people into the movements of the stars, until it was impossible to tell which was which. As she spoke, the same magic that tinged her tales spilled over and touched her face until she blazed so brightly, her listeners were compelled to turn away while her voice plucked aside the veiled darkness of the sky and told of wonders wrapped within the layers of night.

One night the stars were so plentiful they appeared blurred and overlapping, and their reflected light in the water was more dazzling than was the light in the heavens. Sophie stopped her story in mid-sentence. The linen square which now accompanied Caroline everywhere had captured Sophie's attention. She lifted the sampler from Caroline's lap and focused on it before lifting her eyes skyward. It was some time before she spoke, and when at last she did, her voice had deepened and those in the circle had to lean forward to catch her words:

A long time ago, before my people or yours lived on the earth, man moved in unison with the heavens, according to a design outlined each night by the stars; the secrets of the gods were written across the sky for all to see. The seas and tides, the plants and animals, the stars and man moved in absolute harmony, and all knew where they belonged in the universe. There was no friction anywhere on earth. It was an ideal world.

Sophie smiled sadly before she continued.

The people grew in number and in prosperity, and some among them were not content with their place in the heavenly order. These men wished to be greater than their neighbours, and they knew that if only they understood the movements of the stars, they would have power over those on the earth and they would rule. And so these men created fear among the people regarding the reading of the stars and imposed taboos and stringent penalties on those who wished to follow the old ways. No longer was it safe for a woman to leave the shelter of her house on a clear winter night, to look into the heavens and read the meaning in the stars. It was the women who had most to lose, having been trusted by the gods with the secrets of creation. Now they had to trust these men who set themselves above the cosmic order to interpret the message of the gods. In time, only a select few knew how to read the evening sky and possess the wisdom written there. These men called themselves priests and used this knowledge to their own advantage. No women were admitted to their order.

Unbeknownst to the priests was a woman called Malacha who could still unravel the mysteries of the heavens. She had learned the art from an older woman who had befriended her as a child; no one knew Malacha had the knowledge. When she married, she kept her secret even from her husband, for although he was of royal blood, he ruled his people with permission from the priests. The woman had warned Malacha not to trust the priests. It was very lonely for Malacha; she could not share her secret. She had two children, twins: a boy, whom the priests named Mundi and who would, one day, succeed his father and be king, and a daughter, whom Malacha called Astrela. Malacha spent her days at her loom, spinning, weaving, and dreaming of the secrets that she alone of all women still possessed. She was determined that what she knew should survive her death and one day help lead her people back to the old ways, where all men shared the magic that was life. Day after day, as she wove the brightly coloured threads, her children playing about her feet, Malacha found herself weaving a pattern she had not set. She continued letting her fingers guide the design without her interference. When the piece was done and she removed it from the loom, Malacha realized she had, in her tapestry, stitched the code to translating the wisdom of the gods. If one knew where to look, the cipher to this wisdom lay waiting in her stitches. Malacha laughed out loud, and the little girl playing by her mother's feet looked up and smiled.

When Astrela was old enough to hold a needle, Malacha taught her to stitch the pattern that she herself had woven quite unconsciously. She made the little girl stitch it over and over again until the design was imprinted in Astrela's memory and she could transfer it through her needle to the cloth without thought. On the eve of Astrela's wedding day, Malacha took the girl into the desert, and under the watchful eyes of the star-studded sky, she initiated Astrela into the mysteries of the old ways. Malacha pointed out each secret written by the gods in starry letters, and when all the knowledge had passed into Astrela's care, Malacha unrolled the tapestry that had hung over her bed for all these years and spread it on the sand.

Malacha motioned for Astrela to kneel beside her, and when she had done so, Malacha stroked the tapestry and pointed to the heavens.

"Remember this, Astrela: as above, so below."

The girl followed the sweep of her mother's eyes from the woven cloth to the heavens and back again. A smile crossed her face as she recognized the pattern stitched into the cloth as the very one stitched in the stars and written large across the sky. Her eyes twinkled and her fingers threaded an imaginary needle and began to embroider an intricate design in the desert night. Malacha smiled and raised a finger to her lips. The priests never suspected that the secrets they had claimed for themselves were taught stitch by stitch by the mothers of Malacha's line, and passed intact to each succeeding generation of daughters.

A hush settled over the circle following Sophie's story and magnified. Its frail sides expanded beyond the boundaries of the original circle until they enclosed the boat, the sea and the sky itself. Only the steady lapping of the waves against the side of the ship gave some semblance of reality to the group. Inside the enormous bubble they were aware of stepping outside the rules imposed by time and space, a wondrous and frightening place. No one moved or spoke until Sophie's voice punctured the bubble. Her voice was hollow with fatigue and empty of emotion as she jerked the circle back to life. "Excuse me, please. I am exhausted. I'll see you below, Caroline. Good night."

Sophie rose, barely able to support herself, and the sampler slipped to the deck where it lay unnoticed and unclaimed. Her departure broke the spell that had lifted them beyond themselves. The group fragmented into smaller groups and then dispersed, leaving Caroline alone. She retrieved the fallen sampler, placing it gently across her lap. She caressed the cloth with her fingertips, receptive to the shape of each silken knot, while her eyes explored the cryptic sky. Motionless, she formed a small dark pool of humanity in that vast hall roofed in starlight and grounded in the pale shifting prints of stars reflected in the sea. It was as though she had entered an immense room with mirrored sides, where the points of light slid from one star-soaked surface to another, echoing and enlarging the outline of a primeval flame until it was impossible to distinguish the flame from its reflections. She waited. The firmament began to lighten, and the stars faded from brightness into the blue of sky and sea.

There were no more meetings. Sophie no longer appeared on deck after the evening meal, and there was an instinctive communal feeling among those who had been there that that evening's performance could never be duplicated and should not be. It wasn't until the night before they were to dock that Sophie came on deck in the evening again. Caroline's chair was pulled close to the railing and she had the sampler lying across her lap. Without a word Sophie leaned over and removed it for a second time. She touched each letter of the inscription with her long fingers.

"Elizabeth McMaster. Who was she?"

"My mother."

"I thought as much."

"I never knew her. She gave birth to me aboard ship, on the way to Canada."

Caroline's eyes grew large and thoughtful and she whispered to herself. "She looked at this same night sky and wondered at its meaning. She sat on deck and watched the stars move, guessing at their secrets, just like me."

The likeness of their actions delighted Caroline; she could share something of her mother's life. She smiled at Sophie for the first time in months.

"Yes, Caroline, just like you."

Sophie trained her transparent eyes on Caroline's face; the double image of the strange woman of the stream surfaced in Sophie's eyes. She dropped her gaze only when she was certain that Caroline had seen the woman's face.

"Sophie, what are you trying to tell me?"

"Nothing you don't already know. If your mother was from Galway, why are we going to Liverpool?"

SUMMER SCHOOL

for angels: I sit on the dock and wait for the enlightenment that comes like thunder and lightning. We see the illumination in a brilliant flash but must wait for the words. These cosmic analogies are so simple and elegant. I am a child in this larger dimension. I trust the angels. They have made such a commitment to me. They have outdone themselves this week in pyrotechnical displays, giving me everything from shooting stars to rainbows, and finally a most awesome storm… a storm to strike fear into the hearts of men, a storm to cleanse the soul of terror. This place, this space, is *Holy the Firm* for me.

What language do the angels speak? I think they speak in poetry, in moonlight, in the eyes of children and from the tops of trees.

I listened to Peter Gzowski interview Jack Shadbolt, who, at eighty-one, is collecting his paintings for an exhibition. He said, "It is like collecting parts of your past." This struck a chord. What were those two years all about? A spell was cast and then removed. Did I pass some sort of test?

Don't you understand... I don't want to be a second-class man. I want to be a first-class woman. I am feeling tremendous rage with my femaleness, which has let me down dreadfully. Here I have been working so hard to take charge of my life, to make my own decisions and to question which patriarchal decisions are good for me. Having done this, I walked a road which allowed me to be strong psychologically, but physically that same road nearly did me in. At the end of this particular journey, I find myself holding the same hand I was holding at the beginning. But this time I made a conscious choice. What a circuitous route one travels to "know thyself."

I had a lovely waking dream in which I was the page pursued by the pen, and the two were engaged in an act of love (creation). I was too lazy to get out of my warm bed to record the sentences. I have very nearly finished another journal, my third... a record of a middle-aged woman coming of age. I am starting to understand tolerance and learning, an opening up of the senses, and like the schoolboys of pre-war England, a way to understand beauty in a very brutal world. Cyril Connolly's *Enemies of Promise* is a delicate path through a very masculine schoolboys' world, and from it I glimpsed a society that preferred the risks of homosexuality for their young men to the taint of the feminine. Better to send them off to boarding school than to leave them too long under the influence of the mother. What a price western society has paid for this decision.

CHAPTER FIFTEEN

Dublin was not what they expected. The ferry across the Irish Sea delivered Caroline and Sophie to a thriving waterfront and the sights and sounds of a bustling commercial port. Open sheds, stacked to their roofs with baskets of agricultural produce, waited to be loaded into the empty holds of foreign ships. Men pulling wagons piled high with waxy cabbages shouted at other men manoeuvring barrows of smoked hams around enormous barrels of salted fish. Sophie and Caroline had expected a country beaten to its knees by starvation and poverty. Where was the famine? Fifty ships, anchored offshore, waited their turn to enter the harbour and load their holds with the foodstuffs of Ireland. The women watched in confusion as streams of golden grain poured into cargo bays. Why would a country send thousands of its own people on the verge of starvation to a foreign land, when they had enough of a surplus that they could afford to export food to the markets of England and the continent?

The passenger Caroline questioned about the famine was annoyed at her ignorance. "The potato crop failed, not any others."

"Why weren't those starving people..."

The man cut her off. "Their crop failed, not ours. Don't you understand?" He turned abruptly and strode to the far end of the deck.

Sophie and Caroline could not leave Dublin fast enough. Their map pointed to Galway on the west coast as their destination. They booked a compartment on the next train crossing the pinched waist of Ireland.

The grand railway station was home to hundreds of shrunken souls who moved in a weightless mass as Sophie and Caroline made their way to the departure platform.

"A coin please, your ladyship. I've had nothing to eat in days and my wife's in a terrible bad condition." An outstretched hand touched Caroline's sleeve. A man of indeterminate age, whose folds of facial skin concealed a blackened set of teeth and a pair of glittering eyes, faced her. She opened her purse, but when she lifted her head, coin in gloved hand, she found herself swimming in a sea of gray and hungry faces. Hands pulled softly at her clothing and a steady hum of noise buzzed inside her head. Caroline succumbed to their desperation, drawn gently but relentlessly into the current created by their bodies. She heard the blast of a whistle faintly, as though it came from under water, but it had no meaning. Humanity surrounded her. Only when a uniformed policeman caught her arm and detached her from the crowd did she realize she had become separated from Sophie.

"There, ma'am, are you steady now? Mustn't let those beggars shove you around. Nuisances they are, but they mean no harm. Let's get you back to your young friend. Good thing she alerted me. Too many of those beggars are hungry for one person to satisfy their wants. Strangers here, are you?" He didn't wait for Caroline's confirmation. "Must be. No Irishman or Englishman, that's a bloody laugh, excuse me, ma'am, those closefisted English bastards wouldn't help anybody. If you want to help them, you must give me some coins."

Caroline handed him all the coins she had, and he flung the bright bits of copper into the middle of the hunched and silent mob. They reacted like starlings to a feed of breadcrumbs; the clamour echoed and reverberated around the cavernous station and up into the huge vaulted ceiling. Under cover of the noise and confusion, Caroline, escorted by the policeman, slipped away to board her train. Sophie was waiting on the platform.

"What happened? One minute you were beside me, the next you were gone. Are you all right?"

White-faced, Caroline put her arms around Sophie. "I'm fine. I'll be fine."

From the plush depth of the compartment's chairs, Sophie and Caroline watched the soft Irish countryside slide past soot-streaked windows. The land was green and wet and lush even though it was mid-November. Everything, even the air, was coated with a soft mist that curled like silver smoke. Cottages with thick thatched roofs nestled in the distant curves of undulating hills, undisturbed by the movements of man or beast. They had seen no one since the Dublin station, as if the countryside had been put to sleep. All that day, the train rolled smoothly through glowing green country, across ebony dark rivers and past whitewashed villages, stopping only to stoke the burners that fuelled the train's flight. Still, no one, not even livestock, broke the spell. In late afternoon, the satiny texture of the midlands gave way to a rougher landscape, where the fields were dotted with old and weathered stones and the hillsides were steeper and crisscrossed with low stone fences.

Caroline watched from the window. The countryside was so empty. As the train neared the coast, she scanned the stonewalled fields and vacant farms for signs of life. Rocks, lying heavy and still in the fields, became the corpses of hungry peasants who had died after roaming from town to town in search of food. The ditches running parallel to the chalky roads held more bodies, and as she pressed her trembling forehead to the glass, a swollen-bellied child standing beside the ditch reached up and scratched the window of the coach, looking in at Caroline with huge unfocused eyes. She shrank into the rich plush depths of the chair. With shaking hands, she pressed her fingers to her cheeks to steady them.

"Did you see him?'

"See who, Caroline?"

"The starving child clawing at the window of the train."

Sophie looked blankly at her.

Caroline shook her head and passed her hand in front of her eyes. "You saw nothing?"

Sophie stared and mouthed the word "Nothing."

"He was so real. You saw nothing? He looked so hungry, Sophie."

Sophie took the older woman's hands in hers and held them tightly. She wiped Caroline's dirt-streaked face with her handkerchief and they waited for the slowing of the train to tell them they were approaching Galway. Sophie organized their departure, engaging a porter, requesting a hotel, and finally querying a man on where they should begin their search for lost relatives.

"Miss, the English have all the records. They lock everything up in that building over there, and you'll have the devil's own time prying it out of them, but it's all there in great thick books. I've seen them with my own eyes. If it's Catholics you're looking for, you'd best go to the priests. If you're lucky, the Father will take a fancy to you, and if he doesn't, he'll put you on to those that do. The English keep the records, but the Church keeps the people."

I spent a day in Marmora with Sybil. Since the beginning of October, there have been sightings of Our Lady on a farm just outside the town. We went to Mass first. The church was packed and I was the only non-Catholic. It was unsettling to be celebrating the Virgin Mary's feast day, and only men were allowed to handle the important stuff. We were treated like children, and for the most part we acted like children. In the eyes of the angels, we are children: their children. The music was lovely and the people simple and warm. Sybil looks like she does not belong, and yet she does. We left for the Greensides' farm, where Our Lady has been appearing à la Medjugorje in Yugoslavia. There were a thousand people on the hillside by Station #10—the Greensides have made their property into the Stations of the Cross. I felt very holy, and something funny was happening with the sun... it seemed to be pulsating. I saw this, but nothing else, although I did keep getting whiffs of roses. We prayed, even I did, and the visionary, a young Filipina woman called Dorrie, spoke to Our Lady and received a message. I am not sure what I saw or smelt, but I do know that I was part of a spiritual experience... a thousand people, all anticipating the miraculous.

CHAPTER SIXTEEN

Caroline and Sophie were the first people in the registry office the next morning. The clerk looked disdainfully at the two women, who might or might not be related, as they handed him a square of embroidered linen. Whatever did they mean him to do with that? Deciphering information stitched on a piece of cloth was not his job. He could not recall a similar circumstance in all his years at the registry office, but they tried his patience still further.

"Please, sir, do you have a record of an Elizabeth McMaster in your books? We are looking for any information you might have concerning her."

The elder of the two spoke in the flat, uncultured tones of the American colonies.

The thin clerk puffed visibly under the beseeching gaze of the applicants. They were an exceedingly handsome pair. Were they related? He thought that likely— why else would they be travelling together to look for a lost relative? The mother obviously had a bit of Irish in her; what else could explain the red hair and the bright blue of her eyes? No doubt, she'd trace her ancestors to a farm in Donegal or to one of the crossroads towns sprinkling the south of Ireland. The young one, she was a puzzle. She didn't look like any Irish girl he had ever seen, and yet the straight dark hair and colourless eyes could have passed for a strain of Irish. So many foreigners had landed on these shores and stayed, it was difficult to guess the origins of all the Irish. He refocused his eyes on the linen square with the tiny script stitched in.

"Elizabeth McMaster. Not so common a name in this county. There would be McMasters, I believe, to the north and east of us, but not here. Let me check."

He placed a small pair of eyeglasses on his nose and lifted a large leather volume from a shelf concealed beneath the counter. Caroline reached out to clutch Sophie's hand. Her lips moved silently as the clerk's finger pursued the line of names in the open register.

"No McMaster. I thought not. I would have recognized the name if it had been recorded since I came. It's been twenty full years since I was put in charge of Galway." He consulted the sampler's script.

"1802. That was before my time. Those records will be in another book."

He returned in a moment, carrying a large rectangular book with gold lettering down its spine.

"1802." Slowly, with great deliberation, he read the names down the pages. When he had finished all the Mc's, he looked over the top of his glasses at Sophie and Caroline.

"Nothing under McMaster. I should have saved myself the trouble."

He felt sorry for them, and yet he was pleased that he had been right. Still, it was a shame they had come so far for nothing.

"Was there another name I could help you with?"

His bureaucratic air was dashed as Sophie leaned across the oak counter that served as a barrier between the public and its records and urged him to pursue the matter further. The watered silk of her clear eyes undid his firm resolve to dismiss the women quickly.

"There must have been some reason why she stitched 1802 and County Galway on her sampler. It means everything to us to find out something about her family."

The neat little clerk was as confused by the intimation of violence he heard in Sophie's voice as he was captivated by the silky twilight in her eyes. He no longer knew which sense to trust.

"Miss, I will surely try, but I must warn you that it will almost certainly be useless. These ledgers are exact. The Home Government insists on detailed accurate records, and I have never known them to be in error."

Her eyes deepened and a hint of menace washed their surface. He hastened to add, "I'll check the other years."

The women stood taut and erect, stretched between the years until he returned laden with the dusty records of Galway's past. They waited patiently while he turned the pages, running his finger down one line of names and then another. At last he raised his head.

"There is something here that might or might not mean something to you. No mention of an Elizabeth, mind you, but in 1807, a Charles McMaster registered the birth of a son, Thomas, at Kingsmill Manor, County Galway."

Caroline could not reply; she was struck dumb by the names he spoke. Charles, Thomas. She knew these names. These people belonged to her and she to them. Had Sophie not kept a tight grip on her hand, she might have dropped to the floor. She barely heard Sophie's next question.

"Why, thank you. I am sure this is the family we are looking for, even though there is no mention of an Elizabeth. Is there anything else written there that might give us a clue to their whereabouts?"

He dipped his head into the ledger and traced his finger across the page, reading aloud as he moved his finger.

"Charles Rolston McMaster, born in County Roscommon, Protestant, husband of Mary Ellen Strathy, born County Mayo, Roman Catholic. Now that's a bit of news! A Catholic and a Protestant marrying, that's not so common in these parts, and look at this, their son is registered as a Protestant. Mary Ellen Strathy must have taken a verbal beating from her parish priest. They hate to lose any of them, and for sure they want the children. I wouldn't have liked to be in her shoes. Do you know if your Elizabeth McMaster was a Protestant?"

Caroline spoke without knowing what it was she would say. "Yes, she was a Protestant."

He continued, "Then it's likely you've got the right family. She must have been their first-born, and I'm wondering if she was born out of wedlock. That would solve the mystery of her not being registered. Go to the Church of England registry office. They would have had to be married there; no priest would have touched them. Ask the curate to search the records of all the marriages registered between a Protestant and a Catholic for the period between 1797 and 1807 and I'll wager you will find your answer. There won't be many. You had best be setting out for Kingsmill Manor after you have checked the church records. It's not too far, near the little village of

Ballindooly. You can easily hire a cart and driver and look it over for yourselves. Good luck to you."

And with that, he tipped an imaginary hat to the foreign ladies, who were already halfway to the door.

Like Caroline and Sophie, I too have arrived in Dublin. The synchronicity of this is not lost on me. What are the odds of the three of us arriving in Dublin at the same moment, when two made the journey in fiction and over a hundred and forty years ago? My trip has paralleled theirs: we drove straight across the middle of Ireland to Galway, stopping only at Clonmacnoise, an ancient cathedral compound dating from the sixth century. Clonmacnoise was the center of Irish monasticism, symbolized by the ringed Irish cross. The crossover from the old goddess/nature religion into Christianity can still be traced in parts of Irish monasticism. This place speaks so clearly to me. There is the shell of an absolutely beautiful little nuns' church, set apart from the cathedral by a causeway. It is exquisitely carved, and reminds me of the decorations in illuminated manuscripts.

We went to Cong yesterday, where Michael's family has roots. Ashford Castle is there. That part of my life is finished. The exclusive, locked-in-the-castle life that I thought I wanted is a bore. We followed a perky little Jack Russell, who appointed himself our guide, all over town. I loved the Abbey, smashed again and again by the English, but the lovely cloister remains. I have such an affinity for cloisters. Breakfast overlooking Dingle Bay, lambs on the lawn, and water still as a mirror. I think this may be the most beautiful place I have visited. In the distance, on the hill, is what looks like an Irish round tower. There was such a separate culture thriving here, and it was always in harmony with the land. Everything follows the circle, no beginning and no end, the rhythms of nature expressed in the round: round towers, ringed crosses, spirals as carved decorations, and the beehive huts of the hermit monks. Michael and I are moving nicely together, smooth like the landscape, well-worn and well-loved. The Irish children are beautiful. I saw porpoises in Dingle Bay, and just when I thought it wasn't happening, a connection was made with a nun from Smeen. We had a lovely chat about Celtic Christianity and she mentioned that some scholars are convinced that the Celts arrived in Ireland from Egypt. Now wouldn't that make sense?

The Rock of Cashel holds magic... I do believe all the connections between the old religion, the land and the kings were located on that piece of ground, a huge rock erupting out of a hill in the center of a vast plain. No wonder it appeared to be a place of power. One must confront and walk into one's fear in order to feel empowered. I am beginning to understand. Has Andrea always known this?

CHAPTER SEVENTEEN

"And why would you be wanting to go to Ballindooly, my ladies?"

Their driver had been raised, he was quick to tell them, not far from Ballindooly, and his name was Pat. Here was a stroke of luck: a man whose roots were in the place they sought had been practically thrown across their path. Caroline tried to guess his age from what she remembered of his face and what she could surmise from his broad back, not stooped or hunched, and his full head of dark hair under the cap. Life had taught Caroline that men wore their years better than women. Pat might be thirty-five or fifty; if he were fifty, he might have known Elizabeth McMaster. She made the calculations in her head. Even if he were under forty, he might know the family; and he would know Kingsmill Manor. She took a deep breath to slow the pounding of her heart, and tapped Pat on the shoulder.

"Kingsmill Manor. What do you know of it?"

Pat swung around abruptly, dropping the reins. The horse slowed to a walk. His reply was almost rude— not the words, but the way in which he spoke them, disconcerting from a man who had been so affable.

"What would you ladies be wanting at Kingsmill Manor?"

If Caroline was stung into silence, Sophie was not. She snapped back at him, "What difference does it make to you? Your business is to drive us there." She nodded at the fallen reins and the stationary horse. Pat's face reddened and he quickly retrieved the reins, giving the unsuspecting horse a smart slap in the process. They trotted on.

"Are you looking for someone at the Manor, then?"

"It could be that we are."

"And if you were looking for someone there," Pat had entered into the spirit of the game, "would they be folk who live in a manor house or in a cottage?"

Sophie countered with a question of her own. "Would it make a difference?"

"To some, it might."

Caroline could hold back no longer. "McMaster. Is that a name you have heard before?"

Pat slapped the reins lightly on the horse's back.

"No… I can't say I have. I only know what my gran and my mum say about the old castle— that's what we call Kingsmill Manor. A bad business went on there during the hunger, and maybe long before that. My mum warned me never to get mixed up with any folks that lived there."

After a long pause, Caroline asked, "What happened?"

"I left long before the famine came, but people say the castle agent, the one who turned the folk out of their homes, was found dead one morning on the road to Ballindooly, his head smashed in by a rock— by more than one rock, I heard. His horse returned without him to the stables, trembling and in a fine lather. The constabulary came and interviewed the tenants that hadn't been turned out, but no one had seen or heard anything. Sir Rodney threatened to evict everyone remaining if someone didn't tell about what happened, but no one ever came forward. The police report said the castle agent had fallen from his horse and hit his head. He was known to be a heavy drinker." Pat bent to his task of keeping the horse and cart moving smoothly along the pebbled road between the low stone fences.

"But your granny and your mother, what do they say?"

Caroline was surprised at her own boldness. Sophie asked such questions. But when Pat finally spoke, he turned right around in his seat and looked directly at Caroline.

"My gran said it was the women who took care of that man, though she never said how they did it or how she knew. My mother was very cross at her for telling me, but everyone in this part of the county knows the story or thinks they do. It's just that no one talks about it. It's better that way."

Caroline could not let it go. "What makes them think the women killed him? Why is it better that no one talks about it?"

"Why, it's better for everyone."

He swung back to face the road, cutting off the opportunity for further questions.

Ballindooly was but a half day's journey from Galway, and they reached the village before noon. Pat pulled the horse up short in front of what appeared to be Ballindooly's public house, and announced in his finest tones, "Well, here we be, ladies, in the fair town of Ballindooly. Hey, is there no one here to give these lovely colleens a welcome? They've come all the way from across the sea to find their Irish cousins and we've no one to wish them good day? 'Tis shame on you for your bad manners." He cocked his head and adjusted his cap to a jauntier angle. There was no one other than Sophie and Caroline to appreciate his performance.

"They'll all be at their dinners or in church, more likely in church, for what dinner there is doesn't take long to eat. You ladies be aware of how hard this part of Ireland took the failure of the potato crops? They died by the hundreds up here. Whole families starved to death with none to help them. They'll be on their knees, no doubt, those that survived, giving thanks to God Almighty for sparing them the fate of their brothers and sisters."

Caroline's face lost colour, and she might have fallen from the seat had Sophie not placed a restraining arm about her shoulders.

The noon-high sun cast no shadows on the whitened road. The two women shaded their eyes from its bright glare in order to see the cross that topped the church spire standing on the only rise of land in the village.

"Shall we stop here, then, and make enquiries of the local population after we find a drop or two to ease a parched man's throat?"

"It's not far now, is it, to Kingsmill Manor?"

Pat lifted his eyes skyward as if praying for divine intervention. The thought of rolling through a village without stopping for a bite of food and a pint of ale, and it now past twelve o'clock, was more than the man could counter on his own.

Sophie spoke out. "Take us out there and leave us to our business. When you've finished your dinner and the horse is well-rested, come back and pick us up. Here's money for your meal."

The plan suited Pat, although he grumbled good-naturedly. They continued through the village and onto a track that followed the edge of a lake. The lough, for that's what Pat called the lake spilling across the valley floor, was as still as death, and yet the sunlight playing on the water gave life and motion to its mirrored surface. No one spoke until Pat pointed to the castle.

"There be the place you be looking for. Looks neglected now! The master fled to England when the troubles came, leaving the people to fend for themselves. The craven coward! He's still afraid to come back." Pat spat on the ground to show his contempt. "I beg your pardon, ladies."

The castle was covered with ivy. Emerald green leaves trailed everywhere, coating the old stone walls with thick foliage. The plant wandered freely over windows and crawled across the rough surfaces to reach the slates of the roof, where it hung in great green bunches from the chimneys, as if the castle was slowly being swallowed alive by a lush green growth that would in time cause the walls to disappear forever.

Ah, such a place, my place. I can hardly hold the pen, so in tune am I with where I am. I must be close to that mystical third state. I should not even be writing it down; I should simply be. Everything is sound (wind and waves) and touch (sun and sand) and taste; a cookie has the texture and the sacredness of a communion wafer. I know in my bones what the meaning of "eat of my flesh" is: this world is the gods' flesh... bite, enjoy, taste, swallow, fill yourself up on this beautiful, beautiful world. Smell it, crisp and salty; burrow your feet into it; caress it; make love to this world. The ocean is rushing towards me— swelling up and exploding into creamy foam— a continuous cosmic orgasm. I could curl up on this deserted beach and fall out of time. The ocean has an urgency... pounding, and then a long spell of silence. I am ready to face the gods, if that is what is written. Shells like angels' wings have appeared on the edge of the sand, and the sea grapes are spread in profusion, like a sea vineyard. I can hardly focus, so sacred is this place.

CHAPTER EIGHTEEN

The lawn leading to the house rose in a soft wavy incline from the dirt road. It, too, was madly overgrown, and waist-high grass competed with the spreading ivy for full control of the property. Two small stone houses slanting outward had once formed the side walls of massive gates that framed the entrance to the castle. Their windows lacked glass, and holes studded the mortar where wooden shutters and window sashes had been ripped from their postings.

Caroline was the first to light and walk towards the nearest gatehouse. Then something changed her mind, and she crossed the driveway to peer through the sightless window of the further one. Sophie climbed down, leaving Pat free to return to Ballindooly. Caroline started up the drive, setting course and pace, with Sophie following precisely in her wake. She picked her way past the overgrown house without stopping, crossed the courtyard and proceeded to the rear of the castle. There she checked herself. The wreckage that lay unnoticed from the road was spread out here, displayed for all to see. Every second cottage was uninhabitable. Thatched roofs had disappeared along with doors and windows, and no bright green ivy trailed soft tendrils across the broken walls to mask the damage. Shattered stones lay everywhere, evidence of the violent evictions. The tenants in the battered cottages had been driven out and the buildings smashed to ensure that no family would come creeping back. Caroline and Sophie travelled the length of the row of houses and saw that the ones still standing, although rundown and neglected, were at least habitable; from these cottages rose wisps of smoke. The second row of cottages revealed the same degree of devastation. They moved swiftly down the line of cottages until they came to the edge of a field. There, behind and slightly apart from its neighbours, stood one dwelling intact and untouched; yet no smoke curled from its chimney.

Caroline followed the remains of a path through the undergrowth to the front door. She knocked and waited and then entered the unlocked cottage. As her eyes became accustomed to the light filtering through the filthy windows, she picked out the rough shape of a fireplace and the outlines of a table, chairs and a dresser. More things emerged in the half light: dishes, displayed on the dresser, an iron pot suspended from a hook over long-dead coals, and a dark cloak hanging by the corner of the fireplace. She moved slowly and with great care into the center of the room, touching each object, letting her fingers linger on their surfaces, learning their texture through her skin. Those that were small enough she cradled briefly in her hands before holding them up for a closer look. Sophie stayed in the doorway, as Caroline inspected the room. At one end was the fireplace; at the opposite end was a door, which Caroline pushed open and walked through.

"So you be back now, are you?" The voice came from behind Sophie, who spun around to face the speaker. The dark interior of the cottage washed the rich colour from Sophie's lips and face, leaving only a tall slim figure in black and white.

"I thought it was you. I be watching from the window." The woman angled her arm in the direction of the first row of cottages. "When you left us, the 'fret' came over the land. We waited and waited for you to come back, 'til even your own mother lost hope. My old granny watched her pine away of heartbreak until she never got up from her bed. Most of the women said it was Father Egan's curse coming true, but my gran said it was because she had nothing to live for any more. How could you do that to your own mum? You were the last, gran said, to practise the old ways, and when you were gone the goodness drained from the land. She said you should have left someone in your place. Why didn't you? You must have known that when the land died, so would the people. When the potato first failed, we went to the priest and he said it was God's way of punishing us. Gran snorted when she heard. What did he know of the land and its needs? My father slapped my gran and said it was her heathenish ways causing the potatoes to blacken and rot in the ground. Times got worse, and when we had the strength we went to church, but to tell the truth, few had the strength to walk the five miles there and the five miles back, and of that few, none were women or children. The priest stopped coming out to see us, even to bury our dead. When gran died we buried her as best we could and I think she'd be pleased to know no priest had a hand in her passing. The people of Ballindooly spread stories that we were practising pagan rites out here, but it wasn't true, for after you went away there was no one left that knew the old ways. Even gran only knew what she'd heard from her gran. She'd never done the ceremonies herself; she said you needed the sight for that. The potatoes failed again and this time almost everyone died or left. Do you see what you caused?"

Sophie towered over the woman, who could have been anywhere from forty to seventy. Her skin was loose and what hair she had was tightly drawn back inside a grayish bonnet whose strings trailed untidily across the shawl that enclosed her bent body.

"You don't remember me, then?" The little figure stepped closer to the doorway and lifted her face defiantly for Sophie to scrutinize. The tip of her nose reached across her sunken mouth and curved towards her chin. She held this outstretched pose for Sophie's inspection while she continued, "I'm Annie Murphy that was. I was thirteen when you left for America. My granny said no good would come of it, but I thought she meant no good would come for you, not that no good would come for us. Since you left, we have had nothing but bad times and death. First your mother dying, and no one to replace her that had the feeling for the herbs and the will to tend the sick. Then Sir Roger died and that ne'er-do-well that called himself his son came here to live. Your father left soon after. No wonder! The things Rodney asked him to do were the devil's own work. Make the estate pay, he said, make it pay more. Throw them out that can't pay more. You should have seen the families weeping by their cottages, all they owned in the world piled beside them, the sheriff called to batter down the only home they had ever known, nowhere for them to go, and no one to take them in. Oh, 'twas the cruellest sight, and your father tried to stop it, but he got no help. There was no reasoning with that red-haired devil! Your father even called on Father Egan and the Church to stop the evictions; he was that desperate. He hated Father Egan, and still he swallowed his pride and went to him. He got nothing from the Church and nowhere with Father Egan, and mind you, he wasn't asking for anything for himself. He had no one left.

"That was when I got to thinking of what gran had told me about the way it used to be in her granny's day, when the people still worshipped in the old ways and She in turn took care of them. Gran was glad when you began to practise the craft. She hoped the old religion would come back. I tried to remember what she told me and I asked some of the other women, but we knew so little and so much had been forgotten, we soon lost our way. Your father left and what replaced him was worse than the devil himself, all dark and full of drink. He and that Rodney, we were supposed to call them 'Sir,' but none did, only to their faces. Terrorizing the countryside, riding out in the middle of the night shouting obscenities to the sky and shooting at any creature that dared to cross their path, and sometimes they were too drunk to saddle up the horses. There were none would work in the stables once Paddy died. They carried their drinking on inside the house and shot at whatever moved outside the library windows. It was like living in Father Egan's Hell."

Caroline had finished her tour of the cottage while the old woman was speaking. She stood quietly by the doorway and listened to names she knew were connected to her mother dropping from the woman's lips.

"Do you recognize me?"

The crone reached out a callused hand to Sophie's face and gently stroked her golden cheek.

"I was by the lake that day they pulled your brother from the water and pronounced him dead. I saw you go cold and frozen. My gran said you would die, too, but that the sight would live. I was only ten years old that day, but I still remember how I shivered as you walked past me, straight and cold, and I looked into your eyes and they were dead like the eyes of birds that flew against the shining windows of the castle and broke their necks and fell to the paving stones and died with their eyes wide open. You looked like that."

A cry escaped from Caroline, revealing her presence. The old woman stepped across the threshold of the cottage.

"Who might you be? Not come from that bastard Rodney, have you?"

She stepped closer to Caroline and looked her up and down, her sharp eyes coming to rest on Caroline's hair. "You have the look of him about you, but Rodney wouldn't send a woman. He hates us and he's afraid of us. The last we saw of him was the top of his red head as he was escorted from the estate by a detachment of soldiers sent 'specially from Galway to protect the precious landlords from the hordes of starving Irish who'd been cheated and thrown from their homes. He was afraid of the same thing happening to him that happened to that wretched estate agent he brought in." Her chin wobbled with laughter. "Run off the land, he was, like the common criminal he was, by the very people he had treated like rats or worse. Lucky for him it was the men who ran him off. One good thing came from all the suffering and the misery. It surely kept old Rodney from stepping foot on the land."

Her laughter stopped and her sharp little eyes misted with memory.

Caroline took a step forward and a small boy swam towards the surface. In the same instant that he burst into her consciousness, the name "Thomas" broke from her throat.

"His name was Thomas."

The old woman backed out the door and down the weed-choked path, never taking her eyes from Caroline's face.

"Who are you?"

I have finally figured out about men and women. I am so slow. Of course, it is about power. Who has it? Who doesn't? Obviously women had it... what could be more powerful than the ability to give birth? We are the gender that holds the future of the species in our bodies. Western civilization has been the history of men taking power over the power vested in women by their life-giving function. Look at birth imagery and symbolism in art and literature, in which the very essence of giving life is totally subverted in the context of a divine birth; in which the mother plays a secondary role to both the divine Father and the divine Child. There is no question that giving birth is the most empowering event a woman can experience. I remember it well; it was the first time in my relationship with Michael that I felt sorry for him; he could not experience this incredible thing. Somehow the patriarchy got wind of this power and took over the birth process. Once you have stripped women of their most potent source of power, you are once again in control. Sickening. And look at the price western civilization is paying for this insidious little plot.

I remember hearing a story about little fawns found circled in the grass, newborn and presumably abandoned by their mothers. They were rescued by caring humans... but the zoologist who told the story gave a different interpretation. He said the mother deer placed their babies far from them because the newborns have no scent and therefore a predator would not be attracted to them, as they would be to the mother. By grazing away from the baby, she attracts the danger to herself and away from the baby. Is this what mother did for me? And if so, what was the danger? What did mother do to me that I cannot forgive?

CHAPTER NINETEEN

"Who are you?" Caroline heard herself, as if from a great distance, repeat Annie's question, and then ask another. "Who was that child?"

Was Sophie quiet because she did not have the answers, or did she not want to give them to Caroline?

Minutes passed. Sophie was the first to leave. Caroline followed her down the overgrown walk reluctantly. Annie's words had loosened the knots on a strange package that Sophie was somehow tied into. Caroline needed time to think, and she dropped further behind Sophie, letting the girl walk on alone. Sophie, too, was thinking of what Annie had said, but she was not uneasy with it. Fragments from the story held a fascination for her, as though she had heard the same story before and had forgotten it until Annie's words pulled it to the surface.

A soft, persistent tugging on her sleeve brought Sophie back to the path between the double row of cottages. Sophie turned to see a young girl touching her arm. When Sophie faced her, the girl began to speak.

"Will you be staying now? My gran says the land will listen to you. She says with you here, the hunger will have no home to come to."

To Sophie the words sounded queer, but that might have been because the girl's head was bowed and covered by a kerchief, leaving visible only a strip of chalk-white brow bordered by a band of black hair. Sophie wondered if she had heard correctly. She moved closer to the girl. The girl's body was covered from neck to ankle in a ragged shift of homespun; her feet were naked and defenceless against the cold. Sophie shivered.

"Gran says I speak in tongues, but you will understand them. She says I dream true, and what I see, you have already seen. I want to know the things you know. Will you teach me?"

Her kerchiefed head stayed down, but clear sweetness rose in her voice and swelled as no rejection came. "When the standing stones speak, the land will wake from its sleep."

Her words meant nothing to Sophie. They were just words. When the girl spoke again, there was a sense of urgency in her voice. "You must find the face in the water and wear it for your daughter or the stones will never speak."

While the girl was talking, the cottages had emptied, and Sophie found herself surrounded by women and children. She spoke to the one face in the group she recognized: "What does she want? What do her words mean?"

"She wants you to stay and learn the tongue she speaks. You'll teach her all you know of the craft, for you are the only one left."

A great warmth spread throughout Sophie's body, fuelled, she was certain, by the energy directed at her by the women. She felt capable of doing the things the girl thought she could do. Sophie glowed with the splendid brilliance of the shipboard Sophie, and her voice was deep and sure. "And you and the others, do you want me to stay?"

The black cluster of women nodded as one. With this approval, the flames in Sophie's eyes flared even brighter and she searched each face. Some lifted a hand to shield their eyes.

"Where will I live?"

The knot of women shifted and pointed thin fingers in the direction of the cottage Sophie had left.

"There, of course. Where you have always lived." It was Annie who answered, and as she spoke, she propelled two young girls ahead of her so that they stood directly in front of Sophie.

"These two be my grandchildren, the only two who survived the famine of seven in their family. Their mother died first, and then their brothers, one by one. The father had long gone to the workhouse to try and earn a crust to feed his family, but he died there of the fever. These two," and Annie touched the girl who had spoken the strange words to Sophie, and a younger version of her, on their foreheads, "are cut from a different cloth, stronger stuff than the boys. They fought to live, and so they did. The big one is Meaghn and this is Mary Rose."

The elder of the sisters lifted her head shyly, like a young animal surprised by another in a forest clearing, and spoke in a high sweet voice.

"She, to whom all things belong, must give all things back, for in the belonging is also the sharing."

As Sophie stared, mesmerized by the girl and her words, she caught a glimpse of silvered light coming from beneath Meaghn's lowered eyelids. And for the first time since Sophie had left her own people, she felt a sense of belonging.

"I'll stay for as long as you need me, but first I must tell Caroline."

The women nodded and opened their circle wide enough to allow Sophie to slip through.

Caroline was leaning against one of the pillaged gatehouses, lost to time and place. She saw the slender figure skim across the long grass and for a prolonged moment she could not remember who Sophie was. It was odd, this postponing of recognition until the body was close enough to reveal a face. Of course it was Sophie, breathless from her race through the tall grass, her face wild with colour.

"Caroline, we've got to stay and help these women. They think I'm someone else, but it doesn't matter. I can help them. A girl here, Meaghn, speaks in tongues. Have you ever heard anyone speak in tongues? It sends a shiver through your soul, and you are never happy until you can speak with them. Nokomo used to take me to the clearing in the forest where the graves of the ancestors were. On the anniversaries of their deaths, she spoke to them like Meaghn spoke to me." Sophie's eyes grew very clear and large and her voice dropped to a thin whisper. "And Caroline, I heard the spirit people answer Nokomo. I heard them, and Meaghn talks as Nokomo did. I almost know what she is saying. If I could listen harder, I could understand. Caroline, please say that you will stay here with me."

Sophie's body was quivering, and Caroline was reminded of a young hunting dog that has found the scent but has not yet been given the signal by the hunter. It would be impossible to refuse Sophie. She looked over the lake, and Nokomo's parting words came unbidden to her mind. "Take her back, Caroline, to her father's people. It is a beginning." Caroline pleaded silently for Nokomo's wisdom to reach her. Was this where Nokomo meant Caroline to bring Sophie? To this abandoned Irish estate with its handful of wretched women and children? Was this the beginning? The smooth surface of the water was ruffled by a sudden gust of wind, and Caroline saw a solitary figure in a gossamer light canoe paddling across the waves. The wind stopped and the water flattened. There was nothing on the lake. I am too fanciful, Caroline thought. Nokomo cannot come just because I call her.

She remembered what had brought them to this place, and shook her head at her own forgetfulness. Caroline couldn't leave even if she wanted to, not without first finding out all she could about her mother.

She faced the dazzling brightness in Sophie's eyes.

"Yes, Sophie. Of course I'll stay here with you."

It was late November when Caroline and Sophie moved into the cottage. Sophie cleaned and polished windows, while Caroline washed walls, scoured the hearth, and removed layers of dust from oak furniture. When the windows were washed so thoroughly that the pale autumnal sun filling the interior of the cottage caught and held the motes of dust in its light, Caroline begged Sophie to stop, and she turned her attention to the overgrown path. One woman came to watch Sophie pull the weeds away, then two. By the time Sophie had freed the path from the accumulated undergrowth, all the women were waiting at the end of the walk; they smiled shyly as Sophie got up from her knees. One of them produced a twig broom and swept the path.

Caroline watched from the window; it seemed as good a time as any to introduce herself to the other women. She had met only Annie Murphy so far, and that had not been an easy meeting. No one had said hello, or even returned the waves she had given in passing, much less come to pay a visit. She went out and spoke from the front steps.

"Good day. You have met my niece, Sophie, but you haven't met me. I am her aunt, Caroline Paterson. It was kind of you to invite Sophie and me to stay. Now that the cottage is cleaned and aired, we very much hope that you will come and see us." As Caroline advanced down the path, the women retreated. When she reached Sophie, not one other woman remained in sight.

"What have I done?"

"It's not you, Caroline. In their lives nothing good has ever come from a stranger. Be patient."

Caroline tilted her head to get a better look at Sophie's face. Sophie was getting taller every day.

"How do you know that? And if they are so afraid of strangers, why aren't they afraid of you? And where are the men? I find Kingsmill Manor most peculiar. I'm even beginning to find you peculiar."

Caroline went back into the cottage. She had tried, and it was humiliating to be rebuffed again. Even Sophie seemed to have turned against her; she was always in and out of their houses and hardly ever in her own. Caroline would be as wary and aloof with these Irish women as they were with her. And she wasn't going to ask for Sophie's help, either. Sophie had eased into their lives with the instincts of one who has been absent for a time but still retains a memory of the rhythm of their life.

Caroline, left to her own devices, explored the estate, ever hopeful that someone would talk to her about Elizabeth McMaster. Many times she caught the women staring at her, but no longer did she smile and wave at them. She continued about her business, ignoring their hostility until they bent their shawl-draped heads and returned to their work. Their dislike baffled Caroline. What had she done to earn such animosity? She was too proud to ask Sophie a second time. Caroline began to hate to leave the cottage.

It was dark and Caroline was alone, as usual, when she heard a noise outside the window. Listening carefully, she moved quietly to the source of the sound and heard it again. It was a child's voice. Opening the door, she called out a greeting; she could see nothing but blackness. Caroline sensed the child before she spotted him. After patient coaxing, a small boy with a thin white face appeared beyond her doorstep.

"How nice of you to come and see me. Would you like a biscuit?"

He crept closer but remained some distance from the steps.

"Yes, please, mum, and could I have something for my dinner? The smell's so good and I'm hungry, and so are my sisters and my mother."

"You can have as much as you can carry. Come inside while I fill a bucket for you to take home."

He jumped back into the blackness. "Oh, I couldn't do that. My ma would kill me if she knew I was here. She told me never to set foot inside this house when you were home."

"Wait here. I'll be right back."

Caroline filled a tin bucket to its brim from the kettle simmering on the hearth, and wrapped a thick piece of bread, baked that day, in a clean towel. She delivered them— with a warm smile and an invitation to come again— to the small hand that reached from the shadows to receive her gifts. He was gone before she thought to ask his name.

Caroline could never again complain of being alone. Every evening there were three, and sometimes more, children's faces in the shadows. They never knocked, but Caroline could tell when they were there. She would go immediately to the door and open it wide, letting the light from her fire spill across the threshold. She would speak in a soft low voice into the surrounding darkness; soon, one empty bucket after another would appear on the bottom step. They thought themselves well-hidden in the shadows, but Caroline could see them clearly, outlined in the light coming through the door. It was not long before she came to recognize her visitors. There was the boy who had been the first to come, the eldest of the group, maybe ten, though it was hard to tell— the children were thin and undersized. He came almost every night, and was the only one to talk to her. Almost as old was a girl Caroline thought she had seen before, a thin little thing with the most extraordinarily alive face, all eyes and mouth. Caroline had to restrain herself from moving closer to get a better look, but she had learned her lesson with their mothers. The third of the regular visitors was a tiny boy, no more than six, who never spoke and whose freckles seemed to fly off his face with fear whenever she knelt to hand him his bucket. He was so frightened of her that she took pity on him and placed his bucket on the bottom step rather than handing it to him. She never sent anyone away empty-handed, and she never let the children know that she had memorized their features. Caroline would have recognized them anywhere.

I walked along the beach this morning
And heard the ocean breathe

As I walked Four Mile Beach, lots of things fell into place. We come out of the sea, picked clean by salt and sun and seawater... curved and pared to essence... nothing left (no flesh, nothing extra)... salted, as Annie Dillard says in *Holy the Firm*. Everything makes meaning but we must get through the mist. Two more clues from nature: termite mounds are only one-third of what we see above the ground; the nest is two-thirds below ground... it is the same ratio with icebergs. Does this ratio extend to humans? Only one-third of our lives is visible? The second clue came from the bloodwood trees in Kakadu National Park. They are tall trees with a sinuous shape and pure white bark that is so like skin I found myself stroking it. It even wrinkled where the branches began... the sap was garnet or blood coloured, hence the name, and crystallized into little pellets. But it was the shapes that drove me crazy... I longed to be able to draw what I saw... beautiful female forms... some stretched out with their backs arched; some with their arms upraised like Cretan goddesses; and some like the figureheads on a ship's bow. They are breathtaking and awesome. I wonder if I have stumbled into the Garden of Eden, the pre-lapsarian state, before one intellectualized the world in order to dominate it. We came from the sea, and as we evolved we moved inland and lost touch with "our country of origin"... only now and then do we hear the sound of the ocean breathing, and remember where we came from.

Whatever that was has been internalized, digested and resolved... I have no outer edges. I am, in Donne's words, part of all that I have met. I love the sun on my skin... illumination on my mind. I must remember not to want to retain my turn in the sun for too long. Swimming back across the summer magic of the bay, I thought, I have been on a long journey and now I am nearing home, just as Caroline is. Incredible how she and I are taking this journey to our mothers together.

CHAPTER TWENTY

There came a morning when the staples were exhausted. Caroline decided to walk to Ballindooly to purchase what they needed and to make arrangements for their delivery. She was considering buying a cow and some chickens, if livestock was to be had. It would be nice to give the children milk and eggs. It was a longer walk than she had thought, and the wind blowing from the lough was bitter; she arrived in Ballindooly so cold and tired that a cross word would have sent her into tears. She was in luck; the storekeeper was friendly, possibly the first kindly person she had come across since arriving at Kingsmill Manor. Caroline placed her order, chatting companionably. The man was a storehouse of information, answering every one of her questions concerning the purchase of a cow and some chickens, going so far as to offer to send one of the local farmers out to see her.

"Where is it you are staying, then?"

When Caroline told him Kingsmill Manor, he stepped back from the counter, his face puckered in confusion.

"Are the menfolk back, then?"

"No," Caroline said, "there are no men at Kingsmill Manor. In over a month I haven't seen a boy older than ten. Why is that?"

"You've not heard of the road gangs run by the relief agency? All the men and older boys hire themselves out to the government to work on the roads. Each one is fed and at the end of their work detail they are paid a small sum of money. It's not much, but at least they don't starve. Folks at the castle suffered terribly during the hunger, perhaps more than other folks, and that was bad enough."

Caroline lingered by the counter. She wanted him to continue. It gave him confidence, and he posed a question of his own.

"What brings you here? We don't see many strangers in this part of Ireland."

There was nothing hostile in the look he gave her, only curiosity. She chanced the question she had been saving since her arrival at the estate.

"I'm looking for relations of mine by the name of McMaster. I was told in Galway there was once an agent by that name at Kingsmill Manor. I've come to find out whether I am related to this family."

"I remember Mr. McMaster, a fine man and well thought of in these parts, even though he was a Protestant. But you'd do better to talk to my da'. He's seen all the goings and comings at the castle for better than fifty years."

He pointed her to a back room, where a small fire glowed hotly and a chair stood pulled before the hearth. In it was an old man with wisps of white hair covering his pink scalp. He and the huge gray cat asleep in his lap shared the warmth of the fire.

"Da', here's someone to see you."

The storekeeper bent over the old man and stroked his arm until his watery eyes opened.

"Should you disturb him?"

"Oh, he sleeps more than he wakes nowadays. It's good for him to have a visitor, especially one who wants to know about the old days. He would be cross with me if I didn't wake him up to talk to you. He's feeble, but his mind's in good shape. He lives in the past; he saw so many die in the famine that now he only remembers things from before those terrible years. You won't remind him of it, will you?"

She shook her head, for she could not speak. *Saw so many die,* he had said. Tears filled her eyes and she knelt by the old man.

"The lady wants to know about the McMasters that used to live at the castle. Tell her all you know, da'."

A bell from the front of the store sounded, and the storekeeper eased himself from his position beside his father.

"Will you excuse me? I have a customer."

The old man straightened in his chair and leaned closer to Caroline.

"I remember her well. She was a beauty, real Irish, with black, black hair, and eyes so dark a blue they looked like the sky before a storm. She never went to school with us— they were black Protestants— but for all that, she was the prettiest girl I ever saw. The day she left, they waited by the public house for the coach, and I watched her 'til they pulled away. She was a beauty, but she never came back."

Caroline's reaction was electric. She knew he was describing her mother. She had to hear him say it. She had to be sure.

"What was her name, the beautiful girl?"

"Her name? McMaster, of course. I thought you said McMaster. Elizabeth McMaster. I'll never forget the way she looked that day, huge eyes and black curls, bundled in a dark green cloak."

Caroline trembled, and the tears hiding under her bottom lashes spilled down her cheek.

"Do you remember when she left? What year was it?"

The old man leaned forward and gently stroked her wet cheek.

"Don't cry, my lady, old Stephen will remember. I was a big lad then, 'most ready to be married to my Molly. I remember I felt bad thinking how beautiful another girl was when my Molly was waiting for me to marry her. Molly and me were married at Christmas in 1818, and Elizabeth left not long before that time. For sure she and Sir Roger Kingsmill left at the end of October, or early November, 1818. He helped her into the coach, for the step up seemed too steep for her. I always wondered why she left. There were rumours; there are always rumours about a beautiful girl. He was a decent man, though, or her mother and father would never have let her go with him. They were good people. Ellen saved my youngest brother's life when he was just a little fellow and had the croup. My mother told us we were never to say anything unkind about the McMasters, and if others did, we were to stick up for them. It was hard, us being Catholics, and Father Egan hating them. I always wondered why she left. He came back, yes, he came back before the wedding, for he gave us five pounds for a wedding present even though I had left the estate to work in the store for Molly's father. It was the most money I had ever held in my hand. She never came back, though. I would be working behind the counter in the store and look out the window, and for no reason I would wonder what happened to her. There were rumours she died at sea, but I never believed she was dead. That was one of Father Egan's ways of getting even with the Protestants. Was it her you were looking for?"

"Yes," Caroline whispered, "she's who I am looking for. I can tell you what really happened to her if you want to know."

But he was no longer paying attention. His head had dropped and the rhythm of his breathing matched the sheathing and unsheathing of the cat's claws. They were both asleep, but Caroline stayed beside him, loath to leave.

"I'm Caroline McMaster, Elizabeth's daughter, conceived in this place and carried from here under my mother's heart to the ship where I was born."

And saying this aloud, she remembered that with her birth had come her mother's death. "I wish I could have known you."

With a wry smile, she continued, "I wonder what you would think of me."

Caroline took the old man's cold bony hands between her own and rubbed them tenderly.

"Thank you, thank you so very much. I never knew for certain before today."

She touched her lips to the old man's forehead and left the store.

I can feel the heat on my back, a soaking in of sunshine. I am submerged in myth and mysticism, Yeats and Joseph Campbell. Lake of Bays sets the stage for this, the unconscious brought to the surface. Talking it out reveals a lot... holding secrets in impedes clarity of entry to that enchanted place.

I never felt safe as a child. I never felt mother could look after me... she might lose me or let me drown. I always had to double-check on her... a terrible burden for a little girl. I married Michael because I needed to feel safe... he has kept me safe for twenty-seven years. Thank you, Michael; that wonderful feeling of safety has let the little girl grow up.

Such a lovely dream... relaxed, but passionate... a walk through unfamiliar territory but still lovely. I have finally learned not to ask what it means. The vestiges of such a mature innocence are still with me. One must not deny any part of one's nature— the erotic, the sensual, the cerebral, or the spiritual. "I love your breast." It is a lovely statement, use of words, a combination of the emotional and the sensual. Whatever that dream unleashed is not quite poetry, but metred feeling. I saw a pair of ducks swimming near the beach and she was the negative of him... a pale print of his coloured splendour... a black and white movie to his technicolour. Why did nature arrange them so? Was he the decoy, the one to attract the bullets, while she sheltered the young? Too simple, somehow. Is she the shadow to his sun? Is it the dream that lingers? I found a striped feather on the road and at the root it was frayed into angora— is it in the unravelling that something new and beautiful is revealed? That dream was potent. I am sitting up in bed, reading, and I discover to my intense pleasure that I am able to be who I am because I am greatly loved... not just loved, but greatly loved. Such a lucky woman! Being greatly loved makes all things possible, even the lonely offbeat honest road that I must walk.

In my childhood and young womanhood, my guides were faulty. My parents, my educators, my religion all wanted something from me. They wanted my youth, my beauty, my intellect and my innocence to uphold the status quo, their vision of the world. Their version was fenced, patriarchal and restricted. Did they do the best they could? I wonder. The loon in the bay just gave the most haunting cry; my blood tingles when I hear him.

ANNIE

Annie lives inside me
Looking up from under tangled hair.
She puts a dirty finger
On the wingtip of a bird.
Annie's not alone, she's with
An unkempt man, wearing filthy jeans.
He doesn't like me staring
At Annie's open face.

I watch and wonder at the two of them.
Who holds who in thrall?
Is he her husband, father, lover?
Does he keep Annie safe from all of us?
Or does he fear we will discover
The secrets Annie shares?
I do not know, although
Annie lives inside me.

BRITANNIA AND I walked into Ragged Falls, sauntering along the bank until we could go no further. The leaves are off the trees... they are stripped down to structure, and it is very beautiful to see them without the physical distraction of the leaves. It is not sad, but as though the structure points the way to something else. We climbed down so we could hang over the falls... the spray rose in the air, catching the sunlight and creating a rainbow. Do we use this analogy— the lovely placid river channelled between and falling over huge rocks before becoming once again a tranquil pool in the basin below— for the journey of our lives? Is this the celestial essence, turned into energy by the current and the narrowing harrowing passage through the rocks? Something is released into the air on the way down, so the celestial essence is lost by the time it reaches the lower pools. One must be in the right place (perched on a rock, hanging over the water) if one is to have a chance at inhaling this heavenly substance.

CHAPTER TWENTY-ONE

"You have all seen the face of the Goddess."

Sophie's face was turned to the fire, away from the circle of women.

"Remember yourself as a child, skipping across the freshly turned fields, carrying wildflowers in your hands. Smell the spring air, feel the warm wind on your face. Dig with your fingers in the damp richness of the earth."

Caroline, standing in the doorway, watched as even the oldest woman in the room sniffed the air and let the memory of a soft April wind play about her face. But Sophie's first words held no meaning for Caroline. Who was this Goddess?

Sophie continued, in the lavish tones of the accomplished storyteller: "Reach deep inside yourself; remember how you felt the first time you knew yourself to be a woman. Think. How special and overpowering. For each of us, that time was different and yet the same, for at that moment the second face of the Goddess was revealed to you. As woman, she is very beautiful." Sophie paused. "As you are."

A collective smile warmed the room as each woman released her own golden memory of individual glory. Their memories floated to the surface, perfuming the air with the scent of blossoms. Caroline, unnoticed beside the door, thought of Daniel and the splendour she had known as his desire described her beauty and her power. She grappled with that memory even now and leaned against the door frame, weak with wanting him.

"Some of you have seen the third face of the Goddess. For some of you, she still waits."

Sophie's voice surged with promises, and she turned from her contemplation of the flames to place her arm about Meaghn. The girl's body was rigid with concentration, her eyes riveted on Sophie. She reminded Caroline of the young Sophie of the Ojibwa campfires. That girl, too, had consumed a storyteller's every word. Caroline caught herself. A young Sophie! Had it only been a year since she had watched Sophie drink in Nokomo's every word? It was queer how quickly Sophie had assumed Nokomo's mantle of authority.

"And her third face, Sophie?"

Caroline had spoken aloud. The faces in the circle revolved to where she stood, half hidden in the shadows. Caroline shrank from meeting their many eyes. Sophie stood to answer Caroline, the same Sophie who had returned from her night alone in the woods, the one who had stepped into the clearing with the bird perched on her wrist.

"You ask about the third face of the Goddess, Caroline. Let me tell you. I had a daughter and I lost her. It doesn't matter how. I was deranged with grief. I looked everywhere for her. One day I heard a cry, and knew it to be hers. I went to her; don't ask me how I found her, or perhaps, how she found me. What matters is, she called to me and I came, and I will stay with her until she no longer needs me. There is a bond, Caroline, between mother and daughter, that defies time and place and can never be denied. It is in that bond, Caroline, that one sees the third face of the Goddess. I have seen Her."

The tension in the room was rising, gathering. Just as Caroline felt it must surely crest and smash about her head, bringing her and everyone around her crashing down, Sophie relinquished her hold on Caroline and spoke once again to the group.

"As you sing to your new daughter and cradle her against your breast, the Goddess will come to you in her third face, at her strongest; nothing, and no one, can defeat Her. At this moment, your face and Hers are one, and the life you have given birth to is Hers as much as yours. The three of you are linked forever, in this life and beyond."

Spellbound by Sophie's words, but no longer held against her will, Caroline raised her head to look at Sophie, knowing almost certainly what she would find there. The same girl who had lived once before in Sophie's face looked back at Caroline with solemn deep blue eyes. Caroline glanced wildly about the room to see if anyone else had noticed, but the room was even, and no sudden shifting of attention betrayed a stranger's presence. Caroline watched the women listen to this storyteller as attentively as they had listened to Sophie. She was certain they did not know they had lost Sophie.

"And the face that floats on the water without a life of its own?"

Meaghn's question captured the attention of the dark-haired stranger. Caroline leaned forward. Surely Meaghn would react to the girl using Sophie's voice. She, who had followed Sophie's every move, would not be fooled. As Caroline watched, Meaghn's expression did not change. It seemed incredible to Caroline that she alone, in the room full of women, knew that Sophie had been replaced by another.

"The face that floats on the water is the fourth and final face of the Goddess. She comes in this face only to those who are lost and truly search for Her."

The dark-haired girl who shared Sophie's voice dropped her eyes and whispered. Only those who were listening intently heard her final words: "And only to those who pay Her price."

The girl who shared Sophie's body folded her hands in her lap. Whatever she had come to say was finished. The women rose as one and filed silently past Caroline. No one looked at her or spoke. When everyone had gone, Caroline went to the figure seated by the fire and gently touched her on the shoulder.

"Sophie? Is it you?"

And once again it was Sophie who looked back at Caroline.

"Who told you about the Goddess? I never heard you speak of Her before tonight."

"I think that I have always known of Her, but tonight is the first time that I have shared that knowledge."

They did not speak of Her again.

Sunday morning on the dock... a solid white sky lifting to reveal this paradise of lake and shore with no one in it... truly God's creation. I came down early, thinking I might catch a glimpse of angels leaving, but I missed them. I don't think they like to be caught. They like to do the surprising.

This was the day for the most awesome of confrontations; I felt I could no longer avoid this meeting or I would die, and this awful violence would triumph, but the massive confrontation did not take place. I simply could not rage and claw and scream. I have written it out in *The Illuminated Manuscript*. In the quantum realm, the observer plays a crucial role in bringing about the situation that she observes. This translates seamlessly into the creative realm. The writer or artist plays a crucial role in bringing about the situation that she writes or paints, but this same phenomenon occurs in life. More often than not, we miss this crucial connection. I must perform my role, negating the violence put into play all those years ago.

CHAPTER TWENTY-TWO

It was in the children that Caroline first noticed the improvement. Their faces had lost the hollowness that frightened her so, and their clothing was not as shabby or as dirty as before. It pleased her to see her efforts bearing fruit. Even the cottages had lost their hangdog look. They were whitewashed for the first time in years, and starched curtains hung in the windows. Caroline was still regarded with suspicion but with less hostility, and the women no longer hid inside their houses when she passed. She was able to observe their actions as she moved about the estate; it was in the women themselves that the greatest change had been effected. They moved with a purposefulness that had been missing when Caroline and Sophie had first arrived, and in their interaction with one another there was a kindness that had not been there before. It was hard for Caroline to give a name to what she sensed, but the women seemed to share a common past. And it was more than that.

Caroline had pried the rusted lock from the outside room at the rear of their cottage, guessed at its former use, and focused her attention on the neglected room. When it was ready, she invited Sophie to share her find. It was worth all Caroline's efforts to see the look on Sophie's face as her eyes swept the shelves neatly lined with jars and baskets and the scrubbed surface of the huge oak table.

"Oh, Caroline, it's a stillroom! Just what we need. I've been wondering what we would do with winter almost here and everyone still so weak. We'll want remedies to treat the sick, and you have solved the problem for me all by yourself. How can I thank you? I'll speak to the children. I'm sure they will want to gather herbs for you. Tell me what you need."

Every day after that, when Caroline had finished her chores, she went to the stillroom to prepare whatever tonics or syrups Sophie needed for that day. And always, when she opened the door, there were bundles of herbs placed carefully in the center of the oak table. That she never encountered the donor or donors was a mystery, but not one that caused her any worry; Caroline was growing accustomed to the clandestine atmosphere of the estate. If her benefactors wished to remain anonymous, so be it. She had a syrup to deliver to a cottage where Sophie had cradled a croupy baby in her arms all night, and she turned to the task at hand, knowing that when she finished, Sophie would coax warm milk laced with Caroline's soothing herbal mixture down the infant's cough-roughened throat and the baby would reward both their efforts with a milky smile of contentment and fall asleep in Sophie's arms. And there was much more to Sophie's activities, some of which could be seen from the window in Caroline's stillroom. In the winter-shortened afternoons, Sophie gathered the older girls from their household tasks and took them into the threadbare fields. There she turned the tired soil with her golden fingers and showed the girls how to feed the earth with the crumpled limestone that circled the fields like lace. Caroline watched from the window as the estate gained strength under Sophie's supervision.

The dark wet Irish winter ran its course and passed into spring. Annie Murphy came to their cottage and told Sophie, within Caroline's hearing, that this was the first winter in her memory that not one death had come to diminish their tiny community.

That same evening, as the light faded and the pale prints of the early stars surfaced in the purple sky, a slight figure ran up the cottage walk. Caroline, attuned to the sounds of children, rose from her chair to investigate. As was her custom, she spoke into the shadows surrounding the open door.

"What would you like? Are you hungry? Wait there, I'll be right back."

But instead of an empty bucket being placed on the bottom step, Meaghn stepped out of the twilight. Her eyes were silvered and she spoke in a whisper. "Please, mum, get Sophie. I must talk to her."

"What is it, Meaghn? Are you all right? Come in."

The girl shook her head, and a shower of silver light spilled from her eyes. Caroline retreated, but not so far from the doorway that she was unable to overhear what Meaghn had to say to Sophie.

> She guards the gate
> between the worlds
> and speaks in stone
> to those who listen.

"Meaghn. So you have found them. Take me there."

Sophie walked through the open door and stretched out a hand to Meaghn. They spoke a language Caroline did not understand, and once again Caroline was an outsider. She watched them cross the fields behind the house until she lost them in the blackness. Wherever they were going, Caroline wanted to be with them. She ached with loneliness.

Each morning, before she tackled the needs of the stillroom, Caroline took the cow out to one of the abandoned paddocks where the grass was thick and lush. She returned for her in the late afternoon. She brought the animal into the stable and talked companionably into her soft brown side as she milked her. After the cow was bedded down in a stall ankle-deep in clean straw, Caroline attended to the chickens. She let them loose to roost in the tumbledown piggery behind the stable. They were not as good company as the cow, and yet their antics pleased her. This day, as she scattered grain on the ground, she called to them, trying to attract their attention. She walked backward, throwing the grain out in front of her until she saw the ground grow dark. She was standing in the shadow of the castle. It had been a long time since Caroline had come so close to it. Almost without thinking, she walked up to the overgrown walls and idly plucked at the ivy clinging to the stones. She uncovered a broken window pane. Poking out the shards of glass, she lowered her head to peer inside. The room showed only filtered blackness.

"Do you want to go in? I know a way."

The childish voice came from behind her. Caroline blushed at being caught peeping through a window.

"Follow me. I've been in there lots of times. I come here when they won't let me go to the mountaintop with them. They don't want me near the stones, either. They say I'm too young. So I come here and explore inside the castle. It's got ghosts, but I'm not scared."

Caroline smiled at the child's boasting and allowed herself to be led across the courtyard to the front of the house. She didn't remember the name of her guide, but recognized her as Meaghn's younger sister. Caroline thought she was a plucky little thing to be going into the old castle by herself. She couldn't be much more than nine or ten years old. Caroline wasn't sure if she had the courage to enter that huge abandoned building.

"Duck your head and crawl under this hedgy part. When you feel the edge of the stone wall, stand up flat against it and slide yourself along 'til you feel a ledge. I'll lead the way. If you get stuck, just whisper 'Mary Rose' and I'll come back and help you. Here we go, then."

Mary Rose wriggled under the thick undergrowth and disappeared, with Caroline close on her heels. When Caroline's fingers encountered the window ledge, she had a moment of panic. What was she doing, breaking into the old castle? A small pair of hands appeared over the edge and Mary Rose issued further instructions.

"Hoist yourself over the ledge. I'll pull you up from inside."

Between her own efforts and those of the girl, Caroline found herself in the green darkness of a large room, with Mary Rose beside her.

"I've got a candle, but I don't want to waste it. Anyhow, granny says you can see in the dark. Is that true?"

As the child was talking, she was leading Caroline by the hand across the room.

"No, I can't see in the dark. What does your granny take me for, a witch?"

The child bluntly dropped Caroline's hand and swung around to face her.

"Gran says you know things you shouldn't know. She and Meaghn talk about it. I hear them talking about other things, too. They tell their secret things when they think I'm asleep."

The switch from dark to light was so abrupt that Caroline had to shield her eyes from the brightness of the candle flame. When she dropped her hands she was face to face with a portrait of a young man. Both the artist and his subject were gifted; the good-looking young man with the arrogant tilt to his head belonged in the castle. He reeked of ownership, and a painted cruelty in his eyes made Caroline wonder what he had done to provoke the artist. She stepped back sharply from the portrait, nearly knocking over the child and her candle.

"Who is he, Mary Rose? Who is this man?"

"Don't you know him? Why, he's the owner of the castle, Sir Rodney Kingsmill. I thought you would recognize him. That's why I brought you. Take another look. I'd know him anywhere, and I was just little when they ran him off the property. The women say you look like him, and you surely do."

Mary Rose held the flame closer to the portrait and, unarmed, Caroline confronted the man in the painting.

She barely breathed the words, "Do the women hate me because I look like him?"

"It's more than that. They think you are his bastard, come back to claim the castle and the rents."

The girl blew out the candle and Caroline heard her bare feet pat across the stone floor. She stayed where Mary Rose had left her, stunned by her uncanny resemblance to the man in the painting, and the beginning of a terrible knowledge. He was a devil, this red-haired Rodney. She knew what he had done to the people on the estate. No wonder they hated her, if it were true and she was his flesh and blood. That was the question. Was she his flesh and blood? The thought made her cringe. Alone in the empty castle, at least no one could see her. Rodney Kingsmill, her father! No wonder the women feared and hated her. She hated herself. And her mother, the mother she had come so far to find, how could she have loved such a man? It didn't make sense. How could her mother? It was disgusting. How could she allow such a thing? Didn't she know? God, one had only to look into his eyes. How could she have allowed herself to make love to such a man? Caroline spoke out loud, asking the questions over and over again, until one word stuck in her throat. Allow. How could Elizabeth McMaster have allowed Rodney Kingsmill to make love to her? Allow. Allow. Maybe she hadn't, maybe he'd forced her! Maybe this was the key to her birth! It wouldn't be the first time a landlord's son had forced himself on an employee's daughter. The French even had a name for it, le droit du seigneur. An age-old, ugly story. Caroline could swear it was still practised, albeit clandestinely, in the culture of today, as it had been for centuries. Caroline left the castle in a loathsome frame of mind, scarcely conscious of where she placed her feet.

Some distance from the castle, she was intercepted by the village priest, the first man she had seen at Kingsmill Manor since her arrival. Caroline was in no mood to be gracious. He spoke first.

"You have wrought a miracle here at the Manor. I hope it's not the devil's work you're doing."

The priest knew exactly who she was. They inspected each other in the spring sunshine on the path between the rows of cottages.

"It's true I am not of your faith, Father, but surely even your Church could not credit the devil with the rosy cheeks of these children or the renewed vigour of their mothers." She waved one arm to encompass the women they could see, some working in their gardens, while others were standing in their doorways watching the exchange between Caroline and the priest. Her wave included the jumble of children playing about the cottages.

"Of course it's the Lord's work, Mrs. Paterson. It's just the transformation is so astounding, I have been puzzled. I've heard of the miracles you and your friend have worked here, and I felt it my duty to investigate. Is the young lady available? I would like to extend my thanks to her as well."

Before Caroline could reply, one of the women, sweeping her walk, stopped to answer the priest.

"She's in her bed, sleeping. She was up all night tending a sick baby. She never shut her eyes the whole night long. Now don't you be disturbing her."

This was news to Caroline, who had seen Sophie and Meaghn climb the hill behind the cottage just after daybreak. She caught the woman's eye, but said nothing.

"Of course I won't disturb her. Have you come from the castle?"

He turned and walked away from the cottages. Instead of replying, Caroline accompanied him across the overgrown courtyard to where the massive front door of the castle was hidden in the ivy. They were followed at a slight distance by the women; behind them came the children, with Mary Rose at the head. The priest paused to take in the ivy running wild over the walls, and to muse out loud on the rundown condition of the castle. The winter months had not slowed the growth of the ivy; rather, the wet weather seemed to have accelerated the proliferation of leaves. Even the windows had disappeared inside the thick green ropes of trailing vines. The stone exterior was so blurred and softened by the ivy's lavish growth that the old castle had taken on the appearance of some ancient monument reclaimed by nature, whose original use had been forgotten.

"I suppose I should communicate to Sir Rodney the miserable state of his house. It is surely safe for him to return to Ireland."

The priest spoke reluctantly and to himself, but his words carried to the women who stood at a respectful distance. The eyes of the black-shawled women crackled at his words, and Caroline felt the force of their unspoken anger beat against her back. She was astonished the priest did not flinch at their fury.

"Yes, I must notify Sir Rodney about the condition of Kingsmill Manor. He must be advised. It's a shame to let such a fine property deteriorate."

The priest's sigh, following his decision to make contact with Sir Rodney Kingsmill, signalled his own distaste for the absentee landlord. The priest had not been unaware of the nocturnal terror practised by Rodney and his agent, nor had he been ignorant of the scale of the brutality used in the Kingsmill Manor evictions. As the priest saw it, his duty was to notify the gentleman as to the condition of his house and let him decide whether he wished to reclaim it.

"You wouldn't have him back?'

The thought of the man who might be her father coming to KIngsmill Manor sickened Caroline.

"I beg your pardon?"

"I said I cannot believe that you would allow, much less invite, a man of such wicked parts to resume life on this estate. Tell me I am mistaken in what I heard you say."

The priest took a step back from Caroline, and was about to respond, when Annie Murphy detached herself from the clutch of women who had gathered. She stepped in front of Caroline and eyed the priest, shaking her finger at him to underline her message. "It would be better for him and for her and for all of us if he did not return here, Father."

Her words hung suspended between her bent frame and the black-robed figure of the priest for all to hear, until, dismayed at her own boldness, Annie ducked her head and slipped back inside the knot of women. The priest looked first at the women and then at Caroline, confused. Had he been threatened? And if he had, which woman was responsible?

I am reading Anne Stevenson's biography of Sylvia Plath, *Bitter Fame*. The creative imagination in the female cannot survive the rigidity of the male-imposed myth of woman as Eve, the nurturing maternal figure created to sustain man. In this myth, the female imagination must surrender, go mad or die. There are no other choices. We must create a new scenario, one in which both male and female imaginations are allowed to take flight.

I met Mary and David Kent's granddaughter for the first time. Her name is Caroline. She is enchanting, a precious little creature, very articulate and not at all shy with adults.

Life keeps rolling along, like rowing in an eight; you cannot stop the motion when you are tired or want to take a closer look at a certain moment. Such a shame that humans had to introduce measured time into our existence. The seasons were so nice. I am mesmerized by William Blake. It's all I want to do— read him, read about him, read all around him. Somehow I must join in with the larger world, the world of mental forms... not intellectual forms, but of the soul. I am coming face to face with my own aging, not mortality so much as invisibility. Does one become less visible as one ages? Do we just pale out... like Thel, in Blake's *Book of Thel*? What keeps the outline clear? It is not the body. Perhaps the mind? The soul? How and what is the soul?

I am watching a leaf fall from a tall tree... at first it is a piece of yellow light (sunshine) floating from the heights, then it picks up speed and spins quickly to the ground to join the other fallen leaves. A human life? Set into motion by a time cycle (seasons), loosened from its source, floating, but always with the final destination in view... does life speed up as we age? Do we land like leaves on the ground, to rot and mulch and feed the earth, to send nourishment back to the tree? It makes sense, but it saddens me. Ride the air; don't resist it.

CHAPTER TWENTY-THREE

The interlude with Mary Rose and its aftermath with the priest robbed Caroline of what peace of mind she had gained over the winter. The painted implication of Rodney Kingsmill's role as her birth father and the worse possibility of his return ate away at her. Caroline no longer worked in the stillroom or cared that Sophie had not been to the cottage in two days. With only passing interest she noted a line of dark-robed figures cross the fields and thread their way up the steep hill to the old mountaintop. Her comment was offhand and to herself: "There'll be just children in the cottages tonight." It took a minute for the information to sink in. Caroline dropped to her knees, scooped up a live coal from the hearth, placed it in a tin bucket and left the cottage without bothering to shut the door.

By the time she had made her third trip into the cow's stall, the animal did not even lift her head as Caroline bent and gathered straw from beneath her hoofs. She carried this bundle, as she had the previous ones, to the place in the hedge that Mary Rose had shown her. Pushing the straw through the bushes, Caroline crawled on her hands and knees after it. When she felt the rough edge of the castle wall with her fingers, she gathered an armload of straw and stood up, using her back and shoulders to guide her as she inched along the stone wall to the window ledge. Once there, she threw her bundle of straw through the opening and eased herself into the room.

This time her eyes were conditioned to the darkness, and she could see the outlines of the room. Shelves rose from the floor to the ceiling, covering the wall space. From her place by the window she could discern rows and rows of books. It surprised her that she had gained entrance to the castle through the library, but then she remembered the story Annie had told, of Sir Rodney and his loutish agent shooting out the library windows during their drunken binges. Good, she thought. Picking up as much straw as she could carry, Caroline moved across the stone floor, bits of straw flying with each stride. She went without hesitation to the portrait of Rodney Kingsmill, dropped her armload of straw at his booted feet, and faced him eye to eye, for he was almost life-sized. It was a battle of her will against his, and once again he seemed to triumph, for she was the first to turn away. Caroline knelt and touched the live coal to the straw heaped about his boots, and watched impassively as the fire brought into focus the painted image of herself. The flames leapt higher and higher in their efforts to reach Rodney Kingsmill, and in minutes he could no longer twist away and save his likeness from the flames. Caroline waited until the last bit of paint had run from his face before effecting her own escape. She had almost stayed too long, for the fire moved swiftly, nourished by the rows of old books and carried on bits of fallen straw to the farthest corners of the room.

Outside the inferno of the library, the night was mild and still, and the sky was steeped in stars. Caroline ran down the drive and through the missing gates of the estate. She did not once look back, and only stopped when she could no longer catch her breath. She sank in a heap and buried her hot face in the soft grass that rimmed the lake, but it failed to draw the fire from her overheated skin. The coolness of the water appealed and she leaned over to bathe her face in its frosted depths. The moon's reflection traced a pale path across its surface, but Caroline, with her burning face submerged, saw its track from underwater. There, illuminated in the moonlight, was a dark-haired girl who glided from the bottom of the lake in a froth of silvery bubbles as Caroline looked down in fascination. The girl swam close enough for Caroline to see her face, the same face that had emerged from Sophie's face on two occasions. She could no longer be called a stranger. Caroline closed her eyes. When she opened them, the girl's face was floating on the surface of the water, and Caroline was close enough to hear silvery peals of laughter issue from her lips and to see her own reflection in the girl's black-bordered, moonlit eyes. It was an invitation to a waking dream that Caroline accepted. Caroline swam effortlessly through the unresisting water to where the girl floated above a carpet of tiny polished shells. The dark-haired girl held Caroline in the center of her eyes while she extended her long pearl-tipped fingers into the pile of luminescent shells and scooped two handfuls from the profusion on the bottom of the lake. She let them drip through her fingers like tears. Caroline hung motionless above the gleaming shells, caught and held like time itself in the girl's silvern eyes. She could have stayed forever, but it was not to be. Caroline had come too far to stop, and reaching down, she plucked one perfect shell from the many clustered beneath her outstretched hand and gave it to the girl. The girl took the curved and opalescent shell, kicked her slender feet and rose from the depths in a cloud of silver bubbles that trailed behind her like great luminous wings, leaving Caroline to surface on her own.

Awakening from her dream, Caroline left the lake and walked wraith-like through the seaweed grass of the lawn. The tall strands parted at her passage and regrouped behind her; from the lakeside, it would have been impossible to tell that anyone walked there. The rows of cottages gleamed whitely in the moonlight like teeth, and darkness obscured the holes left by the shattered wrecks of the evictions. There was enchantment in the landscape which Caroline no longer needed to deny or escape; its magic washed through and over her. When she reached her own cottage, exhausted, she sank into a chair, untied her shoes and closed her eyes. When Caroline woke, she thought someone had placed a map on the mantelpiece. Propped there, in the fluctuating light from the fire, was the outline of the lake, the castle and the cottages, but not everything was familiar. Caroline crossed the room for a better look. When she picked up the map, she felt the knotted stitches with her fingers. It was her mother's sampler that she held. On closer inspection, she saw it was indeed a map. How stupid of her to have missed it. Each stitch, taken individually, told nothing of a landscape, but taken as a whole, read from a distance, they clearly created a map of the estate. One had only to look.

Caroline's fatigue vanished. Clutching the sampler, she left the cottage and crossed the black soil of the freshly turned fields. The earth clung to her bare feet in a moist embrace. She travelled upwards, through the rocky high meadows, pausing only to read the directions stitched into the map. They, and the moonlight, guided her to the slit in the rock face of a steep limestone wall. Caroline was trembling. Whatever lay on the other side of the wall was not of her world, but of her mother's. The map on the sampler was designed to show the place where the two worlds touched. It was her mother's legacy to her.

Caroline slipped inside the enclosure and gasped with pleasure. Stones, like giant stitches, were set as precisely on the mountaintop as were the stitches on the sampler, giving an intimacy to the landscape. Even the vastness of the night sky seemed accessible to Caroline, for it was the very one embroidered by her mother, with the stars following the same pattern as those stitched to the sampler. Never had Caroline seen stars so close, and she tilted her head backward, revelling in the primeval drama above her head. Stars in intricate formations winked saucily and shifted positions before her eyes, to form yet another complex pattern. It was a world within a world she saw, created and then dissolved into another world in the flutter of an eye. The magic in the heavens was infinite and dazzling and it required an enormous effort for Caroline to pull her eyes away and observe her immediate surroundings.

She stood on a grassy plateau, inside an immense arena roofed by stars. In the far corner of the field, flames outlined the blackened figures of dancing women. The light crept part way up the towering stones which served as the outer boundary of a huge circle. The fire cast monstrous shadows of the stones on the moonlit whitened walls and dwarfed the stick-like bodies of the dancers. Caroline watched, still as the stone monoliths, while a solitary white-gowned figure rose from behind the leaping flames and slowly executed a series of difficult steps. Caroline saw the scene enacted simultaneously in sharp relief in miniature around the fire, and magnified to an infinite degree in the shadow sequence which played against the limestone walls. As her mind and eyes adapted to the dual vision, the other dancers stopped their movements and knelt to form a second circle inside the standing stones. A wreath of flowers crowned the head of the lone dancer, and as she revolved around the flames, her long straight hair flared out about her body like glossy black wings. At some specific point in the dance, she paused and cocked her head as if listening for instruction, before sinking gracefully to her knees. The women in the stone-edged circle watched as she spread her arms up and out to either side of her flamelit face, as if communicating with the stars. Both worlds stood still and waited.

Caroline chose this moment to move across the grass of the enclosure to shelter in the shadow of an upright giant stone, one of two that formed a natural entrance to the circle. The central figure of the piece had not moved, nor had her acolytes; even the fluid shifting of the stars was checked. Caroline was unaware that her presence had brought the ceremony to a halt. She placed a hand against the huge stone to steady herself and stiffened suddenly as energy, stored in the stone for centuries, entered her. Her body twisted and silvered in the moonlight, and as the waves of energy built beneath her hand she was spun into the circle. Designs in alternating bars of flame and shadow flowed across her face and skin, as if the stones had waited for her touch to unleash their reservoirs of power. The circle surged to life. The white-robed leader sprang from her kneeling position to lead the pulsating line of black-garbed women threading through the ancient stones. As the dancers came within touching distance of Caroline, two figures broke the line to catch her hands and take her in. She fit her movements to theirs, and her feet to their steps, and all the while she tried to keep the spinning figure of the leader within view. The girl's robe and hair spread out from her spiralling body in differing directions, and her slender form translated music, heard by listening feet since time began, into a series of explicit movements. As Caroline danced, her feet were retracing a story. Her first steps told of the old ways and the old religion, of the time when the Goddess ruled the world and all men listened to Her voice. They told of standing patiently on the mountaintop, waiting for the sun to rise, and of the Goddess speaking to them in the sun's golden tones, telling them of winter's death and promising them a green and growing land. Then, all respected Nature's laws, which were Her Laws, too, and shared what food there was in the shallow years. The steps of the dance told Caroline that women were especially cherished by Her, for in them was Her life sheltered. Each year when the sun returned to give life and warmth to the land, the people celebrated and at these celebrations the Goddess chose one woman to lead Her people and keep them from falling away from Her ways. Then the steps changed tempo and a wild story was stamped out by the women's feet, of armies marching across the land, stripping it bare and leaving death in the fields. The women were frightened and hid in the caves from the invaders. No longer was She worshipped openly, for those who came brought their own God, and He would not share His house. Those women who dared to speak Her name and worship Her in the old ways were burned alive by men who carried their God nailed to a cross. The ground scorched her feet; Caroline leapt higher to escape the flames. When she could stand the heat no longer, the beat slowed, the rhythm relaxed, and the story she heard through the soles of her feet was of the gradual death of the old religion. In time, the people and the land adapted to the ways of the Roman God, and the Goddess was forgotten by all but a few old women who remembered only what their grandmothers had shared with them in whispered tones when they themselves were giving birth.

Absorbed in the story relayed to her in the steps of the dance, Caroline lost sight of the girl who led the dancers. It was only when she stopped to rest by a great smooth-coated stone that Caroline saw Sophie again. The girl melted from light into shadow, reappearing as the flames shot higher. She danced faster and faster; her feet never stopped tracing the patterns of antiquity, until she stood directly in front of Caroline, and Caroline could see in her transparent eyes an ancient wisdom. Caroline wanted more than anything to speak to her, but before she could gain her feet, the girl was gone, her robed figure dissolving inside a flight of flames.

Caroline caught and held her breath. No one could pass through those flames and live, yet as she looked, a girl glided from the fire and moved with an easy grace to the stone where Caroline waited. The girl stopped in front of Caroline and knelt before her. A smile swept across her face, and Caroline's reaction was one of rapture. This time she knew who it was who smiled at her. It was the face floating on the lake, the face of the girl in the stream, the girl who shared Sophie's face, a girl who was no longer a stranger. Caroline thought it quite natural that she should be gathered in her arms. It was not the first time that she had held Caroline. For a single moment, as Caroline lay cradled in her mother's arms, Elizabeth brushed back the layers of purple blackness that filled the sky, and showed eternity to Caroline.

In that moment Caroline saw a moving line of women and saw herself among them. Holding her hand on one side was Emily. She had not known until now that it was Emily who had broken the line to take her in, for this Emily was young and vibrant, not the death's head Caroline had last seen. It was good to see her happy. Emily touched Caroline lightly on the forehead.

"I am so sorry, Caroline. I loved my life too much to give you yours. I was wrong. Can you forgive me?"

"That time is long gone. You were a mother to me when my own was looking everywhere for me. You kept me safe, Emily, and think on this: if I had married Daniel I never could have left him to find Her. When I found Daniel's grave, I thought my life was over and I hated what you had done to me, but I never hated you." She kept hold of Emily's hand and turned to the woman who waited for her on the other side. "Thank you, Caroline, for bringing Sophie home. I knew we could not keep her, and yet, until you came, I had no way to send her back."

Tears welled in Caroline's eyes as she saw Nokomo holding her other hand.

"I should thank you, Nokomo. You gave me courage when I had none, and loaned me Sophie to bring me home. I think I am beginning to understand some small part of what you tried to teach me. No sooner do I decode one set of signs than another appears. It is a fathomless design, and yet the threads are human."

"Caroline, there were times when I despaired that you could ever learn what is every girl of the tribes' birthright, but I was right to persevere with you. We know Her by a different name, that's all."

The veil dropped into place, and ever so delicately, Elizabeth released her hold on Caroline and searched her face.

"You have come a long way, my child, longer than I thought it possible for you to travel. I have watched and prayed that you would find the way."

As Elizabeth spoke, Caroline heard the echo of a cherished voice. She closed her eyes and dreamt of that time. Elizabeth's lips curved in the softest of smiles as she bent over Caroline's peaceful form. She smoothed the tangled copper hair from her daughter's brow and brushed her lips against her forehead as she had longed to do. The last words Caroline heard her mother speak before she drifted into sleep were, "You, too, belong to Cerridwen."

Caroline, restless in her deep sleep, tossed and turned her face towards the ground. Her fingers gripped the loosened soil around the base of the huge stone and a sigh rippled from her throat. In her dream she was a great dark field full of secret growing female things. Inside her dream, she spoke of what she saw and felt.

"I love the rich earthy smell of the plants that root around me. I move my hands to bring the soil to my nostrils, and my fingers, buried in the freshly turned soil, lose their flesh and dissolve into the warm wetness of the earth. It is where I belong. I renew the earth with my body and She in turn renews me. It is the way of the Goddess. I am whole at last. She has connected me to roots that have no beginning and no end and yet are everywhere. Wait. Listen. I feel bare feet across my face and I wonder, do they come to nurture me or will I nourish them? They pass and I understand it matters only that they come. Am I dreaming, or in dreaming have I woken from the sleep of centuries? In either case, I feel no fear, for I have seen the face of eternity, and She is kind."

When Caroline woke, it was morning, and she was alone. Elizabeth, Nokomo, Emily, and the other women had vanished. The bonfire was a pile of emptied ashes flickering faintly in the pale golden light. Only the great standing stones remained as Caroline remembered, worn smooth with the touch of hundreds of human hands. She closed her eyes and the drifting dreamy wholeness of the night returned, cradled in her being, waiting to unfold like babies' hands. Everything had changed, everything but the great gray stones and Elizabeth's sampler. Caroline picked her way across the meadow and slipped neatly through the concealed entrance. Her mother's sampler was no longer needed, for in the clear morning light Caroline's newly washed eyes saw everything. She stood on tiptoe, stretching her arms skyward, and laughed with the sheer joy of being connected so intimately to all the life spread out before her. The green high meadows and the dark brown fields met and merged until it was all but impossible to know where meadow ended and field began. Deeper in the hollow of the valley, she saw the gleam of whitewashed cottages, and in the distance, shreds of mist retreating from the lake. Or was it smoke? From this distance she could not tell. Caroline left the wider canvas of the valley and bent her head to examine what lay beneath her feet. In this fashion she inched down the mountain with her eyes unfocused on anything but the tiny patch of ground over which she moved. Kneeling to inspect each thread of grass, each winged flower and each rounded pebble, she made slow progress down the mountain path. The sun had travelled one-quarter of the way across the sky before she reached the fields where the women usually worked. There was no one there. At the edge of the first field, she bent and gathered handfuls of the clotted dark earth, letting them separate and fall between her fingers, liking the feel of the dirt in her hands. She loosened the soil around a shiny green shoot and observed the earth slide away from its delicate sides. Touching the feathered lace of one embryonic leaf, Caroline marvelled at the faint but identifiable pattern veining its surface. Had She marked everything with Her own design?

In the distance, two lines of figures walked up the drive towards the castle. Behind them lay the lake. Caroline watched, and as the gap between them lessened, she could see that it was a procession. In the lead was a girl pulling a red wagon. Caroline was too far away to see what the wagon contained or to distinguish the features of the girl. It might have been Elizabeth, or Sophie, or Meaghn. Caroline was curious, but by the time she crossed the fields and reached her own cottage, there was no sign of them. They had vanished. As she rounded the corner of her cottage, Caroline became aware of an odd noise coming through the opened windows. It had pitch and volume, but it was more than sound, for it vibrated and filled the air with echoes of itself. Caroline could not recognize the noise, nor should she have, for she had never heard the sound of women keening. She went into her cottage. There was no one in the main room and yet the noise intensified in tone and strength, emanating from behind the closed door to the bedroom. Caroline stepped cautiously across the room until she was just outside the door where the sound originated. It stopped abruptly, and the sudden silence was more dreadful than the noise. The door opened, and Meaghn stood in the doorway. Behind her, grouped about the bed, were the women of the estate. Meaghn went to Caroline and put her arms around her, drawing her gently inside, towards the bed.

"I found her this morning, floating at the edge of the lake."

Caroline did not want to hear. She shook her head. She would wake before it happened. It was not to be. Meaghn still faced her.

"Caroline, you must know. Sophie is dead."

And Caroline screamed across the room.

"Why, why, Sophie?"

Meaghn pressed her fingers into Caroline's shoulders until the crushing pain of loss had loosened its grip and Caroline could hear again.

"You ask what should not be answered, Caroline."

Caroline remembered another time, another question, and the same reply.

"Will Sophie ever come back, Nokomo?"

She had her answer now, and shuddered at the anguish she had caused. Nokomo had known, had always known, that Sophie would not return. Still, she had had the courage to let her go.

It was more courage than Caroline thought she possessed.

"Come and say goodbye to Sophie."

She let herself be led by Meaghn. The women parted to let her pass, and the keening resumed. The girl on the bed had been both mother and daughter to Caroline. Sophie lay still and white in the soaked robes of last night's ceremony, her black hair spread out in straight lines across the pillow. Her eyes were wide open. They glittered with the silver of new coins, coins that had been placed there as payment for the boatman to ferry the dead woman from life to death. Caroline leaned over and kissed the cold forehead of the girl with the silver eyes.

"Goodbye, Sophie. I shall miss you. Thank you for bringing me home. Without you, how would I ever have found my way?"

When Caroline straightened, the women crowded in the tiny room were all watching her. She smiled at them and they smiled back. Meaghn joined her as she left the room and walked through the cottage into the May morning. Caroline's life had made its first full circle, and it was her turn to take up where Elizabeth had left off all those years ago. It was an ancient sisterhood she had joined, the links of which swung back and forth in time in an unbroken chain. Steeped in such thoughts, Caroline walked arm in arm with Meaghn until the girl stopped her, touching her delicately on the cheek.

Meaghn smiled at Caroline and opened her eyes so widely that their brilliance spilled over and fell in sparkling blue fragments to the ground.

"Caroline, you wear the face in the water."

"Yes, it is my mother's face. And now it belongs to me."

When women assume power, they step outside the boundaries of their society. What they find becomes their story.

So many things I would love to save run through my hands like water; I can trap only a few of them. Oh, to write one's own thoughts always, but think of Ann and dying suddenly and having someone read your thoughts. God, even in a journal, one tidies up. Why?

You pushed me into a form that suited your life, your needs, and you bought off your conscience by saying to yourself, "she has time." Is it any wonder that she makes patchwork quilts, writes short stories or poetry and paints miniatures or watercolours? You probably never thought about the form she had to choose for her creations. Your rules, your time, my space... never again!

A clear golden day with cool notes, but still in summer dress. I am sitting topless on the dock. Old people try to maintain the status quo, conserve, hoard... dealing with what was. The trick is to look forward, outward, share, change, challenge, try... never to hold on to something that has served its purpose. Growth is change. To stop growing is to die... that's what old is, giving up the hope of change.

I am alive in every nerve end, even my fingernails. Spend your life in large sums, throw pennies to the crowds... the only coin of reality is life.

I am sitting up in bed in a lovely old inn in Vermont. Mike is at shooting school. We are part of the pampered rich and I wonder where it will all end. Overdressed, overfed and underconscienced men and women sleepwalking through the rooms of this beautiful place. Inane conversations ring me on every side. France must have felt like this before the revolution, and Russia, too. Were they as unconscious as we are? The air is crisp and mountain clean and the sun shines on a perfect green and white village. Shall I just curl up and enjoy this, and refuse to think of how rapidly we are rattling along to our destruction? The perfection seduces you. I have tried to understand and I can only posit that this (the green lawns and shutters, the white clapboard cottages and picket fences) is a white Anglo-Saxon male vision of perfection. There is no room for blacks or Turks or wild old women who dream of caves and power. It is a lovely place of mowed order and tall statues to the dead (men, of course), so clean and sterile and antiseptic that all the old wealthy WASPs rush to be here. It is their vision, after all, but the key is old, finished, done with, over. Their children do not want their vision. They want their own, in Europe or Africa or China or space. Their vision is travelled and compassionate. I prefer theirs. Once you start to look beneath the ordered structure, you realize that they are just keeping us at bay. The breakthrough could come at any moment.